MW01222618

THE JERICHO WALL

THE JERICHO WALL

Chike Momah

To order additional copies of this book, contact:
Xlibris Corporation
1-888-795-4274
www.Xlibris.com
Orders@Xlibris.com
106463

DEDICATION

To my wife Ethy and our Children:
Chidi (and his wife Ifeyinwa), Adaora, and Azuka
And their Children
And to the Nigerian community
In the
United States of America

BOOK ONE

CHAPTER 1

C hief Nathaniel Anigbo was in his element as he presided over the wedding reception. If he loved weddings, he loved wedding receptions even more. And if he was privileged to chair the function, it was like icing on the cake. Indeed, because of his widespread reputation for generosity on such occasions, it was an icing that he enjoyed with some frequency. His social standing in the Nigerian Igbo community of New Jersey was considered by many to be truly second to none. His friends liked to say that he and his wife deserved, more than any other couple, the privilege of first refusal of the chairmanship of any significant social or festive gathering of the clan.

For him, this was no ordinary wedding. He loved the bride, Nonye, as he was wont to put it, "to death". She was his niece, an only daughter of his sister Ngozi Uguru, widowed now for about a decade. Not a few persons had hinted at the striking resemblance between uncle and niece, and there were those who thought that Nonye was his daughter. He got quite a kick out of that supposition, not least on account of Nonye's comeliness. And unless absolutely pressed on the issue, by those who harbored some lingering doubts, he let them wallow in their ignorance.

To his left, demurely twiddling her gold pendant and necklace, sat his wife Ekemma. She looked resplendent in a long orange-colored gown that hugged her figure without being overly tight, and sewn from material with intricate designs. Her head-tie, of the same material, sat like a crown of many folds, uncertainly, on her head. Her husband Nat had in fact warned her against making too abrupt a movement of her head, or her crown could come tumbling off its perch. Her smile, the merest lifting of one side of her mouth, lit up her face and gave it a radiance that was at once warm and serene.

On a sweet impulse, and so gently her husband initially paid no heed to the action, she slid her right arm under his left arm, which rested on the table.

She reached for, and clasped his left hand, and intertwined her fingers with his. He turned, looked tenderly at her, and smiled.

"I know," he said gently. "I know. Weddings always have this effect on you."

"You don't have to tell the whole world," she rebuked him in a sharp whisper.

"Oh, Mma, I'm sorry," he whispered back, looking around him. He always called her Mma.

"That's okay," Ekemma said. Then she pointed, even as she slowly disengaged her fingers from his. "Look who's coming—"

"The MC himself," said Nat, taking a peek at his watch. "About time we got started."

As if on cue, both the Chairman and the Bridegroom rose from their chairs as the Master of Ceremonies approached the high table. Chuka Okpala had a jaunty, almost haughty, air about him. Time was, when Nat Anigbo could just barely stand him and his exaggerated self-assurance. That time was now happily long past. Chuka Okpala had fairly earned his reputation as the best MC in the community. He was so well regarded in this role that some, putting sweetness of sound above denotation and literalness, often addressed him as "*MC Emeritus*". And he loved it! Several of his friends were convinced that he could make tons of money if he charged a fee for his MC services. They pointed to Nigerian communities elsewhere in the country where MCs, like Disk Jockeys, were adequately compensated. But Chuka would have none of that. "My MC skills are not for sale," he would say. "And, besides, DJs often have to lug heavy and expensive equipment with them. I only bring myself, and my smooth tongue."

He walked up to, and stopped directly opposite the bridegroom. But when he spoke, he turned to the Chairman. " *Ugo-Oranyelu*," he addressed Chief Anigbo by his titular name, in his well-practised, most affable voice. "I'm sorry for the slight delay. But the woman bringing the kolanut and sundry other things got caught up in a bad traffic go-slow along route 22."

Nat Anigbo lifted an eyebrow in mock surprise. "That would be—let me see—Mrs. Mordi, no?" He lowered his voice as if he was sharing a very private joke. "And you believed her? The woman is always late—to everything. But thank God she's here at last. What do you say we start, Mr. Bridegroom?"

Nnanna smiled expansively, clucking humorously. "Let's not be too hard on her—at least, not today, eh, Nonye?" he said, turning to his bride. "As the Chair said, thank God she's here, and we can proceed."

"All's well that ends well," Nonye chimed in. "Let the fun begin."

The big banquet hall, large enough to sit five hundred, had filled almost to capacity. The Celestial Gardens, an elaborate structure that catered exclusively to banquets and conventions, had several halls that could be adjusted to fit any occasion—small or large—by the use of sliding partitions. Because of its strategic location at the junction of two important roads in the heart of Highland Park, route 27 gave it easy access from all points in New Jersey. Its brochure boasted a parking space for three hundred vehicles. The perimeter of its grounds was lined principally by maple trees, whose palmate leaves look like human hands with the fingers splayed out. Copiously leafed in the spring and summer, and gloriously colorful in the autumn, the trees heightened the visual attractiveness of the Celestial Gardens.

It was a lavish wedding reception. Nat and Ekemma, as surrogate parents to Nonye, had not even bothered to discourage the popular notion that this was going to be "the mother of all weddings" in the Igbo community of New Jersey. Everybody who was anybody, as the cliché has it, was invited. Nat brought his sister Ngozi, the mother of the bride, over from Nigeria for the wedding. Surprisingly, but fortunately, the American Consulate in Lagos, Nigeria, had given her a visa without demur. Ekemma, magnanimous as always to her husband's niece, had assured Nonye that her mother would be present at the wedding. "That's the least we can do for you," she told a beaming Nonye. "It wouldn't be right if she's not here for her only daughter's wedding."

Now, as the festivities were about to commence, Ngozi smiled from ear to ear. She sat next to her kid brother Nat, her grateful heart full to bursting point. She let her eyes take in the enchanting view: the rich variety and the brilliant colors of the women's outfits; the understated majesty of the archetypal Igbo jumper, most of which sported the *isi-agu* or other animal-head motifs; the voluminous, billowy *agbada* and *shokoto*, the traditional Yoruba ethnic outfit, though there could not have been more than a negligible handful of Yorubas present.

The crowd was ebullient, smiling and laughing and tittle-tattling in excited anticipation of an enjoyable evening. And the little children—hordes of them! Ngozi could not recall ever seeing so many children at any wedding reception she had attended at home in Nigeria. Their restlessness was palpable, as they gamboled between the tables, and on the dance floor, though not necessarily to the rhythm of the raucous music supplied by the DJ.

This was Ngozi's first visit to the United States. "My cup of blessings is full and running over," she had softly muttered to Nonye, as mother and daughter posed for photographs earlier that afternoon. "If I die tomorrow, I know I'll have few regrets." To which Nonye, smiling indulgently or frowning by turns, responded just as softly: "Mom, please! No one's going to die. You know I don't like to hear you talk like that."

Teary-eyed with the emotions that assailed her from time to time, Nonye wished that her dad had lived long enough to see this, the happiest day of her life. Her father Tagbo had doted on his daughter, but he had known, long before his death, and when she was barely into her teens that, unless a miracle cure was discovered, the cancer that was ravishing his body would rob him of the joy of seeing his two children progress from their childhood to maturity.

Nonye was thankful for God's mercies, manifested to her in many different ways. She was thankful for her uncle, and surrogate father in America, Nat Anigbo. It was Uncle Nat who first set her feet on the road to her American odyssey by persuading her mother to let him take her to the United States not quite a year after she graduated from her high school, Queen's School, Enugu. She was thankful for her Aunt Ekemma, who might easily have resented the strong bond of affection between her husband and his niece, but instead—and like him—loved her almost as a daughter. She was thankful for her brother Somtochi who, at nineteen going for twenty, had just completed his freshman year at Rutgers—the State University of New Jersey—thanks to a soccer scholarship worth a few thousand dollars. And again, Uncle Nat had had a lot to do with Somto even applying for admission to the university, and the wheeling and dealing with coaches that yielded the financial aid.

Above all else, Nonye thanked her stars for leading her, with inexorable steps, to Nnanna. She could not now bear to even think what might have been her future if she had not undertaken that fateful trip. A trip that had seemed, at the time, wasteful of her resources, and for which Uncle Nat had roundly upbraided her! A trip that had taken her from sea to shining sea, across the entire breadth of the United States, for the wedding of her friend Chinyere Mordi's friend—Ann, a girl she barely knew! But she had learned, from the many twists and turns her life had taken up to this point, not to unduly question her God and her *chi*—that personal, guardian spirit in which her Igbo people so strongly believe—about why she was where she was at any major moment in her life's journey.

That had been a most momentous trip to Los Angeles. She had sat next to a young man who, for the first hour out of Newark, was as taciturn as a dummy—until Chinyere Mordi came down the aisle from her seat, for a brief chat, and was surprised to see him.

"Nnanna!" she exclaimed, hitting him familiarly on his shoulder. "I didn't see you when we were boarding. Don't tell me you're also going to LA for Ann's wedding! I didn't—"

"Who is Ann?" he asked, smiling.

"Oh, sorry. I just assumed—"

"That's all right, Chinyere. I'm going to LA for a brief visit. You might call it a vacation. Who is Ann?" he asked again.

"Just a friend," said Chinyere, and then pointed to Nonye. "Do you two know each other? But why am I even asking? Nonye, let me introduce you to a friend I've known almost since the first day I arrived in this country, Nnanna Onwuka. He's Assistant Professor in the African-American Studies Department—or whatever they call it—at Rutger's university. At their Newark campus, I believe. Nonye, don't be fooled by his shyness. It's just an act. Half the young ladies in New Jersey—"

"Chi-Chi, you've come with your trouble and your loud mouth." Nnanna's rebuke sounded harsh, but he was laughing. "What have I done to you?"

"Nothing much, except you're sometimes too shy for your own good." She turned to Nonye: "Can you believe that this man teaches African literature in the university? What he doesn't know about some of our great African writers can be accommodated on the point of a pin. And he's a bit of a writer himself. You should hear him talk about—"

"That's enough already, Chi-Chi! You're embarrassing me."

But Chinyere was not yet done with him. "Nonye," she said, smiling at the memory, "you should have been there the day Nnanna was elected assistant secretary of our *Aniagu* union. The secretary, Celestine Nwachi wanted him as assistant secretary because she hoped to profit from his writing skills, so that when she does her minutes of meetings and other union correspondence, he might be persuaded to look them over and edit them so they read better. The moment she nominated him, there was a loud cry of "unopposed!" before poor Nnanna could decline the nomination. That's a true story. You're still very new in the union, so you've not yet gotten to know some of our executives, especially those who like to keep a very low profile—like Nnanna here."

Nonye, through all of this banter, sat quietly, arms folded across her chest. When she finally turned to look at Nnanna, short-sleeved, and sitting to her left by the aisle, it was as if she was seeing him for the first time. She was immediately affected by his good looks, and his aura of great physical strength, with biceps that clearly bespoke several hours of weightlifting at the gym. There was a velvety quality to his voice that recalled the singing voice of the superlative Nat King Cole.

In the upshot, in very quick time, she fell hopelessly in love with him. And when Uncle Nat became aware of the ripening fondness between his niece and Nnanna, he was quite delighted that Nonye had not heeded his opposition to her LA trip. Nnanna was very highly regarded within the Igbo community, as an upstanding young man, and very respectful to his elders. There might have been a few within the community who were surprised that Uncle Nat seemed to go somewhat out of his way to encourage their courtship, but Nnanna and Nonye were not among them. Nat Anigbo was well known, among his friends, to be strongly in favor of encouraging the Igbo children of the Diaspora to find love and marriage preferably within the *Igbo* or, failing that, at least the *Nigerian* communities.

Their romance had progressed from that chance encounter to this, their glorious July 20, 2002 wedding day. Nnanna knew what a debt of gratitude he owed to Nonye's friend Chinyere, who remained a constant friend to both of them, and helped keep their feet firmly planted on *terra firma*. Close to one full year had passed since that fateful flight from Newark to Los Angeles.

Nnanna looked across to the Chairman, and said: "As my bride just said, let the fun begin. The hall is full."

Chuka Okpala spread his arms wide, and then pointed to his chest. "The MC's here, that's me," he intoned. "So let's go. The kolanut is here. The Pastor's here. The microphone—where did I leave it? I had it in my hand a moment ago—"

"The DJ—what's his name—Magnus Aneke, he has it," said Ekemma, pointing.

Indeed the DJ had the microphone, and was waving it to and fro, trying to attract Chuka's attention.

Chuka turned and regarded the DJ in silence for a moment or two. "How did the fellow get his hands on my microphone, and how did he even know I was looking for it?" he asked the Chairman, but did not wait for his reply.

He walked briskly over to the DJ's corner, some fifteen or so paces to the left of the high table, and took the microphone from the DJ, none too gently, but with a sharp laugh.

"*Eneke-nti-oba!*" he addressed the DJ, using Magnus's nickname, and wagging a finger at him as one would at a naughty little kid. Magnus Aneke earned his sobriquet only because of the phonetic similarity between *Aneke* and *Eneke*, an aquatic animal whose ears (*nti*) are reputedly a wasted and superfluous organ. "From this distance, and with your music loud enough to wake our forefathers," he said flatly, "you could not have heard my conversation with *Ugo-Oranyelu*. You must be a lip-reader, or something."

The DJ laughed raucously. "*Nnamenyi*," he said, addressing the MC by his praise-name, "why are you surprised? You and me, we have done this thing many, many times. Don't you know what those who speak English call body language? Just the way you stand, or twist your body, or wave your arms, or scowl, are like words to me. You don't need to—"

But he was talking to Chuka's back. With short, quick strides, Chuka took the center of the dance floor, and lightly tapped the microphone two or three times. Then satisfied it was live, he coughed twice to gain the attention of the crowd.

"I probably don't need to introduce myself again," he announced. "But for the benefit of those who just got here, my name is Chuka Okpala, *Nnamenyi*—"

Shouts of "MC Emeritus!" rent the air and reverberated across the hall. Chuka smiled from ear to ear.

"Thank you! Thank you all! But we have to get a move on. First, let me also again introduce the Chairman for this reception, and his beautiful, elegant wife—Chief Nathaniel and Mrs Ekemma Anigbo. Chief Anigbo, *Ugo-Oranyelu Aniagu*, as most of you know, is the President of the umbrella Igbo organization, Nzuko Ndigbo, here in New Jersey, popularly known as NNNJ. More importantly, for this occasion, *Ugo-Oranyelu* is the uncle of the lovely bride, Nonye and, since about two hours ago, the uncle-in-law of the personable bridegroom, Nnanna Onwuka. Secondly, I have to apologize on behalf of the bride and groom, and their families, for the late start. This is not your usual late start for which our community is commonly known, and for which we should all be properly ashamed. We thought we were ready to start at least an hour ago, after the roll-call for the high table. But a little hitch developed, and we had to take care of it. Our sincere apologies."

He cleared his throat, even as his eyes swept the hall from end to end. "I believe the officiating priest has arrived. Oh yes, there he is, our good Rev. Dr. Nweke Emenike. Sir, you were not here at the roll call, but that's okay. We knew you were otherwise engaged in the Church after the wedding service. I hope you do not mind saying the opening prayer now, and then you may take your seat at the high table."

He stopped and waited for Rev. Emenike to join him, and then held out the microphone to him. Rev. Emenike, standing just about five feet six inches at his most erect, was plump and balding. He took the microphone, crossed himself with a rapid motion, and signaled to the crowd to rise to their feet. As they rose to their feet, many men knew to also remove their caps from off their heads. The few who did not know were quickly nudged, by those who did, to do likewise.

"Lift up your hearts!" the priest urged the assemblage.

"We lift them up unto the Lord!" the crowd intoned.

Rev. Emenike's prayer was short and succinct, and was only notable for his earnest entreaty to the Blessed Virgin Mary, Mother of God, to intercede on behalf of the newly-weds so they might be blessed with as many children as their hearts desired. Nonye and Nnanna exchanged rapid glances, and smiled. Children had been lately a subject weighing on both their minds, and which they had discussed endlessly. Nonye wanted at least four children; Nnanna consistently held forth on the economic imperatives of no more than two. "Especially if we're lucky to have a boy and a girl," he would say.

Uncle Nat claimed the privilege, as the oldest member of the bride's family present at the reception, of performing the kolanut invocation. He got no argument on the issue from the MC, or from the groom. Nnanna and his paternal uncle, Sylvester Okoye, a physical therapist, who had come all the way from Seattle, Washington State, had pretty much agreed that that was how it was supposed to be. Besides, Nat Anigbo's financial contribution to the cost of the wedding feast was truly beyond generous. Nnanna had argued, but somewhat perfunctorily, that among the Igbo, the standard practice was that the groom and his family principally bore the brunt of the expenses for the reception. "Don't waste your breath," a smiling Nonye had told him when they talked about it. "I know I'm very special to uncle Nat. Besides," she had added, with a look and a smile that brooked no further argument on the matter, "this is America! Here the bride's family carries the main burden, I'm told. Please let Uncle Nat do his thing."

He did. His kola-nut invocation followed the traditional pattern. He prayed for the marital happiness of Nnanna and Nonye. He echoed the prayer of the Reverend Emenike that God should bless the couple with children. He prayed for the safe return of the guests to their homes after the reception—that nothing should cause anyone, male or female, to stumble on the road.

Then he continued, glancing briefly at Reverend Emenike, and half-smiling: "We know that our ancestors, from the great beyond, are benevolently watching over all of us, and what we are doing here and now. I call on them to come take their share of this kola-nut. I say they are the saints in our Igbo traditional theology and world view. I hope what I'm saying does not trouble our Reverend brother Emenike, who is a proud successor of the European evangelists who brought Christianity to us. I am calling on our ancestors in this invocation because we continue to respect them as our forebears, and I see no conflict between that profound respect and my Christian faith. I should stop here because those who go to Church say that the sermon for the evening worship should not be long, because it is already late. And Ndi-Igbo say that if the kola-nut invocation is too long, our forefathers and those long-gone before us will refuse to partake of it."

When it came time to make the traditional Chairman's opening remarks, he seized the opportunity, or he would not have been Nat Anigbo, *Ugo-Oranyelu*, to "do his *other* thing"—hold forth passionately on a subject very dear to his heart, a subject on which he was ever ready and willing to take on the opposition.

"When I look at my beautiful niece Nonye, and his truly engaging husband today," he told his audience, "I see something that is exactly as it should be, as it is naturally meant to be. We must keep all those endearing human qualities within the large Igbo family. I am happy for them—and for myself, on account of my niece. Let those who say that the great wide world has become a global village hold fast to their point of view, and God bless every one of them. But let us never forget, as our people say, that the lizard that leaves the relative security of the tree trunk, and runs around, might well become a prey to a dog."

"*Ugo-Oranyelu-Aniagu!*" several voices called out loudly. Aniagu was the name of his village in Anambra State, Nigeria.

Nat, all smiles, raised his red chieftaincy cap in respectful acknowledgment of the acclaim, bowing modestly to his right, center and left.

Okocha Anigbo, aged twenty-eight, sat at table no. 1, reserved for the groomsmen and bridesmaids. Supporting his chin in the cup of his left hand, he was pensive as he listened to his dad expatiate on his favorite subject, which had lately become the principal topic of conversation between them. And which was why he had lately begun to cut down on the frequency of his visits to his parents. Okocha was not at all sure if his old man suspected anything. But no visit now went by without his dad alluding to the fact that his first son was fast approaching the next logical stage of his life, his next and looming rite of passage: marriage. And not just marriage, but marriage to an *Igbo* girl!

He quite understood that his dad's concern was natural. Not a few of the older members of the Igbo community's cultural associations had spoken to him quietly about this aspect of his life, and had dropped hints—sometimes directly, mostly obliquely—about this or that girl, who might make a *great* or *good* wife for someone like him. No one, it had struck him again and again, seemed to talk about a *loving* wife. He knew that the concept of love and marriage was not entirely foreign to his Igbo people, but he could not help wondering how deeply it was ingrained in the Igbo psyche.

He listened and watched abstractedly as the reception program followed its familiar course. But he perked up a little when his aunt Ngozi, called upon to say a few words to the bride and groom, startled everyone by bluntly declaring that her strongest wish was to return to America within the next nine months.

"I'm telling my daughter and my son-in-law to give me my first grandchild in nine months from now," she announced with a straight face. "I want to do my first *omugwo* before anything happens to me. God knows I thank Him for His many blessings, and I don't want to be greedy. Just the chance to come back to America to do the traditional thing and help my daughter look after her baby in the first year or so of its life. That's all I ask for. A chance to do my first *omugwo*! And there's my son Somtochi too, who has been in the university for just one year. But who knows when *he* will marry?"

Okocha paid scant attention when Nnanna, as usage required of the groom, groped Nonye's legs, under her voluminous wedding gown, in search of the garter. He was distinctly unenthusiastic about participating in the throwing of the garter, and was persuaded to line up with his fellow young bachelors only because he was one of the groomsmen, and it might have seemed ungracious and churlish if he had not. In the event, *he* caught the garter. But that was only because he could not have avoided catching it. Nnanna, his new cousin-in-law, had seemed—quite deliberately—to lob the thing in his direction, where he stood almost head and shoulders taller than his very excited rivals. He had indeed only thrust out his hand as a pure reflex.

"You're the next bridegroom!" several voices shouted, amidst the general hilarity, customary on such occasions.

Nnanna came to shake hands with him "You're a lucky son-of-a-gun," he told Okocha as they gripped hands.

"How so?"

Nnanna pointed to the girl who had earlier caught the bouquet. "Look at her, Okocha! That's why. Ifeoma's beautiful, isn't she? I know scores of young men who would—"

"Ah, yes, Ifeoma. I see she's sitting with her folks—"

"Of course," said Nnanna. "Are you forgetting—?"

"I'm forgetting nothing. I know Nonye gave Ifeoma her blessing. I've no doubt Ifeoma asked Nonye to let her sit with her parents. That's okay with me. More space at our table for everybody."

"What do you have against her, man? Like I was saying, there are scores of young men who would have given anything to have caught the garter."

"Nnanna, man! You know I'm not one of them."

"I know?" asked Nnanna softly. "But relax, man! You know this is never serious—just fun."

"I know it's fun, but—" Okocha said, and paused, shaking his head slowly from side to side. "You know, man," he whispered, "it might not be just fun for Ifeoma. You know what's going on, no?"

"No, I don't," said Nnanna, deadpan.

"Oh, yes! You do. You courted my cousin—let me see—at the very least, eight or nine months—"

"One year—just about," said Nnanna. "So, what?"

"There you go! One year! Well, you can't have courted her that long without knowing about Ifeoma. The two moved pretty much in the same circle of friends with that blabbermouth—what's her name?"

"Easy now, Okocha. I think I know the lady—"

"Yes, you do. Chinyere Mordi, no less. And you don't have to tell me she was the busybody who brought you and Nonye together—for which I am eternally grateful to her."

"You are?"

"Well, isn't it because of her that, today, I have a new and wonderful cousin-in-law, you, Nnanna Onwuka? Actually I should call you my *brother*-in-law. Nonye is like a sister. I don't see her any other way. And, talking of sister, Nonye is staring at us right now. Must be wondering what we're talking about."

Nnanna swung round, smiled, and waved discreetly to his bride, who sat demurely at the high table. Turning back to Okocha, he said: "Sorry, man. Love and duty call. We'll talk some more later about Ifeoma." They embraced in a quick motion. "Meantime," Nnanna quickly whispered into Okocha's ear, "Ifeoma is waiting, man."

Okocha watched Nnanna walk back to the dais with brisk, lighthearted steps. And watching, he felt an overpowering surge of jealousy. Jealousy, that Nnanna had found love from within their Igbo community, to the obvious and gushing delight of most of the notable personalities within that community! But especially his, Okocha's, father! And with that thought, his eyes were irresistibly drawn to Ifeoma Ndukwe, where she sat with her parents and their friends. "God!" he said to himself, "she *is* beautiful." For a moment or two, he wondered if he should do as Nnanna suggested, and go talk to her, but not out of any real desire to chat up a pretty girl. Rather, as the catcher of the garter, he had the notion that he was supposed to follow the community's wedding reception usage, and go through the motions of linking up with the girl that had caught the bouquet.

He hesitated, then looked towards the dais and saw Nnanna making repeated motions of his head to him, clearly in the direction of Ifeoma's table. Even the bride, his cousin Nonye, seemed to have been caught up in the mood of the occasion, and was, like Nnanna, gesticulating to him. This did not surprise Okocha. He had known, for quite a long time, that Nonye and Ifeoma were close friends, and Nonye had—on several occasions—sung her friend's praises to him, with the rather unsubtle objective of linking them up in a love connection. He loved Nonye like a sister. But he knew that she opposed his friendships with American girls, White or Black.

An uncharitable thought suddenly crossed his mind. He began to wonder if Nnanna and Nonye had colluded in some way to pre-determine the trajectory of, first the bouquet, and then the garter, in the hopes of entrapping Ifeoma and himself. And he concluded—perhaps to his eternal shame if he concluded wrongly—that his cousin and cousin-in-law were guilty as charged!

"Where's Tatiana when I most need her?" he asked himself wretchedly. "She should've been here by now."

Tatiana's paternal Grandmother, Wyomia, whose plane was scheduled to land at the Newark International Airport by five pm, had apparently expressed a strong wish that Tatiana should be there to receive her. "Granny knows I have a wedding reception to attend, and with you," Tatiana had said, when they had discussed the matter a day before the wedding. "You know she adores you.

But she sees nothing wrong with my being just a tad late. Okocha, I'm really sorry to have to do this to you but, me and my Granny, there's a special bond between us, as you well know! And I don't want to disappoint her." Tatiana had even wanted him to accompany her to the airport, if he could have managed it somehow. But she knew he couldn't. This was Nnanna and Nonye's wedding day, for crying out loud! There was no way he was going to miss even one minute of the celebrations!

He had thought long and hard about the matter, and had finally decided that the reception was going to be their occasion for *coming out*; an occasion to declare to the community, and especially to his parents, that Tatiana was his girlfriend, and there was nothing anyone could do about it. He hoped it would be a watershed of sorts in their relationship. He was under no illusions about what his father's attitude to Tatiana would be, but he desperately hoped that his mother would be more charitable and accommodating. "I'll be late perhaps two hours, three max," Tatiana had sworn to him earlier that morning. But then she had added, with what she meant to be a knowing smile: "With your Nigerian sense of time, I'm sure two or three hours will be nothing to worry about."

Okocha looked at his watch. It was already well past nine pm. He shook his head sadly, biting down on his lower lip. "I should have remembered about—how do they say it—*colored people's time*." He smiled faintly, and walked with resolute steps towards Ifeoma's table.

CHAPTER 2

Ifeoma Ndukwe watched as Okocha approached her table. Her smile was demure, but her eyes sparkled. From the moment he had caught the garter, and the significance of that catch had been noisily proclaimed by her friends, she had been in a state of subdued animation. She briefly allowed herself to indulge in a self-deluding fantasy—a fantasy in which she was romantically linked up with the engaging Okocha. He was, without doubt, one of the most eligible bachelors in the Nigerian and Igbo communities of New Jersey.

She knew she was in her own world of delusory imagination. She knew this because, as her friend Nonye repeatedly, and rather indelicately, loved to put it, "Okocha has the hots for an *Akata* girl," the Igbo community's favorite but unflattering term for the Black American—male or female. Ifeoma resisted a strong urge to turn to look at her father, who sat immediately to her right. She knew her dad, and that, at that precise moment, he would be watching her narrowly, to see how she was reacting to young Okocha, as he came and stood behind her, but slightly to her right.

"Can I ask for the first dance—?" Okocha began, but was interrupted by Ifeoma's dad.

"Too soon, young man!" Mr. Ndukwe said sharply. "The Chairman has not yet opened the floor for dancing."

"You're right, sir," Okocha said, bowing modestly. "I was merely asking Ifeoma in advance—"

"Dad!" Ifeoma cut in, but she was smiling. "This is a wedding reception. It's the Bride and Groom who will dance first, not the Chairman, before the guests can do so."

"Of course I knew that," said her dad, as he reached for a big bowl of roasted peanuts, placed centrally on the table, and pulled it closer to himself.

He scooped some of the nuts into a paper napkin, which he held in his left hand. "What I meant—"

"*Nnanyelugo*," Ifeoma's mother, Gloria, called out to him, using his praise-name. "Why don't you concentrate on your peanuts? You don't have to explain what you meant." She had a hand half-cupping her mouth, in a deliberately half-hearted effort to suppress her giggles. Mr. Ndukwe pretended not to notice her.

It was an awkward moment for Okocha, who stood rooted to the spot, transfixed. Standing in the narrow space between the tables, and slightly behind Ifeoma and her dad, he was relieved that neither could see his face at that moment. He should not have yielded to Nnanna and Nonye's pressure, he chided himself. He was desperately searching for a dignified way out of the impasse when Ifeoma stood up and placed a gentle hand on his shoulder.

"You can certainly have the first dance, Okocha," she said sweetly, "when the floor is open. Dad's just pulling your leg."

"Thank you, Ifeoma. I'll see you later."

Okocha threw a quick glance at Mr. Ndukwe, bowed gently but uncertainly to him, then immediately spun round and carefully wound his way back to his table.

From just this brief interaction with Ifeoma and her parents, he ruminated, he thought he knew the score with her family. He had heard rumors, and now he believed those rumors had been confirmed, that Ifeoma's dad and mom had opposing attitudes towards him. And was it not Nonye, no less, who had more than merely hinted that whereas Ifeoma's dad had some misgivings about him, her mom Gloria unabashedly looked forward to the prospect of having him as a future son-in-law?

Okocha sat quietly, resting his head in the cup of his hands, elbows on the table. He went into a brown study, pondering what he needed to do to avoid the impending clash of wills with *his* dad when his old man found out about Tatiana. Or did the old man know something already, and was merely toying with his, Okocha's, emotions? He did not know what to think, other than that his dad probably already suspected something, and chose to bide his time. But that was not at all like the father he knew. On a subject as important as his son's girlfriend, the senior Anigbo would have taken the bull by the horns, and put him on the spot. Squarely! No quarter given! None expected!

Suddenly he half-raised his head, and gritted his teeth. And, at that instant, he was convinced that the decision he had made, relating to Tatiana and him, was the right decision. It was a decision that had at first startled him on account perhaps of its audaciousness but which, on further reflection, seemed the most natural course of action in his circumstances. He would be a son worthy of his dad; a chip—in more senses than the merely physical—off the old block! Tatiana, when he told her about his intentions, declared herself ready to go along with it. "But," she had added, "you will have to do this in whatever way you choose, in your own style."

This was surely going to be a night of nights! In his state of mind, he could hardly wait for Tatiana's arrival.

A gentle touch, and the voice of his brother Kanu, sitting immediately to his right, brought him out of his reverie.

"I don't how many times I have to tell you this," Kanu said softly, placing a hand on Okocha's arm. "But you shouldn't have gone to Ifeoma's table—"

"Who says?"

"I know you're my big brother," Kanu said, with a sarcastic smile. "But you don't seem to understand our girls."

"And you do, kid brother? First-hand experience?"

"Sh-sh!" Kanu whispered fiercely, and pointed. "Don't look now!"

Too late to stop himself, Okocha jerked his head in the direction of Kanu's finger, and saw Ifeoma walking towards them. She was smiling beguilingly. Out of an innate sense of gallantry, Okocha made to rise from his chair, but was restrained by a firm hand pressure by Kanu, who clucked disapprovingly.

"What d'you think you're doing?" Kanu asked in a tone of exasperation.

"What I'm doing?"

"Let her come to you," Kanu counseled earnestly. "You've really got to watch it with our girls. She might get the wrong idea if—"

"Oh, shut up, Kanu!" said Okocha, as he quite deliberately rose from his chair, shrugging off his brother's restraining hand. He turned fully towards Ifeoma.

"What's up?" he asked, with a smile.

Ifeoma pointed towards the High Table. "I believe the Bride and Groom are ready for their dance. We should be ready to go and support them." She turned to Kanu. "Hi! Kanu. *Kedu?*"

"I'm doing okay, thank you," replied Kanu, noting—with mild amusement—the challenging tone of her question, which she had posed in the Igbo language. "I didn't hear the Chairman announce that the Bride and Groom will be taking the floor."

"Neither did I," said Okocha.

"There wasn't an announcement," said Ifeoma. "I've been watching Nnanna and Nonye, and they seemed to be signaling in a manner that suggests they are ready for their dance."

Okocha smiled indulgently, and said: "I think we should wait until they actually take the floor. They have the Best Man and the Maid of Honor sitting close to them. *They* are the best placed to give immediate support, if needed."

"But, Okocha, you and me, we are the closest to them. Shouldn't that count for something? You're very close to Nnanna. I know you think of him more as a *brother*-in-law than a *cousin*-in-law."

"Nonye told you?"

Ifeoma smiled. "What if she did? Isn't it true?"

"You got me there," said Okocha. "Doesn't matter, anyway. What matters—"

At that moment, the voice of the MC came over, loud and clear. "The Chairman says the Bride and Groom will now take the dance floor for their first dance ever as man-and-wife. Please give them the entire floor for a moment or two, and then you can all come forward to show your support in our usual way."

In less than no time, the dance floor was crowded, with everyone pressing forward to reach the newly-weds. Those lucky enough to get really close to them pressed several single dollar bills on the foreheads of the Bride or the Groom—in that peculiar Nigerian practice commonly called 'spraying'.

Okocha and Ifeoma were among the first to reach Nnanna and Nonye. After a quick, very brief exchange of hugs, Okocha took out a wad of crisp, very clean dollar bills. Smiling radiantly at his cousin Nonye, he swiveled and pirouetted, and undulated his body to the pulsating rhythm of musician Sonny Bobo's *Old Skool* beat. Simultaneously, he pressed his dollar bills, one at a time, on her forehead. Ifeoma, not to be outdone, danced sinuously opposite Nnanna, and pressed her dollar bills on his forehead.

Other dancers, seeming to recognize the special bond between the Groom and Okocha, and between the Bride and Ifeoma, held back a little. A few, impatient to do their thing, spun their wads of dollar bills in eye-catching, high-flying arcs, with the bills falling in a showery flurry all over the newly-weds and those nearest to them. Only those persons who had acquired the necessary dexterity, or those who thought they could, engaged in this spectacular display of flying dollar bills. And, of course, in doing so, they made quite sure that the Bride and Groom, as the beneficiaries of their largesse, saw them *in the act*. Or there would have been little or no purpose in their showmanship! The falling dollar bills, trampled upon indiscriminately by the throng of dancers, were picked off the floor as quickly as possible by young kids, armed with plastic bags, scrambling for the bills in some kind of competition to see who would pick up the most.

After 'spraying' the Bride and Groom, Okocha and Ifeoma lingered awhile on the dance floor and, like others, began to dance. Ifeoma, consonant with the literal meaning of her name, danced beautifully, and with beguiling grace and effortless charm. Okocha was searching for the appropriate words to compliment her on her dancing virtuosity when he felt an insistent touch on his shoulder, and turned.

"Easy, bro!" It was Kanu, his toothy smile lighting up his face. A mere step behind him was Somto, his face expressionless, his eyes darting from Okocha to Kanu.

"What are you doing here?" Okocha paused long enough to ask, his face and voice emotionless.

"That's an odd question to ask your brother," Ifeoma observed. "Of course he's here to spray Nonye and Nnanna."

"He doesn't have any money. He's just a flipping high-school boy!"

Kanu giggled. "Dad gave us some dollars—me and Somto," he said conspiratorially. Then he added, coming really close to Okocha, and lowering his voice, doubtless in hopes Ifeoma would not overhear him, "I envy you, big brother."

So saying, Kanu took out a small wad of dollar bills from the breast-pocket of his embroidered Igbo jumper, held both arms aloft, but bent at the elbows, and swayed and gyrated his way towards Nonye and Nnanna, his dollar bills flapping with the rhythmic motion of his arms. Somto, with a shrug and a gesture to Okocha, also took out his wad and followed closely behind Kanu.

"You're a little hard on your brother," Ifeoma said, after they had danced in silence for a long moment. Her eyes held Okocha's steadily, with a light and a twinkle that seemed to bare her soul to him. It was one of those moments when words were superfluous, and body language—the sometimes conscious, but mostly unconscious gestures of human communication—said it all. Watching the unaffectedly sensuous and sinuous grace of the beautiful girl who danced opposite him, Okocha needed to tap into his reserve of will-power to resist even the merest temptation to look at Ifeoma as anything more than a good friend of his cousin Nonye.

Conversation was difficult on account of the ear-shattering volume of the music. But there were couples who placed a high premium on holding some sort of a conversation in the midst of the din. These couples had perforce to cut down on the freedom of their dance movements, typically individualistic, and dance almost cheek-to-cheek—a style alien to the West African *high life* dance. Okocha pulled Ifeoma so close to himself that they were able to talk directly into each other's ears. Nevertheless, every spoken word was a shout, pitched high enough to have a chance of being heard.

"Never mind about my brother. He can take care of himself. You didn't hear what he just whispered into my ears. But I can tell you this. He finds you a very beautiful girl. And he's not alone. Half the young men in this crowd right now would give body and soul to be in my shoes."

Ifeoma inclined her head to one side, smiling in appreciation of his compliments. "You think so?" she asked softly. "But what about you yourself? Are you saying you have no body and soul to give? Or—"

She paused, and looked intently at him with a mischievous glint in her eye. "A penny for your thoughts!"

"What do you think I'm thinking?"

"Perhaps you're thinking what I'm thinking," she challenged him.

"Oh, come on, Ifeoma. You know what I mean."

"I'm not sure I do," she countered, still smiling. Then pausing again to gain his full attention, she asked him a question completely out of left field. "Is what you said anything to do with you and Tatiana?"

"Who—?" he started to say, then paused and, in a very subdued tone of voice, asked: "You know about Tatiana?"

"Surprised?"

"Who—how did—?"

"I give you one guess, and I bet you'll be wrong."

Okocha sighed. "Of course, Nonye!"

"Wrong!" She had quickly decided that this was not the time for complete honesty as to what Nonye had—or had not—told her about him and his *akata* girlfriend.

"Who else? Nonye knows how it is between me and Tatiana."

"She may know, but she didn't tell me anything," Ifeoma cooed into his ear, but loud enough for him to hear her above the din. Then she held up an arm. "I don't want to keep you in suspense any longer. I heard about Tatiana from your dad. There!"

If she had hit him with a punch flush on his jaw, the effect could not have been more dramatic. His mouth fell open, and stayed open while he struggled to collect his thoughts.

"My dad?" he muttered hoarsely. "But that's impossible! He doesn't know—. But wait a minute! Why would my dad, even if he knew, tell you anything? Have you two been talking about me?"

Ifeoma, pausing in her undulations, put out a hand and placed it on his shoulder. "I didn't say he *told* me; only that I *heard* about her from him."

"What kind of talk is this?" Okocha asked in frustration. "He didn't *tell* you! But you *heard* about her from him! What's that supposed to mean?"

"Simply, that he was not talking directly to me. I merely heard what he said about you and Tatiana when he was talking to somebody else. I just happened to overhear the conversation."

"You mean you just happened to be eavesdropping. Perhaps you came to our place to see your friend Nonye—"

"Okocha, please! This has nothing to do with my friend. It wasn't even at your place, but mine. You know my dad is the Socials Director of Nzuko Ndigbo—"

"Yes, and my dad is the President," said Okocha, his tone of voice noticeably alarmed. "The two of them were talking about me?"

Ifeoma pulled slightly away, and looked blankly at him, her lips exaggeratedly clamped together. She had the look of someone who feared she had spoken too much and out of turn. Then she moved closer to him, placed her mouth a mere inch from his ear, and said: "I'm not saying anything more. You want to know more, talk to your dad."

"You read my mind," said Okocha with a levity he did not at all feel. "That's exactly what I intend to do."

He held her at arm's length, his dance moves slower and more controlled. "What do you say we concentrate on the dance, and forget about conversation?"

"Let's!" Ifeoma said. "I'm fagged out competing with Sonny Bobo and his Old—whatever they call it."

"*Old Skool*," Okocha said. "But the man is a beautiful *high life* musician."

"The best," said Ifeoma, "if you ask me."

For the next several minutes, they focused on their dancing, with hardly a word spoken between them. Ifeoma was radiant, as Okocha knew she would be, dancing with him. This was not a question of conceit, he said to himself. He knew Ifeoma had a soft spot—a *very* soft spot—for him, which was very flattering and all that. But as he peeked at his watch for the umpteenth time, and wondered what was keeping Tatiana, he knew it would be cruel to do, or say, anything to Ifeoma that would encourage her to hope that there might be the possibility of a romantic relationship between them.

He had made that very clear indeed to Nnanna. And even if Nnanna was too dense—which Okocha knew he was not—to understand his drift earlier, when they talked about his catching of the garter, Nonye knew. If Nonye knew, Okocha reasoned, chances were good that Nnanna also knew. Nonye knew well enough about Tatiana that she had mounted a strong, tenacious opposition to what she so uncharitably called his love affair with an *Akata* girl. Such was Nonye's obstinate opposition to Tatiana that she appeared determined to leave no stone unturned to push and coax him into Ifeoma's arms.

Suddenly Okocha felt, rather than saw, someone's eyes on him, and looked up. And there, not quite three feet from him, were his cousin Nonye and his new cousin-in-law, Nnanna. The latter had his eyes firmly set on him, and the eyes were smiling radiantly. Nnanna nodded his head twice, thrice, as if in approval of something, and the wicked wink that accompanied the nods left

Okocha with only one thought: that Nnanna approved of what he, Okocha, was doing with Ifeoma.

The music suddenly began to wind down, and then stopped. Then the MC, Chuka Okpala, tapped on his microphone a few times, and gained the attention of the crowd.

"Thank you all, Ladies and Gentlemen," he announced. "It's time now for dinner. We have two service points, and it would be appreciated if guests can line up in an orderly manner at whichever of the two service points is closer to their tables. We will do this table by table. I have some assistants who will call your tables, when it is your turn. Please do not rush. There is enough food here to feed a battalion! The High Table of course will be served where they are. We are taking care of that."

CHAPTER 3

Dinner was well under way when Tatiana Karefa finally showed up at the wedding reception, two hours later than she had promised Okocha. Her hair—a wig actually—was disheveled, but her face was flushed with excitement. Okocha recognized the signs. Tatiana loved parties, especially if she was with him. More so if the occasion was a wedding!

They had been together at two previous weddings. Those were weddings of two of her African-American friends. On both occasions, Tatiana had been the one invited, and he had happily agreed to go with her, as her companion. She had so enjoyed the receptions, and been so gushingly overcome with emotion during the wedding service on the second occasion, that she had unrestrainedly dissolved into tears.

"This has to be the supreme moment in a girl's life," she had said, dabbing at her eyes with a frilly handkerchief. "My wedding day—whenever that happens—will be the happiest day of my life. I just had my bachelor degree, but it is as nothing compared to something like this. I can only hope I'll be mature enough then not to be as silly as I am now, shedding tears. You know what I'm sa-a-a-ying?"

Since then, she had only occasionally alluded to the subject of marriage, and usually in an indirect manner. But, in many different ways, she had left him in little doubt that, as their mutual affection grew, he was the star around whom she orbited. Her unalloyed joy in his company gave him immense and reciprocal pleasure. But it also gave him pause. As he watched and savored her increasing devotion to him, it was borne in upon him that hers was not love to be toyed with, or trampled upon and cast away at a whim. She gave him her love wholeheartedly and without equivocation; she accepted his love just as simply and unreservedly.

He met her in the corridor, just as she was about to walk through a door at the rear of the reception hall. He had been on the lookout for her, having twice received her cell-phone calls as she approached the Celestial Gardens. The second call told him that she was at the front desk of the facility, and would expect him at a rear entrance to the hall. Not for the first time, Okocha wondered what life would be like without the convenience of the cellular telephone system!

Tatiana walked into his arms for a bear hug that lasted long enough to fleetingly raise eyebrows all around them, and to evoke taunting remarks from a handful of acquaintances. In spite of her disheveled wig, she looked lovely in her close-fitting, flowered gown that reached down to just below her knees, and accentuated her softly curvaceous figure.

"First things first!" she said, at the end of their embrace. "I have to set my hair right."

"Let's get to our table first," said Okocha, "so you can at least rest your feet, and put down your handbag. Never mind the hair. You look gorgeous!"

"Spoken like a man!" Tatiana retorted, with a smile. "You don't know I have the things I'll need for my hair in the bag? Won't take long, honey. See you in a jiffy. Love you."

She made a beeline for the Ladies' room, looking back only once, to wave daintily to him as she disappeared into the rest room. He stood where she had left him, and waited. Soon he felt his body begin to tense up, as the significance of the occasion began to assert itself in his rather sluggish mind. It occurred to him—as he wondered how the night would go—that he had not the slightest idea how Tatiana would react to a situation that was going to be perhaps stressful for *him*. Stressful, that is, unless he was able to constantly remind himself that he had made the right decision to let his community—his world in every sense that mattered to him—know about Tatiana and himself!

Tatiana re-emerged from the Ladies' room with a new face. Amazing, Okocha reflected, how a simple touch to the hair here and there could so transform a woman's face as to render it almost unrecognizable from one moment to the next. Her hair was now brushed back, and gathered in a disciplined bun at the nape of her neck. She looked even more fetching, as she once again walked into his arms, and then let him lead her by the hand to his table.

He had not bothered to seek permission from his cousin Nonye or from Nnanna about seating Tatiana at the table reserved for the bridesmaids and groomsmen. He had known ahead of time that Ifeoma, and at least one other bridesmaid, had been allowed to sit elsewhere in the hall. So, there was not going to be any problem finding a chair at his table for Tatiana. He had, however, told his table companions about Tatiana, and that she would join him there. And his table companions had, by acclamation, approved of his intentions. "We'll finally get to meet your girlfriend," one of the bridesmaids said, with a wink and a smile that said she had known all along that he was up to something.

As soon as they reached the table, Okocha gestured towards his table companions, and said: "Introductions are due, I suppose," he announced to the group. "But I think I'll just rattle off the names for now. It isn't as if Tatiana will remember any of the names hereafter, unless she interacts often enough with any one of you. So, if it's okay with you all, I'll just say this is Tatiana Karefa. Tatiana," he said to her, as he rapidly indicated each person as he called out the name, "meet Chuck (as in Chukwudi, not Charles), Okwudili, Ugoada, Chinonso, Nneka, Nwakego, Ifunanya, Benedict, and last, but not least, Mike." Everyone shook hands with Tatiana, and assured her they were pleased to meet her.

Okocha then pulled out the chair next to his, and held it for Tatiana. Tatiana smiled her appreciation, but pointed to the dance floor.

"Let's dance," she said, as she deposited her handbag in the chair. "I'm sure I've missed a whole lot of dancing. And as you know, dancing is one of my favorite things."

"Sorry," said Okocha. "Dinner is being served, as you can see. People are already lining up at the service points, for the food."

"Who are those people dancing?" Tatiana persisted, pointing again to the dance floor.

"People who do not listen to the MC's instructions," Okocha told her. "The MC announced that this is dinner time, not dancing. But some people will do what they want to do, irregardless."

She took the chair he offered her, and looked around the hall. "Wow!" she exclaimed. "This is a very large crowd."

"Yes, and that's why there are two serving points," said Okocha. "And if I'm not mistaken, it'll soon be the turn of our table to go line up. I hope you're hungry, unless of course you've dined with your Granny—"

"At the airport?"

"I didn't say that. But when you took her home—"

"I didn't. A cousin who went with me to the airport did. They both knew—everyone at home knew—I had another engagement. I came here straight from the airport, as I believe I promised you I would. Perhaps you forgot—"

"I didn't," said Okocha, peeking at his watch. "I just didn't expect you to be *this* late. But I shouldn't be surprised. Isn't this what they call *colored people"s time?*"

"Getting your own back on me, honey?" she asked, laughing. She leaned towards him. "It's a shame you don't want to dance now. Might have served your purpose too. You know what I'm sa-a-aying?"

"No, I don't know what you're sa-a-a-ying," he said in his best imitation of her drawl. "Served my purpose? What do you mean?"

Tatiana smiled sweetly, then lowered her voice even more, and spoke directly into his ear. "Well," she said, "I might have misunderstood you. But I thought you had decided that this was going to be our night to—how did you put it—to come out to your folks, to let your community know that you and me, we're tight."

"I love the way *you* put it," said Okocha, laughing softly. "*You and me, we're tight.* That's neat. True also. But I didn't mean to do so in quite the way you are suggesting. Our dancing together at the wrong moment will not tell anybody anything, except perhaps that some people will say that Okocha's girl is the most beautiful girl in the hall."

Tatiana's face broke in a beaming smile. "I love it when you talk like that. Don't ever stop, you hear? Talking of food, I don't know about you, but I'm hungry! And I see you have my favorite snack there on the table. That's your Nigerian cookie. You call it—no, don't tell me—*chin-chin*, no?"

He nodded. "Right! Please help yourself."

Tatiana reached for the bowl of *chin-chin*, drew it closer, and helped herself to a moderate handful. "I love the different ways these cookies are shaped. It adds to their attractiveness. Great taste too. You make them with flour, you told me, and—"

"Eggs", Okocha said, as she hesitated. Then he pointed to a wooden snack bowl. "Try our Nigerian peanuts also. Your American roasted peanuts don't taste anything as good as ours—as you well know. Too processed, if you ask me." So saying, he pushed the bowl towards her.

"Must have cost an arm and a leg to import enough of the peanuts from Nigeria for this large crowd," Tatiana said, looking around her, her gaze taking in the entire hall. "There are so many tables—"

Okocha, the expression on his face conspiratorial, shook his head. "Only two or three tables," he whispered into her ear, "have been served with these special peanuts—the high table of course, and this table for the groomsmen and bridesmaids. All other tables have only your American version. Trust me."

"Your peanuts are certainly the best I ever tasted," said Tatiana. "But for the moment, I'll stay with the *chin-chin*. Don't want to overstuff myself too quickly. You know what I'm sa-a-aying?"

In the brief lull that followed, as she snacked on the *chin-chin*, Okocha began to reflect on what his best strategy should be, to achieve his grand design. Timing, he said to himself, would be key. Of one thing he was sure: Tatiana could not help him with this problem. She could not possibly have the natural, instinctive feel for the psychology of his people and of the moment that he thought might be critical in his calculations. He was not even sure about his own instinct for the apposite moment to make his move. He wondered if indeed there was such a moment. In the end, he thought his best tactic would be quite simply to play it by ear. To go as the spirit moved him. In a word, to put himself in the hands of his *chi*—that divine and personal spark of vitality that had shaped his life and destiny up to the moment.

One of the MC's assistants approached their table. "You're next!" he announced, pointing to the food serving station close to their table. "When you've been served, please don't try to return to your table the way you went. Let's do it in a sort of circular motion."

Okocha immediately stood up, and took Tatiana by the hand, and helped her up. They had barely taken a step when Kanu and Somto came up behind them. Kanu then put a hand on Okocha's shoulder.

"Hey, guys," he said in his most affable voice, "I don't think I'll be here and see you and Tatiana standing in this long food line. Tell me what you want, and I'll do my best to see you get it. What are younger brothers for, if not to help their big brothers?"

Okocha smiled, and turned to Tatiana. "He's doing this for you, and you only, believe me," he said. "But thank you, Kanu. And you too, cousin Somto! Kanu, you're a good kid brother. Tatiana, we'd better accept promptly before he has a chance to change his mind."

"He wouldn't dare—", Somto began to say.

"As if I would!" said Kanu, in the same breath. "Tatiana, if you're not sure what you want, you can leave it to me to bring you a good selection. I believe you like our *moi-moi*—that's a bean-cake—and fried ripe plantain, no?"

"Right on both counts! I suppose Okocha told you—"

"Not really. But we sometimes talk, you know."

He took their orders, and even refused Okocha's offer to accompany them so as to help carry the plates of food. Kanu had no doubts whatsoever that his big brother had made the offer, at best, only tentatively. Calling on one of the younger bridesmaids, Uzoamaka, to accompany them, Kanu led the way as the two cousins set off to join the long queue of hungry guests.

Tatiana and Okocha instinctively turned to each other and their eyes held for a brief moment. Tatiana then pointed a finger backwards over her shoulder, as her face lit up in a subdued but contented smile.

"Your brother, Kanu," she said softly, whisperingly. "I believe he likes me."

Okocha shook his head slowly, and put his mouth close to Tatiana's ear. "He doesn't *like* you, Tatiana. He *adores* you!"

"You're kidding me, Okocha—"

"Trust me. Kanu's one of the few persons in the family who know about us. And he's strongly supportive. He's a tough cookie, that one. Sometimes he thinks *he* knows better than I do what's in *my* best interest. But that's okay. He's the best kid brother one could ask for."

"I can see that," said Tatiana. "I remember the day, not so long ago, he kind of scolded me for something I did—"

"For something you did *not* want to do," Okocha corrected her. "Or rather something you would not let me do. If memory serves, that was the day I was going to—how do I put it? Actually it was the first time I decided to take the bull by the horns, and introduce you to my folks. I remember I had let Kanu in on my plans, and he was very gung-ho about it. But at the last minute, so to say, you surprised both of us by advising that I not do so. Kanu—"

"Surprised you?" asked Tatiana. "How so?"

"Because this is America," said Okocha. "America, the land of freedom and human rights! The land where women's rights and the feminist movement have found their most radical expression! If I must tell you the truth, Tatiana, neither of us had expected you—an educated, sophisticated, young lady of America—to be *that* reluctant in the situation."

"Don't blame me, honey," said Tatiana, laughing. "If you're looking to blame anybody, blame yourselves—I mean, your community. You know you and I, we've talked endlessly about how you guys—"

"Meaning us Igbo people?"

"You know what I'm sa-a-aying? Yes, you Nigerians! How you react whenever one of you—and as far as I can tell, usually the men—starts seriously dating an American! What's that name you call us?"

"*Akata* girls," Okocha said, and burst out laughing, drawing the attention of their table companions, who turned to look wonderingly at him.

"Yes, *Akata!* And I won't ask you again what it means—"

"Thank you, Tatiana. Truth is, as I've frequently told you, I have no idea whence that word came into our language. When I first heard it, I thought it applied to West Indian girls."

"I don't even like the sound of it," said Tatiana. "I just know it's a derogatory word. That's part of the reason I thought you shouldn't rush into anything. You know what I'm sa-a-aying?"

"Well, it's been more than one year since then," said Okocha. "Do you still see any reason my folks should not meet you?

"None!" said Tatiana emphatically. "Let's do it, and see what happens."

Okocha had been so wrapped up in his conversation with Tatiana, he did not notice Nnanna approach.

"What's up?" Nnanna asked. "What are you two whispering about so earnestly?"

"Isn't it amazing?" asked one of the Groomsmen, Mike Egbuna. "For the past several minutes, Okocha and his American girlfriend seem to have forgotten that they have table companions." He had spoken in Igbo, causing Tatiana to look sharply at him.

Okocha got up and, taking Tatiana's hand, helped her to her feet. "Nnanna, allow me to introduce Tatiana Karefa, my—"

"I know," Nnanna interrupted, with a wave of his hand. "She's your girlfriend, no?"

"Man, you surprise me," said Okocha. "Tatiana, this here is the Bridegroom of the day, my newly-minted cousin-in-law, Nnanna Onwuka."

"It's my pleasure to finally meet you," said Nnanna, first shaking hands with Tatiana, and then, on an impulse, pulling her to him in an embrace. "You're beautiful, as I knew you would be," he added, at the end of the embrace.

"You knew?" asked Tatiana demurely, looking fleetingly at Okocha.

"Man," interjected Okocha, "you'd better not try to explain this. Let's just leave it as you said it. Tatiana *is* beautiful."

There was mutual understanding in both their eyes as Okocha and Nnanna looked at each other. Not quite two hours earlier, as he was urging Okocha to approach Ifeoma, Nnanna had claimed he was not aware of what was going on. Okocha had understood this to mean that Nnanna did not know about Tatiana. That declaration had been a surprise to Okocha, in light of the fact that Nonye had met Tatiana at least once, if not twice, and was well aware that he and Tatiana were dating. And what Nonye knew, it was a safe bet Nnanna also knew. Now Nnanna had finally acknowledged the fact that he knew about Tatiana, even if he had never met her before.

Mike Egbuna coughed loudly two or three times, to draw Okocha's attention. "What was that name again?" he asked.

"Which?"

"Her last name. Tatiana what?"

"Karefa," Tatiana herself answered, stealing a glance at Okocha.

Mike Egbuna looked around the table, with an odd kind of expression on his face. "Am I the only one here who thinks the name sounds like *Okoroafo*?"

Okocha and Tatiana turned to each other. Simultaneously, each pointed to the other, and lifted up an arm. Then, to the evident surprise of everyone around the table, they exchanged high-fives—not just once, but two emphatic times.

Nnanna leaned towards Okocha and Tatiana. "Looks like you've got to explain the high-fives. Have you two been discussing the matter?"

"Have we indeed!" Tatiana asked rhetorically, even before Okocha could get a word out. "I remember it was on our second date that Okocha first told me that I might be an Ibo girl."

"Yes indeed," Okocha said. "I told her that her family name Karefa might well have been derived from the Igbo name Okoroafo, obviously corrupted in the process of transmission through the centuries, from one generation to the next."

Mike Egbuna stood up, and knocked twice on the table. "Ladies and Gentlemen at this table," he proclaimed, with a comical air of importance, "I'm sure I speak for everyone here when I say to Tatiana Karefa that we welcome her *back* into the clan, as our long-lost sister. Tatiana, let me reintroduce myself. I am Michael Egbuna, currently and for the past several years, the honorable Treasurer of our—that is, me, Nnanna and Okocha's—home-town association in New Jersey, the Aniagu Kindred Progressive Union. Aniagu is our home town in Nigeria."

He paused and looked around him. His eyes shone, and there was mischief in them. When next he spoke, he reverted to the Igbo language.

"I'll dare to predict," he said, looking Okocha directly in the eye, "that perhaps soon—two, three years—we may have the great pleasure of welcoming her into our Union, who knows?"

His eyes avoided Tatiana's, but held Okocha's challengingly. But Okocha was not at all sure if Mike was seriously challenging him to make some sort of a statement about his future with Tatiana. It was of course entirely possible, Okocha said to himself, that the fellow might have had a beer or two too many. He shook his head, smiling, but kept his eyes on Mike.

"Who knows, indeed?" But he merely mouthed the words—like Mike, in Igbo—without giving them utterance, moving his lips silently. Then he took Tatiana by the hand, and turned to Nnanna. "Please tell cousin Nonye that we, Tatiana and me, we'll come to the high table after we've eaten, to say hello to her—"

"And to your dad and mom?" Nnanna asked, his expression quizzical.

It was not so much the question, as the puzzled look that went with it, that affected Okocha deeply. He stared hard and long at Nnanna, even as his hold on Tatiana's hand unconsciously tightened. He became aware of this only when Tatiana began to struggle to withdraw her hand from his.

"Sorry, Tatiana!" he quickly apologized, letting go of her hand. "It's his fault," he added, turning and pointing accusingly at Nnanna.

"What did I do now?" Nnanna asked softly, with a smile that was strangely at odds with his raised eyebrows.

"You can't fool me with that fake innocent look, man," Okocha countered, just as softly, leaning towards Nnanna. "I know you're up to something."

"Please, Tatiana," Nnanna said, raising his voice, "could you excuse us for just a moment? I'd like to consult Okocha about something. It won't take long, I can assure you. I'll return him to you in a matter of minutes. It's really a man-to-man thing that you don't want to hear, believe me."

Okocha turned to Tatiana, and appealed to her with his eyes. "I hope you don't mind?"

"Not at all, honey," she said graciously. "But wait a moment. Here comes our food. Thanks a lot, Kanu, Somto, and you too—I forget the name—"

"Uzoamaka," said Kanu.

"Thank you, Uzoamaka. I really appreciate this."

"I don't know how I can thank you two guys," Okocha said, looking from Kanu to Somto. "If there's—"

"Don't worry, I'll think of something," said Kanu, smiling mischievously. "In the meantime, here's your food."

So saying, he deposited the tray he was carrying on the table, and gestured to Somto and Uzoamaka to do the same. Then he selected two of the four plates, placed one before Tatiana, and the other before Okocha. "This is yours, Tatiana—*moi-moi*, a little bit of *jollof* rice, and fried plantain. Okocha, this is yours. You asked for yam *foo-foo* and *egwusi*-soup. Enjoy!"

"Thanks a million, bro!"

"I don't know where you're going," Kanu said to Okocha. "Don't take too long—"

"Or the food will be cold," Somto added, and turned to Uzoamaka. "Thank you very much, Uzoamaka!"

"Please excuse us," said Nnanna, looking appealingly at Tatiana. He put an arm around Okocha's shoulders, and led him away from the table.

As soon as they reached the long spacious corridor, Okocha held out an arm and stopped Nnanna in his tracks. "You son of a gun!" he said. "You know more about this thing than you're willing to admit. You sure didn't call me out here to consult me about anything. This is about Tatiana and me, no? So spit it out! What's going on? Should I or shouldn't I take her to your high table? You foresee any problems or what? C'mon man! You know something. I can see it in your eyes."

Nnanna hesitated, looking everywhere but at Okocha. In the end he threw up his arms, and sighed. "Guilty as charged!" he said. "I suppose I have no choice but to tell you. Yes, it's about you and your American girl. Your old man saw you and Tatiana walking into the banquet hall. And I heard him swear under his breath—"

"What did he say?" Okocha asked breathlessly.

"Nothing," said Nnanna, his eyes shifting from side to side. "Nothing that I heard clearly. But he was visibly unhappy. And I saw your mom put an arm around his shoulders."

"Go on, man!" Okocha pleaded. "You can't stop now. Are you saying I shouldn't—?"

"Oh, I don't know!" Nnanna said, in desperation. He ran his left hand uncertainly from the front to the back of his head, and stared at nothing in particular for a moment or two. From Okocha's dad's dark mutterings when he saw his son walk into the reception hall with Tatiana, Nnanna suspected that there could be trouble. "I don't know what to tell you. I'll admit I'm not as ignorant of Tatiana as I—well—pretended to be. Nonye has let me in on some of the goings-on. But as to your dad and mom—your dad especially—from what our entire Igbo community has heard him say openly on many occasions, I doubt he'll be particularly thrilled that you're dating an *Akata* girl. And if you take Tatiana this openly to the high table to, as you put it, say hello to him, he'll surely misread the whole thing, and think you're challenging him. Is that what you want?"

Nnanna paused and, this time, looked directly into Okocha's eyes. "Nonye has not said anything clearly about whether your dad even knows about—"

"He knows!" Okocha declared emphatically. "He knows everything!"

"How would you know—?"

"I just found out, only a few minutes ago, right here at this reception. Ifeoma told me. She overheard her dad and my old man talking about the matter. So, man, what to do now?"

"Don't!" Nnanna said. "If you want my advice, don't rush into anything now! Give your dad a little more time. But something tells me my advice is a trifle late, no? I see something in your eyes that I don't like at all. I don't know what you had in mind, bringing her here this openly, and then you want her to meet your dad and mom. Watch out, my friend! There may be the devil to pay, if you're not careful. Do you hear me, Okocha Anigbo?"

"I hear you," Okocha said, gently putting both his arms on Nnanna's shoulders. "I hear you loud and clear, man. But this thing between me and Tatiana has reached a point of no return. What's that our proverb about not letting the fear of defeat stop one from engaging in a worthy fight?"

Nnanna looked into Okocha's eyes, and smiled. "I'm impressed that you're familiar with that proverb. You know, sometimes I forget that you actually grew up at home before your folks moved to America."

"I was in high school," Okocha said proudly, "when dad finally got his green card, and moved the family to the U.S."

"So I've heard," said Nnanna. "But of course you have become so Americanized, it is sometimes difficult to believe you're not American, born and bred. You sound totally American! And talking of American, you're All-American in football—and that's a game we don't even play in Nigeria. I hear you took to the game as fish takes to water."

Okocha waved a dismissive hand. "Forget all that," he said. "That was then! This is now! Listen, Tatiana must be wondering what's keeping us." He paused, then pointed over his shoulder towards the reception hall, and shook his head. "Nnanna, man!" he said. "The die is cast, as they say. This is the moment of truth because, in the next several minutes, one of us two—my old man, or myself—one of us is going to have to draw a line in the sand. It's going to be either *his* way, or *my* way. I think I've shilly-shallied enough. I have to do this for Tatiana and myself. It's not fair to her for me to go on like this."

Nnanna looked down meditatively for a long moment. Then he lifted his head, stared briefly at Okocha, and shook his head slowly. "What can I say?" he asked rhetorically. "Good luck, man. May *The Force* be with you!"

"I'll need both."

"But you look so calm and composed," said Nnanna. "If I were in your shoes, I know I'd be a bundle of nerves."

"And you think I'm not?" Okocha responded, and stretched forth both his arms towards Nnanna. "Look at my hands, and tell me again I'm calm. In fact, you'll have to excuse me because nature calls urgently and I must answer."

"I'll see you later," Nnanna called after Okocha as, without further ado, Okocha spun round and headed hurriedly to the nearest rest room.

CHAPTER 4

O kocha stood in front of the rest room mirror and, for a long moment, stared unseeing at his reflection. Then he took a small comb out of his jumper pocket and mechanically ran it several times through his hair. He finally came fully awake to his surroundings when a careless stroke with the comb scraped a tender tissue at the back of his right ear, causing him a searing pain. He looked again at his reflection in the mirror, smiled with some satisfaction, and went through the quite futile motion—a long established habit—of patting down his close-cropped hair. There was a time, in his first and second years of high school in America, when he favored the *afro*—the long, bushy, but scrupulously well-rounded and tightly curled hair style, that was even then no longer the rage it had been a decade or two earlier. But he had adopted it, as some sort of a symbol of his closeness to his African-American soul brothers. A rather sad smile played gradually across his face as he ruminated on what he now thought of as his early years of immaturity in the United States.

Years of immaturity! He turned the phrase over and over in his mind. They were years when he had mostly toed the line, in strict obedience to his father's strictures relating to a whole host of matters, from the rather mundane to the more serious issues of morality—especially sexual morality. No physical fights with schoolmates, or team mates, whatever the provocation! Absolute obedience to those in authority over him, at school or on the playing field! "A Christian kid like you," his father had pontificated, "walks away from trouble, from other boys, and from your teachers and coaches, unless someone is asking you to burn your fingers over a flame, or something of the sort! And, especially, watch your steps with the girls. Satan—and his henchman, the devil—can come at you under different guises. Be warned!"

He had mostly had little or no trouble from the regular schoolboy bullies who, perhaps taking one look at his superb physique, steered clear of him. The problem was of course that the very same physical attributes that had persuaded the bullies to keep their distance, created its own—quite delectable—problems from another angle: the fair sex. The girls simply would not—or could not—keep *their* distance! And it was, inevitably, in this regard that he had, with bothersome frequency, fallen afoul of his old man's rules of conduct. His dad, especially in those early years, only had to see him in the company of a girl to unleash a torrent of denunciations, and dark mutterings about the wages of sin.

Whenever the subject of girls came up in their conversations, his dad had seized the opportunity to preach and moralize endlessly. But the old man, to judge by his impressive build and quite transparent virility, and the many times Okocha had espied him ogling the ladies, must have been something of a ladies man in *his* time. Okocha had even overheard his mom now and again tease his dad with remarks—to be sure always lightheartedly made—about this or that woman who had preceded her in his affectionate esteem. But his dad had a ready and unvarying response to the tease: "Bottom line," he would say, "is that none of that mattered, because the girls went away when I did not follow through as no doubt some of them had hoped I would."

Okocha did not know if he could always believe his old man's consistent denials about that period of his life. It was of course possible, Okocha reasoned with himself, that the mores of his days, growing up, might have made it relatively easier for his dad's generation to obey the seventh, and most titillating, of the Ten Commandments handed down to the Biblical Moses more than three millennia ago: *'thou shalt not commit adultery'*. Okocha had, on one occasion, dared to point out to his dad that nowhere in the Ten Commandments had it been expressly stated that sex between consenting *unmarried* adults was forbidden. To which his father had retorted that there was only a thin line between fornication and adultery, and that the former, perhaps slowly, but inexorably, led to the latter.

He heard the sound of approaching feet, and quickly pulled down two segments of the paper towel. He wiped his hands and, squeezing the paper towel into a ball, threw it with an inborn athletic skill into a trashcan some distance away from him.

"You play basket-ball?" the new entrant asked, holding the door of the rest room open, and looking admiringly at Okocha.

"A little bit," Okocha replied, with a grateful smile. "Thank you very much."

His mind was in turmoil as he emerged from the rest room. It remained in that state of uncertainty until he reached his table. But one look at Tatiana, and his doubts melted away, replaced by a firmness of purpose which he knew he would need if he hoped to have the merest chance of success with his dad and mom.

As if drawn by a magnet, Tatiana rose from her chair as he approached. She looked into his eyes, and took the hand he held out to her. His fingers closed on hers as, for a very brief moment, he spoke to her with his eyes, and she replied with the faintest of nods, and a smile that was as heart-warming as the bright sparkle that lit up her eyes.

"But what about the food?" she asked, pointing to their two plates.

It was only then that Okocha noticed that she had not touched her own food.

"You have not eaten?" he asked her.

"I was waiting for you, honey."

"Then you're not as hungry as I had thought you would be," Okocha told her. "However, the food can wait. What we must do now cannot. Let's go!"

Without another word, Okocha led her by the hand away from their table. He walked with the assured steps of a man who knew that the very few steps he needed to reach the high table represented probably the most crucial, the most important steps he had ever taken in his entire life, up to that moment.

Because they were among the earliest to be served, the high table dignitaries had mostly dined. Okocha saw his father nonchalantly picking his teeth—undoubtedly with one of a little stock of toothpicks, which he seemed always to have in one or the other of his jumper or trouser pockets on these festive occasions.

Notwithstanding his renewed tenacity of purpose, Okocha felt his heart begin to go pit-a-pat as he and Tatiana neared the high table. He was angry with himself, but he knew he could not afford to lose his cool, no matter what. He recovered much of his aplomb when Tatiana gently pressed his hand, which she held in hers. Okocha turned to look at her, wondering whether, and how, she had sensed that he was beginning to be affected by the situation. Her smile, in answer to his unspoken question was, mercifully, all he needed to recover his composure.

He had not felt the need to discuss tactics with Tatiana. He did not think any particular tactic would guarantee the outcome he sought. Indeed he sought no particular outcome to which he could give a name. Other than Nnanna, no other person at the reception knew he was about to make very public what only a handful of individuals—including apparently, and most importantly, his dad—already knew: that he and Tatiana were for real, and that what they had between them was the real thing!

Instinctively, he steered Tatiana towards the end of the high table farthest from where his dad and mom sat. By this maneuver, he hoped to be able to greet several of the dignitaries, and introduce Tatiana to them, before he had to face his dad. But even as he did this, he felt his eyes irresistibly drawn to Nnanna, where he sat with his bride Nonye, in dead center of the table. Okocha knew that Nnanna would have his eyes riveted on him, because he, Nnanna, alone was privy to the unfolding drama, and had expressed some reservations about it. But when their eyes met, Nnanna promptly looked down and away, shaking his head slowly and sadly. Nonye was the one staring fixedly at him, with eyes in which amazement and disapprobation were mixed in about equal proportions. "No surprise there," Okocha murmured to himself. "Nnanna must have told her."

Okocha, eyes firmly set on Nonye, inclined his head to one side and made a gesture of helplessness with his free hand—a gesture which he also hoped would tell her that there was now no turning back; that his course was set, and his purpose irreversible.

He had not reckoned with his old man. At just the moment he turned his eyes away from Nonye, he heard his dad call out his name. The booming voice stopped him in his tracks and, when he turned, he saw his dad beckoning to him peremptorily. The imperial bearing and magisterial gestures of his dad did not surprise Okocha. What did, was the smile on his dad's face. Okocha rubbed his eyes and looked again. The smile was still there.

"Man proposes, but God disposes," Okocha muttered to himself, but to Tatiana he whispered: "Let's go meet my old man. This might well be our moment of truth."

He shrugged imperceptibly as he and Tatiana swung round and headed towards his dad and mom. His father's eyes held his unwaveringly. The smile was, and remained, inscrutable. Okocha went immediately on his guard against reading too much into that smile. He knew his dad, and had now and again seen how his smile could, in the blink of an eye, change into a scowl so dark and deep as to seem not just chilling, but *un*human.

"Who's your friend?" Mr. Anigbo breezily asked his son. "Your mom and me, we'd like to meet her."

Okocha stole a quick glance at his mom, who responded with a faint nod, as if in confirmation of what his dad had just said. Talk about the moment of truth! In the brief second or two which was all the time he had to think about it, Okocha decided to speak *his* truth, strongly believing with his Igbo people that 'truth is life', or, as his Christian religion had taught him, that the truth would set him free.

Okocha put an arm around Tatiana's shoulders, so that they stood side by side, with only the width of the high table separating them from his parents.

"Dad, mom," Okocha intoned. "May I introduce Tatiana—that's Tatiana Karefa. She's my girlfriend. Tatiana," he called to her, and pointed to his dad and mom. "Meet my parents."

For just a brief moment, time seemed to stand still, but his dad's voice quickly shattered that illusion. "Pleased to meet you, young lady," the senior

Anigbo said, extending a hand to Tatiana, who grabbed it happily and with a radiant smile.

"And I'm pleased to finally meet you guys," Tatiana said, shaking hands with Okocha's dad. When she turned to do the same with his mom, she found her smiling sweetly, but holding her right arm stiffly by her side.

"A handshake isn't good enough for me," Okocha's mom said, gently shaking her head. "You'll have to come round to this side of the table so I can hug you."

"With pleasure," said Tatiana. "Okocha, shall we?"

They went, and each received a warm-hearted hug from Okocha's mom. "You're beautiful, my child," Ekemma Anigbo said to Tatiana, then turned to her son, "Okocha, you should bring her to the house. This is not the right place or occasion for any kind of conversation."

"You can't imagine how much I've looked forward to this day," said Tatiana. "I'm just so thrilled to meet you and Okocha's dad."

Mrs. Anigbo's smile was expansive. "So am I, to finally meet you—"

She stopped abruptly, as her hand flew to her mouth. Quickly recovering from her slip of the tongue, and in a voice that had changed to a damage-control cadence, she said: "I mean, it's a pleasure to meet you."

Okocha leaned towards his mom. "It's okay, mom," he said in an undertone to her. "I know."

He embraced her a second time and then turned to his dad. "We, Tatiana and me, we thought we should come to the high table to greet you guys—"

"'You *guys*'?" His dad's voice was querulous. He did not like the word, *guy*, which he believed to be an indication of how far his two sons had become Americanized.

"Sorry, dad," Okocha quickly said, in a voice that might have sounded genuinely penitent were it not for his somewhat sardonic smile—a smile with which his old man was all too familiar. "I meant to say—"

"Okocha, I know what you meant to say. It's okay. Get along with you both now!"

Okocha was familiar enough with his dad's manner of speech to recognize that though the words might have sounded harsh, the serene expression on his dad's face took the bite out of them. Okocha thought he knew why: his dad was enjoying himself, as he always seemed to do at wedding receptions, especially when he was in the chair. Okocha was now glad that he and Tatiana had started their high table encounters with his dad and mom. From that point on, Tatiana's introduction to the others was something of a breeze. Even his cousin Nonye, though she did not exactly bubble over with enthusiasm, nevertheless received Tatiana with decorum and even a touch of cordiality.

Nnanna was his usual cultured self and, having of course met Tatiana earlier, was convincingly warm to her at their reintroduction.

*   *   *

Tatiana and Okocha ate their food in silence, but Okocha's was not the silence of contentment. He was, by turns, meditative, acutely puzzled, guardedly optimistic, or—at the other end of his emotional spectrum—rather deflated. His emotions, constantly changing, chased one another fleetingly across the befuddled theater of his mind.

From moment to moment, he asked himself how he might best interpret what had just happened. There was that inscrutable smile on his dad's face, as he shook hands with Tatiana. Tatiana, an *Akata* girl with whom his son was obviously very seriously involved! Okocha did not, for one second, believe that his old man would have missed the import—the deliberately staged significance—of his introduction to Tatiana. This, at a wedding as important to him as this was—the wedding of a favorite niece, Nonye, to a favorite son of his New Jersey Igbo community, Nnanna. And then, there was his mom! For a woman of her gentle nature, it was perhaps not totally surprising that she had warmly embraced Tatiana. However, she had not only complimented Tatiana on her beauty, but had requested that he bring her to the Anigbo home. Last, but not least, Nonye, long an advocate of Ifeoma as his girlfriend, had been the soul of courtesy to Tatiana.

All this, Okocha reflected, did not necessarily add up to a ringing endorsement of Tatiana as a future Mrs. Okocha Anigbo. It was clear to him that, shorn of all peripheral considerations, the prospect of his marriage to the American girl was—or would soon become—the core concern of his family, especially his dad. Okocha was on his guard against the temptation to view the evening as anything more than a passable achievement—a so-so beginning to his moves to bring his girl into the family fold. The damper on his optimism was—and remained—that inscrutable, enigmatic smile on his old man's face, at the crucial moment of his first meeting with Tatiana. He knew his dad; knew too that the old man's instincts would rebel against the American girl, and her ilk, as prospective daughters-in-law.

Tatiana broke into his thoughts. "You know something, honey?" she asked. "Perhaps you've been a tad unfair to your dad, you know what I'm sa-a-ying? He seems an okay guy to me."

"Please don't judge that book by its cover," Okocha said, shaking his head meditatively. "He has his moods and, in a thing like what we're embarked on, I suspect it isn't wise to jump too soon to conclusions. If it's his smile you're thinking of, I know the old man well enough to fear that those smiling teeth could easily change to the fangs of a carnivore."

"That's a very harsh judgment."

"I'd rather start there, a little negatively," Okocha said, frowning, "and look upwards, than start with unfounded optimism, and then watch everything go south."

CHAPTER 5

Chief Nathaniel and Ekemma Anigbo lived in a large, two-storied, five-bedroom house, surrounded on every side by trees that blossomed in spring and summer, and with a garden full of flowers carefully chosen for their exquisite colors in the growing seasons. Chief Anigbo, who hated Botany as a subject in his high school years, and knew next to nothing about flowers, engaged the services of a part-time gardener, and paid him rather more than his wife thought they could afford. The house was located in a very respectable neighborhood of Woodbridge, N.J., close to the intersection of El Pam Boulevard and Interstate Route 1. It was conveniently close to the Woodbridge Mall, one of the better known malls in the state, which was just under a mile away. Ekemma loved to spend time in the mall, dawdling, buying very little, but stopping now and again to refresh herself at a McDonald's, a Burger King, or any one of a handful of other restaurants that were strategically located on both floors of the huge structure.

Chief Anigbo sat meditatively in his chair, in his living room. This was his *king's* chair, intended mostly for his exclusive use, especially when there was company. And there seemed to be always company, which was an indication of his social status and significance in the Nigerian and Igbo communities in New Jersey. To the left of the king's chair, there was a love seat, next to which, in an L-shaped arrangement, was a long settee. A commode, directly opposite the king's chair and the love seat, had space for a twenty-one inch television set, and a glass-enclosed cupboard on either side of the T.V., with shelves on which were displayed a number of African artifacts. Among these were two twelve-inch delicately sculptured human heads, of Igbo-Ukwu pedigree, and a matching pair of terracotta heads of Ife (Yoruba) origin, acquired and proudly show-cased by the Anigbo family.

Against one wall, directly behind the long settee, and in some kind of isolated grandeur, was a *chaise-longue* which, despite its fancy name, was but a long chair, marketed under its French name. It was a sofa with only one arm rest. A longish oval table, glass-topped, stood in the approximate middle of the sitting room, but conveniently close to the chairs. Framed family photos hung from three of the four walls of the room, or sat atop the commode.

In his mind's eye, he saw the room full of people. His people. He loved the noise and bustle of ordinary conversation, and sometimes even of discord, so long as the members of the union could maintain a reasonable level of civility to one another. His sitting room had become, over the years, the stand-by venue for the gathering of the sons and daughters of Aniagu, the name of their village in Nigeria. They named the association the Aniagu Kindred Progressive Union, New Jersey, and held their meetings on the third Sunday of every other month.

Evidently, neither the originator of the association's name, nor the general assembly when it voted to approve it, had given any thought to the fact that its acronym, AKPU, spelt the Igbo word for cassava (or manioc) which at home in Nigeria, is generally regarded as the poor man's food. No matter! Too late to change the name, the association members had no option but to ignore the muted sneers of their fellow Igbo. And they sometimes countered the sneers by pointing out that if one inflects the pronunciation of the acronym differently, *akpu* denotes solidity in one of its senses.

Chief Anigbo derived much pleasure from participating in the meetings of AKPU, of which he was one of the founding fathers and was, for the first four years of its existence, the President. Which was how it came about that his house became the favorite venue for their meetings. The collective will had been that the venue would rotate monthly to different family homes, but only a handful of members volunteered their homes. In the event, Chief Anigbo, strongly supported by his wife Ekemma, had little option but to offer his living room as a stand-by venue for the bi-monthly meetings in the calendar year.

As the President of AKPU, he had succeeded in giving the union a significant presence in the community of Igbo associations that dotted the New Jersey landscape. On relinquishing his AKPU presidency, it was a given that he would ascend—and he did—to the presidency of the umbrella Igbo organization in New Jersey: the Nzuko Nd'Igbo of New Jersey (NNINJ but, somewhat illogically, better known as NNNJ). Unopposed at the election, and voted President by spontaneous acclamation, Chief Anigbo, in his acceptance speech, had declared that the centerpiece of his tenure would be the promotion of an awareness, among the Igbo youth, of their cultural heritage in all its aspects: language, traditions and family values.

To those ends, he had spared no effort to ensure that the Igbo Class, taught fortnightly in Spring and Summer, was well provided for. The classes did not teach the young ones only the structure and grammar, or the phonemes and phonetics, of the language. Almost equal emphasis was accorded to the teaching of Igbo culture and traditions. His primary objective, which had lately become an obsession, was to ensure that both of his sons, Okocha and Kanu, ultimately spoke Igbo conversationally. But beyond that goal, he hoped they would live their lives as dyed-in-the-wool Igbo men, and marry from within the ethnic family. As he had done. As his father—and *his* father before him—had done.

Okocha, his first son, spoke Igbo adequately before the family relocated to the United States. For that, he was thankful to God, and to his ancestors—who, he liked to say, watched over him and his family from the great beyond.

His second son, Kanu, was another matter. Kanu was a great kid but, unfortunately, he had unavoidably been literally uprooted from his natural traditional milieu when his Igbo cultural underpinnings were as yet largely unformed. Poor Kanu! He had cried endlessly, inconsolably, when he realized that he was going to leave his friends behind, to go live in a strange land. Not coincidentally, the youngster was what someone in the Igbo community disparagingly referred to as a cultural floater. To be sure, Kanu had acquired a smattering of the language, but that was principally because dad and mom had established it as a matter of deliberate policy that they would speak to their children, as often as possible, in Igbo. Which, Chief Anigbo was surprised to find out, was not as easy as it might have seemed to them initially! It was even more difficult to compel the children to do likewise. Even Okocha! In the end they had been forced to accept what they had been powerless to prevent: that Kanu, especially, was probably never going to speak Igbo conversationally. This, notwithstanding that he had an elder brother who spoke it passably. And notwithstanding the Igbo classes, which he attended fairly regularly, but which in recent months had functioned in fits and starts!

The situation was even more troubling and challenging in matters of the heart. He had probably never thought of himself as a shining example of the modern man in outlook and opinions, but he believed he was moderately open-minded in a general, undefined sort of way. He had been only mildly concerned about the rumors of Okocha's brief dalliances with the odd American girl or two. That was, until he got wind of Okocha's serious involvement with Tatiana! He had not been prepared for his revulsion at the notion that his son would seriously fall for an American girl! He was literally taken aback by the depth of the aversion he felt, and by his conviction that he would probably never be able to overcome it.

It did nothing to improve his mood when he discovered, on broaching the matter to Ekemma, that she—the mother of his sons—had known about Tatiana for some time, and had not breathed a word about her to him. He could not imagine the reasons for her strange behavior, since she knew well enough how he felt about their young Igbo boys and girls marrying Americans;

in particular, how he must feel about Okocha and Kanu seriously dating American girls, which was but one step to marrying them. He knew that she, too, felt pretty much the same way, even if less vociferously. They understood each other—at least he thought they did. To the extent that they had discussed the—to him—looming nightmare scenario in which their sons would get hitched to American girls, they had been of one mind that it would probably be easier to take on Okocha first. When the family relocated to America, Okocha was more mature, as the older brother, and therefore understood better than Kanu did, about the way things are supposed to be done.

"I didn't take the rumors seriously," Ekemma said to her husband. She sat by herself at one end of the long settee. "Why would I? Nat, it's not as if this is the first time we've heard that our son was carrying on with an *akata* girl. And every time, it's proved to be a brief affair, and nothing came of it."

"You're right, Mma. You're absolutely right." A smug smile lit up his face. "A young man like Okocha would be one hell of a catch—"

"Stop it, Nat!" Ekemma thundered, but she was smiling with her eyes. "Okocha is not the only good-looking boy in the place."

"He may not be. That's true. But there's something real special about that boy. Sometimes, when I look at him—"

"You see yourself!" said Ekemma. "I know a self-satisfied smile when I see one."

"Sorry, Mma! Can't help it. I wonder what he might have done if he'd played professional football. Half the young ladies in New Jersey would have been hovering around him, like those groupies swarming around rock groups—"

"That's why you wouldn't let him—?"

"Not at all! I don't know about others, but this Nigerian," he said, and thumped his chest, "this Nigerian—I mean—this *Igbo father* has his priorities for his children—"

"And it's education, education, education, before all else, right?"

"Right! And I'm not ashamed to put education ahead of money where my kids are concerned."

"You talk as if Okocha couldn't have managed both," said Ekemma, staring at her husband with a steely gaze that she knew from experience often made him uncomfortable. "You know very well that these days, colleges insist on their football players also taking their academic studies seriously."

"That's what they all say."

"That's what they do, too!"

"How'd you know, Mma?"

"Why didn't you ask Okocha himself?"

"And if I did, what do you think he'd have said, woman? Mma, please, enough of this argument. Look where the boy is today. A great job in one of the best financial houses in the country, Union Bank of Switzerland, better known as UBS, the *'You-And-Us, You-Be-Us'* people. That's a great ad, by the way." He paused, looked at his watch, and frowned. "It's already three o'clock. Okocha's supposed to be here by now, no? Said he'd come see us about some matter—"

"Must be about the girl—er—"

"Tatiana," he said, shaking his head at her. "Don't tell me you've forgotten the name. Especially as I know you knew her name before we met her yesterday. By the way, did you hear the buzz around the hall—?"

"I did," said Ekemma. "Something about her family name being really the Igbo name Okoroafor, but of course mispronounced by Americans."

"I'm tickled by the possibility she may indeed be descended from an Igbo ancestor."

"Would that make her less of an *akata* girl to you?"

"You would like to know, Mma, wouldn't you? I don't think I care for that sarcastic smile. Nor for that word, *akata*, either. Anyway, I hope he's not bringing the young lady with him. That would be a bit awkward—"

He stopped and looked mechanically around him, as if he suddenly thought of something. "And talking of awkward, where's that boy, Kanu. I don't think it would be a good thing for him to be around when we talk with Okocha—"

"You've nothing to worry about, Nat. The boy, as we talk, must be at least ten miles away from here, visiting a friend. I told him he could go."

"You? Told him he could go? You, who never seem to want him going off on his own? But wait a minute. I think you knew exactly what you were doing, Mma. Good for you, girl! Cleared the coast exactly when we needed it cleared because of Okocha's visit."

They heard the buzz of the doorbell, quickly followed by a key turning in the lock of the front door. Mechanically, they both got up from their chairs, and moved together towards the front door. Okocha stood still for a moment, magnificently framed by the doorway, a picture of such natural elegance that a smile lit up Ekemma's face.

"Talk of the devil!" said Ekemma.

"Okocha, finally! And alone, thank God!" Chief Anigbo whispered to Ekemma. Aloud he said, smiling and wagging a finger at her: "Our son is not the devil."

"I see you've been talking about me," said Okocha, walking into his mom's embrace, "and, no doubt, Tatiana?"

"Right on both counts, son," said his dad, hugging him warmly. "You've been to Church, I hope?"

"Straight from there!" Then with a mellow smile, he added: "I know better than to come visiting you and mom, on a Sunday afternoon, without first fulfilling my *Sunday-Sunday* obligation."

"Right on! A sure prophylactic against hell-fire in the afterlife," said Chief Anigbo.

They all laughed, as Chief Anigbo held Okocha at arm's length, the better to look him over. Okocha liked his colors somewhat understated. He wore his favorite dark brown embroidered jumper over black trousers, and sported a pendant, dangling from which was a silver cross. At his dad's mention of hell-fire, he touched the cross reverently.

"As always, son, you look good."

"A chip off the old block, no?"

"Who're you calling old, son?"

"Easy, boys!" Ekemma called out, with a radiant smile. She loved it whenever her husband and her son talked to each other familiarly. "Okocha, you know how your dad can sometimes pluck a quarrel out of thin air. So, watch out, son. I alone reserve the right to call your dad old, to his face. Right, Nat?"

"I don't know about that, woman. What, if I returned the compliment?"

"You wouldn't dare!"

"Thought so!" Chief Anigbo turned to Okocha, and pointed to the love seat. "Welcome, son. Make yourself comfortable. We've been expecting you." He peeked at his watch. "What kept you so long? It's past three."

Okocha also looked at his watch. "Only fifteen minutes past. That's no big deal, dad. We're Nigerians—and that says it all. And besides, I'm coming to visit my dad and mom, not going to some official appointment—"

"That's okay, son," Ekemma interposed. "I'm your mom, and I say you can be as late as you like, so long as you come regularly to see how we're doing. By the way, are you hungry? I imagine you haven't had lunch, no? You are an *okokpolo*. Sometimes when I see you, especially when you are engaged in some strenuous physical activity, I remember the song that cautions an *okokpolo* against dancing too vigorously as, by definition, he has no wife to cook him a meal."

"Don't worry, mom. I'm all right. I stopped on my way here and bought a hamburger, and a bottle of coke. That's enough for one meal."

"Hamburger? You know I don't like—." Chief Anigbo stopped, looked sideways at Ekemma, and quickly added: "Sorry, son, I know I must stop telling you what to eat and what not to eat. Please forget about it. What I really wanted to say was that you surprised us yesterday, bringing your girlfriend to introduce to us. What's that her name—?"

They were not prepared for his answer, which he delivered with a straight face, and in a voice that was teasingly solemn. "Okoroafor! Tatiana Okoroafor."

His dad and mom looked at each other, eyes dilated in wonder.

"What was that?" his mom asked.

"Don't tell me you did not hear what at least half the guests yesterday were talking about."

"We did," said his dad. "But we didn't expect to hear you mention that name."

"Dad, mom, Tatiana may well be an Igbo girl," Okocha said, struggling to maintain a straight face.

Chief Anigbo laughed merrily. "It's certainly an intriguing possibility, what with the slave trade and all that. Who knows?"

"Should make a difference, shouldn't it?"

"Good try, son. Good try. I don't know about your mom, but—"

"Dad, please! I know what everybody in our community knows. That Chief Nat Anigbo is the fiercest advocate of Igbo boys marrying Igbo girls—or, at worst—but even that, God forbid—other Nigerian girls."

"Guilty as charged!" Chief Anigbo raised his right arm. "I freely admit I've always dreamed the impossible dream, if you see what I mean. Of course I'm aware that ethnic purity is now all but impossible. It was never possible, except perhaps in the earliest times. But who knows what happened then?"

"Dad, that was then. This is now. We are talking about me and Tatiana. You know now that I love her and—are you ready for this—I would like to marry her. You've now met her. And dad, you've known about her for some time—"

"Who—how—?"

"Doesn't matter, dad. You knew, and that's a fact." His eyes held his dad's, challengingly, unwaveringly. "Dad, mom, my question to you both is this: don't you think that in this day and age, your attitude to where a man may find a wife is somewhat *passe*, outmoded?"

"Maybe," said his mom.

"Doesn't matter," said his dad, in the same breath.

"I'm confused. Either it is, or it isn't. Dad, mom, the world has indeed shrunk to a global village as far as marriage is concerned. I listened to you yesterday, as you made a sarcastic comment about the global village thing. And even then, I had an idea you were talking to me. That was before I found out that you knew about me and Tatiana. So, indeed, your remarks were directed at me, your son."

Chief Anigbo got up from his chair, went to the commode on which the television stood, pulled out a drawer, and took out a packet of cigarettes. He selected one, and inserted it between his lips. Then fishing out a lighter from a trouser pocket, he lit up, and took a long drag on the cigarette. He blew a spiral of smoke towards the ceiling, and then slowly, with deliberate steps, returned to his chair. He knew that Okocha and his mom had disapproving eyes glued on him, and that his theatrics had their full attention.

He blew another spiral of smoke towards the ceiling, and then turned to Okocha. "Son," he said, slowly spreading his arms wide in a grand gesture. "The world may be a global village to you. But I have been around, and I know things are not as simple as you may think. If you marry this girl, you may be jumping into a river that is deeper than you know. We say that the sea does not swallow a person with whose legs it has not come in contact. Put differently, you may discover that you are like the tortoise that is gearing up to negotiate a deep river that drowned elephants. How do you plan to do it? Fly or jump over it?"

Okocha regarded his dad in silence for a moment or two. Then he addressed his mom. "Mom," he said solemnly, "do you share dad's opinion on this matter?"

"Would you be shocked if I said I do and—er—I don't?"

"Not really," said Okocha. "I suppose I know some people are seriously conflicted on the question."

"If I must tell the truth," said his mom, "the one thing that bothers me is how we would relate to our prospective American in-laws."

Chief Anigbo laughed out loud. Okocha was surprised that his dad could seem to be enjoying himself when the issue under discussion was as weighty as it obviously was to all three of them.

"Son, I know what your mom is concerned about. She's thinking, when she dies, will her American in-laws be willing and able to come to her funeral ceremonies? You know that, for our people, it is awfully important that in-laws are involved."

"As a matter of fact," said his mom, "in-laws are family. They're even more than just family. I'm sure you must remember what our people say, that one's in-law is one's *chi*, don't you? Isn't that a reason to be extremely careful into which family you marry? Marriage is never simply between two individuals, the man and the woman. It's between two families. Okocha, please don't listen to anyone who tells you differently."

"That's probably an important reason our people don't like to marry from foreign lands," said Chief Anigbo.

"And in this matter," said Okocha, "I suppose foreign includes other Nigerian tribes—"

"Okocha, don't use that word 'tribe' again!" his dad interrupted him. "You ought to know that White people typically use the word when they want to emphasize how primitive we are."

"Sorry, I should have said—er—other Nigerian ethnic groups."

"Or just simply, other Nigerian peoples! Yes, I mean the Yoruba, Hausa, and even our closest geographic neighbors, like the Efik-Ibibio, Bini, Ijaw and so on. And you're telling us you seriously want to marry an American girl."

"Wouldn't it make a difference if she has an Igbo forebear?" Okocha asked, smiling impishly.

"You know, my boy, you can only go so far with that argument. You know that, like other peoples, the Igbo have a taboo against marrying a blood relative. If your—er—Tatiana is indeed descended from an Okoroafor, how can you be sure she's not related to you. When you look at an African-American today, don't you sometimes wonder if you may be looking at a long-lost cousin?"

"That's a good one, dad. That's really good. However, I have yet to hear of a family in our village, or those villages around us, who use the name Okoroafor. But just in case you are really serious, what was that play on a Broadway theater in New York? *Six Degrees of Separation*, or something like that. I didn't see the play, and I never understood what that title meant. But here, dad, we're talking about as many as possibly *three centuries of separation*! Come on, dad!"

"I'm sorry, son, but you must know the word our people use for Americans, White or Black? *Akata*, or some such word. I wish our people would stop using that word. I don't know what it means, and I doubt many—who use it—know. I only know that its use is uncomplimentary to our American hosts. Let's just say that an American is an American, and that's all there is to it."

"Something is lost in all this argument, dad, mom. What is it you really want for me? My happiness in life, or my blind conformity to our antiquated ways of looking at life?"

"Of course we want your happiness," said his dad. His mom nodded vigorously in agreement.

"And you think an Igbo youth finds happiness only in marrying an Igbo girl? Is happiness what we younger ones see when we look around us, and see some of our Igbo families? I don't want to mention names, but dad, mom, you know what I'm talking about. You know that I know how many families have brought their domestic problems to you, and sometimes even to the union."

Okocha got up from his chair and went to his mom. He knelt by her, and put both his hands on her lap. "Mom, yesterday, you said something when I brought Tatiana to the high table. D'you remember what you said?"

She looked at her son, and then at her husband and, suddenly, she did not know if she wanted to answer her son's very simple question. A question she suspected that her son would insist that she answer. A question to which she was well aware both of them knew the answer. "Bring her to the house," she had told him. But did those five simple words signify acceptance of the *akata* girl as her son's serious girlfriend and—which was for her even more troubling—her presumptive daughter-in-law?

"I told her she's beautiful," she finally mumbled, her eyes averted from her son's.

"You did, mom. But you know that's not what I'm talking about."

She threw up her arms in desperation. "How am I supposed to remember every single thing I said, when a hundred people were talking all at the same time?"

Chief Anigbo sniggered. "What's a hundred people talking at the same time got to do with remembering what you said to Okocha and his girlfriend?" he asked. He sat, totally relaxed, in his well-upholstered chair, his legs and feet fully extended and resting comfortably on a pouffe. His face wore the same enigmatic smile that had troubled Okocha from the moment he took Tatiana to the high table and introduced her to him. His old man was clearly enjoying himself at the expense of his mom.

"Nat!" his mom called out, fixing her husband with a stare that might have felled him if stares could kill, and that asked on whose side he was.

"Mom, it's okay. You know how dad can tease. Maybe you should get your own back on him, and ask him why he's doing something he knows he shouldn't be doing—smoking."

Chief Anigbo laughed out loud. A crackling burst of laughter that shook his tall powerful frame, and that lasted for a long moment. His cigarette dropped from his lips, and Okocha sprang to his feet and quickly retrieved the stub from the floor. He crushed it and deposited it in the ashtray on the center table.

When his laughter subsided, his dad looked at him for a moment or two, and then said: "Son, you're observant and smart. Sometimes, when I listen to you, it's as if I'm listening to myself talk. It's as they say, that the offspring of a snake is usually long."

"And you're that snake?" asked his wife.

"What can I say?" Chief Anigbo asked with a smug smile, adjusting his body into an even more comfortable position in his chair.

Okocha was silent, as he went back to the love-seat. As he looked from one parent to the other, it suddenly struck him that he had seldom seen them sharing the love-seat. That thought immediately refocused his mind on Tatiana!

Tatiana, or—to put it another way—his love for the American girl, was a powder-keg that could blow up in his face, if not handled adroitly. The agonizing question for him was how adroitly to handle a situation that was not deliberately of his choosing. A situation into which his guardian and guiding spirit, what his Igbo people would call his *chi*, had led him! He had had no power to control his emotional response to a stimulus as beautifully packaged—in *his* eyes—as Tatiana Karefa. Whatever defined a girl's allure in the eyes of a boy, she had *it*, for him! Okocha told himself it was not just her external, physical appeal that made her irresistibly attractive to him. There was something about the way her face lit up when she smiled; something about the sparkle in her eyes; something about the warmth that seemed to emanate effortlessly from the totality of her being! He had dated other girls before Tatiana, but none had had the soothing, steadying effect on him, as had Tatiana.

Briefly, he wondered about Ifeoma Ndukwe. But he quickly dismissed any thought of seriously comparing the two girls. Tatiana had burst into his world of reality almost literally out of the blue. Ifeoma suffered in comparison because she had been—in a manner of speaking—pushed into his focus by persons eager to see both of them linked romantically. In other words, he reflected, he would have had—in Ifeoma's case—to make a *deliberate* choice of dating her, which would have introduced a certain degree of artificiality into what should be—in his view—spontaneous and unrehearsed, to be fully and artlessly savored.

Okocha shook himself out of his reverie, rose from his chair, and went and stood in front of his dad. His bearing was calm, his eyes respectful as he looked at his old man. His voice, when he began to speak, was firm without being strident. As he spoke, he looked from his dad to his mom.

"Dad, mom," he began, "as I have said, I know why I'm here. Mom, you told me yesterday to bring Tatiana to the house, although you seem to have forgotten. But that's all right. I'm not sure if you meant for me to bring her here today. But I decided I'd come alone. I didn't think it would have been fair to her to thrust her into the middle of this type of conversation. What we three need to have is an honest open talk about her and me, and about where she and I think we are going with our love for each other."

Chief Anigbo saw a mellowness in his son's eyes that struck him to the core of his heart. He loved his son, and would do anything for him—especially where his welfare was at issue. But, in this matter, he knew now, if he did not know it before, that his perspective was anathema to Okocha. And because he knew that his son was a chip off the old block, he sensed that they were rushing headlong towards an irreconcilable disagreement that could tear them apart. But he also knew that he could not, if he valued the continued respect and esteem of his Igbo community, hold out vociferously and endlessly on the virtues of marriage strictly within the Igbo group, only to give his son an easy pass to go with his heart, and marry the American girl of his dreams.

He cleared his throat. "Son, the question I want to ask you now is probably as important a question as I have ever asked you. And I want you to think carefully before you answer." He looked across at his wife, his eyes asking her a question. She nodded gently in response. He cleared his throat again. "This is my question, son. It will help your mom and me know exactly what we are dealing with here. Okocha, are you really—and I mean really—thinking of marrying the girl? I need a straight, categorical answer."

For a moment, Okocha seemed confused. Then he smiled faintly, shaking his head. "Thinking? I'm not thinking—"

"You're not? Then what have we been talking about? What's the problem?"

"You don't understand, dad. I've gone well beyond the stage of *thinking* about it. I've *decided* I want to marry her. She's the only girl for me in the whole wide world. She's the girl with whom I want to share my life from here on. What remains—and this is very important to me—when the time comes, I would like to have your blessing, yours and mom's."

He stopped and, on an impulse, went down on his knees to his dad. For a brief moment, he cast his eyes down. When he looked up again, his eyes were teary.

"I've never taken an important step in my entire life," he said, looking from his dad to his mom, his voice charged with emotion, "without your support and blessing. You have been my guide and protector against all the odds I have encountered. You have helped shape the decisions I have made about my life, even though some of those decisions have gone against what I really wanted to do, to be. Professional football, for example. I had set my heart on it. And if I had stayed with it in my junior and senior years in college, I might have had a good shot at being drafted by one of the football franchises. But, dad, you put your foot down against the very notion—as you loved to put it—of your son frittering his life away playing a boy's game. You don't know how many times I heard you say something like that, and it hurt badly. Dad, mom, I'm a grown man now, and I need—no, I *have* to make some of the important decisions about the way forward for me. Marriage—"

"My son," his dad interrupted him, placing a gentle hand on his shoulder, and then making him get up off his knees. "You're Igbo. You don't kneel to anyone but God. My son, marriage is an institution, among the Igbo, that is bound by tradition and customs. It isn't something a young man—or girl—is entirely free to get into, at his whim. There are all manner of considerations that have to be weighed in the balance. Above everything else, we—that is, your mom and me—we have a certain responsibility to try to guide you as you make some of the important decisions about what you do with your life. It is your life, true. Not mine or your mom's. You might call it part of the job description, but it is what God, or nature, has tasked parents to do for their children. It puzzles me often why the young don't want to listen to their elders.

They think they know everything. It is as if they think they can be on the ground and yet are able to tell which birds, flying high over their heads, are pregnant."

Okocha shook his head slowly, side to side, tight-faced. Then he looked down, covered his face—his eyes, nose and mouth—with both his hands, and stayed like that for a moment or two, as if silently praying. When he lowered his arms, there was a calmness in his face and a quiet dignity in his bearing, as his eyes bored into his dad's. "The world has changed, dad. We both know that. Even our Nigerian, our Igbo world is changing. Don't get me wrong, dad, mom. I know that a people, any people, should hold on to their customs and traditions. I just happen to believe that we, as a people, should begin to look critically at our old ways of doing things, and change what's outmoded, what can no longer meet the needs of the modern Igbo man or woman. Dad, mom, we've talked now, for the first time really seriously, about marriage, which is something about which you both—especially you, dad—have been on my case. I am now pretty close to taking that step, but I see it isn't going to be easy. Why don't we leave it there for now? We'll talk again soon. And I'm sure when we do, you'll not miss the opportunity to remind me, for the hundredth time—"

"That what an old man can see, sitting down, the young cannot see, even standing up!"

Okocha laughed, but not scornfully. "Except, dad," he said, "and you taught me this proverb also, that a man may rest his head on whichever of his two arms he chooses. Doesn't this mean that—at least in certain things—a man can do what he wants to do, the way he chooses to do it?"

"Not in marriage, son!" Chief Anigbo said, emphatically. "But, as you said, we'll talk again."

CHAPTER 6

Kanu and Somtochi were first cousins who, from the moment they came together in Chief Nat Anigbo's family home, connected well. Somtochi was the older of the two, by somewhat less than one year. But Kanu had lived much longer in the United States, and tended to take the lead in whatever they did together.

Two weeks had gone by since the wedding of Nonye and Nnanna. They were in Kanu's room, snacking on fruits—cheries, plums, grapes—from a big glass bowl on a table set between them. Suddenly, Kanu pushed the table further away from him and towards Somto, got up, and stretched himself.

"I'm sick of these fruits," he said. "Since you came to live with us, it's been almost nothing but fruits, fruits, and more fruits—all because of your never ending regime of healthy foods for your athletic program. I thought I was done with this stuff when Okocha moved out. Do you have to keep it up, even during the summer vacation, when the coach is not watching you?"

"What can I say, Kanu? It's just habit. If I were to gorge on your cookies and doughnuts, I'd be sick."

"Anybody would, Somto. But enough of all that." He looked at his watch. "Would you like to come with me? I'm going to see Okocha. There's an urgent matter I want to discuss with him. In fact you have no option but to go with me. As far as I can see, you're not busy right now."

"And he won't mind if I come along with you? If it's an urgent family matter—"

Kanu looked surprised. "What family are we talking about? You don't seem to understand that you and me, we're family. Your mom is my dad's sister. What more family do you want? Where are we now? In my dad's house. You have your room. I have mine. We live like brothers. I know that during the academic session, you'd prefer to move to a campus dormitory, like other students. But I'm glad you live here, and commute to your college. I need a brother my age—well, more or less my age—and you're it." He paused because of the way Somto was looking at him. "Why are you smiling like that?"

Somto continued to smile, shaking his head gently. "You know, Kanu, for a young boy—er, okay—man, your age, you're—I don't know how to say it—you talk wise."

"'Young boy your age', did you say, Somto? See who's talking! You're only one fucking year—sorry, please excuse me. I shouldn't have used that word. I should have remembered who I'm talking to—a Nigerian only recently arrived in America from the backwoods of our dear old country."

"Er, Kanu. Easy on Nigeria, please."

They both laughed, comfortable and relaxed in their relationship and easy friendship. Sometimes, as was the case now, Somto considered it his patriotic duty and obligation to defend the honor of his country. But when he did so, it was often with an air of mocking insincerity.

"What I was trying to say, Somto, is that you're only one year older than me. And you're saying I'm wise for my age. As if I'd be much wiser in, say, one year from now. Wisdom, my dear Somto—"

"Doesn't necessarily come with age, I know."

"Exactly. And that's why I need to talk to my big bro. Let me see. You know about him and the American girl, don't you?"

"Of course. Who in the family doesn't—?"

"Now you're talking, Somto! Now you're showing me you know what I'm talking about when I say 'family'. Yes, everyone in the family knows. But not everyone approves—"

"Like your dad—"

"Yes, and your big sister, Nonye."

"You mean, Mrs. Nnanna Onwuka!" Somto said, with a mock serious expression. "Are you sure you're old enough to call her by her first name? Just joking, man! I know this is America. But seriously. What's it you want to talk to Okocha about? Are you one of those opposed to him and Tatiana?"

"What are you talking about?" Kanu's eyebrows were raised in surprise. "Quite the contrary, man. Haven't you noticed, in the past week or so, that my bro has not been quite himself? Whenever he has come visiting, he has not said much, and he looks rather sad and worried. That's not the brother I used to know. I'm sure all this stuff about a true-blood Igbo man not marrying an American girl—"

"*Akata!*" Somto interjected.

"Call her what you like. I prefer *American* girl. It's just been a constant barrage of opinions—mostly unfavorable—by even persons who have no stake in who Okocha marries. It seems to be getting to him."

"He's human."

"He is. That's why I have to talk to him, and in his apartment too, where nobody will disturb us."

"So why do you want me to come along?"

"'Nobody' doesn't include you. You want me to go on repeating myself? You're family. Besides, I think I can use a backup. I want somebody who can help me talk sense into him, and encourage him to marry whom he chooses, and live his life the way he wants to—"

Somto held up an arm. "Hold it there, Kanu! Are you quite sure I'm the backup you want for this purpose? Is that supposed to mean that you believe this bumbling Johnny-just-come agrees with you?"

"You mean Johnny-come-lately. Same meaning."

"Whatever!" said Somto, in his best imitation of the apposite body language. "As I was saying, you seem to believe I totally agree with you about Okocha and—what's her name—Tatiana."

"You don't?"

"You've forgotten so soon you're talking to someone who just got to this wonderful new world, raw and primitive, out of the backwoods—or whatever you called it—of Nigeria. I may have been already one full year in America, but what's one year compared to your dozen or so years? Please don't interrupt, and let me finish what I'm saying. Where I recently came from, our parents still have some say—quite *some* say, I might add—in who we marry. Most of my relations at home—that's the men—went through that process. Doesn't mean we don't fall in love, like you Americans—I mean, you Nigerians who've grown up in this American culture. Yes, we fall in love. But we also know that marriage sometimes doesn't follow love quite as night follows day. What I'm saying is that my mind is not quite made up about the rights and wrongs of the matter. I'd certainly love to see Okocha marry his girl—"

"That's it!" said Kanu triumphantly. "That's all that matters. You must come with me." Then he added, with a laugh: "Bring your native wisdom with you, if you like. Just come! There's serious work waiting for us, and this is no time to hesitate."

"When exactly do you plan to go see Okocha?"

"Today, now! Let's go!"

"What's the hurry? You're afraid if you don't do it this instant, you'll lose your—how to say it—nerve? Is he expecting you?"

"Of course. He knows I'm coming. This is America, man. He may be my bro, but I have to respect his privacy enough to at least call him—"

"Meaning, Kanu, that we're not in Nigeria, where you just get up and go knocking on another person's door?"

"Of course!" said Kanu, with a laugh. "Even if it's a brother. We're in America. Things are done differently here. I know this place. I know the people inside-out. They're not like us—I mean our people. When you've been here a few more years, you'll understand better."

"I understand, Kanu. It's okay. Our people say that a chicken, newly arrived in a strange land, said it had better stand on only one leg, until it has taken proper stock of its new environment. That's what I'm doing."

"Somto, I'm impressed by your use of our Igbo idioms, even when you're speaking English. You know the language well."

"I try, but are you surprised? Don't forget I completed high school before I came here. Even so, I don't speak Igbo that well, though I was certainly better than many Igbo kids my age at home, who can barely speak it. It's a shame."

"That's what Okocha has often told me. I was very young when I left Nigeria. And here I am. I know this country better than my own."

He paused, and looked steadily at his cousin for a long moment. "I suppose we should get ready and go to Okocha's. I'm sorry, I should have asked you before calling him. But I'm lucky it's okay with you. You're still enjoying your summer vacation from all those hefty volumes of books you people have to read endlessly in college."

"You wait till September, my dear freshman-to-be, and you'll find out how it is."

"Enough talking, man." Kanu looked at his watch. "It's four-thirty. He's expecting me by six. Your car, or mine?"

"If I must go with you, it'll be my car," said Somto, smiling. "And for an obvious reason."

"You don't think I'll concentrate adequately on the road?"

"You got that right, man. I don't want you driving me, with your head full of chaotic thoughts, because of Okocha and Tatiana."

"That's because you don't know me. But that's okay. You drive."

*   *   *

Okocha had a two-bedroom apartment in the Rolling-Hills Village, in the township of Franklin, Somerset County, New Jersey. The estate was lush with greenery, and it was this that gave it much of its appeal and respectability. Okocha had chosen his place of abode with an eye to its natural scenic beauty, the spaciousness of its rooms, and its proximity to the two most important things to him at that point in his life: Tatiana's home, and his work place—in that order of importance. Indeed, Tatiana had helped him with his search for a suitably located apartment.

If his dad had not counseled otherwise, he would almost certainly have already bought a bungalow or a two-storied house. He had seen one or two that he liked very much, especially those that had dormers. For some obscure reasons, dormers appealed to his sense of architectural beauty. He loved the way they project vertically from the sloping roofs. Whenever he passed a house with dormers, he wondered if there was someone in there peeking at him from the curtained security of the rooms from which the dormers projected. But his dad had counseled that he not rush into buying a house. This, notwithstanding that he had a handsomely paid job! And notwithstanding the easy credit facilities available to him in the UBS! "Wait a few more years, son," his dad had said. "You're still very young, unmarried, not really sure what you want out of life." Okocha wondered what marriage had to do with the matter. The way he saw it, if indeed it turned out that his wife, when he married, did not like his house, they could always purchase another.

Two years had rolled by since that conversation with his dad. And in the meantime, like a bolt from the blue, he had met and fallen in love with Tatiana. And his life, and priorities, changed. He still occasionally thought about buying a house. But as the weeks and months rolled by, all he could think about—all he even *wanted* to think about—was Tatiana. Latterly the two of them had begun to allow the subject of marriage to creep into their conversations. It seemed at first that they were feeling each other out on the issue. It did not entirely surprise him that Tatiana had been more forthright in expressing her feelings than he had been. He had quickly observed, since coming to America, that American girls were infinitely less timid about such matters than their Nigerian counterparts, among whom he had grown up, though he was barely into his teens when he had had to leave Nigeria.

His thoughts turned to Tatiana's parents, and her grandmother, Wyomia. Tatiana had just turned three when her grandfather, Alex Karefa, suffered a stroke that left one half of his body paralyzed. He never recovered from the stroke, and died within a few months, notwithstanding the earnest endeavors of his doctor, and the devotion of his wife Wyomia. Alex's son, and Tatiana's dad, Philip, was a very devout Baptist. Corpulent and jovial, he was always looking to crack jokes with Okocha except, notably, when the younger man thought to poke fun at his strict fundamentalist beliefs, which Okocha, mischievously egged on by Tatiana, sometimes tended to do. Okocha was always well received by Tatiana's mom, the ever courteous Edna. But the suspicion lingered in his mind that her courtesy did not necessarily signify total approval of him as her daughter's boyfriend. If his relationship with Tatiana progressed to the denouement for which he naturally hoped and prayed, would her mom Edna unreservedly support her daughter's decision, and accept him as a son-in-law? He could never tell, from the never-changing, humorless expression on her face, and the way her eyes silently flitted from her only daughter to him, what thoughts lurked in the innermost recesses of her mind and heart.

Grandma Wyomia was an altogether different matter. She welcomed him, whenever he met her, with open arms and a truly warm heart. "You sometimes remind me of Alex," she once said to him. "Give an inch or so, he was just about as tall as you, my boy. And he had your tightness of body and your broad shoulders. God sure don't make them like that hardly anymore." Okocha was not quite sure what she meant by 'tightness', but he recognized a warm and sincere compliment when he heard one.

Suddenly, he remembered that Tatiana was due to visit in about an hour, and he had not yet tidied his living room. His bedroom too! He did not think of himself as ordinarily an untidy person. It was just that Tatiana loved to see every piece of furniture, every book or magazine, every cushion, every photo album, of which he had close to half a dozen, and even the TV remote control, in its allotted space! She liked order, but was not compulsively obsessive about it. He respected that quality in her, though he sometimes wished she would let him live—as he had once delicately put it to her—"with a little, tiny bit of disorder" around him, so long as it was kept within manageable limits. That simple, uncomplicated request had had the strangest effect on her. She had laughed heartily, and went on laughing until he put both his hands on her heaving shoulders. Then, with tears in her eyes, she had said something that touched him deeply: "You are such a darling person, you know, Okocha. You are just so down to earth. I love you so very much because you are not afraid to be who you are."

Not quite a month earlier, about a fortnight before his cousin Nonye's wedding day, he had—in a deliberately casual tone of voice—asked Tatiana if she would like to move in with him. He had not expected her reaction. She was silent for an uncomfortably long moment, as she sat demurely, sharing the love-seat with him, in his sitting room. She covered her face with her hands. "I thought you'd never ask," she first said, looking up and gazing into his eyes. "Thank you, Okocha, for asking." Then, seemingly illogically, she had turned him down. "I can't," she had said. "And for a very good reason. My folks would kill me if I did. They are very religious, and you know that." Of course he knew that her parents were strict, uncompromising Baptists. With true simplicity of heart, they avowedly believed that every word in the Bible was the word of God; that God's wrath, such as He had visited on the twin cities of Sodom and Gomorrah, was intended as a warning to those who would stray from the straight and narrow; that every man would surely reap what he has sowed; and that everlasting life was the reward for those who loved their neighbors as themselves, but not carnally. He had, for quite a while now, enjoyed a relationship with them that was comfortable enough for him to occasionally engage in a lighthearted and friendly disputation with them on some of the more rigorous tenets of the Christian religion.

The buzz of the front door bell brought him to his feet. He quickly arranged the three albums lying haphazardly on the center table in a neat pile, and picked up a handful of music cassettes, and shoved them out of sight on the lower shelf of the same table. He straightened himself, looked around him to make sure everything was as it should be, smiled with satisfaction, and then went to open the door. Kanu first brushed past him, and then apparently remembered his manners, and turned back and enfolded his big brother in a bear hug. Somtochi, more hesitant, smiled and said his 'good afternoon' to Okocha, very deliberately wiped his feet on the front door rug, and accepted Okocha's embrace happily.

"I can see you forgot that I was coming to see you," Kanu said accusingly. He looked at his watch. "It's—"

"Doesn't matter what the time is, you're always welcome, little bro," said Okocha graciously. "Somto, it's good to see you. How are you doing?"

"Not too badly, cousin Okocha. I hope we didn't come at an inconvenient time. You must be a busy man—"

Kanu interrupted him. "Doesn't matter if he's busy. I know my brother. He's always glad to see me, and he'd better start getting used to your visits too, because this is going to be our—and I mean you and me, *our*—second home. I know he'll like it. Trust me!"

Okocha smiled indulgently, and waved them into his living room. "I didn't exactly forget you were coming, Kanu. It's just that of late my mind has been occupied with all sorts of little problems. I'm glad you came. In fact it may be the best thing that has happened to me today. Somto will get to really meet Tatiana for the first time—"

"Oh, my God! She's coming?" Kanu asked, wide-eyed with surprise.

"Does that bother you?"

"'Course not! I just didn't know, that's all. You're right, big brother. Somto will have his first chance to really meet and talk to the goddess of love, who's been lately the principal item of news in the family."

"Kanu, no one can say you've ever had a problem with your mouth," Okocha said, with a smile. "But the things you say! I never heard anyone describe Tatiana as a goddess of anything. Anyway, you'll soon get a chance to tell her so, to her face. And, if I know you—"

"You don't know me nearly as well as you think. I might suddenly develop cold feet, and vamoose before she comes. What do you think I am?"

"A talker! That's for sure. But forget all that! What's your news? I hope you've come to bring me good news. I need some cheering up."

Kanu turned to Somtochi, spread his arms wide and pursed his lips. "What did I tell you, Somto—eh?" To Okocha, he said: "I thought we'd have all the time in the world to chat, but with Tatiana coming soon, we—Somto and me—we need to hurry up just a little."

"I didn't say she's due this minute," said Okocha. "Let's all sit down and relax. And even if she meets us talking, what's the harm? You didn't come to malign her, did you?"

Somtochi laughed out loud. "Him, malign Tatiana?" he asked, pointing to Kanu. "Wait till he tells you why we're here. Malign her! Indeed!"

Okocha turned and gave his full attention to his brother. "Ball's at your feet, little bro. Out with it!"

"Still thinking football, I see. I tell you, if I'd had any say in that matter—"

"You couldn't have, because you were this little," said Okocha, his right hand stretched out and positioned only a foot or so above the floor. He graciously added, to mollify his brother: "If you allow for some exaggeration, of course!"

"A *lot* of exaggeration, Okocha!" Kanu stared with disapproval at Okocha's hand. "All this football controversy took place only a couple or so years ago."

"Now who's exaggerating, Kanu? But that's okay. By the way, you know where to find your favorite snacks. Ask Somto what he'd like, and maybe you both can go help yourselves from the kitchen."

"What about you, bro? Nothing for you?"

"No, thanks. Good of you to ask, anyway."

Kanu and Somtochi needed no further urging and, in no time at all, they were both tucked into some cookies and a bottle each of coca-cola.

Kanu silently took several sips of his drink, lowered his bottle, and exhaled mightily. "As you know, I like my coke with all the works," he said, beaming.

"With all the works?" asked Somtochi. "What's that?"

Okocha laughed. "It's his way to say he likes his coke *regular*, not *diet*, or whatever else they do to make it healthier. I see you are both settled comfortably with your drinks. How about we start talking."

"What else have we been doing?" Kanu asked, smiling impishly. "Okay, sorry bro. You're right. Let's talk."

He paused for a second or two, cleared his throat importantly, and said: "It's about you and Tatiana, Okocha. I'll go straight to the point, because I don't want the great girl to walk in on us before I've said my piece. I have a very simple question for you, big brother Okocha. And it is this: what the hell are you waiting for?"

"Waiting for?" Okocha asked, his expression reflecting his puzzlement. "What exactly—?"

"That wasn't what we agreed—" Somto started to say.

Kanu chuckled gleefully. "Couldn't resist injecting some drama there. All right, fellows. Seriously now, what both of us—Somto and me—what we want to say to you is really quite simple. Marry your girl! Or rather, go ahead, ask her to marry you, before anybody has a chance to make you change your mind. We—both of us—know what's going on. We know," he said, with a quick glance at Somtochi, "that you love her, and she loves you. And there's nothing anyone can do to change things between you two. Not dad or mom, not Somto's sister Nonye, nor our new cousin-in-law Nnanna. We know that none of the above, all close family members, are in favor of you and Tatiana." He paused, laughed briefly, and continued. "Even non-family members want to interfere in what does not concern them. Take Ifeoma Ndukwe. She's Nonye's friend—a beautiful girl, to be sure—she, too, is opposed to Tatiana. But the whole world knows where *she* is coming from; she wants you for herself. The entire Igbo community in this state, it seems, is watching our family, waiting to see if our dad, *Ugo-oranyelu* as they respectfully call him, will let his son marry an *akata* girl, when he is always loudly proclaiming his opposition to the very idea of such marriages. Well, Okocha, my brother whom I love and esteem more than—"

"You have no other siblings, Kanu," Okocha laughingly interrupted. "You have no choice but to—well—love me, or—hopefully not—hate me. I'm sorry to interrupt you, but I believe you've said what you and Somto came to tell me. Anything else is padding! And that was quite a mouthful, even for you, kid brother. I love you; you know that. And I thank you both for coming to give me your support." He paused, turned to Somtochi. "I take it you too—".

"I totally concur with what Kanu said," Somto said, nodding vigorously.

"Well, I thank you both, very much," Okocha said, his voice betraying a trace of emotion. "I really, really appreciate it. More than you know! Kanu, I'm glad you came, and that you came with our cousin. Thank you, Somto. God bless you!"

"What about me?" Kanu spread his arms wide, looking up to the ceiling.

"God bless *both* of you!" Okocha said with a chortle.

Kanu stood up from his chair. "Come on Somto, let's conclude this matter properly. I know my brother will not let us down, or he knows he'll cease to be my role model. Nothing more need be said."

Beckoning to Somtochi to follow his example, he stepped towards Okocha. Somtochi came and stood by his side, and together they pulled up Okocha. Then Kanu opened wide his arms, and smiled as Somtochi did the same. Simultaneously, they both wrapped their arms around Okocha in a bear-hug that lasted a long moment.

Okocha was quite winded at the end of the embrace. He inhaled deeply, and then exhaled. "Kanu, you are the best brother I could ever have wished for. You too, cousin Somto. You are one in a million. I needed—no, I still need all the support I can get. My mind is of course made up. When the moment is right, I intend to pop the question to Tatiana, and I hope and pray she'll—"

"She will," interjected Kanu, resuming his seat. "Trust me on this."

"I am reasonably optimistic," said Okocha. "But of course, as you both know, there are always two sides to every question. I never forget that Tatiana has a family, who—for all that they are usually courteous to me—may have their own attitude to these matters. I never assume anything until I am on solid grounds."

The door bell buzzed, and Kanu leapt to his feet. His excitement showed on his face, as he leaned towards Okocha, and asked in a hoarse whisper: "Are you going to ask her today? Now? While we're still here? It might well be the right moment. And please remember to ask her in the time-honored manner, like a proper gentleman—on your knees."

"Oh, shut up, Kanu!" said Okocha, but he was smiling. "You seriously believe I'll ask her while you and Somto are here? Sorry, no chance of that happening."

Somto rose from his chair. "Kanu, I think it's time for us to vamoose. We've said what we came to say. Okocha, thank you very much, and I wish you good luck, if you decide that this is the day. Come, Kanu. Time to leave."

Kanu hung his head, to dramatically demonstrate his disappointment. "Okocha, I thought you said this would be my opportunity to tell Tatiana that she's a goddess—"

"I did, didn't I? You can still stay long enough to tell her whatever your heart desires. She might even love to hear you call her a goddess."

"She might, Okocha, but not today," said Somtochi. "There's a time for everything. Kanu, I think we should leave now. Hold your compliments till next time around." He reached for Kanu's hand. "Come on!"

Kanu willingly submitted to Okocha's embrace as they said their farewells. Okocha led the way to the front door, where a smiling Tatiana, head scarf tied babushka-style, first kissed Okocha, hugged Kanu, and shook hands with Somtochi, with whom she was not very familiar. Kanu, all smiles, held the door open as Tatiana stepped into the apartment.

"Bye, Goddess!" Kanu called out, still smiling.

The salutation stopped Tatiana dead in her tracks, as she was reaching to take Okocha's hand in hers. She spun round, but only in time to see Kanu shutting the door with one hand, and waving with the other, a roguish grin splitting his face from ear to ear.

CHAPTER 7

Okocha silently led Tatiana to the love-seat, and made her sit by him, her hand still in his, a puzzled expression now creasing her brows. Okocha knew that the question was coming before she asked it.

"What was that?" Tatiana pointed towards the door, as she lowered herself mechanically into the seat. "Did Kanu just call me a goddess, or am I beginning to hear things?"

Okocha laughed. "Don't mind my little brother," he said, waving his arm dismissively. "He says whatever comes into his mouth."

"Oh, so you heard what he said?"

"Of course I did. But it's not serious. You know how he talks."

"But what did he mean, goddess. No one ever called me—"

He put a finger to her lips, and firmly held it in place, shaking his head the while. He looked deeply into her eyes, and what he saw in those orbs told him that this was a contest he was going to lose. He knew she would not stop asking—or wondering—until she knew the full story. So he did not resist when, with a slow deliberateness, she pried his restraining finger from off her lips, and guided it to his lap, and held it there. She was smiling sweetly.

"There!" she cooed into his ears. "You'd better start talking, baby. You know I'll get the story out of you sooner or later."

Okocha's head and shoulders drooped in an exaggerated show of surrender. "I suppose I've no choice but to tell you what in fact I told Kanu he should tell you himself. But the fellow chickened out, and left me carrying the can."

He paused, lifted his head, and shook off his slouching posture. "Kanu said you are the goddess of love—or words to that effect. He said—"

"Goddess of love!" she echoed breathlessly. Her face suddenly shone with an unusual and incandescent light as her lips parted in a smile of pure contentment. Then, just as suddenly, her smile disappeared, and was replaced by a frown darker than he had ever seen on her face.

"Goddess of love!" she repeated, looking askance at Okocha. "I hope he—or rather, did he say it as something positive? I'll be mad as hell if he—"

"Easy, Tatiana! You know my brother worships the very ground on which you tread. I assure you he meant it positively when he said to Somto that you are a goddess—"

"Of love." Tatiana spoke the words softly, nodding her head repeatedly, and pursing her lips. "And, speaking of Somto, I hope I'll have a chance to get to know him better. He seems a great lad. And I'm keeping my fingers crossed for luck that he'll look at me with more kindly eyes than his sister."

"Nonye?" Okocha said. "I shouldn't worry too much about her. I know she actually likes you, even though she has her private reasons for—how do I say this?—for pretending otherwise. Nonye is like a sister to me. So is Somto—I mean, he's like a brother. I know I have him on my side."

Okocha stopped suddenly, jumped to his feet, and dramatically slapped both sides of his head. "What am I doing?" he asked himself aloud, and hit himself one more time. "I'm sitting here, jabbering away, and overlooking the most important thing I have to do—"

"Like what, honey?" Tatiana asked with as straight a face as she could manage. She knew what his response would be.

"Like elementary hospitality, my dear girl! We Igbo place a high premium on hospitality when we have strangers visiting—"

"Me, stranger?"

"Come on, Tatiana. You know what I mean. This isn't the first time I've used that word when I should have simply said 'visitor'. I've been here how many years now, yet I 'm still very much a Nigerian the way I sometimes talk. Come to think of it, I should perhaps stop thinking about you as a visitor. This is virtually your second home. You know you only need to say the word, and it is done. Because you and I practically live together, I have been exerting myself to keep this place tidier than I used to. I even know what you would like to snack on right now, as we speak. I have your special snacks in the kitchen. We can talk while we munch, no? There's cashew nuts—the type you like, roasted and unsalted. There's baby-carrots, nicely packaged, and broccoli, and a selection of dips—cheese, onion, or vegetable. I've already taken the OJ out of the fridge, so that it's not too cold when you drink it. What's so funny, girl?"

Tatiana was laughing, and rocking her body as she did so. Okocha, after a brief moment of pretended seriousness, joined in the laughter. It was a scene oft repeated between them, though the context and the words spoken changed fractionally from one day to the next.

"You know," Tatiana said, "I can listen to you all day, the way you can dramatize even the most ordinary speeches—"

"It was a little speech there, wasn't it?" Okocha asked, preening himself.

"You certainly speak your lines as fluently as the great Denzel Washington himself. You could take a trip to Hollywood, and see what you can make of it. You have the looks too!"

Tatiana, her fervor spent, allowed herself to be lovingly enfolded in Okocha's powerful but tender arms. They stayed locked in this tight embrace until she was almost out of breath. He kissed her lightly, then released her—slowly and unwillingly. He led her by the hand to the kitchen, and made her sit at the breakfast table. Then he set about bringing the snacks out of the fridge, refusing her offer to help him.

"I would hate for you to risk smudging or breaking your daintily manicured fingernails. I just want you to be comfortable, dear. Today, I have a story to tell you. It is a story you must know only too well. The only reason it is worth my recounting it to you is that my Episcopal pastor, last Sunday, used the familiar Bible story in a way I had never before heard it used by other preachers. The way he used the story struck me as something that should be of interest to you and me."

"And this was last Sunday? That's almost a whole week ago! And you held it back from me till today. What's today?"

"Saturday. That's only six days ago. Have you forgotten that, somewhat unusually, I've not seen you for a few days? In fact, since—"

"Since you asked me to move in with you, right?"

"Don't remind me of that conversation. Anyway, I respect your feelings on that subject, though not necessarily because your folks—how did you put it?—something about killing you if you shacked up with me. You Baptists take yourselves too seriously, if you ask me."

"Thank you, OK baby," Tatiana said, her eyes tender, and her smile positively angelic, as she gazed on him. She had latterly begun to call him OK baby, and did he love it! It seemed, in a way he could not explain, to bring them closer together, in a tighter bond of love.

"You want to hear the story now?" Okocha asked.

"Yes! Oh, yes! You said it's a familiar story, and that it's important to you and me. Can't wait to hear it."

"Sorry, dear. But you have to wait just a little bit more. I absolutely have to change into something more comfortable. This polo shirt is much too tight." He wriggled his body, twisting and turning, and pulling at his figure-hugging, high-necked shirt, which he wore casually over his khaki trousers. "Give me just one moment. Be back before you can say—er—Denzel Washington!"

In less than no time, Okocha was back. In place of the khaki trousers and polo shirt, he now sported a short traditional Igbo jumper, modestly embroidered, and a pair of matching pants, of the same light-blue, flowered cotton fabric.

"That certainly feels better, don't you think?" he said, executing a little pirouette.

"You looked good as you were, but you look even better now," said Tatiana, smiling. "But where's the Nigerian cap that usually goes with this outfit?"

"Don't need to wear it when I'm in my home. Hey, dear, I see you haven't touched your snacks. Anything the matter?"

"I'm not in a hurry. I suppose I'm not really hungry, come to think of it. Would you, by any chance, consider we go out a little later, and have a normal dinner in a restaurant. And then you can tell me the story. What's the time?" she asked, peeking at her watch.

Okocha waved a dismissive hand. "Forget about the time. And a restaurant is the worst place to tell my story. Let's just enjoy the snacks, and we can talk as we munch."

"How about we first thank the Lord for what He has provided for us."

"Right on!" said Okocha. "I always remember that when I'm with you, I forget to pray at my peril. Wouldn't dream of being in breach of your family tradition."

Tatiana said a brief prayer, and they fell to. Her eyes were glued on him expectantly. But when he continued to eat his carrots in silence, she could no longer take it.

"What about your story? Or are you going to make me wait for ever for it?"

He smiled impishly, as he slowly guided a small carrot into his mouth. He avoided her eyes as he began to chomp it. After a little while, he stopped the noisy mastication, interlinked the fingers of his hands in front of him, and gazed over them at her. He held this pose for a moment or two, and then made a sound of clearing his throat.

"My story is not a long one. It's just the way I chose to present it to you to arouse your interest. It's not even *my* story in any sense of the word. It is the story of the Israelites during—or rather, close to the end of their famous exodus from Egypt."

He paused, and reached across the table and took and held Tatiana's hands in his. "Are you listening, my dear? Father Connery—that's my Episcopal Pastor—was preaching last Sunday, and he recounted the story of how the Israelites took the ancient walled city of Jericho. You know the story. They crossed the Jordan after countless years of wandering—"

"Forty years, to be precise," said Tatiana.

"I don't know about its being forty years *precisely*. But that doesn't matter. Between Egypt and Palestine—or should I say, Canaan—the Israelites, first under Moses, then under his successor Joshua, lost all their men who were of fighting age when they left Egypt, because they had disobeyed God. And, as punishment, He had said that that generation would pass away before the Israelites reached the Promised Land."

Okocha, as he spoke, continued to munch on the carrots, which he first dipped in a bowl containing his favorite vegetable-dip. Tatiana, for the most part, sat quietly, her elbows on the table, and her head resting in the cup of her hands. She focused intently on the story-teller.

"The rest of my so-called story is quickly told," Okocha said. "The Israelites, led by the Ark of God, and with the invisible hosts of the Lord hovering overhead, marched round the city of Jericho—I believe they did so seven times, or was it eight times. No, it must have been seven times. Seven seems a sacred number, and features in some Bible stories, including the creation story, and the Seven last utterances of Christ on the Cross.

"Anyway, the Israelites marched around the city once a day, for six days. On the seventh day, as I already said, they marched around it seven times. Then at some sort of a signal given by Joshua, the priests blew the trumpets, the Israelites gave a great shout and, lo and behold, the ancient city's walls came tumbling down. That was how Jericho was captured."

Okocha paused again, threw some cashew nuts into his mouth, and munched in silence for a very brief moment. His eyes held Tatiana's, tenderly, the faintest of smiles on his lips. Then dipping his right hand into the pocket of his Igbo jumper, he produced a small Bible. He opened it, and found what he sought—*Joshua*, chapter six. He did not read from it, but merely kept a finger there, so he could easily return to the text, if he needed to.

"This is a very familiar story to anyone who knows his Bible, as I'm sure you and your Baptist family do," he began again. "But, Tatiana, this is where Father Connery gave the story a whole different set of meanings. Which is why, dear girl, I am—perhaps needlessly—retelling the story to you now."

"I'm listening, OK baby. Take your time."

"What I have to say now is, I sincerely hope, not a misrepresentation or distortion of what the good Father Connery said last Sunday. If I understood him correctly, he drew some sort of a parallel between the walls of that ancient city, and the walls that modern man needs to break down; the sometimes artificial walls that mankind has built to divide one people from another—"

"The Berlin Wall!" Tatiana said brightly, her questioning eyes seeking his confirmation.

"Right on, girl! That's a great example, though I don't remember the pastor mentioning that famous wall. That wall has of course been torn down and, as the whole world knows, its fall changed East-West relations, hopefully, for ever. Father Connery had other examples of what he meant. He mentioned walls of sins and iniquities that have tragically separated us from the grace and mercy of our Lord. He pointed to walls that need to be torn down to free a people from the shackles of what he called the antiquities—ancient customs and traditions that would not let a people march with positive and firm steps into the future." He paused, and then gently touched Tatiana's hand, which was now resting idly on the table. "Do you begin to see what I'm talking about? As I listened to the Father explaining his story, my mind immediately went to my own people—"

"Nigerians?"

"No, Tatiana. Not Nigerians, but to my own Igbo people. We have our customs and traditions, and our old ways of doing things; ways that need some overhauling. That's a crusade that has to be undertaken, by the young generation of the Igbo."

"I hear you, baby. I hear you loud and clear. But if you're thinking of taking on your people's traditions, that's going to be one heck of a job, if you ask me."

"Funny you should say that, because—yes, my dear girl, I'm *asking* you. But I'll get to that in a moment. It's not as if I am talking about taking on the entire range of our customs; just a tiny part of it. That part that I can attempt to influence from my own little, inconsequential corner. It will take much, much more than an individual's effort to attempt anything more ambitious. It will probably take the effort of more than a whole generation of determined Igbo youths, to move us forward, and out of the quagmire in which we, as a people, are currently bogged down. You're right, Tatiana. It would be one heck of a job. We do not have a Joshua to lead the charge, or the heavenly hosts hovering over our heads. We do not have the priests to blow the trumpets, or even a crowd of people to raise a shout that will bring any walls crumbling down. But, I'm okay in what I plan to do, because I have you."

As he spoke, he rose from his chair, and went and stood by her side. First, he untied the babushka from under her chin, and then, very casually, his left hand reached inside the pocket of his jumper.

"Tatiana," he said solemnly, taking her hand. "I love you. You must know that I have loved you since the day I first set eyes on you. You are my world. That's why I now ask you: Will you marry me, Tatiana? But before you answer me, I need to warn you that we must expect our own little wall of Jericho. It is a wall that springs up from family to family, depending on the attitude of parents, and sometimes of relatives who do not want to see their old ways in these matters crumble before their very eyes. It is a wall that would not let our young Igbo persons find love where their hearts lead them."

Very gently, he pried open her right hand, and placed a small velvety casket in her palm. "Will you marry me, Tatiana?" he asked again.

Tatiana's eyes glazed over in exultation, as she first stared at the casket, and then placed it, unopened, on the table. Then she got up and, immediately, Okocha's arms opened wide and enfolded her.

"You didn't need to ask me twice, baby," she said softly. "But just in case you're keeping count, I'll answer twice." She took a deep breath, struggling to compose herself. Then, in a tremulous voice, she gave him the answer he sought, and for which he had prayed unceasingly: "Yes, baby! And, yes, again! That was quite a speech, OK baby. Perhaps a little bit melodramatic, but I can see that this thing—breaking down walls, as you call it—is very important to you. So I say a big Yes, and that's my third yes, because it seems preordained that I should be involved in breaking down this particular wall. I'm now convinced that it wasn't just happenstance that brought you and me together. You know what I'm sa-a-ying? I will be your partner in your crusade. I'll marry you because, of course, I love you! I've loved you for ever, if you must know."

Before he fully realized what he was doing, he had pulled her to him in a smooth move. Their mouths came together in a long, lingering kiss.

When they came up for breath, Okocha laughed and said: "My kid brother, Kanu, would have given an arm to see us now. He had hoped I would do this while he and Somto were still here. And he even seriously cautioned me to pop my question in the proper gentlemanly style and manner—"

"Meaning on your knees?" Tatiana asked, laughing.

"Precisely."

"So, why didn't you?"

Okocha hesitated for a moment, then said, searching her face anxiously: "Because I'm Igbo. The Igbo man does not kneel to anyone but God."

"Isn't that one of your ancient customs that need changing?" Tatiana asked, tongue in cheek.

"No, dear girl. That's something to hold on to, for ever!"

She fell into his arms again as they were both convulsed with laughter.

Moments later, when they had regained their composure, Okocha led her back to the love-seat. Without breaking their embrace, he made her sit by him. They sat like that, tightly holding each other, alternately kissing and gazing into each other's eyes. Occasionally, Tatiana daintily wiped her mouth, and his, with a tissue which she extracted from her purse.

"OK baby," cooed Tatiana into his ears, "you can release me now, and let me take my first look at your little box—"

"It's yours now," said Okocha, with a laugh. "Remember? I gave it to you."

"Of course, of course. And do you know why I didn't even look at what's inside—?"

As she spoke, she got up from the love-seat, and went and picked up the casket from the breakfast table. She carried it, unopened, back to the seat she shared with him.

"Because it's yours now, and there's no hurry. You have all eternity to gaze at it."

She placed the casket on the center table, and turned to him. "No, OK baby. It's because I needed to give an answer to the most important question I've ever been asked, without the need to know the karat-measure of whatever is in that box. You know what I'm sa-a-a-ying?"

"I think I do," said Okocha, smiling. "And now for the second most important question I need to ask. What do I do next? You know what I'm—"

"Stop it, OK! But seriously, my answer is that you'll have to decide what you want to do. If I understood anything from our conversations in the past on this subject, it's you who have to determine how you apply your Igbo customs at this point. But I know I don't have to tell you that. I just hope it's not an additional wall to scale."

"Oh, no! It's not another wall, per se. It's an integral part of the same wall that arises culturally whenever an Igbo man faces this situation."

"Meaning—?"

"Meaning, my dear girl, that the same wall that would discourage me from marrying a—how do I put it—a *foreigner* like you, would also not encourage my dad and our blood relatives to do the cultural thing and go with me to your parents' home to do what we call *knocking on their door*, as a first step to our asking for your hand in marriage."

"*Our*, did you say? *Our* asking? How many of your relatives want to marry me? What's going on here? Did I say something funny?"

Okocha was laughing so heartily that for a moment or two he was unable to speak. Then he regained his composure, and smiled at her. "Yes, Tatiana, you may not have intended it, but you're funny. I honestly thought that I had mentioned something about our Igbo tradition of knocking on the door of a girl's parents' home. Bottom line is that marriages—in our tradition—are contracted between two families, not so much just between two individuals, like me and you. It is a family to family thing. We come and knock on your door, to let your family know that one of us—that's me—wants to marry you. Simple actually, though the protocol can sometimes be fascinating to watch."

"Wow! I don't believe we've ever gone into all the details that I need to know as a prospective wife of an Igbo man. You'll have to explain quite a lot more—"

"I will, my dear girl," said Okocha reassuringly. "I will. There are any number of things an Igbo man's wife must know, like how to cook *egusi* soup, for example. But for now, the main point to bear in mind is that, unless my family—my dad especially—is agreeable to what I want to do, he most likely will refuse to have anything to do with going to knock on your door."

"And does your tradition provide some way out of such an impasse?"

Okocha stared blankly at her, shaking his head sadly. "If there is, I'm ignorant of it."

"That's terrible," Tatiana moaned. "So, what does all this mean for us?"

"Simply, that I'm more or less on my own. And when I enter into that mode of operation, it becomes part of my individual effort to help break down that proverbial wall of prejudice and fear that keeps one people apart from another. In the teeth of my dad's opposition—should he react as I suspect he will—very few of our relatives would be willing to stick their necks out, and accompany me to see your people."

"How many of these relatives do you even have, here in America?" Tatiana asked softly.

"Other than the immediate ones around me—my brother Kanu, and my cousins Nonye and Somto—none that I know personally. My aunt, Nonye's mother's visit will end in another week or so. No, I don't have that many relatives in the country that I can run to, to help me out." He paused, as a thought struck him. "Hold it there! Did I just say that there was no way out of the impasse? That's not totally correct. I do believe there's something I can do, to somewhat make up for the lack of relatives. I can ask my friends—my close friends—to step into the breach."

"Even if your dad doesn't—?"

"Even if he doesn't approve, yes. Some of these friends, I'm sure, will give me their open support, if I can judge by what they've been saying about us—you and me. Some of them are already married; some are not. Those not yet married can look into the future, and they must know that they could one day find themselves in a similar situation."

Tatiana was pensive as she tightly held his hands, which rested in his lap. Her eyes held his tenderly. "I suppose the only other question I want to ask is, is this process—what you call knocking on my parents' door—is this something you absolutely have to do with a bunch of your people?"

"Let me put my answer like this: any self-respecting Igbo man would certainly want to do the traditional thing, and do it as closely to our time-honored way of doing these things as possible. Yes, it is important to me that I do not come, all by my lonely self, to do the traditional knocking on your parents' door."

He paused for a brief moment, in thought. When he next spoke, his voice was pitched low, but it was intense.

"All of this brings me to the unavoidable corollary to all the questions we've been asking ourselves and discussing. What will *your parents* say when I ask them if I can marry you? What is the African-American culture in these matters? Will they be able to give an answer to my question without your wider family being present and participating?"

Tatiana seemed surprised by the question. "Honest to God, I don't know. My Karefa forebears may indeed have been Igbo—as you and some of your friends have loudly speculated. But centuries of slavery have taken care of any vestiges of Igbo culture and traditions that we might have brought with us to America. Slavery, surely the cruelest institution ever invented by man, systematically wiped it all off "

"Very sad indeed. But it leaves one last question. Tell me, Tatiana, what will we do if both of our families give us the thumbs down?"

Tatiana nestled closer to Okocha as she whispered her reply. "We'll sure cross that bridge when we get to it, won't we, OK baby?"

Okocha enfolded her, one more time, in his arms. "You can say that again!"

She picked up the casket from the center table, and gazed at it silently for several moments. "I suppose I can now take a peek at the little box, if it's okay with you."

"But of course, dear."

Tatiana opened the little box, and her eyes immediately lit up. She took the ring out of the box, and stared at it, fascinated by its silvery smoothness, and the sparkling diamonds embedded in it. She wrapped her fingers around it, and carried it to her heaving chest.

"I love you, OK baby. Couldn't have picked out a lovelier ring myself."

"I try to please," said Okocha humbly, "the best I can."

CHAPTER 8

"There's something you don't seem to understand, son," Chief Anigbo declared rather vehemently, "though you must have heard me talk about it over and over again. We don't customarily marry from distant lands. We simply don't. It's pointless reminding me that our Igbo men have been known to marry Yoruba women, or Ghanaians, or Ethiopians, or even Americans. Even our women have done the same. All I can say is: to each, his own. But you've been present, here in this house, when I've discussed this and related subjects with others of our community. Everybody knows where I stand on the issue."

"Yes, I've heard, dad," Okocha said. "But I don't seem to recall—"

"Recall what, Okocha?" Chief Anigbo asked, his tone sharp. "For a young man with the kind of brains I know you have, you are acting strange. Do you not recall the day—just over a year ago, I believe—when *Nze* Ahamefule came to see me with his son—what's his name, Ochia. Ochia was sitting there, where you're now sitting. You don't remember?" He paused, staring at his son. When Okocha remained silent, he shrugged. "Wonders will never end! I think what you have is selective memory. You just don't want to remember an inconvenient incident."

"Dad," Okocha said softly, "you say you remember that Ochia was sitting where I'm now sitting. I wonder where I was sitting. But I'm not asking it as a question, to test your memory. You are my dad, and I must not challenge you like that. One thing I remember clearly. Ochia was, at the time, thinking of marrying a girl from Sierra Leone. I know Ochia well. He told me his dad was totally opposed to the marriage, and kind of dragged him to come see you, as you're one of the elders of our Igbo community here in New Jersey."

"You're right, Okocha," Chief Anigbo suddenly exclaimed, pointing a finger at his son, by way of emphasis. "You're absolutely right! I remember now. I believe what happened was that we were expecting you to visit that afternoon, and indeed, you came. But that was later, much later, after *Nze* and his son had left."

Okocha exhaled with a soft whistling sound. "Thank God," he muttered under his breath. Aloud, he said: "As I said, Ochia told me about their visit, and what you said to them—"

"I knocked the idea right out of his head," Chief Anigbo said proudly. "And as you said, he was going to marry this Sierra Leonean girl—a girl from a brother West African country. Told him what I just told you that, as a rule—indeed one can say, as a matter of our Igbo traditional way of life—we do not readily marry from outside of the Igbo group. Would you believe that there are some Igbo villages whose people do not marry from certain other Igbo villages—"

"No!"

"Yes, Okocha. People from a particular village or town will say they do not marry from so and so village, perhaps because of the way the people perform certain traditional rites that might seem obnoxious to them. Things like that. Anyway, fortunately for Nze and his family, young Ochia took my advice—and his dad's, too—and within a matter of months, he found a nice Igbo girl. Their wedding, you'll remember, took place just a month or so before Nonye and Nnanna's."

Ekemma, Okocha's mom, sat in silence, listening with rapt attention to her son and his dad. From the moment Okocha had intimated his desire to come to the house to speak with them about the American girl—that was three days earlier—she had suffered sleepless nights. Three sleepless torturous nights, during which her mind and heart had been buffeted and tormented by what was clearly shaping to be for her, a looming, endless tragedy. Unless of course a miracle happened, and Okocha allowed himself to be dissuaded from taking the irreversible step!

The three of them—father, mother, and son—were closeted in the family den. It was a Saturday of uncertain weather, with the sun struggling to peek through dark, lowering clouds. Okocha's mood seemed to match the weather. In an already hour-long session of rather bitter argument, mostly between father and son, Okocha's face had remained as tight as she had ever seen it. Even an occasional attempt at levity by his dad failed to elicit anything but a tight-lipped response from Okocha.

It was just as well, she reflected, that Kanu and Somto were not present, especially Kanu. Kanu had not been particularly reticent about expressing his opinion on the matter in hand, and did not seem to care who was listening to him. Or not listening! Matters had reached a point where his dad refused to listen any more to what he disparagingly dismissed as Kanu's rantings. "What does it matter how the boy feels?" he had asked Ekemma, not quite two days earlier. "He's only exercising one of his American freedoms."

She was not at all surprised that her husband had sternly instructed Kanu to "make yourself scarce". And Kanu, perhaps himself not wishing for an open conflict with his dad, especially in the presence of big brother Okocha, had decided to go to a local movie theater. Ekemma was sure that Somto, for reasons not totally unconnected with the delicacy of the situation, had happily agreed to go with him. *"The Shawshank Redemption"*, one of Kanu's all-time favorite movies, with Morgan Freeman in a stellar role, was showing.

Ekemma looked long and hard at Okocha, and her puzzlement was palpable. She kept asking herself why Okocha did not—or would not—understand the obvious advantages of marrying a good Igbo girl. The Ndukwe girl, for example. Ifeoma Ndukwe had everything: good looks, good character, a pedigree of unsullied, irreproachable parentage! Ekemma, however, thought she understood a little bit about the psychology of the situation. It was perhaps predictable that Okocha would react negatively to Ifeoma, because she had been—in a manner of speaking—pushed at him from multiple directions. But there were other girls besides Ifeoma. Quite a few in fact, if one allowed the catchment area to extend beyond New Jersey, to include the contiguous states of Pennsylvania and New York. One only had to participate fairly regularly in the festivities and other social functions of the Nigerian communities, which the family did—indeed as far afield as Washington, DC. The girls were always there. Scores of them in fact!

Ekemma had decided that her best line of action would be to self-effacingly let her husband do most of the talking. She was basically of one mind with him on the simple question of whether or not to allow Okocha marry the *Akata* girl. It had to be prevented, almost no matter the cost. She had repeatedly asked herself if she was prepared to face the possibility that her son—if thwarted in his plans—might turn his back on the family. Okocha's generation was different from hers. It was a generation nurtured on the ideas of the liberty and independence of thought and action such as her generation never dreamed of. A generation, especially in America, that literally challenged the authority parents had enjoyed, since the beginning of time, to map out and shape the routes the lives of their children would take.

She shook her head, smiling sadly as she remembered a scene in a favorite sitcom in which an irate African-American father told an errant son: "I brought you into this world, and I can take you out of it"—or words to that effect. The look on the son's face, as he listened to his dad's bombast, told his old man that that was what his words were: hot air! She smiled even more miserably as she recalled a real-life drama in which a petulant teenaged girl threatened to *divorce* her parents because they would not let her have her way on her choice of a boy-friend—a young man of very dubious character, whose rap sheet was a mile long. What was the world coming to? She wondered.

There was, however, one thought that seriously troubled her with regard to Okocha and Tatiana. She was concerned that her position was perhaps an untenable one, if judged by the concept that happiness is the primary goal most persons seek in choosing their life-partners. The notion of procreation as the biblically ordained goal of marriage was now rather *passe*, and fell woefully short of the preoccupations of the present generation of young Nigerians.

Okocha's gentle voice brought her out of her reverie. "Mom!" he called out to her, engaging her attention with eyes that seemed to slice through her heart and soul, and a smile that was at once warm and challenging. "You've hardly said a word all afternoon. I know dad's position on this matter, even though he thinks I don't understand what he's saying. What about you, mom? I remember asking you the same question some time ago. I'm asking you again. Do you believe, like him, that my generation is condemned to doing things only in the way your generation, and those before you, did them?"

Ekemma hesitated, looking helplessly from her son to his dad. She clasped and unclasped her hands, and then began to twiddle her thumbs.

"C'mon, Mma!" Chief Anigbo cried out when he could no longer stand her silence. "Tell Okocha what you said the other day when we were discussing this same subject with my sister Ngozi. You remember? That was two or so days before she left to return to Nigeria. You were surprised she was upbraiding me for—how did she put it—being so old-fashioned in my views of marriage. I wasn't surprised; not really. Ngozi had always shown a tendency to give the young ones their head when it comes to such matters. But you reacted as I knew you would. You didn't seem to lack for the words to express your feelings then. Now, Okocha is here, and he's asking you and, suddenly, you're acting dumb."

Ekemma found her voice. "It's not being dumb. It's just that I'm not sure how to respond to a question that hasn't really been asked. Like the frog, I don't know what I'll say, and water will fill my mouth."

"What question has not been asked?"

"Okocha has not told us if he has actually talked with the girl—"

"Tatiana," said Okocha, when she seemed to hesitate.

"Yes, Tatiana. Thank you, Okocha. You have not told us if, and when, you will ask Tatiana—you know—"

"If she will marry me?" Okocha asked. "Dad hasn't allowed me to get to that point of my story."

He rose from his chair, and went and stood by his mom. Then kneeling down, he reached for, and took her hands in his. Holding firmly to them, he looked directly into her eyes. When he spoke, his voice was gentle but firm, as a glow spread across his face, and a radiant smile curled up the corners of his mouth.

"Mom, dad," he said brightly, turning briefly towards his dad, "I have finally asked Tatiana to marry me, and she has accepted."

A silence descended on the room. And the silence was like the silence of the tomb. Chief Anigbo fell back deeper into his king's chair, and raised both his arms and interlocked his fingers at the nape of his neck. Ekemma slowly but steadily removed her hands from the grasp of Okocha's hands. Okocha, after a brief moment of attempting unavailingly to hold her eyes, slowly rose from his kneeling position, but remained standing by her.

"You did?" his dad finally asked.

"And she said yes?" added his mom.

"Yes, to both questions," Okocha said.

"And what do you expect me—us—to say?"

Okocha turned fully to his dad. "I had to tell you exactly where we stand in this matter—"

"Where *you* stand, son. Not us."

"I have asked the girl I love to be my wife, and she—"

Chief Anigbo interrupted him. "We heard what you said. She accepted your proposal. We are not deaf. It is you who are playing deaf. But I'll let your mom say something. Ekemma!"

"What do you want me to say?"

Chief Anigbo laughed. "Are you an echo, or what? You just repeated the exact same words I said a moment ago. Mma, this is your chance to say to your son what you've repeatedly told me—"

"That's not fair, Nat. Because I told you something privately—"

"You don't understand, Mma. There's no more privacy in this matter of where our son marries from, or whom he marries. Okocha has told us what he has done. We need to tell him how we feel about it, both of us. The boy knows how I feel. He knows the only answer I can possibly give him. But I see getting you to say something now is like pulling teeth. So, though I don't really think I need to say what he already knows, I will do so."

He paused and sat up straight in his chair, placing each arm on an armrest. "Okocha," he said, "will you please come and stand in front of me, because I don't want to strain my eyes as I look directly into yours. And I expect you to also look me straight in the eye as we talk now. You and me, we are alike in many ways. If I am a leopard, so are you. As we say, a leopard does not breed a hyena."

He waited until Okocha came and stood in front of him. Then he rose from his chair, and put both hands on Okocha's shoulders. "My son," he said, "I love you. And I know your mom also loves you. But if she's strangely reluctant to speak to you directly on this issue, I'm not. So now, I speak for both of us, your mom and me."

He paused, and cleared his throat, staring intently at his son. "How well do you know the girl's family? I ask because, as you are well aware, we never rush into marriage before we find out everything we can about our prospective in-laws. And if they want to, they too can check us out. That's quite simply how it is with the Igbo. What kind of people are we marrying into? Are they a respectable family? Was there ever insanity in their extended family—not just their—what's the word?—yes, their *nuclear* family. Or a murderer? Are they from a stock of freemen, or slaves—?"

"Excuse me?" Okocha burst out. "Did you say—?"

"Yes, I said 'slaves'. But I know it's different in Tatiana's case. I don't mean 'slaves' as in the African-American situation. But that's one of the problems. If she has Igbo ancestry, as some of our people here believe, and his name was Okoroafor, who was this Okoroafor? What part of Igboland did he—?"

"Dad!" Okocha could no longer restrain himself. "I can't believe what I'm hearing. Aren't you carrying this thing too far—this Igbo tradition of—?"

"Like I said, son, the African-American thing is too muddled up for the usual process of checking out families. So I won't raise some other questions I'd have liked to ask."

"Like what, for example?" Okocha asked, with a short sharp burst of laughter. "This is getting a tad unbelievable—"

"You've noticed, I hope," Chief Anigbo said, with an intriguing smile, "that Tatiana is not totally black. She has white blood in her. One could ask who the white forebear might have been—?"

"But you're not asking?" Okocha asked, smiling.

"Not really, but it is intriguing. Could this forbear be what was called an indentured servant, who was not much better than an African slave, and might indeed have been a criminal in Europe before being shipped out to the new world as an indentured servant?"

Okocha burst out in a peal of laughter, and went on laughing until he noticed he was the only one doing so. His mother, Ekemma, was looking down silently at her hands which she held together, fingers intertwined, in her lap. Chief Anigbo continued to stare at his son.

"I must say," said Okocha, "I'm glad you're gracious enough not to ask, because probably no one could have given you the answers you seek."

"Son, you can be as sarcastic as you like, but we are what we are. Come here, my boy." Chief Anigbo pulled Okocha into a hug that endured for several moments. Then he let go. The cadence of his voice, when he next spoke, sounded a trifle tremulous to Okocha. But there was no hesitation in his manner, no stumbling for words. "Here's our answer to the question you haven't really asked us, but which was clearly implied in what you just declared to us. No, Okocha! Do you hear me, son? No! No! No! You do not have our blessing to marry your *American* girl. You'll never have it! I don't know how our ancestors will react, if I said yes to you. They'd probably turn in their graves, and that's the last thing I want to happen. So, there! You have our answer. The question now is: will you do as we have told you, and stay away from this Tatiana girl?"

Okocha sighed, his eyes boring into his dad's. They stood like that for a long moment, in silence. Then Chief Anigbo removed his hands from Okocha's shoulders, and let them drop to his sides. After a momentary hesitation, Okocha turned away from his dad, and went back to his mom's side. He again knelt by her, and took both her hands in his.

"I know, mom, how you feel about me and Tatiana," he said very gently. "I can see the pain in your eyes. So you don't need to say anything now. I'm really sorry about the pain and anguish I've caused you and dad, by the very simple and innocent act of falling in love with the wrong girl—wrong, of course, from both your perspectives. I love you both very dearly. You've been the best parents I could have wished for—in absolutely every respect, except this one thing. Dad," he said, turning to him, "I don't know if I'm quite the leopard you mentioned moments ago. But there may be something in the way you put it. All I know is that I am in love with Tatiana, and we have agreed to marry. I cannot see my way to—how do I put this? I cannot now go looking for another girl to marry. I fervently hope you both will take some time to think this thing over. And, hopefully, you will come round to my point of view—that my generation and the generations coming after us, cannot live our lives bound hand and foot by the traditions and customs of our ancestors. And this, irregardless of the crying need for some of those traditions to be changed or discarded, as unsuited to the modern Igbo world."

Ekemma tightened her hold on Okocha's hands. "Okocha," she pleaded, "please, please, think carefully before you do this thing. It's great to be in love. I think I was in love with your dad—"

"You can say that again!" Chief Anigbo interrupted, with a self-satisfied smile.

"Okocha, don't mind your dad, and his new American talk. As I was saying before I was interrupted, I would not have married him if I wasn't—you know—"

"It's okay, mom. You loved him. And I know you still love him."

"I'm not so sure of that," Ekemma said, looking daggers at her husband, though her smile said the opposite. "Main thing is that we, also, know what love is. But we cannot throw away the ancient wisdom of our people just because we are in love."

"Go on Mma!" Chief Anigbo exhorted her, lowering himself into his chair. "Talk to him! Maybe he'll listen to you. And while you're at it, you could remind him about what we say, that the chicken that plays deaf and obstinate will, when it is too late and it is in the soup pot, and cooking over a fire, wish it had listened to wise counsel."

"If he doesn't listen to you," Ekemma countered, "is it me he'll listen to? Okocha, please listen to your dad's counsel. Everyone in our community listens to him. Many seek his advice. And why do you think this is so? I'll tell you. He is that person who is most frequently called upon when, as it is said, a cow is being pursued, because people believe he has either some ju-ju power, or at least the rope with which to catch and secure the cow. Please listen to him."

Okocha slowly withdrew his hands from his mom's. He then embraced her, stooping over her, and encircling her with his arms. Straightening himself, he turned to his dad, and opened wide his arms. Chief Anigbo, rising to his full height, and standing eye-ball to eye-ball with Okocha, embraced him, and held on to him for a long moment.

"Dad," Okocha said, solemn of face, and earnest of voice, "this is my moment of truth. I hear you, dad. But I'm afraid that in this matter concerning Tatiana, I must go my way. You mean well for me, I know. But this is *my* life. I'm now old enough to make this major decision myself. However, it is my prayer—it will be my unceasing prayer—that one day, you and mom will bless my decision, and be happy for me and Tatiana. I hope I haven't lost you."

"Seems like there's nothing more to be said," said Chief Anigbo. "At least for the moment. Tomorrow is another day."

"Just one more thing, dad, and I am done—for now." Okocha said, and briefly hesitated. "In spite of everything that has passed between us today, now, I will dare to continue to hope and pray that you will eventually consider going with me to knock on the door of Tatiana's father's home? This gesture, on your part, would mean a lot to me, and to Tatiana."

"How so?"

"Because it will show me that, in spite of our differences of opinion on this issue, you are still my dad, and that our father-son relationship is basically intact. I am not the first young Igbo man to want to marry an American girl. And God knows, I will not be the last. Dad, mom, you are not forgetting, are you, that we Nigerians are no longer what we used to be decades ago—just sojourners in America? For an increasing number of us, we are here for keeps, dad. Many of us, including you and mom, Kanu and myself, are now naturalized Americans. Some of us, including even our girls, have enlisted in the armed forces of this country. I personally know an Igbo girl who did. It follows, doesn't it, that our horizon in the matter of marriage, and where we may find love, like it or not, has expanded beyond any Igbo parent's control. That said, I am totally comfortable with our Igbo tradition of going to knock on the door of the parents of the girl I wish to marry. It is one of those traditions that we must hold on to, if necessary with hoops of steel, as some poet or the other once put it. Dad, mom, I know you will not abandon me just because I fell in love with this girl."

For a heart-wrenching moment, he held his dad's eyes. But there was now only silence between them. And a sad smile—more like a grimace actually—on his mom's face. He turned, and walked towards the front door. At the door, he stopped, spun round and, with tears in his eyes, said: "Dad, mom, I love you both. And I hope you love me enough to rethink this matter and give me your full support. I need your support as I've never needed anything in my life. But if you finally choose to deny me what I ask of you, I'll know then that I'm on my own. But you will always be my mom and dad."

He closed the door behind him.

CHAPTER 9

Tatiana held the door open and stared, open-mouthed, at Okocha. Okocha, who knew she would be surprised, smiled evenly and leaned forward to kiss her on her right temple.

"What are you doing here, OK baby?" Her voice was without emotion, but her eyes briefly smiled at him. Then she looked over his shoulders, her eyes scanning the road where his car was parked. "You're alone?"

"Can't a fellow come by himself to see his girlfriend?"

"His girl-what?"

"Sorry, I meant fiancee."

"That's better. C'mon baby! You can do better than that kiss on my head."

"I thought you didn't—"

"Stop thinking! Show me!"

Their mouths met in a brief but intense kiss.

"Who's that, Tiana?" A voice from inside the house asked.

"That's dad!" Tatiana whispered hoarsely to Okocha. Aloud, she said: "It's okay, dad. I'll be right back! Okocha baby, I wasn't expecting you—"

"You weren't," said a voice behind her. "But I was."

"Was that what you were trying to tell me yesterday—?"

Her dad, Mr. Philip Karefa, put a gentle arm around her shoulders, and offered his right hand to Okocha, who took it with a respectful bow. "Thank you, Tiana," he said in a baritone voice. "Please come in, O'kcha?" he said, giving the name a tang that was peculiarly American. "You're welcome, young man. And let me ask, as usual, did I say the name—you know—?"

"Not too bad, sir," Okocha said, deadpan.

Tatiana giggled, looking from her dad to Okocha, eyes dilated in wonder and curiosity. "What's going on?" she asked.

"Nothing much," Okocha replied, with an awkward smile, guilt written all over his face.

"O'kcha had called some days ago and said he'd like to chat privately with me," said Philip Karefa. "Tiana, you were supposed to be out, to do your nails or something. That's what your mom told me."

"I see," Tatiana said, in a tone that belied her words, her brows furrowed in thought. "I see," she said again, nodding her head.

"What now, girl?" Okocha asked her, smiling. "You mustn't be late for your appointment, you know."

"Was it you made the appointment for me, *Mr.* Anigbo?" Tatiana asked, stiffly and exaggeratedly formal, turning fully to Okocha. A half-smile played around her lips. "If you think I'll just go away like a good little girl, you have another think coming. You want to talk to *my* dad, in *my* house, about *me*—I mean, about *us*—you'd better believe I want to be there. So, what do you say we get on with it, dad?"

Philip Karefa looked at Okocha, smiled and shrugged his big shoulders in surrender. "If you know my daughter—and I imagine you do, O'kcha—you'd know in this matter, it would be pointless to try to argue with her. She's as stubborn as they come. So, please come in, and make yourself comfortable."

With a smile and a wink to Tatiana, Okocha followed her dad into the living room. He was now quite familiar with the simple but well-appointed living room. The chairs were upholstered in a mauve-colored fabric, smooth to the touch. A chandelier, with eight bulbs, hung from the dead center of the ceiling. A wide-screened television set—Okocha thought he had seldom seen one wider—stood on a table in the far left corner of the room as one entered from the front door. But there was something in the room that he had not seen on his previous visits: sharing the corner with the TV set was a life-size bust of an elderly-looking, luxuriously mustachioed African. He stared at it.

"It catches the eye, doesn't it?" Mr. Karefa said with a smile, pointing to the bust. "That's my grandfather, popularly known in the neighborhood where he lived for many, many years, as Uncle Thomas. He was the first of his family to earn a high-school diploma. Made the family mighty proud. He didn't go to college because, in his time, very few of our people did. No money too. But he made something of himself in the limited world of business accessible to him, with a small franchised store in the ghetto in which he had grown up, selling a variety of household goods."

"That's really wonderful," Okocha enthused. "I have a lot of admiration for those African-Americans who rose above the racially-inspired limitations they suffered, to make their mark on this American society. It couldn't have been easy for them."

"That's the understatement of the century, O'kcha. It was like hell!" Mr. Karefa paused, breathed in slowly, and then exhaled even more slowly. "Just thinking of it—the general hardships imposed on us, the insufferable degradations—makes my blood boil. You probably don't know this, but our family—some sixty or so years ago—moved up North from the Deep South. It was granddad Thomas," Mr. Karefa pointed to the bust, "who decided enough was enough, and took his family out of the South. Today, the South ain't so bad for our people, and my father always said he preferred the relatively warm southern climate to the freezing cold of New Jersey winters."

He stopped, looked keenly at Okocha, and shook his head sadly. "I'm awfully sorry, O'kcha. I seem to lose my cool whenever I get started on this subject. I should know better than to ramble on and on—"

"Not at all, sir!" Okocha said hastily. "I understand. The grim experiences of the not-so-distant past are hard to forget."

"OK baby," Tatiana said softly, "That's why you mustn't get him started down memory lane."

"O'kcha didn't get me started on anything," her dad quickly jumped to Okocha's defense. "*I* started *me*, all on my own. Anyway, enough of my blabbering. O'kcha, you are very welcome to my home, as always—of course so long as you are not here to talk religion or anything like that! It's a shame," he added, with a quick glance at Tatiana, where she sat by herself on the love-seat, "you and me cannot have our conversation as privately as we had hoped. But that's all right. Tiana, where's your mom? Be a good girl and go tell her O'kcha is here. And while you're at it, might as well get us some drinks. O'kcha—"

"No drinks for me, thank you, sir. I just had my lunch before I came."

"But that's no reason not to have a beer or something."

"He's not much of a drinker, dad. I thought you already knew that? Hardly touches alcohol. I'll get him a ginger-ale when he's had time to settle down, and we've talked a little."

"*We*, Tiana?" Mr. Karefa asked with a smile. "This was supposed to be a strictly—"

"I know what it was supposed to be, dad. And I promise to be—how to say it—as inconspicuous as possible. Okay, guys? I'll go call mom." She rose from her seat. "And don't, neither of you, think to start talking behind my back. I'll be back in a jiffy. Mom!" she called out loudly as she walked out of the living room.

In the silence that followed, Okocha studied Mr. Karefa. He knew Tatiana's dad to be a good-humored middle-aged man. But he also knew that the man could, in an instant, turn irascible when provoked. So he was never quite sure which Mr. Karefa would receive him when he came to visit. A somewhat heavyset light-complexioned African-American, he was sometimes in ill humor, almost sour-faced, and unwilling to swap jokes, especially those jokes that tried to make light of the black man's burden in an unfriendly world. And jokes that lightheartedly questioned the seriousness of his religious convictions and practices. Today was different, Okocha quickly reminded himself. Today's visit had a serious purpose. Quite simply, his future with Tatiana was on the line. This was decidedly not a day to take unnecessary risks; he had to play it by ear.

In little or no time at all, Tatiana was back, with her mom, the amiable Mrs. Edna Karefa, trailing behind her. Edna seemed to walk with an unusual degree of sluggishness, as if she was reluctant about something. But she smiled expansively when she walked into the living room and saw Okocha.

"Here's mom!" Tatiana announced. "But before you start your conversation, there's something I want to ask Okocha to clarify for me. He told me, when I last saw him—that was about three days ago, wasn't it OK baby—something to do with—"

"In good time, Tiana," Mr. Karefa told her. "In good time. You can ask him as we talk. Let your mom first welcome O'kcha."

Okocha was already on his feet, as Tatiana's mom came up to him, and hugged him enthusiastically. "You're always welcome, my boy," she said to him. "You know that, don't you."

"Yes, ma," he answered, with a smile.

Edna sat at one end of the settee, holding on to his hand for support, as she lowered herself into the seat. "Is everything all right? Tiana said you're here to speak with Philip—"

"We were just about to get started," Mr. Karefa said. "O'kcha—"

"You've never said his name right, have you, Philip? It's not really all that difficult."

Philip gave his wife a stern look. "You're bugging me, woman! You know I do the best I can with African names. Sometimes they're as difficult as Polish names. How's a guy supposed to get his tongue around them? Anyway, stop interrupting me. I want to ask him what he wants to talk to us about." He gestured to Okocha to start talking. "Over to you, young man?"

Okocha shifted in his seat, looking nervously from Tatiana's dad to her mom. Then his gaze settled for a long moment on Tatiana. He made to get up, but was stopped by Tatiana.

"You don't have to get up, OK baby—unless you've come to make a long speech or something. Dad and mom know where we're at—you and me—because I've told them pretty much everything. I hope that's okay with you."

"Everything?" Okocha asked. "You mean—?"

"Everything! Yes, OK baby. I hide nothing from them, as I thought you knew."

Okocha smiled radiantly, nodding emphatically. "Thank you, Tatiana. I appreciate it."

He was silent for a moment or two, as he struggled to collect his thoughts. Then looking from Tatiana's mom to her dad, he cleared his throat nervously. "As she said," he began, "she has told you everything. Tatiana has done me the great honor of agreeing—let me put it this way—she has agreed *tentatively* to marry me. I say tentatively because of course it depends on how things develop from here on. The reason I wanted to talk with you today is that we Igbo people have our customs and traditions in these matters and, no doubt, you have yours." He paused, and nervously twiddled with his fingers for a moment. "This isn't as easy as I'd hoped it would be. What I'm struggling to say—"

"O'kcha," Mr. Karefa said gently, stealing a quick glance at his wife, "it's okay. Take your time. I know it's never easy when the subject of marriage comes up. Try to relax. Remember, Tiana has already briefed us a little bit. She's tried to tell us about your people's customs in these matters, but I guess she doesn't know much, does she?"

"Thank you, sir. Let me merely say that, in our way of doing things, the next important step is that my family will need to come to see you and your family—"

"Tiana told us something about that too," Edna said, looking at Tatiana for confirmation.

"Wait just a minute!" Tatiana cried out. "I need to ask Okocha about this, and I'm not sure it's a question I should ask him in front of you guys. Is it okay if I talk to him in private? Won't take long."

Mr. Karefa shook his head emphatically. "No side-talk, please. You can ask him any question you like, Tiana. But you should do so right here and now. As a matter of fact, your question may be of interest to me and your mom. I might even have a few questions of my own. So, girl, what is it?"

Tatiana hesitated for a moment or two, her mouth working as if she was struggling to get the words out, and her haunted eyes focussed questioningly on Okocha. "I'm not sure I should—unless *he* tells me to go ahead. It's better—"

"What is it, Tatiana?" Okocha's eyes held hers. "You seem so serious."

Suddenly, Tatiana's eyes lit up. "I think I've found a way to ask my private question publicly." She turned to her dad and mom: "Sorry, guys. I might be cheating, but I have to do what I need to do—you know what I'm saa-aa-ying?"

She did not wait for their reply, but went and sat between her mom and Okocha. She placed her hand gently on his lap, leaned towards him and, in a clear voice, asked her question. "OK baby, my question is—are you ready for this? Is this the *iku aka* thing?"

Okocha's eyes dilated in amazement and exhilaration, as a happy smile suffused his face. The intonation was not perfect, but Tatiana's articulation of the Igbo phrase was as clear as if he had spoken it himself. "No, Tatiana," he replied. "We're not yet there."

"What's going on here?" Mr. Karefa wanted to know.

"Nothing, sir." Okocha said. "I must apologize—"

Mr. Karefa interrupted him. "For what, Ok'cha? If apologies are due, they should come from my daughter, I should think."

"I can explain, sir," Okocha said. "Tatiana was confused about something I had told her, and needed some clarification from me. It was an innocent question."

"Wow!" said Mrs. Karefa. "Any question that could put such a wide grin on your face must have been a whale of an innocent question. So, it can't be so bad as to need an apology from you."

"I was thrilled and overjoyed, ma," Okocha explained, "that Tatiana could so easily pick up an Igbo expression just from hearing me use it two or three times."

Tatiana laughed contentedly. "T'was actually more like twenty or thirty times, to be truthful."

Mr. Karefa cleared his throat noisily. "I wish someone would tell me what's going on."

Okocha and Tatiana exchanged glances. Tatiana pursed her lips, and made a hand and eye gesture in a silent question. Okocha answered with a quick wink and a hand gesture that told Tatiana to relax.

"Sir," he began, "it's really very simple. You said earlier that Tatiana had told you and her mom about some of the ways my Igbo people conduct themselves in these matters, and that the very first step we Igbo take is for a family group to visit with the parents of the girl."

Tatiana could no longer restrain herself. "I told them everything! At least, everything you told me. I mentioned about what you called knocking on the door. Remember?" she asked, looking from her dad to her mom.

"You did," said her mom. Her dad nodded his affirmation.

"Although dad had said something yesterday about Okocha coming here, he did'nt say it was today. And when he suddenly showed up a few minutes ago, it was already too late for me to call him and ask any questions. Mom, you told dad about my nail appointment—"

"I did?" her mom asked, looking questioningly at her husband.

"So he said, mom. And he fixed the time for Okocha's visit so I wouldn't be in."

Mr. Karefa laughed softly. "I didn't know you're a mind reader, Tiana."

Tatiana smiled at her dad, shaking her head gently. "I didn't know if he was coming by himself," she went on. "Or with his family. I didn't know if he requested to speak to you privately—meaning, when I was out. So, when he came by himself, I absolutely had to ask him if he had come to—as they say—*knock on my father's door*, and if so, what caused him to go against the Igbo practice of coming with a group. That's what I just asked him—whether this visit is to knock on our door. OK baby, you have some explaining to do."

"No problem," said Okocha, with a short laugh. "My visit today, the reason I asked to come to speak with your dad—and of course your mom—is, first and foremost, to try to fix a date for the family or group visit." He turned to Mr. Karefa. "Also, sir, to give you some hints about what happens typically when the Igbo come to knock on the door of a girl's home. We always recognize that there are two sides—two families—involved in the discussions. Which is another reason for this visit. I would like to ask what might be expected of me as the suitor for your daughter's hand—that sort of thing."

"You really need your family to come with you?" Mr. Karefa asked.

"It's actually just a matter of tradition, sir. I'm not myself very knowledgeable about some of the details, for the simple reason that I have been directly involved in this sort of thing only once—when a young man came to my father's house to knock on our door. But it is a frequent topic of conversation in our Igbo community."

"That's very interesting," Mr. Karefa said. "I'm highly tickled by the prospect of such a visit. Quite fascinated, in fact. Tradition is something the African-American has badly missed out on, these many centuries—I mean, whatever sense of tradition we brought with us from Africa, but which has been lost for ever. It's a shame! That's why I'm very intrigued by what is happening between you and Tiana. It gives me—us—a chance to experience, at first hand, some of the things one hears only from time to time, and always at second hand."

"At second hand, sir?"

"Yes, O'kcha. In fact, only recently, I heard from a friend whose daughter married an African—not sure if he was Nigerian—that there are what he called protocols peculiar to Africans which are important to them in marriage matters. So I would like to know what your people's customs are, so I can show adequate respect for them."

"It all adds some flavor, doesn't it," Edna added, "to what would otherwise be almost a routine event?"

"There's just one problem for me," Okocha said, and stopped. He fidgeted, clasping and unclasping his hands nervously.

"What's the problem, young man?"

"Perhaps nothing much, sir. But ideally, my dad should be the leader of the family group that should come to 'knock' on your door, if you see what I mean."

"But—?" Mr. Karefa asked.

"I don't know how to say this, sir. But it is something that will soon become obvious to you and Mrs. Karefa. Tatiana is partially aware of this, but I'm not sure if it's one of the things she has told you."

"Why don't you get whatever it is out of your system, and then we'll know if Tiana has mentioned it? Is your dad perhaps hesitant about something?"

Okocha turned to look at Tatiana, sitting quietly now by his side, her hands clasped in her lap. At the same moment, she too turned, and their eyes met. She smiled and nodded encouragingly, which lifted his spirit and restored his aplomb.

"I'll just come out and say it," Okocha said. "My dad will, more than likely, not lead the group. He's still struggling with the idea that I plan to marry a non-Igbo girl."

"He's opposed to your marrying Tiana?" Mrs. Karefa asked, staring at Okocha, and then at her daughter. "She didn't—"

"I didn't mention it," said Tatiana, "because I wasn't altogether sure about it. I've had a sense that Okocha's dad didn't quite approve. But a parent will sometimes oppose his or her child's wishes in these matters. What's important is what Okocha and I do from this point on."

"Is that right?" Mr. Karefa asked his daughter, speaking slowly, pointedly drawing out the words. "Is that what O'kcha also thinks?" He turned to Okocha, and there was something in his gaze that gave a hint of displeasure. "You want to marry my daughter, but your parents do not approve. How are we—her mother and me—supposed to react to that?"

Tatiana quickly reached for, and took Okocha's hand in hers. "Dad, you know that's not a fair question to ask Okocha. You can't seriously expect him to tell you how you should react. We're telling you and mom how his dad feels. I expect you to tell us how that makes you feel. I can't imagine that you too would oppose us, would you?"

"Tiana," her mom said, "you and us—we have talked, and you know we would not want to make unnecessary difficulties for you and Okocha. All we desire is that, if you marry him, which we kind of assumed to be a sure thing, you will find lasting happiness in your new home."

"What about your mom, O'kcha?" Mr. Karefa asked. "You've mentioned only your dad so far. Does your mom think differently than him? Because if she thinks like him, do you think, for one moment, that we'd be willing to encourage our daughter to walk, with her eyes open, into the arms of a hostile mother-in-law? That's going to be quite messy, I can assure you."

Okocha sat quietly, looking from one interlocutor to the other. He could not truthfully answer the question regarding his mom, whose seeming opposition to the marriage might well be rooted in an unwillingness to disagree seriously with his dad. Her plea to him to think very carefully before taking the irrevocable step was couched in rather vague language. Tatiana, for her part, had nothing negative to say about Okocha's mom, who had been quite nice to her on the only occasion they had met.

"There's something else I would like to share with you both," Mr. Karefa said. "Something I do not believe I've ever shared with Tiana."

"What's it, dad? You make it sound as if it's a grave matter."

"It is, Tiana. It is. It's to do with—how do I say it? It's to do with us and them."

"Us and them, dad? Who's *them*? Okocha's people? What have they done now?"

"It's actually what they did, centuries ago, to their brothers and sisters. They sold our forebears into slavery. And this is what galls some of us, but we don't often show it to the outside world, especially to our brothers from Africa. But it has created some resentment among us, and that resentment sometimes surfaces when, as now, O'kcha's dad says he doesn't approve of his son marrying my daughter. I don't know about others, but this great-great-grandson of an African slave, who took a lot of shit from cruel slave-masters, does not take it kindly when a brother African acts like this. O'kcha, it's not your fault—nor even your dad's. But some of us can't help feeling bad when we find ourselves in this situation. It's as if he is telling me my daughter isn't good enough for his son. That's like adding insult to injury, if you get my meaning."

"Oh my God!" Okocha murmured, letting his head fall forward, and covering his face with both his hands. He stayed like this, looking down at his feet, for a moment or two. No one spoke. Then Tatiana put her arms around his shoulders, and held him close.

When Okocha finally looked up, he saw Mr. Karefa's eyes focussed on him, but there was no longer any trace of bitterness in his gaze. "Sir," he said tremulously, "it's a cultural thing. At home it is not very common that persons from one ethnic group marry into another. Even among us Igbo, there are instances where people from one town or locality do not marry from another Igbo town. I have sometimes heard people say "Oh no! We do not marry from such-and-such a village. Sometimes it is not clear why this is so."

"OK baby, it's all right," Tatiana cooed into his ears, looking strangely at her dad. "I've never heard dad speak like this. I don't for one moment believe he intends to—"

"Quite right, girl," said Mr. Karefa. "It was only a momentary thing. Like I had to get it off my chest. O'kcha, my boy, it's okay. I'm happy—I really am—for you and Tiana. It's of course your decision what you want to do in the face of your dad's opposition. Are you listening, O'kcha? Give us the details of your—what did you call it? Knocking down the door?" He smiled at his own joke. "And we'll take it from there."

Okocha's face broke out in a wide smile. "It's knocking *on* the door, sir," he said softly. "Thank you very much, sir. I will always remember your generosity to me, in spite of the past. Indeed, I don't know what else to say than to thank you from the bottom of my heart."

"You're welcome, son. As to you and Tiana, as I have said, you're welcome to come with your group, even if your dad doesn't come with you. You didn't answer my question about your mom. But I s'pose we'll just have to take our chance on that, and hope for the best. I'm pretty confident, if your plans go through, that my Tiana will charm her out of any ill feelings she might have. It's going to be all right. I'll even consider talking to your old man, and see whether I can make a difference."

He paused for a long moment, as his eyes focussed alternately on Okocha and on Tatiana. He was smiling now, nodding repeatedly as if satisfied that all was well with the world. Then, suddenly, he slapped his thigh. "There's something I almost forgot to ask you, O'kcha. Tiana once mentioned something about the name Karefa. That some among you believe it is a corruption of a Nigerian name—"

"Igbo, dad," Tatiana cut in. "And the name is Okoroafor." She turned to Okocha. "Did I say the name right?"

"Yes, Tatiana. Almost perfectly."

Mr. Karefa laughed. "H'm!" he muttered. "The two names do sound suspiciously alike. So there might be something there." He shook his head slowly. "I don't think I should try to get my tongue around the Igbo name. But that doesn't matter. What does, is that if indeed my forebear was Igbo, all the more reason to do our damnedest to do this thing as your people's tradition requires. We must respect *your*—" he laughed shortly, "and *my* Igbo tradition."

Tatiana was teary as she went and knelt before her dad, and threw herself into his arms. Okocha, following her example, went to her mom and embraced her.

CHAPTER 10

Chikezie Odogwu's honorific title, *Afulu-kwe*, derived principally from his reputation in his Igbo community as a doubting Thomas. "You can't get anything past him," Chief Anigbo once told Okocha, "without showing him incontrovertible evidence to support your claims." Okocha had a profound respect for Mr. Odogwu, who had succeeded his dad as the President of their village union, the Aniagu Kindred Progressive Union, otherwise known as AKPU. But that was not the only reason for the deep respect. Mr. Odogwu was one of only two or three persons in the community who could stand up to Chief Anigbo on any issue, eyeball to eyeball, and tell him when to get off his high horse.

On the second Saturday following Okocha's meeting with Tatiana's parents, the monthly meeting of AKPU was held at the residence of the Odogwus. As President, Mr. Odogwu had formally ended the meeting, and the members had been invited by Mrs. Odogwu to help themselves to a buffet dinner. Mr. Odogwu whispered into Okocha's ear, inviting him to an upstairs room for a private chat. Then—as imperceptibly as he could contrive—he made a prearranged signal to his wife. Gesturing to Okocha with his head and eyes, Mr. Odogwu led the way to an upstairs lounge. Okocha followed about half a minute later—a necessary delay, to avoid arousing any suspicion among the membership.

Mr. Odogwu did not prevaricate. "Is this true, what I'm hearing?" he asked Okocha, his voice notably soft and anxious.

"What—?" Okocha countered, smiling.

"What you're on the point of doing, young man, in direct defiance of your dad," Mr. Odogwu said in a fierce whisper, though he knew they were alone in the room.

"You're referring to my intention to marry an African-American, no?" Okocha's smile faded, replaced by a deep frown.

"Yes, Okocha. I hear you're going to see her parents. You remember you brought her to the high-table at your cousin Nonye and Nnanna's wedding reception, and introduced her to all of us at the high-table, where I was very privileged to sit."

"Privileged? You're too modest, *Afulu-kwe!* You couldn't not have been called up to sit there. You're the President of our town union."

"You're very kind," said Mr. Odogwu, smiling contentedly. He lowered his voice even more. "She is a great-looking lady, to be sure. But for you to be actually preparing to set out, more or less on your own, to do the traditional knocking on the door of her parents' home, that's an act of considerable courage. Good thing your dad isn't at this meeting today, or I'd not have been able to have this chat with you—"

"He's not feeling too well today, as I thought you knew."

"I know. He called me earlier today and told me. But, young man, are you absolutely sure about what you're doing—perhaps I should have said, what you're about to do? Your dad, *Ugo-Oranyelu-Aniagu*, should—by rights—lead your family group—and the emphasis is on *family*! You know that, I'm sure."

"I do. But there's a serious problem—"

"I know," said Mr. Odogwu. "I've heard. And that's why I'm asking you, are you sure you want to go this route, as our American friends like to say? Dear boy, are you quite sure? I'm perhaps not quite old enough to be your father, but I take you as a son. You know that, don't you?"

"I know, and I appreciate you very much. But, to answer your question, I'm fully aware of what I'm doing, and I'm totally convinced it's the only option open to me. What else can I do?"

It was then that Mr. Odogwu threw his bombshell. "Young man," he said, looking quickly over his shoulder as if fearing that someone might walk in to interrupt them, "I'd have done exactly the same thing, if I was in your shoes." He paused, and looked Okocha up and down, and then focussed on his shoes. He smiled expansively, and said: "Of course, your shoes are too damn big for a man of my relatively small stature. But I'm serious. And not only serious about what I just said, I'd have loved to be part of the group going with you to knock on the door of your girl's home."

"You can't possibly mean—"

"But I do, young man. Unfortunately—and that's the hardest part of it all—you know I can't, because if I did, your dad will kill me. You understand, don't you?"

Okocha cast his eyes down, momentarily dazed, and remained silent for a long moment. Mr. Odogwu searched his face anxiously. At length, Okocha looked up, and the radiant light that shone from his face was not the least bit dimmed by his teary eyes. Yielding to an overpowering impulse, Okocha went and enfolded the older man in a bear hug.

"*Afulu-kwe*," Okocha said tremulously, "you cannot possibly imagine how uplifting to me your words are. I fully understand what you're saying about your not being able to go with me to see Tatiana's parents. I really do. You've been such a close friend to my dad, and seemingly for ever, that it would have been somewhat disloyal to your long friendship for you to do so. The only thing I'd like to ask of you is that you do not totally desert me, whatever happens."

"Young man," Mr. Odogwu said, "that's not asking much of me. I'll tell you one more thing, and this is strictly between me and you and these four walls, as they say." He gestured towards the walls, and continued: "For the moment anyway. For some time now, I've been having some discussions with your dad about you and your American girl. I have no intention to ease off him—at least not just yet. Perhaps no member of the community understands where I stand on this matter of marriage. And I decided not to tell you about it—until now. My wife, after some haggling, finally came round to my way of thinking. The crux of the matter is that I disagree with your dad, and it's possible he alone, in our association, knows this. I've never raised my voice with him when we talk about it, but he knows I feel just as deeply about my convictions as he does about his."

"I just don't know what to say, *Afulu-kwe*," Okocha mumbled, a big lump in his throat. "I never imagined what you're telling me now. I don't even know how to thank you."

"No thanks are necessary, my dear Okocha. There's still a long way to go, as I believe you must know. Let's leave it there for now. Tomorrow is pregnant, as we say."

*　　*　　*

Mike Egbuna leaned on the steering-wheel of the Dodge minibus, and looked sideways at Okocha, sitting to his right, on the front passenger-seat. Then turning fractionally backwards, his eyes took in the rows of faces, some eight or nine, in the motley group of friends. The facial expressions were a study in contrasts. Some were aglow with excitement at the unfolding drama; a few looked nervous and ambivalent, as if uncertain about the wisdom of the venture on which they were soon to be embarked. Some faces—those not wishing to show their innermost thoughts—were studiedly blank. But whether excited or hesitant or calm, all were united on the purpose for which Mike Egbuna and Okocha Anigbo had painstakingly assembled them. One among them—a very valued friend, Okocha—was about to exercise his most critical and fundamental natural right: his God-given and inalienable right to want to marry the girl of his choice. Not the girl of his father's—or mother's—choice! Not a choice dictated by the vaguely sacred traditions of his forefathers as to where he might or might not seek a wife! Each person in the group had avowedly and strongly supported Okocha in this venture, which they declared to be an undertaking of unassailable merit and virtue. Indeed it was Mike Egbuna, not Okocha himself, who had taxed each member of the group to search his mind and soul on the issue. It was a process by which he set great store, and Okocha had not needed Mike to twist his arm to agree to go along with it.

"It's okay, Okocha," Mike said, taking a long look at his friend. "Relax, and you might get to enjoy the events of this day, as they unfold. I promise you, it will be all right."

Okocha smiled nervously. "That's easy to say, from where you're sitting," he said. "I wish I could be as confident as you are."

"Man, trust me. What do you think will happen when we get there? You think your dad might come storming in to ruin everything? Or is it Tatiana's dad? Do you fear he's changed his mind? You told me he said he might talk to your dad—"

"And he did," Okocha said. "At least, he tried to, and even left a message. Unfortunately, he gave the game away by saying he was calling about me and his daughter, Tatiana. He went as far as asking if they could meet to talk things over. Not surprisingly, my old man never called him back. Tatiana told me her dad thought he'd perhaps overstepped some Igbo traditional bounds of good behavior."

"Anyway," said Mike, "Mr. Karefa is on your side, from all indications. Your mom, and her mom too, I'll wager, can only play secondary roles in all this—though I have no doubt that behind the scenes, what they say and feel go a long way to determining how these matters go. In any case, Tatiana's mom—according to what you've told me—is also solidly on your side."

"No problem there," Okocha said, waving an arm for emphasis. "It's my mom—"

"Your mom isn't going with us—or is she?" Mike asked, looking steadily at Okocha. "I didn't think so. If your dad isn't coming, your mom naturally won't."

Mike paused, his brow furrowed in thought. "You know, man," he said in a soft whisper, looking quickly over his shoulder, "I feel really honored you asked me to lead this group. You don't have to tell me you chose me because our more elderly personalities are extremely reluctant to be seen—as it were—challenging our respected *Ugo-Oranyelu*, Chief Nat Anigbo, your dad. Can't say I blame them. Your dad is a formidable individual—"

"But you're not, like them, also scared of him."

"Is that a question, or a statement? Doesn't matter anyway. No, I'm not scared of him. One of the privileges, I imagine, of being a young independent man, generally regarded as an *I-don't-care* kind of person. You know what I mean?"

"Are you telling me something I don't know?" Okocha regarded his friend for a moment or two before raising an arm for a high-five salute. They both laughed happily.

"I should really salute your wife, Eunice, not you, because I'm sure she was the one who finally persuaded you to do this. Eh, Eunice!" He waved to Mrs. Eunice Egbuna who, modestly sitting close to the rear of the minibus, was engaged in an earnest conversation with Mrs. Akudola Okpala.

"Is that what she told you?" Mike cut in, before his wife could as much as get a word out.

"What did I tell him?" Eunice asked, eyeing her husband.

"That it was you made me come along for this *iku-aka* trip to Tatiana's father's—"

Eunice laughed out loud. "And if I did," she said, still laughing, "are you saying that's not true?"

"Uh-oh! I'm in trouble," Mike whispered, singsong, to Okocha. Aloud, he said: "I merely asked him a question, Eunice. I didn't mean—"

"I know what you meant, Mike. But that's all right. I know when to look the other way. Otherwise you and me wouldn't have enjoyed so many years of happy marriage. Take note, Okocha dear—for the future."

"I hear you, Eunice!" Okocha said, amid general laughter. "My dad likes to say that to see, and pretend you didn't see, is a sure foundation for a healthy marriage."

Mrs. Akudola Okpala coughed loudly, causing her husband Chuka to look up sharply. He sat in the middle of the minibus, two rows behind Mike and Okocha. Unusually for him, he had sat rather quietly, absorbed in his own thoughts, hardly saying a word to anyone since he boarded the minibus. Now he craned his neck the better to see his wife because, when she coughed—as she did now—with a rapid burst of emphatic sounds, he knew she craved attention.

"Akudola, dear!" he called out to her. "Out with it!"

"What's your problem, Mr. M.C. Emeritus?" Akudola glared at him, even as a smile softened the severity of the scowl. "Or are you like the emaciated person who reacts whenever a proverb mentions an old and tattered basket?"

"Hey! Everybody!" Chuka Okpala's eyes scanned the occupants of the minibus. "You're my witnesses—all of you! My wife is accusing me of not knowing how to look the other way. Can someone please ask her why my neck always hurts if it's not because of constantly looking the other way?"

"If your neck hurts, my dear husband, only you and your *chi* know how many girls you've been twisting your stiff neck to look at."

Amidst the pandemonium of laughter that erupted, someone suggested to Chuka Okpala that this was an argument he was not likely to win. Whereupon Okocha, though still convulsed with laughter, raised his arms aloft, and begged for peace.

"Enough, guys, please!" he cried. "I get the message. Marriage is an adventure that calls for a good dose of humor."

The laughter subsided gradually, and stopped. Mike then surveyed the assembled group, and did a quick count. "We are still expecting three—or is it four persons? Trust some of our people to be late, no matter how important what we're doing might be." He turned to Okocha, and lowered his voice. "By the way, Okocha, do you expect Nnanna? You two always seem to be inseparable," he concluded, laughing softly.

Okocha did not immediately respond to the question. Instead, he looked around anxiously. "Kanu should be here by now," he muttered, frowning. "Where the—?"

"Hello, big bro!" It was Kanu who, with Somto, had just then hopped into the minibus. They quickly took the seats they had earlier claimed for themselves, directly behind Okocha. "Where's our in-law, Nnanna? I don't see him here." His eyes scanned the group as he spoke.

"Kanu! At last!" Okocha's voice was stern. "Thought you'd forgotten. But better late than never—"

"Hold it there, bro! Somto and I were here before you showed up. We had a small business to attend to. That's why—"

"That's okay, Kanu. I know I wouldn't want to do this without you. Thank you for coming along, cousin Somto. No, Nnanna is not going with us."

"But I thought he said he would," Somto said, surprised.

"Quite right," said Okocha. "He said so, indeed. But he and I know that that would be an almost impossible act of defiance, on his part, against my dad, because of Nonye. I found myself in the odd position of persuading him not to go with us. I literally had to *beg* one of my best friends not to accompany me on a mission that means life itself to me. Nonye—"

"You'd have had nothing to worry about," Somto said, "on account of my sister Nonye. Nnanna had worked on her, and finally obtained her grudging consent to give her support to you. If she hasn't—you know—told you so herself, it's obviously because of her friendship with Ifeoma Ndukwe. And because of your dad too, I imagine. You know what I mean?"

Okocha's smile was radiant. "I do, and I'm glad about Nonye's support. Thank you, Somto. No, Nonye never breathed a word about this to me, though

I was with her and Nnanna as recently as yesterday, when I finally persuaded Nnanna not to join this group."

Mike Egbuna stood up as best he could from his cramped driver's seat, and spoke to the assembled group in the minibus. "I think we should be on the move. Now! We're almost all here, and we cannot wait any longer for the—I think, two—slackers. We're expected at Mr. Karefa's in about a quarter hour from now, at four o'clock. And this is a drive that may take us as much as twenty to thirty minutes, depending on the state of the traffic. Today being Saturday, we may be lucky in that regard. But we can't wait any longer."

"Hey Okocha!" It was the voice of Chuka Okpala, pitched—with accustomed and practised ease—at its most raucous. "What's the great hurry? Are you supposed to return this bus tonight?"

"No, *Nnamenyi*, Mr. MC Emeritus," Mike quickly cut in. "But that doesn't change anything." He turned the key in the ignition, and the vehicle responded with a soft and healthy sound. "Fasten your seat belts—"

"What seat belts?" Chuka Okpala asked, amidst uproarious laughter.

"You know what I mean," Mike shouted, above the din, as he prepared to release the handbrake. "Okocha, are we all set to go!"

"I just hope our friend Luke is—as we talk—already at his post," Okocha muttered, as if he was talking to himself.

"What are you muttering about, big bro? What post?"

"Oh! Of course you didn't know, Kanu. But Tatiana and I talked, and we agreed someone from the community should be with her folks—you know—to help and guide them through the traditional ceremony, and explain things as we go along. She herself picked Luke Okobi for this purpose. They were classmates in their first year in college, although Luke is much older than even myself. So she knows him well."

Mike made an impatient sign to Okocha. "Are we going or not? I'm waiting for you to give the word."

"Let's!"

Mike stood up, assuming an important air, as he cleared his throat. "Everyone please mark this date on your calendar: Saturday, October 26, 2002. On this day you all participated in the most important day, bar his birth-date, in the life of a very dear and worthy friend, Okocha Anigbo. Let's go! And may the force be with us!"

*   *   *

In his sitting room, Mr. Karefa clasped and unclasped his hands, and stared uncertainly at his interlocutor. Luke Okobi returned his gaze, smiling compassionately. They stayed like that for a long moment. Then Mr. Karefa shook his head.

"It's almost impossible to digest all this stuff you're telling me," he said. "It's easy for you because you probably do it like every other day—"

Luke Okobi laughed heartily. "Not at all, sir. Only once in a long, long while. Haven't participated in this kind of thing for maybe eighteen months or even two years. It's not every day that someone from my community goes knocking on the door of a prospective in-law's house."

"Forgive me," Mr. Karefa quickly apologized. "I meant that you are thoroughly familiar with the custom. But, for an American, as you must know, it's—" He stopped, shaking his head, both his arms raised in a gesture of defeat.

"I know, sir," said Luke. "I fully understand. That's why, when your daughter suggested to Okocha that I be asked to help you and your family, I knew I had to take it easy with you, and go through the process step by step, slowly. I believe you and Okocha agreed that I should first attempt to give you the broad picture; then, as his visit unfolds, to stick by your side, and explain things to you." He looked at his watch. "I believe they are due within half an hour, no?"

"Uh-huh!" Mr Karefa nodded, also peeking at his watch. "Time goes fast when one is anxious. I'm glad Tiana and O'kcha came up with the idea of sending you to help us. Otherwise, I don't know what I'd have done. I'd have been all at sea—that's for sure. You understand, this is something I've been looking forward to, from the moment O'kcha explained how you guys do this marriage thing. I've wanted to be a part of it since then, and don't want to make an awful ass of myself when the moment comes."

Luke laughed softly. "I won't let that happen, sir. As we've agreed, I'll sit close to you, though it will be as if I'm not there. Whatever I want to explain to you, I'll simply whisper into your ears. Remember that it's been agreed that the whole thing will be kept as simple as possible. I shouldn't worry. Just try and relax, and you'll get to enjoy the experience, sir. Trust me. All our friends in our community are just as excited as you. Few thought you'd be willing for us to go through with our traditional—"

"Why not? Some of us African-Americans welcome an opportunity, such as this, for a taste of what we left behind in Africa so many centuries ago. It'll sure add some color and excitement to our drab and monotonous lives."

"I hope you enjoy the experience, sir," Luke Okobi said. "I really do, though you might find some of it somewhat odd. For example, though your daughter is the reason Okocha is coming here with his group, she is not supposed to show herself until the exact moment when she should, if you follow me—"

"You lost me there, Luke," Mr. Karefa said. "What do you mean, the exact moment?"

" Simply, that she should wait in another part of the compound and building—"

"You mean, like hiding?"

"We don't think of it as hiding. Er—how do I explain this? It's just how it is, sir. She waits until we reach the moment when it is appropriate for her to emerge. In the simplified form we are talking about, when it's time for her to come out and welcome Okocha's group, she'll be escorted only by her mom, and not—as is our custom—by a horde of the women and young girls of the family—"

"In my family, there are only Tiana and her mom anyway," Mr. Karefa observed with a smile. "Tiana mentioned something about her mom accompanying her at some point, but she obviously left out the part about hiding or anything like that. How will I know when it's time for this—er—coming out?"

"Sir, that's why I'm here," said Luke, laughing. "Please, not to worry too much. I'll do my best to explain as we go along. Tatiana has been well briefed by us about this; which, I suppose, is why she knew not to be here with us, waiting to welcome Okocha's group. In fact, sir, I do believe you've got the hang of it already. Trust me, sir, the whole thing will go like a breeze."

Just then the honk of a vehicle was heard, and Mr. Karefa jumped to his feet. "They're here, Luke! Let's go meet them."

CHAPTER 11

Okocha Anigbo, with Mike Egbuna shoulder to shoulder with him, led his group into Mr. Karefa's sitting room as Mr. Karefa, with a courteous bow, held the front door open. Okocha quickly cast his eyes around the room, and noted the dozen or so folding chairs that had been positioned on one side of the room, to augment the seating for the occasion. Most of the folding chairs were placed opposite the armchair, and directly in front of the television. As all were aware, on an occasion such as this, there was not likely to be any television-watching.

"Please make yourselves comfortable," Mr. Karefa said to his guests, his eyes focused on Okocha. "I trust the seating is adequate for your visit. Do you expect more—?"

"No, sir," said Okocha. "We have everybody here." He paused, turned to his group, and pointed to the folding chairs. "Those are for our group. Feel free to sit on any of them. But whatever you do, don't sit on the armchair. Or the two-seater."

"Must be for Tatiana and himself!" Kanu whispered to Somto, and sniggered.

"Shush!" Somto whispered back fiercely, looking anxiously at Okocha. "Have you no respect—?"

"Relax, man! This is going to be fun. I can't wait for the ceremony to start."

"Hello, Luke!" Mike Egbuna greeted, his arm raised in a salute. Luke silently raised his, in acknowledgment.

Mr. Karefa took the armchair, and Luke Okobi the folding chair placed close to it. While Okocha and his group were sorting out their sitting arrangement, Luke leaned towards Mr. Karefa, and whispered in his ear: "Remember what I told you, sir. As soon as they're settled down, you should welcome them as we discussed."

"I remember well, Luke," Mr. Karefa said, putting a reassuring hand on Luke's shoulder. "And I'll do it with as straight a face as I can contrive, right?"

Luke nodded, smiling conspiratorially. "Right on, sir! This is the first of the special moments in this ceremony."

When he looked up, and across the room, at Okocha's group as they took their seats, he saw Okocha's eyes fixed on him. Their eyes met, and Okocha nodded faintly. Luke smiled and nodded back.

"It's time to start, sir," he whispered, leaning towards Mr. Karefa, his left hand marginally obscuring the movement of his lips.

Mr. Karefa coughed loudly, to clear his throat. "I welcome all of you to my home. When, a moment ago, I heard the honk of a vehicle outside my front door, I knew I had visitors coming here. I know O'kcha quite well, though I'm told I've never said his name right, eh, O'kcha? But I do my best, and that's God's truth. How y'all doing?"

"Fine!" a staccato of voices rose in reply.

"That's good," said Mr. Karefa, his face expressionless, impenetrable. "Very good! It's not often that a person like me has so many visitors, all coming together. Never happened before, best's I can recall anyway. I can see you all mean well, but perhaps someone will be so kind as to tell me why y'all here." He stopped and, just barely turning his head, glanced at Luke. When Luke replied with a soft nod and a wink, Mr. Karefa finally smiled at his guests and leaned back fully into his chair.

Mike Egbuna rose from his chair, where he sat next to Okocha, and then turned to look at his companions, before stepping slightly forward. "We thank you, sir, for welcoming us to your home. We heard what you said, about not knowing why we are here. That's exactly what we expected, because it is for us, as your visitors, to explain what brought us here."

He looked again at his companions, and received affirmative nods from several heads. "My name is Michael Egbuna, but my friends just call me Mike. Okocha Anigbo, sitting here to my right, is the reason we are here. He asked me to be the leader of his party—er, this group—and I was delighted to accept. I was delighted because he told me he has finally decided to move his life forward. He knows he cannot do this by his lonely self. When he told me that he has finally found the person that will help him live the life that God means for all of us to live, I rejoiced with him. He called his friends together and told us that God led his search to a wonderful girl who, sir, happens to be your daughter. By our tradition, if a boy meets the girl he wants to marry, he knows he has to meet the girl's family first. But he also knows that he should not go, by himself, to talk to his prospective in-laws."

He paused again, when he felt Okocha slightly tug at his jumper. Their eyes met very briefly, but in that brief moment, Okocha softly mouthed two words in Igbo: '*uka mgbede*'. That was all he needed to say, and Mike understood what was expected of him.

"I'll keep this short," he resumed, "because, as I've just been reminded, the sermon for an evening church service should not be long. We are very appreciative that you were willing to do this thing our way, but we know we should not talk on and on, as if we were at home, in our country. So to put the matter as simply as I can, it is because of your daughter, Tatiana, that we have now come to your home."

"Wow!" said Mr. Karefa, eyes wide open, his face aglow. "That was some speech! Thank you very much for what you said. You-all know that I'm ignorant of your tradition in these matters, but I have Luke here to help me through the various stages. This is great! It's unfortunate that O'kcha's dad is not here with us. But O'kcha and me, we've talked about it, and my hope is that in time, all will be well."

He seemed suddenly to remember something, and had a quick consultation with Luke. When Luke nodded his affirmation, Mr. Karefa turned to Okocha and his group, tapped his head a few times, and continued: "I forgot something which I believe is important in these protocols. Luke told me that your custom is that I would be expected to welcome you-all with—er—a kola nut prayer, I think he called it. But you want to keep things simple, seeing I am not at all familiar with all that stuff. He also said something about your kola nut understanding only the Ibo language—"

There was an eruption of laughter, which lasted for a while. Mr. Karefa, studiedly expressionless of face, waited patiently until the laughter subsided. "Did I say something funny? Anyway, that's what I was told. It's good you're skipping all that."

"What would have been the point?" Mike Egbuna asked, addressing no one in particular. "In a way that may be difficult for you to understand, it would have been sacrilege to do the kola nut invocation in any other than our Igbo language. The kola nut is intricately wound up with the heart and the soul of the Igbo nation, and is arguably our most sacrosanct object of daily use."

"I understand what you're saying," said Mr. Karefa, "though it might have been interesting to listen to it. However, I suppose we should move right on?"

"Right!" said Luke, in an undertone. "Now is the time for your daughter to make her regal entry. But don't worry, sir. I'll do the honors. She told me where to come and get her and her mom when the moment comes."

"I see," Mr. Karefa whispered back, smiling. "You two already had the whole thing set up. So then, go get her, if this is it." Aloud, he said: "Would you-all please excuse Luke for a second or two. He'll be right back."

With a nod and a wink to Okocha and Mike, Luke walked out of the sitting room, and down a corridor that led to the bedrooms. In very quick time, he was back and, with the faintest of nods, silently resumed his seat next to Mr. Karefa. There was complete silence in the room—the silence of hushed expectancy.

"Here comes your princess!" Mike suddenly sang out softly, slapping Okocha happily on the back. "And what a beautiful princess!"

In a trice, Okocha sprang to his feet, as did the dozen or so persons around him. And though it was not strictly in accordance with any usage, everyone began to clap. Everyone, that is, except Mr. Karefa! He stared, in total disbelief, at his daughter, and then at Okocha. Tatiana's outfit—a two-piece dress—was of the same beautiful light-blue lace fabric as Okocha's long jumper. Her blouse, short-sleeved, hugged her upper body comfortably, narrowed at the waist, and flared out to reach down to a little below her hips. The skirt was pleated, and of ankle length.

Mother and daughter were smiling radiantly as they walked into the sitting room. With one hand, Mrs Edna Karefa held her daughter's hand as she gently led her forward. In her other hand, she carried a bottle of wine. They stopped in front of Mr. Karefa, who rose stiffly and mechanically to his feet, as if pulled up by unseen hands.

"Philip," Edna said, "here's our daughter. You sent for her. And here's the wine." She placed the bottle on the center table, directly in front of her husband, and close to an empty tumbler already on the table. Then she went and sat on the love seat, and motioned to Tatiana to come sit by her side. Tatiana looked at Luke, who nodded faintly, before she took the seat offered by her mom.

"Tiana!" Mr. Karefa's eyes continued to stare in wonderment at his daughter, and his voice reflected his surprise. "This ain't fair, girl. You and O'kcha just stole a march on me, though I see not on your mom, who must have been in on this prank." He gazed at his wife silently for a brief moment, and then asked his daughter: "Tell me something, girl. Not that it matters much now, but when were these clothes made—yours and O'kcha's?"

"Can we talk about that later, dad?" Tatiana's eyes held her dad's steadily, even as an impish smile lit up her face.

Mr. Karefa turned to Luke. "Is this also part of your tradition, that the two young persons make clothes of the same material even before the girl's family has had the chance to say yes?"

Luke laughed briefly and shook his head. "I too am surprised by this—er—development. It's what we call *ashoebi*, when two or more persons wear clothes of the same fabric. That's a beautiful lace fabric—so beautiful one could be forgiven for thinking it was spun in the loom of the gods. Okocha and Tatiana look exquisite in them, don't they? You have a beautiful daughter, sir, no matter in what dress she's clothed."

"You telling me something I don't know? Of course she's beautiful. So, you too were surprised—which kind of answers my question. So, now, what comes next?" he asked, lowering his voice.

"We've now come to the heart of the matter. This is when you pour your daughter a glass of wine. Eh, Tatiana! You know what to do with it, no?"

"I do," said Tatiana, with a smile of contentment.

Mr. Karefa picked up the bottle, and held it up to the light. "I love its color and consistency."

After a quick, quiet consultation with Luke, he uncorked the bottle, and poured a small quantity into the tumbler. Then at a signal from him, Tatiana came and stood in front of him. He lifted the glass of wine, cleared his throat noisily and, raising his voice above the hum of general conversation, made an announcement that Okocha's group had obviously been waiting for.

"I will now ask my daughter to carry this glass of wine to the young man who has won her heart."

Several of Okocha's friends immediately and noisily engaged in a good-natured banter and some laughter as they watched Tatiana approach their group, carrying the glass of wine. Two or three among them held up their hands, and shouts of "It's me, girl!" reverberated within the group. But Tatiana, cool and collected, and with the sweetest of smiles, walked up to Okocha, and stopped. They gazed into each other's eyes as she took a sip from the glass, made a face and, genuflecting ever so slightly, handed the glass to him. Okocha took a long sip, stopped for a moment, and then drained the glass. Yielding to a sudden impulse, he reached for Tatiana, and enfolded her in a long embrace. Mindful of the company, however, he resisted the temptation to kiss her.

Kanu Anigbo, from where he sat directly behind Okocha, had been watching his brother narrowly. Now he leaned forward towards Okocha and touched him. Speaking barely above a whisper, and with a wink at Tatiana, he said: "C'mon now, bro! You can go ahead and kiss her properly. Your new found diffidence is a tad late."

"Oh, shut up, little bro!" Okocha fleetingly turned to glare at his brother, but ended up smiling with him. "Me, diffident?"

"Kanu's right, OK baby," Tatiana whispered into Okocha's ear.

"If you say so, girl. What the heck!" Okocha muttered to himself as he joyfully kissed her. "That's better! Now for your dad."

He reached inside his trouser pocket and took out some dollar bills, which he had put there for the purpose, and wrapped them around the base of the empty tumbler.

"You know what I'm going to do now?" he quietly asked Tatiana, taking her hand gently in his. She nodded in answer.

"What was that drink, big bro?" Kanu asked, pointing to the empty glass. "Can't possibly be palm-wine, though it has the same color. Or is there a local store where one can buy the stuff?"

"You would like to know, wouldn't you, little bro?"

"It's the symbolism that matters," Tatiana said. "There are wines that have the same color as your palm-wine."

"Let's go, girl. Mustn't keep your dad waiting. I see Luke whispering something to him, and pointing to us."

Luke had indeed fully briefed Mr. Karefa about the stages of what he called "this little drama".

"The gift of money is part of the show," Luke whispered into Mr. Karefa's ear. "Doesn't matter how much it is. Main thing is this little drama being enacted between your daughter and Okocha clearly identifies him as the young man who has won her heart, and has now come to seek your permission to marry her."

"Quite an enchanting drama, if you ask me," Mr. Karefa said. "I wouldn't have missed it for anything in this world. I'm glad I opted for it, and will certainly let my friends know about this African tradition. The best part of it, for me, was when I had to pretend, soon after O'kcha and his friends arrived, that I had no idea why they came to see me and my family. That was a great moment!"

"And perhaps," suggested Luke, "substituting Irish cream for the palm-wine?"

"Not really," said Mr. Karefa. "Wine is wine. And the palm-wine has about the same color as Irish cream. Couldn't have used burgundy wine, because of its red color, no?"

"Right, sir! And between you and me, I prefer the taste of Irish cream to that of our palm-wine—"

"You do?" Mr. Karefa asked. "You surprise me. I understand your palm-wine tastes quite nice."

"That depends on the type, and how freshly tapped it is, but there's no time to go into all that now. Here comes Okocha!"

Okocha and Tatiana came and stood in front of Mr. Karefa. Okocha bowed solemnly to him, and turned and bowed also to Mrs. Karefa. Without haste, he placed the empty glass, still wrapped in dollar bills, on the center table, in front of Mr. Karefa.

"Sir," Okocha said, "in our tradition on these occasions, I must return the glass to you empty."

"And with some money, I see," said Mr. Karefa, picking up the tumbler, and slowly peeling off the dollar bills. "Thank you, O'kcha. Thank you very much. Fifty dollars is very generous of you, young man."

Generous? Okocha mumbled to himself, smiling inwardly. What was fifty dollars compared to the bride-price he would have had to pay to her parents if Tatiana was an Igbo girl? And this, in addition to the fifty-dollar gift! He did not want to speculate on how much an Igbo father would have demanded for a girl with Tatiana's education, and her other qualities: beauty, sterling unsullied character, her generosity of spirit, her economic potential! But the obverse was now not uncommon. Frequently, a girl with Tatiana's education would vehemently insist that no bride-price be paid on her head. "I'm not for sale, dad!" she would say.

Mr. Karefa came forward and shook hands with Okocha, and then embraced his daughter. Edna, looking around her with an expression of uncertainty, also came forward and embraced both her daughter and Okocha. "I'm not sure if I'm supposed to do this," she said out loud.

"Who gives a rat's ass if you're supposed to or not?" her husband asked. "Sometimes, woman, you got to do what comes naturally."

"Couldn't have said it any better—or colorfully—myself, sir," Luke said, laughing, as he too came forward to hug Okocha and Tatiana. "Okocha, I believe this brings the day's ceremony to an end—as we all agreed. Mike should, I believe, now make his concluding statement. And then perhaps you, sir," he added, turning to Mr. Karefa, "might wish to say something before we disperse."

Mr. Karefa nodded. "Don't see why not."

Mike Egbuna, on receiving a signal from Luke, got up and came and stood in the middle of the room. He waited there until Okocha, now accompanied by Tatiana, had returned to his group. Kanu found a chair for Tatiana, and with more flourish than was strictly necessary, waved her into it. Mike then looked to his right and to his left, letting his gaze take in the assembled company.

When he began to speak, he seemed very conscious that the lead role he was playing, and what he had to say, were weightier than was customary for him. "I salute everybody present here today for the great event that has just taken place. I know I'm not very good at public speaking, and will therefore say what I have to say without belaboring the issues. What we have all just done is something very dear to the heart of every Igbo man and woman.

"We know that Americans have their own ways of doing these things. But our hosts, Mr. and Mrs Karefa, were willing to accommodate this enactment of our traditional ceremony of *iku-aka*. I sincerely hope they have not found it all a boring experience. I know at least one young Igbo man who married an American girl, but they didn't go through this ceremony because the American family didn't want any part of it. That's why I say to Mr. and Mrs. Karefa, thank you very much, and I say so from the bottom of my heart. The fact that they have allowed their daughter to now sit with Okocha and his group tells us that everything is going to be all right." He looked around him, smiling in all the different directions. "That's what I want to say, and I thank everybody." He took three or four steps backwards, felt for his chair, and sat down.

Mr. Karefa cleared his throat loudly. "This has been a great experience, for me and Mrs. Karefa. I am well aware that you have simplified the protocols. But I am glad you did what you did. Why would I not be glad, seeing that, apparently, many of you believe I have an Ibo ancestor—with a name that sounds like mine—"

"Okoroafor!" Mrs. Edna Karefa said, to the hearing of everyone. She giggled as she said this.

"Woman, will you quit interrupting me. Yes, Okoroafor! That's the name. And I know I said it right. So, if I'm Ibo, what you just did is also *my* ancient custom, however briefly you did it. I thank you all."

He paused, and beckoned to Okocha and Tatiana to come and stand before him. When next he spoke, his voice was mellow, his words were measured but firm, and his face was aglow with pride.

"Tiana," he said, reaching for her hand and drawing her closer to him, "it is my belief that you have found you a good and upright man in O'kcha. I may have some difficulty pronouncing his name, but I have none whatsoever in embracing him as my future son-in-law. Eh, Edna! You with me? If so, step up and do as you and I agreed we'd do."

Edna Karefa was all smiles as she got up from her chair, and came and took Okocha's hand in hers. "You are a fine young man, Okocha. I have no difficulty saying your name correctly. Unlike him!" She flicked her head in the direction of her husband. "However, Tiana's dad spoke for both of us."

Mr. Karefa embraced first Tatiana, and then Okocha. Mrs. Karefa in her turn, did the same.

"I have one more thing to say, and I am done," Mr. Karefa announced. "My one regret is that O'kcha's dad and mom did not participate in this ceremony. I do understand that it is sometimes difficult for people to let old ways die, even in a rapidly changing world. My remaining hope is that one day, his dad will be proud and happy to embrace me and Tiana's mom, and to call us in-laws."

CHAPTER 12

C hief Nat Anigbo stood by his front door, which he held open for a moment or two after Chikezie Odogwu breezed past him into the sitting room. A slow smile curled up a corner of his mouth.

"Please come in, *Afulu-kwe*," he said unnecessarily. "You're welcome."

"We've known each other so long I don't need to stand on any ceremony with you. But thank you anyway, *Ugo-Oranyelu Aniagu*." Mr. Odogwu regarded his friend for a moment, and then shook his head. "I don't need for you to tell me welcome, because by the time I'm done with you today, you may well regret your hasty welcome."

"That means trouble," said Chief Anigbo. "What's the matter, if I may ask?"

"You may certainly ask, and the answer is simple. You!" Mr. Odogwu took one end of the long settee, and leaned back in it, with his fingers intertwined at the nape of his neck. From this very relaxed position, he glared at his friend and sometime mentor.

"Me?" Chief Anigbo asked, slowly lowering himself into his armchair. "What have I done now?"

"You don't know what you've done—and are doing? Sometimes I don't know what to say to you. Over the years, I've learnt quite a lot from you. Not least, how to—you know—deal, or interact with our people. But sometimes I wish I could also teach you a thing or two. But will you listen? That's the question. Will you? There's no need looking at me like that. My question stands."

Chief Anigbo continued to stare wonderingly at his guest, and slowly his face broke in a smile. "I think I know what this is all about," he said softly. "It's about my son Okocha, right?"

"Damn right, it is!" Mr. Odogwu exploded. "It's about your son. What's it we say? Something about you don't need to tell an adult to come out of the hot sun. But in this matter, I feel a strong obligation to warn you—as a friend, of course—to step back from your untenable position, or you'll be scalded by something you don't seem to understand."

"You seem to be forgetting that other saying we have," Chief Anigbo said, shaking his head slowly. "A mature person doesn't spit, and then lick the sputum or saliva back. What I have said, I have said, and see no reason to change my stand."

"I won't give up on you—not just yet," Mr. Odogwu said. "But where's *Lolo*. I may have a better chance with Okocha's mom."

Chief Anigbo laughed shortly. "Since when did you start calling her *Lolo*? And why do you suddenly—"

"You're a chief, aren't you?" Mr. Odogwu asked rhetorically. "You were ceremonially installed a chief of our town, Aniagu, by the Igwe himself. And when the king of the town does that, your wife should be titled *Lolo* or *Iyom*, no? As to why I'm asking about her, I don't want to say anything more unless she's here, so I'm talking to both of you. It's about time someone spoke the truth to you two about a situation you don't stand a chance in hell of controlling. Someone needs to welcome you into the twenty-first century." He raised his voice: "Where—?"

"I heard someone shouting my—" Mrs Ekemma Anigbo entered the sitting room through a door that gave on to the kitchen and the master bedroom. "Oh, it's you, Chikezie. One of my favorite persons, that's what you are. How are you today, *Afulu-kwe*? And your wife, Ifunanya? Have you decided on a praise-name for her?"

"She's fine. We're all doing okay. We may fall, but we always get up, thank God! As to a praise-name, I can't think of any—"

"Well, if you can't think of one, I can suggest two or three—"

"Woman!" Chief Anigbo called out to her. "Why don't you sit down first. Take a seat, and listen to what *Afulu-kwe* has come to rebuke us about."

"Oh dear!" Ekemma said, her expression now mildly troubled. "He's on a war path today, is he? *Afulu-kwe*, what seems to be the matter?"

Chikezie Odogwu covered his face with both his hands, and stayed frozen in that position for a long moment. Then slowly removing his hands, he looked at Ekemma. "*Lolo*, do I have your permission," he asked in a soft voice, "to speak to you two frankly?"

Ekemma looked from her husband to Mr. Odogwu, and back again to her husband. "Of course, you may, *Afulu-kwe*. I expect nothing less from you. I imagine this is about Okocha, isn't it? The entire community can't seem to be talking about anything else."

On a sudden impulse, Chikezie Odogwu rose from his seat, and stood to his full height. At just about six feet, he was only marginally shorter than

Chief Anigbo. He went and stood between Chief Anigbo and Ekemma, who was now seated on the love-seat. He looked at both in turn. His expression was now at its most somber. His lips worked as if he was struggling to get the words out. But when finally he began to speak, there was no hesitation in his voice, which was neither strident nor particularly soft, but was modulated to an even pitch that he hoped would maximize the effect of his words.

"I have known you now for upwards of twenty-something years," he began. "And in all that time, more than any other couple, you have been my role models, both for me as a man, and in my married life. I have watched you both, as you come and go, and continue to watch you, especially in your leadership roles in our community. *Ugo-Oranyelu*, that was why it was, for me, a great and signal honor when I stepped into your shoes, as the president of our Aniagu Union. There is no greater honor for a son of Aniagu, in these United States, than to help our people, especially our youths, find their way in a country as different from ours as black is different from white—and I don't mean that as a pun."

He paused, concentrating his gaze on Ekemma Anigbo. She looked up at him with an expression that was at once tender and attentive, as if she was soaking in every word that came out of his mouth. Chief Anigbo was, by contrast, poker-faced.

"Yes, *lolo*. I said helping our youths find their way," he said. "Not directing or ordering them about how to live their lives. For crying out loud, people, this is the twenty-first century. We should know better than to try to dictate to our young men and women whom they should, or should not, marry."

"*Afulu-kwe!*" Chief Anigbo cried out. "If you really believe what you're saying to us, how come you didn't go with my son Okocha to the American girl's dad's home, to *knock* on his door? Okocha wanted you to lead his group, in my absence, and I know he has the highest regard for you, as one of the more elderly persons in our community. And don't be surprised I know he asked you. There's little that goes on in our small community that everybody doesn't get to hear about. So, why didn't you?"

Still on his feet, Chikezie Odogwu turned fully towards Ekemma, and spread his arms wide. "Is this a question I really must answer? Tell me, *Lolo*. Isn't it obvious why I didn't go with him, to lead his group, as *Ugo-Oranyelu* so aptly put it, to—what's his name—Mr. Karefa's house?"

Ekemma looked like someone caught in a trap. "I don't know what I'll say now and, like the frog, water will fill my mouth."

"Go on, woman," Chief Anigbo encouraged her. "Tell him what you think. You're not a frog."

Ekemma looked frostily at her husband for a brief moment, and then shrugged. "Why not," she said. "*Afulu-kwe*, it seems you didn't want to offend us, by joining Okocha in his venture."

"Exactly, *Lolo!*" Mr. Odogwu said emphatically, half-turning to Chief Anigbo. "Loyalty! That's what this is all about. Loyalty to a couple that's been very good to me and mine. That's why I declined to go with your son to his prospective in-law's home. In this type of situation, I thought my duty lay rather in coming to you, to talk you, if possible, out of your opposition to his intention to marry his American girl. Give me one reason—and this is my challenge to both of you—give me one reason why Okocha should not go with his heart in this matter."

For a moment or two, neither Chief Anigbo nor Ekemma spoke. Ekemma's gaze rested on Chief Anigbo who, with the corners of his mouth curled up in a sardonic smile, was content to stare at his interlocutor.

"Might I suggest a reason for your attitude?" Mr. Odogwu offered. "Our tradition, very likely, no? Okocha, if he's permitted—and I use that word cautiously—to go through with this marriage, would be in some sort of violation of our ancient ways of marrying only from within the Igbo nation. Is that it?"

Chief Anigbo laughed out loud. "You make light of a centuries-old tradition. But, yes! That pretty much sums it all up."

"Well, *Ugo-Oranyelu*," said Mr. Odogwu, "I have a surprise for you. The world has changed, and is changing before our very eyes. And, like it or not, we must change with the rest of the world, or we stagnate and become moribund. Thousands of our boys and girls—what am I saying—perhaps even millions of them live, grow up and go to schools and colleges in places thousands of miles away from our country. Do you honestly—and realistically—expect that when they begin to fall in love, they will be bound by what we loosely call our traditions?" He stopped when Chief Anigbo raised an arm.

"You have a daughter in college, I believe," said Chief Anigbo. "Are you telling me you'll willingly give her her head to marry whomever she chooses, even if it's an American, a German, or a Korean—that sort of thing. Can you stand there and tell me honestly you'd like it?"

"You have a point there, *Ugo-Oranyelu*. I might not *like* it. My natural preference would be that she finds one of our own kind, I'll admit. But that's where it'll end. God, in His infinite mercy and wisdom has blessed me and Ifunanya with two daughters. We are thankful for Udeaku and Janet—the best daughters anyone could wish for. Udeaku is what—twenty years old now. If she was to call me today and tell me she's fallen in love with a Yoruba boy or an American, or whatever, I probably would be sad about it. But it doesn't mean

I'll be prepared to do everything within my power to stop her. So help me God, I won't. If I have anything against the particular individual—"

"Like what?" Ekemma wanted to know.

"Like if I know the person is a bad character—like a philanderer who's been known to flirt with any pretty girl in sight, or a dishonest person, a convicted criminal, or some such scoundrel. In that case, I'd feel obliged to tell my daughter about what I've heard, and strongly try to dissuade her from marrying that individual. Yes, I'll oppose the marriage, but not simply because the fellow is not a Nigerian or an Igbo. We must continue to do our traditional things, like discreetly asking a few questions about a prospective in-law, from persons who know him or her. That's it! And, as God is my witness, that's the principle I hope to follow when the time comes."

Chief Anigbo nodded as Mr. Odogwu spoke. "I truly believe you would do as you're telling me. But that doesn't necessarily make it right, that you'll let your daughters marry into families with ways so different from ours that we can't be comfortable with one another, as in-laws should be. And there's another thing. You know how we always talk about the need to know the road to an in-law's home town, and to go visit with them. But when you look at the distance between Nigeria and America, for example, that's a long, long way to go."

Mr. Odogwu gave vent to a short burst of laughter. "Where do you live, *Ugo-Oranyelu*?"

"What's your point?"

"My point is, do you live in Nigeria or America? Are you thinking of packing up any time soon, and moving back to Nigeria? *Ugo-Oranyelu*, you're making me talk too much about a simple matter like Okocha's marriage to an American girl. I don't like making long speeches, but if that's what it will take to make you see reason, so be it. As a matter—"

"In all the years I've known you," Chief Anigbo cut in, "you've never been known for being brief on any issue. But go on. I'm listening."

Mr. Odogwu stared at his sometime mentor in silence for a long moment, shaking his head. Then he looked at Ekemma Anigbo, and suddenly his face lit up in a smile. "*Lolo* Ekemma," he said to her, "I have faith in you, that you'll ultimately save the situation, and prevent your husband from making a bad mistake—"

"It's not so simple, *Afulu-kwe*," Ekemma countered. "Me and him, we are of the same mind on the matter. I'm sorry, but where he stands, there I too stand."

"And do you agree with him that the distance from Nigeria to the United States is a serious problem for getting to know where your in-laws live, if Okocha marries this girl?"

Ekemma silently spread her arms wide in a 'what-can-I-say?' gesture.

"So it means nothing to you," Mr. Odogwu persisted, "what our people say, that where a person lives is the home he defends with all his might? We all live here, and in fact, many of our people strive daily to attain the citizenship of this country. Your son, Okocha, and his generation of Nigerians in America, will almost certainly live all their lives here. Sometimes we refer to them as some sort of a lost generation. This is the generation that will compel us to have American in-laws, and the sooner we cotton on to that overarching reality, the better it'll be for our community health. Don't you understand that what people say is true, and happening before our eyes? The world is rapidly shrinking to a global village. You hop on a plane in New York, and in—what—twelve or so hours, you're in Nigeria. In my dad's time, when very few people traveled by air, it used to take the same number of hours to travel relatively short distances within Nigeria."

He paused and took a deep breath, his eyes now boring into Chief Anigbo's. Ekemma fidgeted, clasping and unclasping her hands, her gaze focused intently on her husband. Suddenly, Mr. Odogwu dropped to his knees, directly in front of Chief Anigbo. His voice, when he began to speak again, was as soft as a child's.

"I've never in my life—to the best of my recollection—bent these knees to any man or woman. I've never asked the time of day from anyone. But I am appealing to you, *Ugo-Oranyelu*, to give your blessing, however reluctantly, to your son and his American girl. There are no guarantees in life. If you give them your blessing today, there's no knowing but you might regret it down the road, if the two kids show themselves to have been undeserving of your confidence in them.

"I'm not God, or one of His prophets. But this I know. If you deny them your blessing, you'll be denying yourself—yes, yourself—and *Lolo* Ekemma—the joy and excitement of seeing your son take this most important step towards full manhood. Don't we say that manhood comes in turns—like, you today, and your son tomorrow? Are you two listening to me, or am I talking only to the four walls of this room?"

He stopped again, and this time let his head drop forward so he was staring at the floor. He remained in that position until Chief Anigbo came to him and, taking him by one hand, pulled him up.

"*Afulu-kwe!*" Chief Anigbo's voice was emotional as he called out to his friend. "I am deeply touched by your plea. But I don't know why you think you have to go on your knees to a mere me. Who am I that you should do so? I've heard what you said. But what you're asking of me—of us—is something I cannot do. You know me well enough to understand where I'm coming from, on this matter. It's just something I can't and won't do. If I give Okocha my blessing to marry this girl, my ancestors will probably turn in their graves, and that's one thing I will not risk. Call me stubborn, if you like, but I have no other option than where I stand."

Mr. Odogwu, overcome by the emotions that assailed him, excused himself, and walked three or four steps away from Chief Anigbo. He stopped, covering his face with his hands, and remained like that for several moments. Chief Anigbo and his wife could not take their eyes off him. Ekemma, especially, seemed to have been deeply affected by the situation. But she maintained her silence.

Eventually, Mr. Odogwu spun round, and walked back to stand before Chief Anigbo, who was still on his feet. "Listen, please listen to me, *Ugo-Oranyelu*," he said. "Your son Okocha will marry his girl. Their date is set, and the invitation cards have been printed, and there's little you and Ekemma can do now to stop them. Where's my bag? Let me show you what I mean."

He found his bag where he had left it, on the *chaise longue*, and rummaged in it until he found the card. He took it out and waved it in front of them. "See what I mean? This is the invitation card." He opened it out and pointed and said: "Here's the date. Saturday, January 25, 2003—"

Chief Anigbo laughed. "We have the card here in this house. Okocha properly felt he had to give it to us, if only as a gesture of courtesy. But he knows what will happen, come the day. He'll have to marry his girl without our participation."

"I can't believe what I'm hearing," Mr. Odogwu said, shaking his head. "Is that your final word on this matter?"

"Sorry, yes."

"You don't have to be sorry about it, *Ugo-Oranyelu*," said Mr. Odogwu, straightening his body from its slouching position, a new note of firmness in his voice. "Your answer to your son is clear. I am very sad about it, but you have to do what you are convinced is right for yourself. Clearly, I have come to the end of my effort to persuade you otherwise."

Mr. Odogwu picked up his bag once more, and went and shook hands with his hosts. "I hope you two can understand that I, too, have to do what I believe to be right, not necessarily for myself, but for your son. I will attend his wedding. I will do so knowing that you might be mad with me, but that time heals all wounds. Mark my words. In time you may well be sorry you failed Okocha when he most needed your support. Nothing more need be said at this point. I'll see you when I see you—hopefully at the wedding if—God willing—you have a change of heart. Till then, I'll keep my fingers crossed, for luck, that you'll be there."

He raised his right hand, to show them his index and middle fingers crossed, and bid them goodbye. "God be with you."

*　　*　　*

Ekemma Anigbo exhaled slowly, staring wide-eyed at the entrance door, through which their visitor exited.

"What was that?" she asked her husband. "I feel as if I just barely survived a gale-force wind."

"More like a tornado, actually," Chief Anigbo said. "*Afulu-kwe* has no use for kid gloves when he is on the attack. And that's exactly what I expected of him. Other persons will grumble and curse you behind your back; but not him. He's a man after my heart. I like him—"

"I know you do!"

"But you know we cannot do as he has asked us, don't you?" Chief Anigbo's eyes held Ekemma's challengingly. "Don't you?" he asked again, when she did not immediately respond.

Ekemma clasped and unclasped her hands and, unable to withstand the intensity of his gaze, looked away from his eyes. "What do you want me to say? You know I'm unhappy about what our son is doing, but I'm not as sure as you that abandoning him is the only way to show him we are opposed to the *akata*—I'm sorry—I mean the American girl."

"Thank you for remembering that I don't like that word, *akata*," Chief Anigbo said, with a smile. "But about our son Okocha, what other response do you suggest, other than our not being a part of the wedding ceremony? It's not as if we can just order him to do this or don't do that, and expect he'll obey us." He paused and regarded Ekemma steadily for a brief moment. "Why are you shaking your head like that? Mma, I know you are thinking something when you shake your head like that."

Ekemma raised her eyes to her husband's. "If I'm shaking my head, it's not only in agreement with what you're saying, that we cannot just order him, and he does what we say. I'm shaking my head because I'm saying to myself, if you know you can no longer order Okocha around, why don't you—no, it's not just *you*—why don't *we* accept the reality that our son is no longer a mere boy, but a grown man who can now make the important decisions in his life? I think I'm prepared to—"

"Hell no! Ekemma, no!" thundered Chief Anigbo. "You deceive yourself if you think you're ready to let Okocha live his life any way he chooses to. I'm sorry, that's not how I see my—indeed, *our*—responsibility towards him. It's a God-ordained responsibility."

"As always, I agree with you," Ekemma said softly, nodding her head. "It's God-ordained, as you put it. And that's why, when we saw he was giving too much time to—what do they call it—American football, we opposed him, because we feared it would interfere with his academic studies—"

Chief Anigbo laughed. "Funny you should mention that," he said. "What happened later, eh, Mma? Didn't you suddenly begin to argue that Okocha could have managed both, that indeed the colleges try to maintain some sort of a balance between the two pursuits. Didn't you regret your opposition to him, especially when you understood, but too late, how much money he'd have been making as a professional footballer?"

"Nat!" Ekemma shouted. "You know that's not fair. Yes, I regretted later, but that had nothing to do with money. My regret was because, for an unduly long time, Okocha was a very bitter young man. And just when he was coming out of that mood, he met Tatiana, and fell in love with her. And now, history is repeating itself. We are telling him he cannot marry her. Like you, I don't like that he's going to marry her. But, as I keep asking myself, isn't it time to let the boy be? Let him marry whom he chooses—unless, as *Afulu-kwe* so rightly suggested, we know something strongly negative about the girl. Let Okocha make his own mistakes, if this is indeed a mistake." She stopped, and shook her head several times, eyes cast down. "When is enough, enough?"

"Mma," Chief Anigbo said, and smiled. "I know you love it when I call you Mma, not only because it is a beautiful short form of your name, but even more because, as the word implies, you are beautiful. Mma," he said again, "don't you think you've spoken long enough? You've said everything you need to say. I'm glad you stand firmly with me on this matter—"

"That's because I truly am not happy about this wedding, and also because, in public, we need to stand together. But now it's me and you only. That's why I'm asking you, when is enough enough?"

"The answer is: when you look for me, as we say, and I'm no longer there. Mma, that's when enough will be enough for this proud son of Igboland."

Ekemma got up from the love seat, and went and stood in front of her husband. Then she did something she had not done in a long, long time. Before Chief Anigbo knew her intent, she sat down on his knees, as he sat in his *king's* chair. She put an arm around his shoulders, and nestled close to him.

"Nat, my dear but very stubborn husband," she said softly into his ear, "do you think when you're dead, and I look for you and don't see you, that that solves anything? When we're both dead and gone, and our son, in his turn, later joins us up there in heaven, don't you think we'll have a lot to explain to him as to why we opposed him in this most important step in his life on earth? Your *enough* in this life, don't you see, will prove to be *not so enough* in the next. How about that, Nat?"

Chief Anigbo put his long arms around her waist, and pressed her close. "Is this *African romance*, or what? But, whatever made you do it, I love it when you do. As to Okocha's questions when we all meet up in heaven, Mma, don't you remember what it says in the good book? In the next life, there is no marriage, or being given in marriage. That's what our Lord, Jesus Christ, said. To which I add that, if there's no marriage, there are no sons and daughters. We'll all be like angels."

Ekemma growled, and hit him, but not too hard, on his shoulder. "Sometimes, I think it is a waste of my time to try to reason with you."

Just then they heard the front door open and then close. In the next second, Kanu burst in on them, closely followed by Somto. Kanu came to a sudden stop and, open-mouthed, stared at his parents.

"Wow!" he exclaimed, turning to Somto and then pointing to his parents. "I haven't seen you two this close since—I don't know how long. Somto, have you?"

Somto, believing the saying about discretion being the better part of valor, merely smiled and looked away, as his aunt Ekemma struggled to disengage from her husband's encircling arms. Chief Anigbo, with a mischievous wink at his son, and a smug smile suffusing his face, held on to Ekemma for another moment or two before letting her go.

"Relax, boys!" he said. "As we say, nothing your eyes see will make them bleed. But where have you two been?"

"We just met Mr. Odogwu outside," Kanu said, side-stepping the question, and pointing backwards towards the front door. "He seemed rather agitated. What happened?"

"Agitated?" asked his mother, quickly adjusting her clothes, as she went and sat on the love-seat. "What did he say that made you think he—"

"He didn't say much," Somto said.

"Only that we—or rather I," Kanu added, "should do something to make you two see reason. That was all he said, as he entered his car and drove off. But I instantly knew what he was referring to. Isn't it about Okocha's coming wedding?"

"And if it is?" Chief Anigbo asked.

"Dad, mom!" Kanu spread wide his arms, and looked up to the ceiling as if in search of divine support. "You may not know it, but the whole world is against you in this matter—"

"You mean *your* world, no?"

Kanu stared at his dad. "Yes, dad, my world. The world of young boys and girls—I should really say, young men and women—whose ideas about social interactions are infinitely more modern than yours—"

"Kanu!" Somto called out to him.

"It's okay, Somto," Kanu said, smiling softly at his cousin. "It's all right. Dad has always encouraged us to speak our minds on any issues of importance. And my brother's wedding, and whom he marries, are terribly, terribly important to me—to him and mom also, I may add."

He stopped, watching his dad narrowly, because he feared his old man might erupt, at any moment, in an angry outburst. But when his dad remained quiet, eyes fixed intently on him, he gently turned his hands outwards, and hung his head to one side, in a gesture of humility. "I know, dad, mom, that my generation is not as wise as yours, in some ways. But it is the generation that matters the most in this affair, because it is the generation that has no choice but to live according to where the world is, *now*, and for the foreseeable future."

"Who taught you that?" Chief Anigbo asked, his expression at once puzzled and thoughtful.

"Dad, I'm not sure how to answer your question. My guess is that it was you who taught me what I just said. You've often reminded me and Okocha that everything you and mom do is to make our future a better world than it is today. But you want to cling to how you did things in the past, which is a contradiction in terms. We—my and Okocha's generation—we have a more modern perspective on things."

"I hear you, my son," Ekemma said, her eyes, as she spoke, focused on her husband. "But you've got to understand it's not so easy for us—"

"Watch what you're saying, woman!" Chief Anigbo raised an arm to stop her. "This is not a matter of anything being easy or not easy. We have our God-ordained duty to guide our children in accordance with the ancient and tested wisdom of our people—"

"Tested?" Kanu stood rock still as he regarded his dad. "Tested by what, dad? You want a test of the ancient wisdom of our people in the matter of marriage, then please, dad, take a look at how couples, who are both Igbo, live their married lives. From what we see all around us, in our very community, I'd say that on a scale of one to ten, I'd score it at about six or seven. And that's being generous."

Chief Anigbo smiled faintly. "Son, where did you get your stats? And while you're at it, what's the divorce rate in the US of A?"

"Dad, I can't get into an argument with you on divorce statistics, because I know it'll lead to a dead end. But I can say this: if the Igbo girls in our typical Igbo-to-Igbo marriages were not accustomed to taking shit from their husbands—oh! I'm sorry, dad, I shouldn't have used that word. What I'm struggling to say is that we—Somto and me—all we're asking is that you let my brother—no, that you *support* Okocha in this marriage to Tatiana. Eh, Somto? Wasn't that what we agreed to appeal to my dad about?"

Somto came forward and stood shoulder to shoulder with Kanu. He looked from his aunt Ekemma to his uncle Nat Anigbo. Then in a soft but measured tone, he spoke from his heart. And, as he spoke, he wondered from whence he got the courage to say the words he never thought he could ever utter to so formidable a person as his uncle.

"Uncle Nat," he began, eyes unwaveringly fixed on Chief Anigbo, "what I have to say is simply that if you do not support my cousin Okocha and Tatiana—if you do not, at least, come to the wedding service—you may for ever regret it, and I know that I, for what my saying so is worth to you, will be terribly disappointed."

"Somto!" Ekemma cried out. "You don't speak to your uncle like that, boy, after all he's done for you—"

"And for my sister Nonye," Somto cut in, eager to pour oil on troubled waters. "You and uncle have been like a second mom and dad to Nonye and me. I didn't mean any disrespect to him or you."

"All Somto meant to say—" Kanu began to say, but was cut short by his dad.

"We heard what he said, and I know he meant no disrespect. It's just that what he's asking—what both of you are asking of us—is something we simply cannot do."

"Just showing up at the Church service, dad?"

"Yes, son. Just showing up there means we approve. And we cannot do that."

"I can't believe this!" Kanu exclaimed, his voice very agitated, his fingers clenching and unclenching. "Dad, mom, you know Okocha will be terribly pissed off. And if he is, I don't know what he'll do."

"In time," Ekemma suggested, "he might get over it, I think and hope."

"More likely," said Kanu, "he'll feel so badly let down he might decide he no longer has a dad or mom. And if he does, so will I."

"You'll do what, son?"

"You heard me, dad. And don't tell me you'd be surprised. What would I hope for, when my turn comes, and I do not marry one of your Igbo girls? Would you come running to my side? I can just see you—and perhaps mom—throwing up your arms, like, there we go again! Come, Somto, let's go. You know Okocha's expecting us this very minute." He looked at his watch. "We must hurry."

Barely acknowledging his parents, he walked with determination towards the entrance door. Somto cast a helpless, forlorn look at his uncle and aunt, and trudged unwillingly behind Kanu.

BOOK TWO

CHAPTER 13

The bi-monthly meeting of the Aniagu Kindred Progressive Union was slated to begin at five o'clock. At half-past six the president, Mr. Chikezie Odogwu, *Afulu-kwe*, called on the provost to say the opening prayer. The reaction was instantaneous, and predictable. Someone was heard to exhale slowly and noisily. Another member whispered loudly: "Oh, my God!" This was followed by a collective but very brief snigger.

Mrs Ngozi Dike stood up and looked around her, smiling with a deliberate and conscious graciousness. Her face wore her accustomed long-suffering expression. She knew, as did everyone of the dozen or so persons present, that the collective reaction to her was a direct result of her penchant for saying prayers that were usually colorful and jazzy, and frequently a tad long.

She cleared her throat and, in her assertive but quite melodious voice, broke into song, signalling to all the members present to join in the singing:

"Oh Lord, we are very very grateful
For all you have done for us.
Oh Lord, we are very very grateful
We are saying, Thank you, our Lord."

The singing, with a dozen pairs of hands clapping to the rhythm of the song, was lusty and harmonious, and the enjoyment was palpable. At the end of it, Ngozi Dike smiled with satisfaction, put her palms together and, lifting them up to her chest, invited the assemblage to lift up their hearts.

"We lift them up to the Lord!" a dozen voices responded.

Ngozi Dike asked that God be in their midst, and chair the meeting. She prayed for those who, being habitual latecomers, were not yet present. "Watch over them as they find their different ways to join us, whether they are coming by foot or by car, so that they will safely arrive here."

She paused for a second or two, peeking at her comrades. Then, at the top of her lungs, and before anyone quite realized she was done, she exclaimed: "For Christ's sake! Amen!"

"Amen!" shouted a chorus of surprised voices.

"Madame Provost!" two or three voices hailed her.

"Our own deaconess, but without a collar!" a lone voice shouted, amidst some hilarity.

Ngozi smiled with satisfaction. "At least I got my own back at all of you," she mumbled to herself, happy with the unusual brevity of her prayer.

The president called the meeting to order. "I say a hearty welcome to all of you—on behalf of myself and the executives." He turned his head to his right and left, his gaze taking in the elected officers sitting with him at a table on a dais. "As usual, unfortunately, our people never show up on time for anything—".

"Except for their jobs, unfailingly, Monday to Friday," said a voice from the rear of the hall.

"This meeting," the president continued, smiling softly, and shaking his head, "should have started an hour and a half ago. The secretary's circular states it quite clearly."

He held up his copy of the circular, and read from it: "Sunday, April 27, 2003. Time: 5 p.m." He paused, and looked around the hall, as if in search of something. When he found it, he pointed. "There! The secretary's attendance sheet is now going round. Make sure you all sign it, and I hope by the time it gets back to her, there'll be at least thirty names on it. For an association that boasts a membership of close to fifty persons, it is sad that there are only thirteen or fourteen of us here. But the quorum needed is ten, including three officers. We have handily met that requirement. There are five officers present."

"*Afulu-kwe!*" Ngozi Dike called out to the president. "Shouldn't we start with the kola nut invocation?"

"Of course," said Mr. Odogwu. "That's when there is kola nut. Did you bring any?"

"Me? A woman?" Ngozi asked, her eyes widening in a show of surprise. "I know if my husband were here, there'd have been no need to ask. But he's been dead these two years or so."

"We know," said Mr. Odogwu. "We all regret his passing. He was a real blessing to our people and—"

"Where's *Ugo-Oranyelu* when we need him?" Chuka Okpala interrupted, turning his head to look at Mr. Odogwu, on whose right he sat. "He always brings—"

"You don't have to look at me like that," Mr. Odogwu rebuked him, but with a smile. "I know what that scowl means."

"You should." Chuka Okpala smiled impishly, his voice as harsh as he could contrive. "When *Ugo-Oranyelu* was our president—"

"He never failed to make sure we had kola nut," Mr. Odogwu—in a slow sardonic voice—completed the sentence for Chuka. "I know. But he's not here—not yet, anyway. He might bring some, when he comes. And then we can do the traditional thing, however late that might be. I hope he's on his way, but we can't wait for his arrival before we can start."

"That's right," said Mike Egbuna. "Have you ever heard that on *Nkwo* market day, the market takes any notice that somebody or the other is not present. Trading goes on regardless." He paused for a moment, and then added: "This is the third meeting since Okocha's wedding that he's missed."

"Correction!" shouted Nnanna Onwuka. "This will be the third if—and that's a big *if*—he doesn't show up."

Nnanna, Assitant Secretary, sat in the middle of the assembled membership. He had firmly declined suggestions from all around him that he should go sit with the other executives on the dais, arguing that there was room up there for only one secretary, his "boss"—as he called her—Celestine Nwachi.

"Hasn't *Ugo-Oranyelu* gotten over his son's wedding?" Mike Egbuna asked.

"Will you please leave uncle Nat alone? Nonye tells me—"

"And talking of your wife, Nonye, where is she?" Mike cut in. "Where's Okocha? Seems like the entire Anigbo clan, except you Nnanna, are not here. What happened to Kanu and Somto? Those two hardly ever miss our meetings, bless them."

"What about Tatiana!" a voice from the back row added.

"Okocha said he'd bring Tatiana to our meeting and register her as a member," said Mike. Then he added in a complaining voice: "He promised me! I hope—"

"Give the man some space, Mike," said Chuka Okpala. "Let him enjoy a few months of his marriage without you hanging round his neck like a millstone. I remember, when I got married—that's many, many, many years ago, when some of you had not even been born—"

"*Nnamenyi*! Mr. MC Emeritus!" Mike interrupted. "No one wants to hear your life story. We've heard it often enough."

There was general laughter and some back-slapping. Chuka Okpala, after a momentary hesitation, joined in the laughter.

Mr. Odogwu, using his empty spectacle case as a gavel, twice rapped on the head table, to gain the attention of the members.

"The meeting today will be a very short one," he announced. "In fact, the Executive Committee considered postponing it till next month because, as many of you know, there's a major celebration due to start in about an hour from now, at the Celestial Gardens. I know that most—if not all—of us have been invited to the event. Which is as it should be because twenty-five years of marriage to the same person calls for serious celebration. God knows it isn't as easy nowadays as it used to be, in the days of our parents and grandparents."

"How long has our very own *Ugo-Oranyelu-Aniagu*, Chief Anigbo been married?" a voice loudly asked from the floor.

"Just about thirty years," Mr. Odogwu responded. "Why—?"

"Praise the Lord!" another voice proclaimed. "He's a shining example."

"Right," said Mr. Odogwu. "That he is. But let's get on with the business of the day. With your permission, ladies and gentlemen, we'll dispense with the reading of the minutes by our able secretary, Celestine. In fact she mailed the minutes to all members more than a week ago, and she specifically requested that everyone read it before today's meeting, and come here prepared to go straight to amendments and that sort of thing. So let's just say that we take the minutes as read."

He paused and looked around him, seeking general agreement. Several heads nodded. A few faces guiltily stared back at him, mumbling incoherently.

"Any amendments?" the president then asked. "And please make your comments brief. Over to you, Mme Provost."

Ngozi Dike stood up and took the center of the floor between the head table on the dais and the general membership. She looked to her left and to her right, her arms spread out, her eyes asking the question without the use of words.

"Or will someone move that we adopt the minutes?" she asked loudly, when no one spoke.

"I so move!" shouted Chuka Okpala.

"Seconded!" a female voice said.

"Thank you Adaku," said the secretary, Celestine Nwachi, craning her neck in the direction of the sound.

"You're welcome, Celestine!" Adaku said, waving an arm in salutation. "And I just want to add that our secretary's minutes have been so good that there's usually no amendments and corrections. And that's what you get when a woman is—"

Cheers and jeers drowned out her voice. In the midst of the jovial uproar, the president thumped several times on the table with his bare knuckles. "We get your point, Adaku," he said, smiling. "As our first lady secretary yourself, you did good. We all remember that, and we thank you."

Adaku stood up and, smiling radiantly, took a bow, and high-fived two of her women friends who sat closest to her.

The president tapped on the table and then cleared his throat noisily. He held up a sheet of paper. "I hope you all have the agenda for today's meeting.

I see here that the first item on the agenda, after the reading and adoption of the minutes, is *Membership dues*! Yes, very important. This ties in directly with our ability to pay our affiliate dues to our umbrella Igbo organization, Nzuko Nd'Igbo, New Jersey. It's very important we do not let ourselves down—if for no other reason, at least because our own Chief Anigbo, *Ugo-Oranyelu*, is its president."

Slowly, he rose from his chair. "Let me stand up to say what I want to say now. It's something I've said many times, and I do not hesitate to say it again. There's a real and pressing need for a new sense of responsibility among us, especially in this matter of annual dues. It's not enough for a town association like ours to submit a membership list of forty-something members to the NNNJ. We have to back this up by paying forty dollars to the NNNJ for every single member on that list. That's sixteen hundred and more dollars. Those of us who have not paid our annual dues to this association must think someone up here, among the executive committee, mints money. How else can we afford the sixteen or seventeen hundred dollars to cover everyone of us? I ask you!"

He sat down, and motioned to the Treasurer, Mike Egbuna. "I leave it to our able Treasurer to take it from there. Mike, over to you!"

Mike cleared his throat as he stood up. "Like our respected president, I too will stand up to say my piece. As we say, when a person stands up to speak, his words are straight and to the point. This matter of the timely payment of our annual membership dues causes me endless problems. Members simply do not pay their dues when they should. For the benefit of our relatively new members, it's one hundred dollars annually for a married couple, sixty dollars for singles, and thirty for those who're full-time students in colleges. And it's from your dues to this association that we find the forty dollars to pay, per head, to the NNNJ. Fortunately the NNNJ charges no dues for full-time students in colleges. The 2003 affiliate dues should have been paid to the NNNJ by March 31. Today is April 27, and still, half of us, about nineteen or twenty members, are owing us their dues."

He paused long enough to look around him, his eyes moving from face to face, glinting challengingly at some, and scowling at others. "I see the hall is filling up nicely. So this might be the best time to say this."

He paused again, very briefly this time, looking around him to ensure that he had the full attention of the thirty or so members now present. "What I want to say is simple, and it is this." He raised his voice, and fairly screamed: "You guys who don't pay your dues are giving me sleepless nights—!"

"That's simply unacceptable!" a voice rang out from the rear of the hall.

All eyes turned to the sound and, as if at a signal, more than a score of voices let out a great and throaty shout of jubilation. "Okocha!"

Okocha was studiedly expressionless of face, as he walked further into the meeting hall, a gently smiling Tatiana holding on to his arm. They were attired in an *asoebi*—outfits made of the same material, a tie-dye fabric, with light-blue and white strips. Okocha's was an Igbo jumper-and-trouser suit; Tatiana's, a fairly loose blouse and a long skirt, pleated at the hem.

"Mike, man! You were loud and clear about your complaint," Okocha said.

"Must be the accoustics," Mike said, rushing from the dais, slightly ahead of everyone else, to hug Okocha and Tatiana. "You're both welcome. Now I feel better!"

"Were we the ones giving you sleepless nights?" Tatiana impishly asked.

Mike tut-tutted at the very idea that *they* would cause him sleepless nights. "You didn't," he said. "But, truth to tell, I've been waiting and praying for this. It's been—what?—three months or so since your—er—great day. But, as we say, it is when a person wakes up that his or her morning starts."

"Here, Mike," said Okocha, as he handed over a cheque to Mike. "One hundred and fifty dollars. One hundred dollars for our dues for 2003, and fifty dollars for Tatiana's registration as a new member. How's that?"

There was a burst of applause, as several members, including some executive officers from the head table, crowded around the newly-weds, back-slapping and high-fiving them.

From the dais, Mr. Odogwu took in the joyous scene with a dignified smile as he patiently waited for the members to resume their seats. And, still smiling, he watched as Okocha and Tatiana walked up to the dais and stood before him. He then got up, walked around the long executive table, and enfolded them both in a warm embrace which lasted several moments. When he let go of them, his eyes were misty.

So were Okocha's, as he began to speak. "I'll never stop thanking you," he said softly, his voice tremulous, "for stepping into the breach on my wedding day, and being my surrogate dad—"

"You already did so, Okocha—and you also Tatiana," Mr. Odogwu said. "That was the least I could do for you, Okocha, in the circumstances."

"Maybe," said Okocha. "But I'll never forget."

Mr. Odogwu nodded his head reflectively a few times. "Welcome back to our association meeting, Okocha." Then, raising his voice a notch or two, he said: "Attention, everyone! It gives me great pleasure to welcome our newest member, Mrs. Tatiana Anigbo! And I see she hasn't wasted any time paying her registration fee and 2003 annual dues. Tatiana, on behalf of the entire membership of our Aniagu Kindred Progressive Union—"

"*AKPU!*" Tatiana intoned, smiling.

"Yes, *Akpu*, as many call it," said Mr. Odogwu. "As I was about to say, we say a double welcome to you, first for marrying into our clan and thus becoming a daughter of our town Aniagu; and second, for enrolling as a member of—yes—AKPU. I take it, from your smile when you said the word, that Okocha has already told you what the word *akpu*, in ordinary usage, stands for—"

"Manioc," Tatiana said softly.

"We call it cassava," Mike Egbuna chimed in, laughing. "It is a plant of many uses, though it is rather derided as a food by some people. Anyway, I join our distinguished president in welcoming you to our union."

"Come, Tiana." Okocha took her by the hand, and led her away from the dais. "Let's go find seats. We've interrupted the meeting long enough."

Ngozi Dike, provost, laughed. "It's the type of interruption we want. I wish those other sons and daughters of Aniagu who have resisted all pleas to join us, will come and interrupt us as you two just did."

"Oh, oh!" Okocha interjected, half covering his mouth, and the smile that had curled up a corner of his lips. "Are you saying I've been resisting pleas to join—"

"You know what I mean, Okocha," Ngozi said, her face and voice very contrite. "I didn't—"

"Only joking, Ngozi. Of course I know what you meant." He went to her and hugged her warmly. "It's all right."

"God bless you, Okocha. Let me find you two seats—"

"That's okay, Ngozi. You mustn't put yourself out on our behalf. Nnanna is already here, and should have saved two seats for us."

"Right here, Okocha!" Nnanna shouted from the second row of chairs, pointing. "Here are two chairs I saved for you."

"That's a good cousin-in-law." Okocha smiled gratefully. "What can I say? Thank you, Nnanna man."

Okocha and Tatiana embraced Nnanna, who had not bestirred himself when the other members thronged toward Okocha and Tatiana to welcome them to the meeting. They then took the seats Nnanna had secured for them, with Tatiana sitting in the middle. Okocha leaned across Tatiana, to ask Nnanna, *sotto voce*: "How's cousin Nonye doing?"

"She's doing as fine as can be expected," Nnanna whispered back. "She couldn't make it, as you know—"

Tatiana smiled, and Okocha nodded several times. "Yes, we do," Okocha said. "I know she has to take good care of herself. And these meetings can sometimes wear a person out."

"You can say that again!" Nnanna looked around him, and lowered his voice even more. "Seven good months into her pregnancy. She really has to watch it."

"I know my cousin," Okocha said. "She's very meticulous in her daily habits. It would surprise me if she doesn't carry out her doctor's instructions to the letter. Especially in this sort of thing. She'll be all right. The only persons I worry about are my dad and mom. I'm surprised they're not here today. I hope they're fine."

"I too am surprised," said Nnanna, speaking softly. "Nonye and me, we went to see them only yesterday. And I believe your mom said they'd be here today. She said nothing about their being late, that sort of thing. This is so unlike your dad, Okocha, to be this late to these meetings. Either he's coming—and then he's one of the earliest to be here—or he's not. He's missed two meetings already this year."

"Really?" asked Okocha. "I don't know what's going on between me—er, us, Tiana and me—and my parents. One thing is clear—my old man has been avoiding me." Then he added, in a peculiar tone of voice: "Sometimes I wonder why."

"Me!" Tatiana whispered. "You know it, and I know it."

"Tiana, dear, you know, you musn't say that," Okocha said gently, looking around him anxiously, worrying that they might have been speaking too loudly, and attracting unnecessary attention.

"Sorry, OK baby. I know I shoudn't. It's just that—well—I don't know what to do to change things. You know what I'm say-y-ying?"

"Patience, Tatiana, patience," said Nnanna. "A good dose of it, too.'"

"I'll try, so help me God!"

"Amen!" said Okocha. "But, Nnanna, you know it isn't easy to be patient, when you think you're—how shall I say it—more or less a victim of circumstances beyond your control. We—Tiana and me—we did nothing wrong, man. Only fall in love and marry. And now, all this! It's absolutely unfair! But this is not the place and time for this discussion."

"You're right about one thing," Nnanna said to Okocha, putting a hand on Tatiana's shoulder. "You did nothing wrong. And I don't know what you have to do to change things. Tatiana, the change in your father-in-law's attitude will come when it'll come. Always remember that God is in charge, as we say. One day, he'll warm up to you."

"And to me also, I pray," said Okocha, his expression sad and wistful. "The last time we saw him, he seemed, if anything, to be even more irritable than ever before."

"You went to see him?" Nnanna asked. "Or did you run into him at a function or something?"

"Man, we went to the house to see him and mom. That was a week or so ago. I believe it was on that occasion that he first saw Tiana's—er—condition. The moment he noticed it, I swear I saw a cloud pass over his face. He might perhaps not have noticed it had my mom not—kind of—drawn his attention to it."

"And how did your mom pick up on it?" Nnanna asked. Then he slapped his thigh. "But what am I asking? She's a woman, a mother twice over, and would notice what a man wouldn't. I swear if you hadn't told me yourself, I might not—"

"Would you two please quit talking about me as if I'm not here! Yes, Nnanna, if you must know, I'm all of five months pregnant."

"Five!" Nnanna fiercely whispered, looking accusingly at Okocha. "Five months! You didn't tell me—"

"Tell you what, man?" Okocha whispered back. "Anyway, as I said earlier, this is not the time or place to dwell on this matter."

"Sorry, man. But you're getting all shirty about something that's simply wonderful, and for which we should be thanking God."

"I'm getting all what?" Okocha asked softly "But never mind." He looked pointedly at the lower half of Tatiana's trunk, flashed her a happy smile, and winked wickedly at Nnanna.

"Order! Order!" Ngozi Dike suddenly barked out, her voice almost military in its intensity. "There're too many side conversations going on, and no one can hear what anybody else is saying. Order!" she shouted one more time, and resumed her seat, nodding to herself as if satisfied she had quieted the hubbub significantly.

As the meeting continued in relative orderliness, Okocha went into a brown study. Once or twice, Tatiana tried to bring him out of it by whispering endearments into his ear. But soon she recognized that he had moved into a state and zone where she knew he was utterly alone with his thoughts, and finally decided to let him be. This was a humor into which he had lately begun to fall with disturbing frequency. And whenever, at the end of it, she was able to draw his thoughts out of him, his recurring preoccupation had been his parents'—especially his dad's—persistent and worsening alienation from him. On account, she was well aware, of herself; of his marriage to her.

She put a hand on his shoulder, and kept her eyes narrowly focused on him. She stayed like that, patiently waiting for him to snap out of his reverie. But soon she felt herself slowly sliding into her own deep abstraction. There seemed little or no chance, she sadly reflected, that her father-in-law would any time soon get rid of that obsessive antagonism to anything and everything she stood for in his son's life. An antagonism that hung over her happiness with Okocha like a veritable sword of Damocles! Her pregnancy, so far from helping, had indeed seemed to make a bad situation worse confounded. Particularly when the old man found out that the pregnancy had preceded the wedding ceremony by several weeks! That was a moment she thought she would never forget. For what seemed an eternity, he had ranted and raved about the moral decadence of the young generation. And then he had summarily ordered them out of his house and presence.

Her mother-in-law, *Mama Ekemma* she liked to call her, had stood silently by, her eyes sadly flitting from her husband to her son. Mama Ekemma, it was obvious to Tatiana, had not wanted to look at her. Not even when Okocha challenged her directly to say if she agreed with his dad's order. She had merely spread her arms wide in a gesture that clearly said she was powerless to oppose him. But in that fleeting moment, Tatiana had observed, Mama Ekemma's expression had seemed acutely sorrowful and nostalgic.

She came out of her reverie when Nnanna leaned across her to touch Okocha and point a finger backwards.

"Your dad and mom!"

In a trice, Okocha was on his feet. He turned and watched as his dad, stiffly erect, walked with measured steps into the hall, with Okocha's mom Ekemma walking half a step behind him. They were both already attired for the Okwu wedding anniversary banquet, though his dad did not have his red chief's cap on, nor his mother her elaborate head tie. These, Okocha knew from long experience, must have been left behind in their car. Chief Anigbo made a beeline for the head table on the dais. He knew Ekemma would not follow him there but would, as usual, find a seat among the general membership.

To a man, the elected executives rose from their chairs as a mark of respect for their most renowned compatriot. They stood in silence until Chief Anigbo took his accustomed seat at one end of the table. That was where he always sat, indeed where he *chose* to sit. Mr. Chikezie Odogwu would have preferred that they sat side by side, in the middle, with the other elected officials sitting to their right and left. But Chief Anigbo had insisted that as a mere ex-officio, the immediate past-president, he had to really and demonstrably move aside so that his successor could properly take center stage.

Three or four members, with Okocha in the lead, hurried to Mrs. Anigbo's side and offered their chairs to her. She smiled her gratitude for their gallantry, then turned away from her son and accepted a chair offered by a member sitting—it seemed to Okocha—as far away from him and Tatiana as was possible, in the last row of chairs.

Nothing deterred, Okocha went to her and, before she sat down, embraced her. When he turned, he saw that Tatiana was standing right behind him. She too enfolded her mother-in-law in her arms. Mama Ekemma accepted the embrace, and smiled flittingly at Tatiana. Then she sat down and, folding her arms across her chest, stared straight ahead of her, a far-away look in her eyes. The sparkle returned to her eyes only when Nnanna, unhurriedly, came to her to embrace her in his turn.

"How's Nonye?" she asked him softly. "I hope she's coming along nicely."

"Very nicely, thank you, aunt Ekemma. She's absolutely glowing."

"I know. I remember how I felt with my first." She looked briefly at Okocha, and smiled as the memory flooded her mind. "Pregnancy is a very positive thing for a woman. Indeed, as the saying goes, it makes a woman especially attractive."

"To this husband at least," Nnanna said, standing proudly erect, and beating once, twice, on his chest. "Welcome to the meeting. But you and uncle Nat are unusually very late."

"Late? I'm glad we came at all. We had toyed with the idea of going straight to the wedding anniversary celebration. But Nat remembered we had missed the last two meetings of the association." She fished out the circular for the meeting from her capacious leather handbag, as well as her reading glasses. She put them on, and then pointed to the agenda. "At what point is the meeting now? I mean, on the agenda?"

"Item 5," said Nnanna. "The president is hurrying to end the meeting. He has just announced that we need volunteers for the committee to work on the preparations for the AKPU annual banquet in September."

"Item 5!" said Ekemma Anigbo. "There are still four other items on the agenda. And you call that *very late*.?"

"As I said, he's hurrying through the agenda, and we might end the meeting before we can get to the other items."

He smiled indulgently. It was not the first time he had had this type of argument with his adorable aunty Ekemma. And it would assuredly not be the last. Like many members of the diaspora Igbo community, she could not accept the fact of her lateness to any communal activity so long as the meeting or celebration was not totally over, and the closing prayer said. This was a societal malady, Nnanna reflected, to which no one had as yet found a cure.

The general hubbub, evidently caused by the regal entry of Chief and Mrs. Anigbo, quietened significantly when the provost, Ngozi Dike, first and conspicuously positioned herself in the center of the hall, where she commanded the attention of all members, and then raised her arm.

"Order!" she bellowed, and repeated herself. "Order! We're all happy that our *Ugo-Oranyelu* and his *Lolo* have not forgotten us, and are here today. We welcome them. But the president is eager that the meeting move quickly to a conclusion, even if we have to postpone discussions on some items on the agenda."

"Thank you, madame provost," Mr. Chikezie Odogwu said. "As she rightly observed, we are very happy—and I might add, relieved—to see our respected elder statesman, *Ugo-Oranyelu* and Mrs. Anigbo among us today. We honor him, not only as our first and immediate past president, but as the shining light of our organization. Welcome, *Ugo-Oranyelu*. And welcome too," he added, gesturing toward Mrs. Anigbo where she sat, "our beloved *Lolo*, as we continue to call her, since she has refused all our effort to bestow on her a fitting praise-name.

"As I said at the beginning of this meeting, I shall do my utmost to make it a very short one because one of us is celebrating a significant event today: the 25th wedding anniversary of Chijioke and Obiageli Okwu. Chijioke, for the info of our newest members, is the elder brother of our V.P. Chuma Okwu. Chuma is sitting quietly by my side here, but that's just a show. The man is raring to go to his brother's celebration. And so are all of us. As usual, *Ugo-Oranyelu* will be chairing the event." He paused, turned and looked briefly at Chief Anigbo, and continued: "It's too late, I believe you'll all agree with me, to ask *Ugo-Oranyelu* if he brought us kolanuts, as he usually does."

He stopped, and slowly looked around the hall, nodding his head the while. "With your permission, I intend to end the meeting when we have found two more volunteers for the Banquet Planning Committee. We already have three volunteers. If we do not now have two more volunteers, I suggest we give our VP, Chuma, who has accepted to head the committee, the power to select two more persons for the planning committee."

"Can I move a motion that we adjourn the meeting right now?" Chuma Okwu asked, taking a peek at his watch.

"So you can pick the remaining two persons for your committee yourself?" Chuka Okpala asked, with a smile, half-covering his mouth.

"Isn't it against our by-laws for our VP to move this kind of motion?" a member asked from the floor, shooting up from his chair.

"What by-laws?" Mrs. Ngozi Dike wanted to know.

"The AKPU constitution, madame provost," the member replied.

"What you probably mean," suggested Mike Egbuna, "is that the constitution is silent on such an issue. Nowhere does it say that an elected official cannot move a motion."

The member stood for a second or two, then threw both his arms up in a gesture of defeat, and sat down deflated.

Mr. Odogwu cleared his throat, and turned to Chuma Okwu. "Your motion is that we adjourn right away?"

"Yes, Mr. President."

The secretary, Celestine Nwachi, raised her arm. "For the records, who's seconding the motion?" She looked around the hall expectantly.

Nnanna raised his arm. "Me, boss!" he announced. "The wedding anniversary celebration is due to start in an hour. And some members might need to rush home to change into their party outfits."

"Any counter motion?" Mrs. Ngozi Dike asked, standing in her accustomed position, where she commanded the attention of all. She looked to her right and to her left, then turned to the president. "*Afulu-kwe*, it looks like we can vote on the motion."

The vote was unanimous, and then the president called on Nnanna to say the closing prayer.

"Me?" Nnanna protested. "Can I yield to our deaconness? If you want the prayer to go beyond the ceiling and reach God's ears—"

"It's not the length of the prayer that matters to God," Chuka Okpala commented in a half-whisper, but loud enough to reach Ngozi Dike's ears where she stood in the center of the floor.

"I heard that!" she said to no one in particular, disdaining even to look at her tormentor.

*　*　*

Nnanna, Okocha and Tatiana tarried a while as the members, in small groups, filed out of the meeting-hall. Immediately after Nnanna had said the closing prayer, Okocha had whispered to him that he and Tatiana would wait to see what his dad would do.

"I'll wait with you, if only to pay my respects to him," Nnanna whispered back. "But you're not thinking of doing anything—"

"Relax, man," Okocha said, smiling. "We'll not challenge him or anything like that. But we—Tiana and me—we agreed that we would go and stand by my mom, and wait with her until my dad comes for her. And then we'll see."

From the dais, Chief Anigbo watched as his son, his daughter-in-law and Nnanna went and stood by Ekemma, around whom a small coterie of admirers had already assembled. Instinctively he knew that Okocha's action was deliberate and premeditated. He shook his head slowly, and then saw his friend Chikezie Odogwu, *AKPU* president, get up from his chair. Mr. Odogwu came and sat next to him.

"I've been watching you, *Ugo-Oranyelu*," Mr. Odogwu said gently. "I understand how you feel about things. Which doesn't mean I like it."

He paused, looked around the table, and leaned closer to Chief Anigbo. "I'm glad it's just you and me here, because what I want to say to you is for your ears only." A slight pause, then in his familiar blasé, take-it-or-leave-it voice, he whispered fiercely into his friend's ear: "You've got to do something, *Ugo-Oranyelu*, to warm up to your son and his wife. This chill between you and them has gone as far as it should. You need to end it, pronto! Are you listening to me, son of *Aniagu*? If it is a handshake, as we say, it has gone way beyond the elbow!"

Chief Anigbo knew that his friend meant well, but what would he know about how a father might feel if confronted by an obstinately contrary son, in a matter as grave as whom he married? Mr. Odogwu had to have walked in *his*, Chief Anigbo's shoes, to pontificate the way he was doing.

He turned to Mr. Odogwu, looked him straight in the eye for a moment or two, shook his head, and got up from his chair. In a voice from which all emotion had been drained, he said: "*Afulu-kwe*, I thank you for your advice given, as usual, in your no-nonsense manner. But what I do, or don't do, is in the lap of the gods."

He shrugged imperceptibly and stiffened his back as he began to walk towards his wife and son, his friend's plea wringing in his ear.

Okocha watched, with bated breath, as his father approached. Something about the way his old man held his body rigidly, and his vacant, emotionless face, left Okocha uneasy, even as his stomach churned. His dad came close enough so that Okocha could easily have reached out and touched him. But he continued to watch, frozen on his feet, as his dad and mom wordlessly exchanged glances. Then his dad, with a mere flick of the head in the direction of the exit door, walked on without a pause. Wordlessly, but with a deep sigh of sadness, Ekemma rose from her chair, and trudged after her husband.

Tatiana sidled up to Okocha and took his hand in hers, and pressed it. Okocha turned to her, but the light had gone completely from his eyes.

"Let's go, Tiana," he said softly. "See you later, Nnanna, man!"

Nnanna could only stand and stare stonily after them.

CHAPTER 14

The hall for the wedding anniversary banquet was beautifully decorated. Chijioke and Obiageli Okwu spared no expense in their desire to put on a show that would be truly memorable. Not only did they rent a sizeable section of the Celestial Gardens, but the panorama, as one entered the banquet hall, was breathtaking. The sea of round tables, well spaced out, had fawn-colored covers, atop which were square center-pieces, pea-green in color. A flower-vase, with a preponderance of yellow and pink roses, stood on each center-piece.

Unusually, for a diaspora Igbo community event, it started only just about an hour later than the 9 pm schedule. This almost unheard-of near punctuality was, in large measure, due to the severe truncation of the meeting of AKPU. This enabled even those members who had need to first rush to their homes to do so and then show up at the event with reasonable dispatch. The celebration, some of them were heard to mutter, was *their* celebration, seeing that they were, with Chijioke and Obiageli Okwu, the sons and daughters of the same town, Aniagu. Besides, Mr. Odogwu, president of AKPU, had made a deeply moving appeal to the members to show the light in this matter so that others might follow.

"We're all in this together," Mr. Odogwu had implored the members, as the meeting prepared to adjourn. "And, to borrow an American phrase, I am sick and tired of being sick and tired about the disgrace of unpunctuality which has become a hallmark of our people's social gatherings. If the banquet starts late, it is our collective failure as children of Aniagu. So, let us all show up at the event in the next hour or two, and put smiles on the faces of the celebrants. If I may paraphrase the motto of Nigeria's one-time most renowned nationalist newspaper, *The West African Pilot*, let's show the light so that others might follow our example. Chijioke and Oby Okwu are our brother and sister and, as we say, it is in a foreign land especially that this brotherhood thing should be put on full display. So, please, please, let me see you all there in an hour's time!"

Okocha and Tatiana, Kanu and Somto, and Nnanna—without his wife Nonye—sat at a table for eight, with Mike and Eunice Egbuna. Okocha was in a deeply pensive mood, as he ruminated on what Mr. Odogwu had referred to as "this brotherhood thing". Sadly, he did not feel any surge of that noble sentiment. How, he reflected wretchedly, could he feel like a brother to people with whom he mostly only interacted at meetings and parties, when his own father went to great lengths to shut him out? His dad and mom, who had arrived at the hall a little ahead of them, sat at some distance from them, at another table where they were also surrounded by other members of AKPU.

"If things are as they should be," Okocha remarked to Nnanna, "we should be sitting with him and mom at that table."

"Come on, big bro!" Kanu leaned towards Okocha to whisper. "Can't believe you'd seriously want to sit that close to him, all things considered."

"What's there to believe, Kanu. He's still our dad, regardless. No?"

"You're forgetting he's sitting there only until—" Nnanna started to say.

"I know," Okocha interrupted him. "Until the MC summons him to the high table, as chairman for the banquet."

"Uncle Nat always seems to chair these occasions, doesn't he?" Somto said. "I'm awfully proud of him."

"So are we all, Somto," Kanu observed wryly. "So are we all. But that doesn't change anything."

Nnanna turned to Mike Egbuna, who sat next to him. "I wish you'd get on with it!" he said. "I'm sure the celebrants must be getting tired waiting for things to start. The hall is reasonably full and we can start now." He paused and looked around the hall. "Where's the MC? We all got here at about the same time. Ah, there he is, Okocha, sitting cozily near your mom."

At that moment Ngozi Dike came and whispered something to Mike Egbuna. Mike nodded, rose from his chair, microphone in hand, and moved to the middle of the dance floor, close to the high table.

"Ladies and gentlemen!" he called out loudly, the microphone so close to his lips it looked as if he had it in his mouth. "Your attention please! We're just about ready to start. And it is my distinct pleasure to introduce our MC for the evening—"

"MC Emeritus! *Nnamenyi!*" a cacophony of voices screamed from around the hall.

"Right! Chuka Okpala, no less," Mike Egbuna announced, nodding emphatically. "The man obviously needs little or no introduction—"

"Thank God!" several voices shouted in unison, as raucous laughter rolled around the hall.

146

"Thank you all," Mike said, smiling broadly. "You make my job easy. All I need do is hand the microphone to him. *Nnamenyi*, where are you?"

"As if you didn't know," said Chuka Okpala, rising from his chair, and bowing first to Mrs. Ekemma Anigbo, next to whom he had been sitting, then to Chief Anigbo. Then he walked up to Mike Egbuna, and held out his hand for the microphone, which Mike handed over to him with a little flourish.

Chuka coughed, to clear his throat. And, by force of habit acquired over the years as the community's regular MC, he tapped two or three times on the microphone to satisfy himself that it was live.

"I thank my friend, Mike Egbuna," he told the crowd, "for that wonderful introduction—"

"What introduction is he talking about?" Okocha asked, turning to Tatiana and Nnanna.

"That's the way he sometimes starts, as you know," Nnanna said, smiling. "I hope he doesn't take too long introducing your dad and mom, and the other persons who'll sit at the high table."

It was, almost inevitably, a forlorn hope. The seating of Chief and Mrs. Anigbo and the dozen or so other dignitaries at the table of honor took the better part of half an hour. Each couple or individual called up was ceremoniously escorted to the high table by two young ladies, selected for that purpose by the 'committee of friends'—friends, that is, of the celebrants, Chijioke and Obiageli Okwu. The committee had worked assiduously to put the banquet together. The two young ladies danced gently but enchantingly as they escorted the dignitaries to the high table. The dignitaries themselves either walked stiffly, or undulated their bodies to the rhythm and beat of the accompanying West African *high-life* music, as their disposition let them.

In their turn, the celebrants were ushered into the hall by a large group that included their three grown-up children and a coterie of friends. Chijioke and Obiageli, to the surprise and amazement of many guests, were attired, respectively, in a dark-brown western-style suit and a flowing caftan. As a concession to their country of origin, and perhaps to underline that they were Igbo, Chijioke wore a traditional red cap, and Obiageli a toned-down head-dress. Their progress towards the high table was frequently interrupted by friends, who either executed a brief sequence of dance steps and movements, or came forward to embrace and greet them with an attention-grabbing flourish.

In a bit of a daze, Okocha stared stonily at his dad as he invoked the protection of God and of the Ancestors on the gathering, in a kola-nut invocation that was notable for its brevity. Chief Anigbo had, through long and frequent experience, fine-tuned his invocation whenever his age and seniority accorded him the privilege of praying over the kola-nut—usually in addition to his role as chairman for the occasion. He determined, in his own mind, when he needed to be elaborate in the invocation, and when brevity was apposite.

"I hope his chairman's opening remarks will be just as brief," Okocha observed, to no one in particular.

"I know what you mean."

Okocha turned to the voice, and smiled. It was Eunice Egbuna, Mike's wife. A woman who mostly kept to herself, Eunice was making a rare appearance at a community social event. She looked very fetching in her accra-type blouse and long skirt, mauve-colored and with intricate geometric designs. Quiet to the point of taciturnity, she seemed deliberately to want to compensate for her husband's loquacity. She expressed her feelings often only by the way she pursed her lips: with a gentle smile to signify approbation, or a tight face if she did not approve.

If her table companions expected her to elaborate on her statement, Eunice disappointed them. Instead, she focused her gaze on Okocha and Tatiana. Like her husband Mike, she was thoroughly familiar with Okocha's story, especially as that story revolved around the beautiful American girl. Okocha was indeed one of her favorite persons in the community, and her heart totally went out to him in his despairing effort to win his dad's approval of his marriage to Tatiana.

Chief Anigbo rose from his chair in his slow deliberate manner, his eyes moving to take in the entire panorama. The immediate effect was that silence descended on the crowd like a gentle wave that began at the tables nearest to the high table and rolled on to the farthest corners of the hall. When he began to deliver his chairman's opening remarks, his voice was gentle and steady.

He made no direct reference to his own thirty years of marriage to Okocha's mom, Ekemma, which Okocha had thought he would be unable to resist proclaiming to the world. Nor did he—as Okocha had multiple reasons to fear—make even an indirect allusion to what he had latterly begun to call his son's "misguided and reckless liaison with an American girl". A liaison which—he seemed to relish to tell the whole world whenever the matter came up in conversation—was "doomed to fail from the get-go!" Instead, as the occasion required, he heaped praise—indeed fulsome praise—on the celebrants.

"Chijioke and Oby Okwu," he said, winding down, "deserve our wholehearted congratulations on a great achievement: a quarter-century of marriage and, I might add because I personally know it to be true, wedded bliss! It isn't easy, as many couples who've been down that road and survived that long in marriage, can tell you. Our celebrants stand before us today as a shining example of what marriage is all about, and as a standard by which marriages in our community may in future be measured. I have been close to them over the years and I can say, with certitude, that I never heard either say a bad word to the other.

"I give you three hearty cheers to Chijioke and Oby!" he ended thunderously, raising his glass. "Hip! Hip! Hip!"

"Hurray!" some two hundred throats roared.

Glasses clinked noisily, and then—as had become *de rigueur* in the community—a long queue began to form as seemingly everyone present lined up to clink glasses with the celebrants at the high table. Chuka Okpala, in his more irreverent mood, was once heard to liken this procession to a line of Christian worshipers slowly inching their way toward the altar to receive the Eucharist. The difference, of course, was that each person carried a glass of champagne, and the leisurely procession was accompanied by rhythmic *high-life* music supplied by Deejay Magnus Aneke, popularly called *Eneke-nti-oba*. Many swayed and gyrated to the rhythm as they inched forward towards the high table.

When the clinking abated, Chuka Okpala, MC, took center-stage, microphone at the ready. "Your attention, please!" he began. "The chairman has signaled that the celebrants will open the floor for dancing. I'm sure many of you have been waiting for this. But please have patience until the celebrants have danced for a while, and we have all had the opportunity to show our appreciation to them in our customary way. I will give the signal when the floor is open for those who want to dance."

As soon as the celebrants came down from the dais and began to dance, a crowd formed around them, and the customary show of appreciation began. Everyone took out a wad of dollar bills—thick, or not so thick—from their pockets and began *spraying* the bills on the celebrants. This went on for a long while, until the MC announced that those who wanted could join in the dancing. Many did, but that did not, and was not meant to stop the *spraying* of the celebrants.

Suddenly, Okocha looked at Tatiana, and Tatiana looked at Okocha. Their eyes locked for a long moment. Then Tatiana's eyebrows rose fractionally in question, and Okocha nodded his head firmly in answer.

He then pointed to the high table. "My dad and mom are practically by themselves at the high table," he said softly as they both rose to their feet. "This is the right moment, I think. Let's go do it."

"Do what?" Nnanna asked, looking from Okocha to Tatiana.

"What are you going to do, bro?" Kanu asked in a tone of voice that betrayed some anxiety, looking askance at Okocha.

Okocha turned, first to Nnanna, then to Kanu, smiling nervously. "Just watch us, and you'll see," he said, holding up his right hand, with his index and middle fingers crossed.

"For luck!" he added, his eyes sad and wistful.

* * *

The eyes of their table companions were trained on Okocha and Tatiana as they walked towards the high table. But those were not the only eyes focussed on them. Chief Anigbo held his breath as his son, hand in hand with Tatiana, approached. He watched as the two young persons mounted the dais and walked around the table to approach him from the flank. Involuntarily, he stiffened his body as his son's American wife came and stopped behind him, and sensed rather than saw Okocha stop by his mom.

As if on cue, Okocha and Tatiana spoke in the same breath.

"Dad! I'd love to dance with you," Tatiana, bending over, whispered into his ear.

"Mom! Let's dance," Okocha said softly to his mom.

Okocha's mom half rose from her seat when his dad put out a hand and restrained her, so that she flopped right back down on her chair.

"Why?" he asked, turning to Tatiana. "Why do you want to dance with us? Is it to tell the whole world everything's hunky-dory? But everything's not all right. Nothing can be all right between us. Ever!"

He turned to Okocha. "Son, you knew—you *must* have known—the moment you two got up from your chairs to come to put on this charade, what the outcome would be. I'm sorry, but I'm not very good at this kind of masquerade, because that's what it would be if we were to dance with you."

Okocha shook his head sadly and, without another word, took Tatiana by the hand and led her away from the high table.

"Just as we feared," he whispered to her as they stepped off the dais. "But that's all right. Now I want to dance with the most beautiful girl in God's creation."

Tatiana managed a smile. "Woman, not girl! Especially now, what with my—er, how many months of pregnancy is it? And I don't know about being the most—"

"You're even more beautiful now, Tiana. Let's dance!"

Tatiana did not simply place her left hand on Okocha's shoulder as they began to move their bodies to the rhythm of the music. She clung to him, throwing her entire arm over his shoulder and drawing him so close and tight to herself that their bodies fused into one, with barely a chink of daylight between them, head to hip.

After a little while, Okocha said, smiling from ear to ear: "This is the West African high life dance, not your foxtrot or quickstep. We don't have to dance quite this close."

"I have to, OK baby, you know what I'm say—y—ying?" Tatiana said, teary-eyed. "I need you to hold me close, if you love me."

"You know I do."

"Then stop talking, Mr. Anigbo! Hold me and dance!"

And they did! To such effect that they seemed progressively to be unaware of other persons and dancers around them—until Kanu and Somto came up to them.

"What was that?" Kanu asked Okocha, pointing in the direction of the high table.

"What was what?" Okocha fired back, stopping the frenzy of his and Tatiana's gyrations.

"You may be my big bro, Okocha, but I wasn't born yesterday," Kanu said, serious of face and demeanor. "You two went up to dad and mom, I strongly suspect, to ask to dance with them, no? Do I need to ask what happened?"

"You just did, kid brother mine," Okocha said with a grin. He held Tatiana tightly as they swayed their bodies to the beat of the music.

"We watched, as you asked us to do," said Somto. "And we saw everything. Didn't uncle refuse to dance with Tatiana?"

"No surprise there!" Kanu stood stock still, staring vacantly ahead. "The surprise was mom refusing to dance with Okocha."

Somto shook his head vigorously. "Not quite right, cousin," he said. "She appeared to want to, but uncle stopped her."

For a long moment, Kanu stood akimbo, with dancers swirling all around him. He stood like that until Somto took him by the hand, and began to pull him away. After a momentary resistance, Kanu quietly allowed himself to be pulled away from the dance floor.

Okocha's eyes softened as he watched his brother hang his head in sadness as he walked unwillingly away. "That's a kid brother to surpass all kid brothers! What can I do without him?"

"He's a great kid, that's for sure," said Tatiana. "But let's dance!"

"He's been like a rock for me in this whole affair," Okocha said. "I hope I'll be as strong a support for him—"

"What are you saying, OK baby?" Tatiana asked him wonderingly. "Are you wishing he'll also fall in love with an *akata* girl, like you did?"

Okocha abruptly stopped dancing, and held her a little away from him, the better to look at her. He was not as surprised that she had used the *akata* word, as he was that she had said it with a seemingly straight face. On closer examination, however, he saw that what he had thought to be a straight face was really a face as tight as he had ever seen it. And her eyes! The light had gone completely out of them, leaving them so vacant as to appear chillingly lifeless. Then she lowered her eyes and looked away from him.

"Tiana!" he called out softly to her. He placed a hand under her chin and made her turn towards him. "Look at me, dear girl. Please!"

Tatiana raised teary eyes to his. He could see that she was struggling to keep her emotions in check. He leaned forward and kissed her eyes, unmindful of the crowd around them. The kiss might have opened her tear-ducts because, when he removed his lips, a steady stream of tears flowed down her cheeks. Quickly he took out a small handkerchief from a trouser pocket and handed it to her. She dabbed at both her eyes with it, and then her face broke in a sad reluctant smile.

"That's my Tiana!" he whispered into her ears, holding her close. "When you smile, for whatever reason, you light up my world. And it tells me that my girl knows that as long as we have each other, nothing—not even my dad's rebuffs—will stand in the way of our happiness."

Tatiana now began to dance with the sinuous grace with which Okocha was all too familiar. But she still would not let him go, and continued to hold him tightly. He was elated by the closeness of their bodies and by the allure of her movements. Not for the first time, he wondered how she could dance with such ease notwithstanding that, in the best traditions of the West African high-life dance, freedom of movement is the norm.

Okocha let his body fuse into hers, and smiled contentedly as exhilarating sensations coursed through his body. She became, for him, an intoxicating and glorious extension of himself. There were, sure, other dancers on the floor. But they were, at that moment, nothing more than a boisterous, convivial and festive backdrop to his world with Tatiana. A world into which, he hoped, no one—be he or she family, friend or foe—would dare to intrude, trailing clouds of doom and gloom! It made no difference what music played, so long as the rhythm was of the West African *high-life* or the Congo rumba-like *soukous* variety. Okocha and Tatiana paused when the music stopped, but stood where they were, and waited for the next piece to start.

Suddenly Mike and Eunice Egbuna materialized seemingly out of nowhere, and they came with an offer.

"You two love-birds cannot dance for ever all by yourselves," Mike said, placing a hand on Tatiana, to stop her bodily undulations. "I would like to dance with you, and Eunice wants to dance with Okocha. What do you say?"

Tatiana did a little pirouette that was like an exclamation mark to her long uninterrupted spell of dancing with her husband. Then she stepped away from Okocha. "He's all yours, Eunice," she said, smiling.

Mike took Tatiana's hand. " And you're all mine. Let's dance!"

*   *   *

Kanu was twiddling nervously with the hem of his long-sleeved shirt, waiting impatiently for Okocha to come back to their table. As soon as Okocha came close, he grabbed him by the elbow and made him sit on the vacant chair nearest to him. Briefly Okocha thought to protest that the chair was not his, but something in the way Kanu was looking at him stifled the protest in his throat. If ever he saw fire in anybody's eyes, Okocha saw it in his kid-brother's eyes.

"I've got to talk to you, bro!" Kanu said in a fierce whisper. "Now!"

"Now? Here?"

"Yes, big bro! Here and now! I don't care who overhears us. There's a limit to human endurance, and I've reached mine. This thing between you and dad is eating me up. I don't even know how you've been able to take it for so long without blowing up."

He stopped, covering his face with both his hands, breathing heavily. Okocha and Tatiana looked at each other, shaking their heads. Okocha then drew his chair closer to Kanu's, and put an arm around his shoulders.

"If you were in my shoes, Kanu," he said softly, "you'd know it'd be pointless to blow up. You'd know this is a situation that calls for patience and endurance. The old man obviously can't help himself—"

"Can't help himself!" Kanu asked, looking at Okocha narrowly. "What's that supposed to mean?"

"Like being a prisoner of his culture," Okocha suggested. "I should really say *our* culture—yours, mine and his. It's easy for you and me to challenge our old ways of doing things—"

"Dad's not the only Igbo man in this country whose son has married an American girl," Kanu whispered and then shook his head reflectively. "You're right, big bro. This is hardly the right place and time—"

"Damn right, it isn't!" Okocha said. "Listen, kid brother mine, I don't like that you're getting all worked up on my account. I wish you'd listen to me when I say that this kind of thing has a way of working itself out. Trust me. The day will come—"

"I doubt it, big bro! I doubt it. Dad's not your average Igbo father, if you ask me, who'll let the passage of time heal his hurt. Not in this kind of situation."

"So what do you want your brother to do?" Tatiana leaned forward and across Okocha to ask Kanu. "Tell your dad to mind his own business? But Okocha's his business. We all are his business, and that includes me now. You know what I'm say-y-ying?"

Kanu stared at her for a long moment. "You are an extraordinary person. An American, and yet you seem to—" He stopped, shaking his head as he continued to look at her. Then he sighed. "Someone's got to talk to him. It's not right—what he's doing to you and Okocha; indeed to all of us. What's to become of us as a family, I ask you? Doesn't he think about that? However long it takes me, I swear, I'll find a way to tell him how I feel. One of these days!"

"Tell whom how you feel?" a voice asked behind him.

Four heads turned to the voice, with Kanu rising abruptly from his seat.

"Mom!" he cried hoarsely.

"Yes, son. It's me." Ekemma Anigbo spoke softly, her expression puzzled. "What's your problem? Is it your dad and me?"

Okocha smiled expansively. "Mom, how can you ask that? Kanu did'nt mean—"

"Thank you, Okocha," said Kanu. "As always, you watch out for your little bro. But I'll speak for myself. Yes, mom—"

Somto quickly reached out and grabbed Kanu's arm. "Kanu, please don't—"

"It's okay, cousin Somto," Kanu said calmly. "Perhaps this is as good a time as any to do this. We are all by ourselves, as a family, and I might as well say my piece before our table companions return."

He turned back to his mom. "Yes, mom. You and dad, especially dad, need to wake up from your sleep, a sleep induced by centuries of a way of life that does not have much relevance in today's world. I don't know how many times I need to say this, mom, but Okocha's now his own man, whether dad accepts that reality or not."

He stopped and looked from Okocha to Tatiana to his mom. For a moment or two, there was fire in his eyes, but when next he spoke, his voice was as gentle as a child's.

"Mom, I'm appealing to you and, through you, to dad. You both need to let us be, Okocha and me. And," he added, turning partially to Somto, "though he's as yet not fully aware of it, Somto too. We are living and growing up in America. On a daily basis, we meet and—you know—interact mostly with young Americans. We make friends with them—both sexes. Do you and dad honestly believe that, in matters of the heart, which is what all this is about, we have any real choice whom we fall in love with? Do you, mom, seriously expect that any of us is even capable of making a deliberate, calculated choice, when the moment comes, to fall in love with an Igbo—and not an American—girl?"

Ekemma Anigbo was staring at her eighteen-year old son, mouth agape, surprise etched deeply on her brow. "What are you saying, son?" she asked. "What are you—?"

Kanu shook his head as he slowly turned away from his mother's searching eyes, and walked away from the table.

CHAPTER 15

Philip Karefa held the door open with one hand and briefly stared at Okocha and Tatiana.

"Wasn't expecting you guys, O'kcha," he drawled, embracing Tatiana with his free arm. "But you're very welcome. I hope everything's all right." He shook hands with Okocha. "Please come in."

Okocha and Tatiana followed him into the sitting-room. "Thank you, sir," Okocha said. "And yes, sir, we're doing all right. We should have called before coming, but—"

"Dad," Tatiana interrupted. "Okocha was going to call you, but I stopped him. Told him it's about time we gave you and mom a taste of how we often do things in our community."

"*Your* community?"

"Yes, dad. Our community. My new community of Nigerians, or perhaps I should say Igbo people."

"Why don't you sit down, both of you," Mr. Karefa said. "First make yourselves comfortable, and then Tiana can go into her long-winded explanations of her new community."

He paused and watched, with a smile, as Tatiana and Okocha took the love-seat. "That's better. Now, Tiana, what were you saying? But hold it there, girl!" He raised his hand to stop her. "Where's your mom? She probably needs to hear this. Edna!" he bellowed. "Where are you? We have visitors!"

"I'm not a visitor, dad," Tatiana protested, smiling sweetly.

"*You* may not be," said Okocha, "but *I* am. We really should have called before—"

"Relax, son," Mr. Karefa said. "You've nothing to worry about. It was Tiana stopped you from doing the right thing. Edna!" he called out again.

"I'm here, Philip." Edna Karefa walked into the sitting-room, adjusting her blouse which she had evidently had to put on in a hurry. "What seems to be—"

She saw Tatiana and Okocha. "Oh, it's you!" she shouted, making a beeline for them, as both rose from their seat to receive her. Edna first wrapped her daughter in a warm hug, and then reached for Okocha to enfold him too in a triangular embrace that lasted several moments.

"It's good to see you two," she enthused, with a radiant smile that went from ear to ear. "This is a surprise. Hope all's well—"

"Woman," Philip interrupted her, "how do you expect them to be able to talk when you have them in a choke-hold?"

Edna gave her husband a withering look and then released Tatiana and Okocha from her embrace. "It's good to see you," she said again. "It's been a long while, no?"

Tatiana laughed. "Like just five or six days, mom," she said, as she resumed her seat, pulling Okocha down with her. "Or do you expect we can come *every* day?"

"Talking about coming every day," Philip Karefa said, "what was it you were saying about how your—er—community does things. This, I believe, was in reference to your coming to visit with us without first phoning us?"

"Is that a question?" Tatiana asked, smiling expansively. "But, yes, you're right. Thing is, in our community—mine and Okocha's—we're so totally relaxed with one another, it's not unusual that we visit without the necessity of first calling—even if it's just to make sure the people you are visiting will be home. There!"

Her dad and mom looked at each other. Edna smiled, but Philip was poker-faced.

"Tiana," he said, "you sound as if you have fully absorbed the culture, and enjoying it, which is very good."

"What's not to enjoy?" Tatiana said, nudging Okocha playfully. "You said it! I'm enjoying myself."

"Couldn't have said it better myself," Okocha said. "As you can see, we are doing just fine. Tatiana is in beautiful health."

"I see what you mean," said Edna Karefa, taking Tatiana by the hand and gently pulling her up. She then held her at arm's length the better to look her over. "Tiana, my daughter, I can see everything's coming along nicely. Let me hold you one more time, and feel your belly with my hands. Any kicks of late?"

"Plenty! The baby must have inherited OK's love for football—er—I mean, soccer. Must be a boy."

"Are you telling me you don't already know if the baby's a boy or a girl?"

"Mom, we don't want to know. Whatever the gender, God is good." Tatiana turned to Okocha. "OK baby, perhaps you could explain about the Igbo names we have chosen for the baby—*Chioma*, or *Nwachukwu*, if I have pronounced them right."

Okocha smiled, nodding. "To a T, Tiana! Couldn't pronounce them any better myself. As to the meanings," he continued, turning to Mrs. Karefa, "*Chioma* literally means a benevolent *Chi* or—in a deeper sense—God, and in everyday use connotes luck or good fortune. It is usually a name for girls."

"And the other?" Tatiana urged him. "*Nwachukwu*."

"*Nwachukwu* is a child of God, and is invariably a boy's name."

Edna Karefa drew Tatiana once more into a warm embrace, and then let her go. "Today is what—June 6, no?" she asked, patting Tatiana on her bulging tummy. "Barely two months or so to go, I believe." She looked from Okocha to Tatiana. "Doesn't she look unbelievably beautiful?"

"That she does," Okocha said, with a happy smile, taking Tatiana by the hand and squeezing it. "Almost exactly two months to go. I can't wait!"

Philip Karefa snorted. "You can't wait, son? Let me tell you. The doctors can say what they like, but this is not something you can assign a time to. When the baby's good and ready, that's when it'll happen. Not a moment sooner or later."

"Talking of June 6 reminds me," said Edna Karefa, "Father's Day is June 15. You two planning anything for that day, for your dad, Okocha, and Tiana's dad here?"

"We could do the same thing we did for Mother's Day—that was May 11, I believe," Tatiana suggested tentatively. "We could go to a restaurant—"

"Not an *All-you-can-eat* Chinese or whatever, I hope!" Mr. Karefa said forcefully. "I know your mom enjoyed it, Tiana. But thank you, no. Not for me. I'd rather your mom cooked me something special—you know, my favorite—"

"What favorite meal, dad?" Tatiana asked. "You have no favorite meal!"

"Except hamburgers, with cheese," said Edna Karefa. "I could make that for him, if that's what his soul desires. It's his day, come June 15. And you two can come pass the afternoon with us, after your church service. Okocha, how about that? Your Anglican service usually ends at about 12 noon. So you could come around one o'clock, and have a meal with us. Eh, Tiana?"

"But what about your dad, OK baby?" Tatiana eyes were soft, as they looked at him. "Wouldn't be totally fair to him, would it?"

Okocha actually laughed out loud. But it seemed a bitter laughter. "June 15 is more than a week away. We have time to think about the matter. But you know how it is between me and my dad right now. And I wouldn't dream of going to celebrate with him without taking you along. You know that, don't you Tiana? I simply couldn't. And that's the sum of it."

Mr. Karefa suddenly remembered something, and slapped his thigh. "What can we offer you? We can't sit here all afternoon just jawing about this and that. I feel like some drink. So O'kcha, what'll it be?"

Tatiana stepped forward. "I believe I still know my way around here, OK baby. I'll get you a drink. Your usual? And dad, mom, a beer and OJ—or has something changed here since I got married?"

Okocha, smiling diffidently, his eyes on Philip Karefa, nodded gently. "Thank you Tiana."

Philip contented himself by simply waving Tatiana away. "Go do what you have to do. Thanks, girl!"

"OK baby, while I'm doing that, perhaps you can give dad your message," she said, but did not immediately leave the sitting-room.

"A message?" Philip looked at his wife, and then turned to Okocha. "I knew there was a purpose to this unexpected visit." He paused for a brief moment. "O'kcha, what's your message? Hope it's something good."

"Yes, sir," Okocha said, nodding vigorously. "It's actually an invitation to you and mom, from—"

"Your dad?" Mrs. Karefa burst out. "Please say it's from your dad."

Okocha, his face suddenly a picture of misery, looked down and away from Tatiana's mom. "Sorry, mom. No, it's not from my dad. But one of the leaders of our community asked us to approach you on his behalf and extend an invitation—"

"What's it this time? Another wedding?"

"It's nothing like that, dad," said Okocha. "It's just an informal invitation for the two of you to come dine with him and his wife, on a day that'll be mutually convenient. He says to tell you it doesn't even have to be a weekend."

Philip and Edna exchanged a prolonged look, asking each other questions with their eyes.

"Who's this gentleman?" Philip asked. "What's he—or his family—to you and Tatiana? I don't know about her," he added, gesturing toward his wife, "but I must confess I'm tickled pink by this kind of invitation. What's this man to you?" he asked again. "And did he suggest a date?"

"I'm glad you asked," said Okocha. "Mr. Odogwu—that's his name—said he would suggest next Friday. That's exactly one week today. But that's only a suggestion. As to my connection with him, Mr. Odogwu is the president of our town association in this part of America—"

"*AKPU!*" Tatiana interrupted, smiling impishly. "That's the acronym for the name of the association. As a word in daily usage, it means cassava—manioc to you. But the acronym stands for *Aniagu Kindred Progressive Union.* You see—"

"I'll take it from there, Tiana," Okocha held up his hand to stop her, and she smiled and left the sitting-room. "Our town in Nigeria is called Aniagu—"

"Never mind about that, O'kcha!" Philip Karefa cut in. "You don't seriously expect me to remember the name. You know how I struggle to even pronounce Nigerian names, never mind remembering them. So this gentleman is your association's president? Is he related to you—I mean, by blood? And was he in your group when you guys came knocking down my door to ask about Tatiana?"

Edna Karefa burst out laughing, and was soon joined by her husband. Okocha's expression was studiedly neutral. Discretion suggested that he not join in the laughter.

"Knocking *at* our door, Philip," said Edna, still laughing. "Not knocking *down* the door. You'll never get it right, will you?"

"Watch your language, woman!" His voice sounded severe, but a soft smile played at the corners of his lips. "I asked O'kcha a serious question."

"You're always making a mess of his name. It's O-ko-cha, Philip." She pronounced the name slowly, separating its syllables. "It's an African, not an Irish name, for crying out loud!"

Okocha, eager to pour oil on troubled waters, quickly intervened, though he was well aware that the exchange between his parents-in-law was not as serious as it sounded.

"Actually, sir, Mr. Odogwu was not with our group when we came here last year, in October. But I'm quite close to him. In fact he's some sort of a mentor to me."

"But still he didn't come with you when you needed his support. Why?"

"I'll try to explain that," said Okocha. "I had wanted him to lead my group when my dad told me he wouldn't be a part of it. But, at that time, Mr. Odogwu just couldn't get himself to so openly challenge my dad. They were, and still are, very close. But by the time of our wedding, he had told my dad he would do the right thing by me. That's why he was the chairman at the wedding."

"Your dad must have been pissed off something awful, no?"

"He was," said Okocha. "But Mr. Odogwu stood his ground. Fortunately, their friendship is still intact. And I thank God for that."

Mr. Karefa nodded several times. "So this gentleman—" He stopped. "But hold it there, son! Did you just say he was the chairman at your wedding?"

Okocha nodded, smiling.

"So why didn't you just say so instead of spinning me a long tale about—? But never mind that. So this your Mr.—whatever you called him—who's inviting us was the chairman at your wedding. I think I'm beginning to remember him. Do you, Edna?"

"Sure," said Edna. "I remember the man was very firm in the way he presided over the reception. I also remember wondering if he had been a military man, because he seemed to always want things done with military precision. Was he?"

"You mean, a military man?" Okocha asked. "Not as far as I know. He might have fought in our Biafra-Nigeria civil war. That was some thirty-something years ago, when he must have been a very young man; perhaps a teenager. From all accounts, some teenagers saw action during that war. But he couldn't have been a military officer, if you see what I mean."

"Here are your drinks," Tatiana announced.

She walked into the sitting-room, carrying a tray on which were an assortment of drinks and snacks. She placed the tray on the center table, and a can of ginger-ale on a side stool by the love seat, for Okocha.

"Thanks, Tiana," Philip Karefa said, smiling at his daughter. "Bless you, girl!"

"What do you say, OK baby?"

"What else but thank you, of course. I was—"

"Wait a minute!" Philip Karefa suddenly called out. "Wait just a minute! O'kcha, let me ask you this, and I want the truth from you. Did you, or you Tiana, did either of you say anything to this gentleman about my desire to get to meet a few members of what my daughter here now calls her new community? Did you?"

"Er—no, sir," said Okocha, with a quick sideways glance at Tatiana.

"And if we did?" asked Tatiana, in the same breath, glaring at her dad challengingly.

Philip first looked up to the ceiling, and then turned to Okocha. "That's how her mother talks to me, O'kcha. You'd better watch out. You've got you a spirited woman there, O'kcha."

"I know, sir," Okocha said, laughing merrily. "But it's all right actually. I love her for who and what she is, the way you and her mom and God made her."

"I know, too, he wouldn't have me any other way," Tatiana said, nestling closer to him on the love seat they shared and, on an impulse, linking arms with him. "If you don't believe me, ask him."

"No need to ask," said her dad. "I have eyes to see. But, about this invitation, what do you say, Edna?"

Edna seemed to hesitate, staring first at her husband for a moment or two, then at Okocha and Tatiana. Her mouth momentarily worked, but no words came.

"I didn't think I needed to ask you, Edna," Philip said severely. "It's not as if we have not talked about this possibility lately."

"That's true, Phil." Edna's tone was apologetic. "You didn't need to ask me. Of course we'll accept the invitation. I was only thinking about the date the fellow suggested—a week today. Wouldn't want to miss such an opportunity to get close to our new in-laws! I gather, the way Okocha's people look at marriage, we now have a wide circle of in-laws. That's what Tiana tells me." She turned to Tatiana. "Am I right?"

"Mom, I don't remember putting it quite that way," Tatiana began, but was interrupted by Okocha.

"It's all right, Tiana," he said soothingly. "Mom, let me explain. In-law is strictly the same in America and in Nigeria. It's just that we, as a people, can sometimes carry a perfectly simple concept just a shade—no, *shades*—further than you Americans do. A whole village or town will claim an in-law relationship with everyone who comes from another village into which one of them married. It's as simple as that. And then of course, when we are far from home, as we obviously are, living in America, we expect, as an Igbo adage enjoins us, that our sense of brotherhood and sisterhood within our community will be heightened. It's all rather exaggerated, but we mean well. That sense of being brothers helps to foster a spirit of togetherness among us here."

"Makes a whole lot of sense to me," Philip Karefa said. "And very touching too. You know what, O'kcha, please tell your Mr.—er—"

"Odogwu."

"Whatever! We accept his invitation. As to the date—and we'll check our calendar to make sure about this—next Friday should be good for the dinner. Yes, Edna?"

"I think so," said Edna Karefa. "I imagine there might be other persons than just us at the dinner?"

"From what Mr. Odogwu said to me, perhaps two or three others, max," Okocha said. "Tiana and me—we'll be there."

"Would it matter?" asked Tatiana, looking from her dad to her mom.

"Not at all, Tiana," said her dad. "Not at all. Your mom and me—we have no hang-ups about meeting people, even if their ways are different than ours. I think it'll be a breeze. I look forward to—"

"Meeting your new in-laws?" Tatiana cut in, smiling.

"You got that right, girl! Let your Mr.—whatever his name is—bring on the entire Nigerian community in this here country. We'll be equal to the task!"

"I'm glad that's settled," said Okocha, reaching for his can of ginger-ale, and a glass. "I'll let Mr. Odogwu know that next Friday is okay for you."

"Go right ahead, boy!" He paused, and seemed to remember something. "But hold it there! I remember him well now. He had on a Nigerian jumper for the occasion, and carried a big round leather fan with tassels. He looked quite striking in his outfit. I particularly liked the fan. But I'm talking too much! We'll see your Mr. Odogu—"

"*Odogwu*, sir. It's an uncommon sound, however—the *gw* sound. Can't immediately think of a word in the English language with a *gw* sound. So perhaps it should be okay how you said it—*Odogu*. It's near enough."

"Whatever! We'll be there—is all that matters."

"Don't worry, Okocha," said Edna Karefa. "Philip will pronounce the name correctly, or nearly correctly, by next Friday, even if I have to do a surgery on his tongue."

Philip Karefa glared at Edna, but his best imitation of a scowl did not entirely wipe off the grin lurking behind it.

CHAPTER 16

Ifunanya Odogwu stood in the middle of the living-room and, for a prolonged moment, looked around her. Satisfied that the room was spick and span, she nodded several times to herself and bowed her head in quiet contemplation. When she looked up, she was surprised to see her husband, Chikezie, framed against the door giving on to the kitchen, watching her with what seemed a smug smile on his quietly pleasant face. A smile lit up *her* face because whenever she caught him looking at her with that patented smile of his, she knew her world was exactly as it was supposed to be; as she had always dreamt it would be: serene and contented. These were the moments that gave her the strength she needed to navigate the rougher moments of her life with Chikezie.

He liked to see everything in its assigned place in the room, whether that room be the bedroom, the sitting-room, or the dining-room. It had become an obsession with him, but she had learned to live with that humor. Time and again, her friends—those who knew her from her relatively carefree years in college and as an unmarried woman—marveled at the transformation. She mostly let them continue to wonder, contenting herself with the popular and universal maxim: to each, her own! Chikezie Odogwu was not just her world; he was her destiny. And she was thankful that, more than anything else, he was a caring husband.

"Our guests should be here within the half-hour," Chikezie said.

"And I'm as ready as I can be," said Ifunanya. "My only concern is that they all arrive in reasonable time."

"There are three Americans in the mix, and they will show up when they're supposed to. Mr. and Mrs. Karefa and their daughter Tatiana—and therefore Okocha—all four of them can be counted on to show up in good time."

"I suppose I should bring the snacks out now," Ifunanya said. "I've always believed the sight of finger-foods, neatly laid out on the living-room table, gets the digestive juices of guests flowing. I'm sure the Karefas, once they taste our Nigerian groundnuts—"

"Peanuts!" Chikezie interrupted.

"Americans can call it what they like," Ifunanya said dismissively. "It's *groundnuts* where it comes from. Our people hardly know what *peanut* is."

"Sorry, Ifunanya, but it's peanut here."

"Whatever you say!" Ifunanya said. "Main thing is, ours tastes different from what we buy in stores here. Let's just wait and see what happens when our American in-laws are here."

She brushed past Chikezie, who stood his ground, partially and deliberately blocking her way into the kitchen. He smiled when her body brushed his, but quickly moved out of her way when she came back carrying a tray loaded with finger-foods: groundnuts, roasted cashew-nuts and almonds, cut broccoli and carrots, each in its own bowl, as well as an onion dip. She deposited the tray on the center table and then, suspicious of her husband's movement towards the tray, blocked his path.

"Patience!" she said to him. "I don't want you touching any of these before our guests arrive—"

"You can be sure of one thing," said Chikezie. "I'm not going to touch your precious broccoli and carrots."

"I know you hate them. But first help me bring out the glasses for the drinks. Please!" she added pleadingly.

"Where are your daughters? You wouldn't be harassing me now if Udeaku and Janet were here. But you had to let them go with their friends to—what do they call it—a summer camp in some remote part of Florida, a part of America we've never been to. Suppose now, with my clumsiness, I break one or two of the wineglasses as I carry them on a tray? You know with their long stems, they easily tip over if not carried with steady hands—"

"And since when did your hands begin to tremble, Chikezie?" Ifunanya asked, laughing. "Excuses! Excuses! Excuses! Please help me get the glasses out, *oh jarri!*" she ended, lapsing into Nigerian patois.

"Right away, madam!" Chikezie said, with mock seriousness, but nevertheless went to do as bidden.

*   *   *

Ifunanya and Chikezie Odogwu watched as Mr. and Mrs. Karefa tucked into the snacks. From time to time they exchanged glances, with Ifunanya exhibiting a mounting impatience. Chikezie remained poker-faced. When she finally ran out of patience, Ifunanya decided to draw attention to her groundnuts. She picked up the bowl, peered into it for a moment, and put it down again on the table.

"Would you like some more of these?" she asked, looking keenly at Edna Karefa.

"Not really," said Edna. "But they're good. I always enjoy them."

"You do?" Ifunanya asked, rapidly glancing at her husband. "I suppose you know these are not—"

"Oh, I know. They're from Nigeria. Thanks to Okocha here, we've been enjoying them for quite some time now. Gets them somehow from your country, and always makes sure to give us a bottle. They're the best peanuts I think I ever tasted."

Ifunanya, a triumphant eye on her husband Chikezie, emitted a long drawn-out sigh of satisfaction. "What do you say to that, Mr. Odogwu, eh?"

Before Chikezie could get a word out, Okocha said, nodding vigorously: "It's always good to hear that compliment, because it shows there are things we do very well in that blessed country of ours. I'm sure our hosts have been waiting for you to say something—"

"How'd you know, OK baby?" Tatiana rebuked him. "Just because *you* always expect non-Nigerians to compliment you on your peanuts doesn't mean every Nigerian does."

"I'm sorry I jumped—" Okocha started to say.

"That's all right, Okocha," Chikezie Odogwu said soothingly. "As a matter of fact, my wife—"

"Chikezie!" Ifunanya exclaimed.

"It's okay, Ify. I was simply going to say you think these are better than the roasted peanuts one buys here."

"And I say she's damn right!" Philip said. "I've not tasted any peanuts better than these."

Suddenly Mr. Odogwu stood up, pointing to the door. "I think I hear a car pulling up the driveway. Must be our other guests. I'll be back in a moment."

He walked briskly through the door of the sitting-room towards the front door, and waited. Soon the doorbell rang, and he opened the door.

"*Ugo-oranyelu-Aniagu! Lolo!* You're welcome. Please come in."

In a trice, Okocha was on his feet. Then, mouth agape, he hurried towards the door. But before he got there, his dad and mom walked into the room, ahead of their host. Mr. Odogwu was vigorously rubbing his palms together with undisguised glee.

"Dad! Mom! What—?" Okocha began, turning to Mr. Odogwu, but left his question suspended.

Philip Karefa rose slowly from his seat, reaching for, and pulling up Edna with him. Tatiana remained frozen in her seat, staring at her parents-in-law as if they were beings from another planet. Mrs. Ifunanya Odogwu, leaning on the kitchen doorpost, looked on with a faint smile.

"Chief and Mrs. Nat Anigbo!" Mr. Odogwu announced. "Let me introduce you to my other guests, our American in-laws, Tatiana's parents, Philip and Edna Karefa. Mr. and Mrs. Karefa, please meet Okocha's parents, Nat and Ekemma Anigbo."

For a brief moment, Philip Karefa stood stock-still and stared at the Anigbos. Then with the merest shrug of his shoulders, he stepped forward and held out his hand to Nat Anigbo. Chief Anigbo, with a hesitant smile, grasped the offered hand, as they stood eyeball to eyeball.

"We finally meet," Philip said. "You can't imagine how much I've looked forward to this day. How're you and O'kcha's mom doing?"

"Very well, thank you," Chief Anigbo responded, serious of face, rigid of bearing. He then shook hands with Edna Karefa. "Mrs. Karefa," he said softly, "my pleasure."

"Please call me Edna," she told him with a bright smile. "I'm especially happy to meet Okocha's mom. *E-ke-ma*, I believe?" she asked, pronouncing the name carefully. "I hope I said it right. I've heard the name a million times from Okocha and my daughter."

The two mothers, telepathically, opened their arms wide as they came together in an embrace that was noticeably unfrosty. Okocha, watching this first meeting of his parents and Tatiana's parents with barely concealed apprehension, held Tatiana by the hand, as they both stood awkwardly, gaping at their parents.

Mrs. Ifunanya Odogwu now came forward to welcome her guests with a charming smile that said that all was well with the world. Though she had earlier appropriately welcomed the Karefas when they first arrived, she went through the ritual of hugging them again, as well as the Anigbos.

"There can never be too much hugging between friends and those who should be friends," she said with gusto, her gaze taking in the entire assemblage.

Mr. Odogwu, who had not seemed to stop rubbing his palms together for even a moment, stood in the middle of his guests, smiling expansively. He looked from person to person, nodding to himself with obvious satisfaction. He winked at Okocha when their eyes met.

"Ladies and gentlemen," he said, raising his voice a notch or two, arms spread out, "I had to do this. And I couldn't even take Okocha and Tatiana into confidence on the matter. I suppose I could and should say I'm sorry I pulled a fast one on all of you. But I'd be lying in my throat if I did. I did what I *had* to do—what my wife and I *needed* to do—to get both sets of parents together. Okocha, when I told you we'd like to invite your parents-in-law to dinner in our house, and could you help us talk to them, I could see you were very curious about my intentions. I had no choice but to tell you we would be inviting two or three members of our community. But there was no way I was going to reveal to you that the two or three persons would be your dad and mom. I couldn't risk your trying to talk me out of it—"

"I don't believe I'd have tried," said Okocha.

"I doubt I'd have let him try," said Tatiana, "if I'd had an inkling of your plans. I thank you with all my heart, Chief Odogwu—"

"I'm not a chief," Mr. Odogwu corrected her, smiling.

"You are, to me," Tatiana said, with a firm and emphatic nod of the head. "You should be a chief! Okocha tells me you more than deserve it."

"Please don't mind your husband," Mr. Odogwu said. "He's just biased in my favor. That's all."

He looked from the Karefas to the Anigbos. "So here we are! It is my hope we can make the most of this dinner opportunity. What d'you say we all sit down and enjoy the goodies my wife has set before us, here on the table, before we get to the dinner proper?"

Mrs. Ifunanya Odogwu held Ekemma Anigbo by the hand and led her to the three-seater. "*Lolo*," she said to her, "I'll share this settee with you and perhaps Tatiana."

At the same time, Mr. Odogwu waved Chief Anigbo into a single upholstered chair—not his *king's* chair—placed between the love-seat and the long settee. A delightfully multi-colored fabric was draped over the back-rest of the *king's* chair, to set it apart from the rest of the furniture.

"Okocha's no stranger here," Mr. Odogwu said, gesturing toward Okocha where he stood quietly behind the sofa, and looking with scarcely diminished apprehension from his dad to his father-in-law. "Why don't you bring up a chair from the entrance area, for yourself?"

"I will, thank you, sir," Okocha said, but stood where he was until everybody else was seated.

Ifunanya maneuvered Tatiana into sitting between her and Okocha's mom. Chief Anigbo, the ghost of a smile creasing his otherwise placid face, gazed for a long moment at his host, nodded gently two or three times, and took the chair offered to him.

"*Ugo-oranyelu*," Mrs. Odogwu called out to Chief Anigbo, "I remembered you don't care too much for groundnuts. So I made sure I got roasted unsalted almonds for you. I know you love them. And there's everybody's favorite—cashew nuts, also unsalted. But please, everybody, remember dinner is coming. So leave some room for the real thing."

Ekemma Anigbo coughed out loud, to gain general attention. "I was beginning to wonder," she said, deadpan, gesturing towards the center table, "with all these delicious nuts, broccoli and what-not to munch on, whether you didn't cook enough for dinner."

"*Lolo*, you know me," Ifunanya Odogwu countered. "There's plenty to eat. The question is, did you come with enough appetite to do justice—?"

"I'm looking forward to your *egusi* soup," Ekemma Anigbo said, smiling. "The last time we were here for dinner, I licked my fingers all the way home." She nodded her head in happy memory, as she spoke.

"So you might say," Mr. Odogwu proudly declaimed, "that Ifunanya's *egusi* and bitter-leaf soups are what those who speak the Queen's English would call finger-licking good. I'm very proud of her. But our American friends here don't know what we're talking about."

He turned to Philip and Edna Karefa. "Please don't mind us. This is just how we talk. The important thing is that we hope you will enjoy the dinner. And by all means please sample the soup, even if you don't touch the farina *foo-foo*. The soup is good to eat all by itself, and not too peppery. We know we sometimes use too much pepper in our foods. But not this time, my wife assures me."

Okocha kept his eyes on his dad. As their hosts engaged in light-hearted banter with his mom, he noted that his dad sat quietly, letting only his eyes flit from speaker to speaker, his expression mostly vacant, his fingers intertwined and lying lifelessly in his lap. He tried, by various subterfuges, to engage his dad's eyes, but soon came to the conclusion that his dad studiedly and quite deliberately refrained from looking in his direction. He knew his dad; knew that he could be inflexibly uncommunicative when silence suited his purpose, or when he believed that it would be weakness to give an opening to the opposition's attempt to shift him from his ground.

Okocha watched as his dad picked up his favorite roasted almonds, one at a time, and crunched and munched them slowly, with barely a twitch of his facial muscles. He sensed that their host, Mr. Odogwu, was taking his time, and seemed not to be in a hurry to draw his dad out of his self-imposed impassivity. He saw Mr. Odogwu glance at his dad from moment to moment, sometimes challengingly, but mostly appealingly. He saw the way his dad's eyes would rest occasionally on Mr. Odogwu, and he began to wonder when the explosion, if it was on the cards, would come.

"Dinner'll be served in a minute!" Ifunanya Odogwu suddenly announced, rising from her seat. "I hope you all like it nice and hot. I'll just get the dishes out of the oven, and we can eat."

"Can I come and help you?" Tatiana asked, also rising to her feet. "Like Okocha, I too am no longer a stranger here."

"Well, I don't mind at all," said Mrs. Odogwu. "That's very kind of you."

Philip Karefa kept a steady eye on Chief Anigbo, looking away only when Chief Anigbo turned to look in his direction. He resisted his instinctive urge to attempt to break the ice between them; an overpowering urge to say something that would compel a response from this in-law who—probably more than anything else in the world—did not want to be *his* in-law. A number of tentative ideas occurred to him, but he rejected them all. It would be infinitely better, he said to himself again and again, for the frigidity to remain in place, than for him to worsen an already deplorable situation by uttering an inanity. He remembered what Okocha had once said—in perhaps an unguarded moment—about his dad; that Chief Anigbo could, when the mood was on him, turn his face and regard into an iceberg.

"Hold it there, Ifunanya," Mr. Odogwu suddenly said, "before you and Tatiana start bringing out the dishes. What about the kolanut?"

"I was beginning to think I had misunderstood something," Philip Karefa said. "Something, that is, about your Ibo culture. I've heard it from several sources that your people always welcome guests to your homes with kolanuts. Or are you expecting more guests? Perhaps we are not yet all here?"

"Everybody's here. I must say I'm impressed—"

"Shouldn't be, Mr. Odogu," said Mr. Karefa. "If I've heard it once, I must have heard it a hundred times—from you yourself when we were chatting about kolanuts at Okocha and Tiana's wedding reception; from Okocha; from that fellow Luke, during the—what do you call it—ceremony of knocking—"

"*At* the door, Philip!" Edna Karefa interjected.

Philip glared at his wife briefly and quickly looked away. "What was I saying? Oh, yes, thank you Edna. Knocking *at* the door! So, as I was saying, I've heard a lot about the kolanut, and the role it plays in your daily life. Don't forget, Mr. Odogu—if you don't mind the way I say your name—don't forget I myself, quite possibly, could be Ibo, with a forebear who probably had an Ibo name suspiciously like mine—"

"*Okoroafor* and *Karefa!*" Edna again interjected.

"Whatever!" said Philip, waving a hand dismissively.

"My mistake!" said Ifunanya Odogwu contritely. "Excuse me for just a moment," she added as, with rapid steps, she went to the kitchen.

She came back, carrying a plastic tray on which were placed a wooden bowl containing four kolanuts, and a smaller wooden bowl holding a scoop of the delectable *okwa-ose*. This is a thick spiced paste, principally made from the peanut, a pinch or two of the common pepper, ground crayfish, and sauce cubes like the *maggi*, or native spices. The paste enriches the taste of the otherwise tasteless—sometimes bitter—kolanut. She handed the tray to her husband.

Mr. Odogwu cleared his throat noisily—to gain attention—and held up the bowl. But before he got a word out, Philip Karefa held up an arm, as he dipped two fingers into the breast-pocket of his shirt.

"Just a minute, folks!" he pleaded. "Wait just a minute! I have it all noted down in my precious notebook, which I made sure I brought with me for this dinner. That's if I can find the page!"

He thumbed feverishly through the pages of a stubby notebook, as the other persons in the room with him looked on, mostly with curiosity. Chief Anigbo was frowning.

"Here!" Mr. Karefa shouted triumphantly. "I've found it. Now let me see."

He looked around him, and then down at the page and, with one finger carefully tracing the lines of interest, read out aloud. "*The blessing of the kolanut has to be done in Ibo, because it understands only the Ibo language.* That's number one—"

"It's actually *Igbo*, not *Ibo*," Ekemma Anigbo said. "The word is spelt **I-G-B-O** and I've often wondered why it's so difficult—"

"Mom, it is," said Tatiana, with an ingratiating smile. "Much as I myself have tried, and OK is a good teacher, the best I can do is *Ig-bo*, gliding very quickly over the *g* and *b*."

"Not too bad, Tiana dear," said Okocha. "Not bad at all."

"I was going to mention only one other thing, among the five or six points I noted down here," Philip Karefa continued, looking down at his notes, and again tracing the lines of interest with the first finger of his right hand as he read out aloud: "*When the kolanut is produced, all other discussions are suspended until after the blessing.* Right?" he asked, turning to Mr. Odogwu. "This means we should get on with it, I believe."

Mr. Odogwu nodded his affirmation. "Quite right," he said. "I'm intrigued by what you have noted down in that your—what did you call it—your precious notebook. But let me ask Chief Anigbo if we can—just for this occasion—let you tell us what else about the kolanut you jotted down. What do you say, *Ugo-oranyelu?*"

"No problem," Chief Anigbo said simply, his eyes riveted on Mr. Karefa.

Mr. Karefa smiled with satisfaction, and raised his notebook. "I noted here that *a woman plays no significant role in the kolanut ceremony, except perhaps to bring out the bowl or plate containing the kolanuts, and hand it over to her husband. Usually, the oldest man present prays over the kolanut. But—*"

"Which means, I suppose," Edna Karefa interrupted her husband, "that Okocha's dad will be the person to do it, no?"

Chief Anigbo again allowed a faint smile to crease the placidity of his face. "Not this time," he said softly. "As a guest in another man's house—"

Philip Karefa cut in, peering once more at his notes. "Yes. I have it noted down here, that *it is the host who does the kolanut prayer, or blessing, unless he specifically empowers a guest, older than himself, to do so.*"

"And he will ask the older man to do so," said Mr. Odogwu, "if he says he has already broken the kolanut earlier in the day."

"So then, have you already broken the kolanut today?" Edna Karefa chipped in. "Or is a woman not supposed to ask even a simple question like that?"

Mr. Karefa turned anxious eyes on his wife. "Edna! It's best for you, I'd suggest, to just listen and learn. But," he added, looking from Mr. Odogwu to Chief Anigbo, "the woman's question is the question I was going to ask. If you have already today broken the kolanut, will the privilege of praying over the kolanut go to O'kcha's dad? And, on that subject, I'm told that sometimes there can be an intense argument about who's the oldest man present, right?"

"Quite right," Mr. Odogwu responded. "I've been present, at lighthearted moments, when passports have been called into play, even though the birthdates given in that document can sometimes be unreliable."

"So then," Mr. Karefa went on, "if you, our host, have earlier today done the kolanut prayer, it could be said that O'kcha's dad and myself may need to produce our birth certificates to determine who's older. I know both of us are older than you."

Chief Anigbo laughed out loud; a crackling, throaty laughter that reverberated round the room, and went on for several moments. All eyes turned in his direction, wonderingly. Mr. Karefa's were the only exceptions. His eyes, quietly focused on Chief Anigbo, sparkled with a hint of mischief and amusement.

"You? And me?" Chief Anigbo at last calmed down enough to splutter. "And if you're the older of us two, what do you plan to do?"

Mr. Karefa, with the self-congratulatory air of a person who had achieved more than he had expected, smiled broadly and pointed a finger at Chief Anigbo. "Got you there, good and proper!" he said. "I know—and don't have to look at my notes for this—I know I can't—I mean—I'm disqualified from saying the kolanut prayer because—"

"The kolanut understands only—er—their language?" Edna cut in, and quickly turned to Mrs. Ekemma Anigbo, seeking confirmation.

Tatiana, sitting between the two women, was the one that gave her mother a firm nod of the head. "Correct, mom. That'll be the day when dad can do a kolanut blessing!"

Mr. Odogwu cleared his throat loudly, and said: "Tatiana has just about summed it all up neatly. So I'll crave your indulgence for us to get on with it. But it'll be brief.'

He paused, and beckoned to Okocha. "Please, Okocha, come and take the bowl from me, and I hope you know what you have to do with it."

"Sure, sir! I have to take the bowl and show the kolanuts to everyone."

"Very good, young man! I only need to add that your dad and Tatiana's dad should each take one kolanut from the bowl, to take home."

"And each kolanut," added Okocha, with a knowing smile, "when it gets to each home, *will tell the story of where it came from*, as we say."

At length, Okocha brought the bowl, now containing only two kolanuts, back to Mr. Odogwu. Mr. Odogwu picked up one of the two, raised it so that everyone present could see it clearly, and looked from Mr. Karefa to his wife.

"As you both now know, I have to do this in Igbo. But I suspect you already have some idea about the general purpose and intent of the kolanut invocation. I'll also say, to settle one point at issue—and I'll not tell a lie—I have not yet, today, done the kolanut ceremony. So, though I would ordinarily not do so when Chief Anigbo is present, this is my home, and so here goes!"

In a voice of appropriate solemnity, in his Igbo language, he welcomed his guests to his home, and then invoked God's blessings on all four families present. He remembered his daughters, Udeaku and Janet, away in the wilds of Florida, among people that their parents did not know, doing things he hoped would bring only honor to the family. He added a special plea for Okocha and Tatiana, who were just beginning the rest of their lives as a new family, with a child clearly on the way. At this point, he struggled mightily to resist the temptation to steal a glance at Chief Anigbo. He prayed that God would bring the Karefa and the Anigbo families together in a bond of love. In doing so, he constantly referred to the Karefas as "*ndi-ogo-anyi*"—meaning "*our in-laws*"—without mentioning the name Karefa. And as he said this, he looked at Chief Anigbo wistfully, his eyes conveying a yearning that he was sure Chief Anigbo would understand. He then broke the kolanut into four pieces, and took one for himself, and one for his wife. He next handed the bowl to Okocha with a request that he cut the second kolanut into smaller pieces, before passing the bowl around to everyone present so they could each take one piece. Okocha cut up the kolanut as instructed by Mr. Odogwu, and then took the bowl first to his own dad, then to Mr. Karefa, before serving the two mothers and Tatiana. Tatiana made a face, indicating she did not want a piece.

"But Tiana," he urged her, "I know you enjoy it when you eat it with the *okwa-ose*."

"Not today, thank you, OK baby," she said with an incandescent smile, reflexively and gently rubbing her belly. "I have to watch what I eat. You know what I'm sa-a-ying?"

"Of course, Tiana. I'll eat two pieces for the both of us."

"You're just making me an excuse," Tatiana said, "to indulge your appetite for your favorite combination of kolanut and its paste."

Suddenly, Philip Karefa rose to his feet and—with all eyes trained on him—took two or three steps and stood directly in front of Chief Anigbo. Then he turned, slowly and deliberately, and looked first at Mr. Odogwu, then at Mrs. Odogwu. He seemed, with his eyes and his entire body language, to be pleading with them for an understanding of what he was about to do.

Philip held his piece of kolanut in his right hand, which he held out towards Chief Anigbo. And when he began to speak, his voice was gentle but assured; his eyes, as they focused on Chief Anigbo, seemed to be smiling at him.

"Your kolanut, I have since learnt, is offered and broken normally in an environment of peace and goodwill," he said. "Before we are invited to the dinner table by our hosts, I would like us—you and me—to demonstrate the goodwill—or the need for it—between our two families. I ask you, as man to man, as one father to the other father, to rise from your chair so we can talk—at least so I can talk to you—eyeball to eyeball. Chief, would you mind humoring me on this matter? I ask this in all humility."

He paused, his eyes unwaveringly holding Chief Anigbo's challengingly. Chief Anigbo, ordinarily no slouch in taking up a challenge, nevertheless looked long and hard, silently, at his interlocutor.

"Why?" he asked laconically.

"Because I don't want to be talking down to you—if you see what I mean," Philip Karefa said, barely above a whisper. "Please."

"You can talk to me, standing, and I can hear you clearly, sitting." Chief Anigbo looked down at his hands in his lap. "There's no reason—"

"Dad, there is!" Okocha somehow found himself standing side by side with his father-in-law, in front of his dad. He held out both his arms, palms turned upwards, in a gesture of entreaty. "What do you have to lose, dad—?"

In a trice, Chief Anigbo was on his feet, his eyes—smoldering with barely disguised resentment—darting from his son's face to Mr. Karefa's.

"So, what now?" he asked. "What's it you want to say to me?"

Philip Karefa smiled, nodding his head as if satisfied he had scored a point. "Thank you for humoring me, Chief," he said. "I would like to ask one more favor of you—that you be patient and hear me out—"

"Why?"

"Because," said Philip, carefully choosing his words, "what I want to say is of considerable importance to me and, hopefully, to you too!"

"Go ahead. I'll not interrupt you. You have my word on that."

"Thank you very much, Chief," Philip Karefa said, and paused. For a moment or two, he seemed to struggle with himself. His mouth worked, but no words immediately came. Then he smiled as one who was finally at peace with himself. He held his hands behind his back, and intertwined his fingers. His body was rigidly erect.

"What I want to say is soon said. My fingers are intertwined behind me. But you cannot see them because my opaque body is in the way. In somewhat of a similar way, you cannot see the reality of our situation—that you and O'kcha's mom, on the one hand, and Tiana's mom, Edna and I, on the other, are now more or less permanently interlinked. You are prevented from acknowledging this overarching reality by what I understand to be the dictates of your culture and tradition, in matters of marriage. I admire a people who have traditions that they value. It's something we, as African-Americans, have since largely lost. But even for a traditional African like yourself, the world has changed, and continues to change before our very eyes. Scores of young persons from different cultures—and Africans, including your own people, are very much among them—intermarry daily, and the planet earth continues to revolve around the sun. The world has not collapsed around them. If some of these marriages fail, the same fate befalls marriages between persons of the same culture. That, my dear Chief, is a universal truth."

He paused again, now very serious of countenance, looked around him and gestured apologetically with his hand. "I'm sorry if this is turning out to be somewhat of a lecture. But that was not my purpose."

Chief Anigbo, equally stern of face, his eyes boring unflinchingly into Philip Karefa's, symbolically waved aside the apology. "What's your purpose?" he asked.

Philip turned to his daughter. "Come here, Tiana," he called out to her. "Come stand by your husband and me."

He waited until Tatiana came and stood by Okocha, and he then manouevered them so that he stood in the middle, with Okocha to his right, and Tatiana to his left. Next he held each with one hand, and made them take a step forward and stand closer together, as all three faced Chief Anigbo.

"My purpose," Philip Karefa said, "is very simply to ask you, as O'kcha's dad, to join me in giving our blessing to my daughter and your son in their marriage. I will not insult you by suggesting that your marriage customs and traditions are anachronistic. Not at all! But whether we, as parents, like it or not, the world is moving on in this regard, and there's precious little we can do to stop our young ones from falling in love wherever their circumstances open the doors for them. What do you say, Chief?"

For a long moment, there was total silence, like the silence of the tomb, in the room. Very gently, Okocha encircled Tatiana's waist with his arm, and drew her even closer. His eyes were passionate in the intensity of their regard as he looked into his dad's eyes, and as he laid bare his soul's yearning to him, in all its naked simplicity.

"Dad, please do this for Tiana and me," he said softly, involuntarily tightening his grasp of Tatiana's waist.

Chief Anigbo shifted uneasily on his feet, and looked around him. He knew that all eyes were on him and, probably for the first time in a long, long time, he was at a loss for words. Then, suddenly, his face lit up with a smile, even as he shook his head from side to side.

"I see," he said, his eyes focused on his host, Chikezie Odogwu. "I see," he said again. "Is this some kind of a set up? Is this what you all agreed to do—to force some kind of a concession from me?"

"Not at all, *Ugo-oranyelu!*" said Mr. Odogwu. "Ifunanya and me, we invited you and *Lolo* Ekemma just as we invited Philip and Edna. And as I said earlier, it is my hope and prayer that this dinner will afford your two families the chance to begin—however slowly—the process of coming together as in-laws. It would be disingenuous and ridiculous to pretend otherwise. But I planned nothing with anyone. That's the truth, and I swear so on—"

"No need to swear," Chief Anigbo interrupted him, "or you risk forswearing yourself! The good book enjoins us not to swear by heaven, for it is God's throne, nor by the earth, for it is His foot-stool, nor even by your head—"

"I know the rest of it," Mr. Odogwu interrupted him, with a short burst of laughter. "I know I cannot change the color of one hair on my head." He paused for a moment, and looked at Chief Anigbo and Mr. Karefa in turns. Then, sadly, he shook his head. "But we've talked long enough about this matter. And it would seem to be pointless to try to force the issue with you, *Ugo-oranyelu.* I know you!"

"Thank you, my dear husband!" Mrs Ifunanya Odogwu said, happily rising to her feet. "Friends, how about we have dinner now? And if Tatiana hasn't changed her mind, I'd appreciate her help in getting the food out of the oven."

"As if I'd dare, or want to." Tatiana gently disengaged Okocha's arm from around her waist. "I'm entirely at your service, Mrs. Odogwu."

*   *   *

Okocha chewed on his fingernails in stolen moments, when he thought he was sure no one was looking in his direction. He could not recall ever sitting through a dinner as nerve-racking as this turned out to be. He could barely eat. Mrs. Odogwu's *egusi* soup, famously one of the best in the community, tasted almost insipid. With every passing moment, he got angrier. With his dad, who remained obstinately inscrutable and emotionless! And with himself, because he could not understand why, at this far gone stage of his life with, and love for, Tatiana, it still mattered to him that his dad remained unyielding in his opposition! He had watched his dad eat his food as if it was a chore; as if all the compliments he had habitually heaped on Ifunanya Odogwu's cooking were nothing but the insincere and fulsome mouthings of a nodding sychophant.

He agonized over Tatiana, and how she must be feeling about his dad's intransigence. They had lately begun to discuss the adviseability of relocating from New Jersey to Delaware or Pennsylvania, "to put some more distance", as he put it, between them and his parents—especially his dad. Relocation would impose little or no additional burden on their commute to their workplaces. Routingly, hundreds of people commuted from those two states to Trenton, NJ, where Okocha worked in the U.B.S. and Tatiana worked in the New Jersey State civil service.

Tatiana had been the less enthusiastic of the two about relocating out of New Jersey. She was not convinced it was an appropriate step to take, in light of her pregnancy. She had but two or so months to go, she argued, and it would be bad timing to have to find a new doctor. Besides, she pointed out, Delaware or Pennsylvania would put some more distance, not only between her and Okocha's dad, but also between her and *her* parents. And this, at a time when she would assuredly benefit from close proximity to her mother when she would need it the most—in the days and weeks immediately following the delivery of her baby. She declared that, willy-nilly, she had had to come to terms with Okocha's dad's unwillingness to accept the reality of her marriage to his son.

It was something of a relief when the dinner was finally and mercifully over, Okocha said to himself. He did not have to continue sitting opposite his dad, or watch him as his dead eyes—impassive, vacant and stony, with about as much warmth shining out of them as from a tiger's eyes—flitted from one speaker to another!

"OK baby," Tatiana now whispered into his ear as they sat sharing the love-seat, "will you please quit being so nervous. Chewing on your nails—"

"Oh, you noticed?" he asked, eyebrows raised in surprise.

"I've kind of grown accustomed to your body language," she said, with a smile. "Your moods and mannerisms are second nature to me now. OK baby, what'll happen, will happen. We can't, neither of us, do anything about it. Your dad is who—and what—he is. And you and me, we are what we are—married, and with a bun in the oven, as they say."

"What are you two love-birds muttering about?" Edna Karefa suddenly asked, smiling impishly.

"Nothing, mom," Tatiana quickly replied. "Only that it's getting late, and I must to bed in another hour or so. Doctor's orders!"

"You got that right, young lady! It's getting rather late."

Seven pairs of eyes looked up sharply at the speaker, Chief Anigbo. Those were the first words he had spoken directly to Tatiana all through the evening. What startled Okocha the most was that the dozen or so words did not seem to have been spoken in anger. Chief Anigbo spoke in his emphatic baritone, with a firm and approving nod of his head. Okocha and Tatiana exchanged a quick, puzzled glance, their faces registering their natural—and considerable—surprise.

"OK baby," Tatiana said, "it's time to take our leave. But first, I need your help to clean up the remaining—"

"Not on your life!" Ifunanya Odogwu cried out. "Don't need any more help than you've given me. There's very little left to clean up. You've done enough, putting the dishes and things in the dishwasher. You had better leave now so you can have your rest, as your doctor ordered. And," she added with a smile, glancing rapidly at Chief Anigbo, "as your father-in-law just said. It *is* getting very late."

"If you say so, Mrs. Odogwu, though I don't feel so good leaving you to do what's left to be done—"

"We insist, Tatiana!" Mr. Odogwu said emphatically. "Off with you two!"

"Nothing more needs to be said," Okocha said, getting up from his seat, and gently pulling Tatiana up, "except of course that I must thank our hosts, from the bottom of my heart, for this evening. It's been truly a memorable evening, and means a lot to both of us, Tiana and me. I don't even know how we can thank you—"

Chikezie Odogwu interrupted. "Certainly, young man, not by making a long speech. It is enough that you all honored our invite. That's all we prayed for. Drive carefully on your way home. You are carrying more passengers than your eyes can see!"

Okocha and Tatiana exchanged happy smiles, and linked arms as they walked out of the living room.

"See you all soon," said Okocha. "Till then, happy Father's Day in advance!"

CHAPTER 17

The sermon had strongly urged the faithful to be fully appreciative of their fathers because, declaimed the preacher, "your father gave you the most priceless gift one human being can give to another: life!" Rev. Father Connery had paused for a moment, and then had added, with a smile: "Of course father could not have done this without mother. But just about a month ago, we honored our mothers. Today, we honor our fathers. The Bible enjoins us to honor our fathers and our mothers so that our days may be long."

Okocha's problem, as he repeatedly complained to Tatiana, was how one could joyfully celebrate Father's Day with a father who might summarily reject one's good wishes and one's gifts, and throw both back in one's face.

"So, what are you saying, OK baby?" Tatiana's bewilderment was strongly etched on her brow. "That we don't go to see your dad?"

Okocha looked long and hard at Tatiana, and then shook his head slowly. "Tell you the truth, Tiana," he mumbled, "I hardly know what I'm saying. We might be better off not going to see my old man. But you heard what the pastor said." He paused for a moment or two, and then added, smiling: "And I want my days to be long on this earth."

"Good to see you smile, OK baby. That settles it then. We must go see him, and take our present to him—"

"And if he says 'Thanks, but no thanks'?"

"At least we would have done what we should do," Tatiana said. "You and me, OK baby, we're no cowards. We don't run from doing what's right just because we suspect your dad might reject our gift. Let's put a bold face on it."

"So what's holding us back?"

"You, OK baby! You and your doubts!"

Tatiana slowly rose from her chair, gripping the arms of the chair for support and leverage. Okocha quickly ran to her and helped her up, holding her firmly—but tenderly—around her torso, and steadying her as she regained her feet.

"You're good to me, OK baby. Don't know what I'd do without you."

Okocha smiled happily, and gave her a peck on her cheek before slowly dropping his arm from around her waist.

"I put you this way," he said, giving her another peck on her cheek, and gently rubbing her protuberant belly. "So I have to take good care of you."

Tatiana smiled. "Bless you. I'm a lucky girl—"

Their eyes met, and Tatiana laughed. "I mean, woman!"

"You always say that, Tiana. But as far as I'm concerned, you're still the lovely girl I met two or so years ago, except you're even more beautiful now."

"Flattery'll get you whatever your heart desires," said Tatiana. "But we need to hurry now. First, your dad; then, mine! We don't have all day!"

"Quite right, Tiana dear. We don't have all day." He paused and looked around him as if in search of something. "Apropos of which, where, in heaven's name, did I put the car key?"

"The car key?" Tatiana asked, and then pointed as, with deliberate steps, she walked up to him, reached into the breast pocket of his Igbo-style jumper, and took out a bunch of three keys. "OK baby, don't make me start worrying about you. You're too young to—"

"Too young for what?" Okocha shot back, with as impassive a face as he could contrive. "Just because I didn't remember I put the keys in my pocket when I stopped to help you button your blouse—"

"The other day, my dear husband, you took a yogurt out of the fridge and—I don't know why—carried it to our bedroom. Then, minutes later, you came out looking for it all over the place."

"That was funny, wasn't it?" Okocha said, but he was not laughing. He was not even smiling. "You know something? You're right, Tiana. Sometimes I don't seem to know what I'm doing. I'm feeling so crushed by my dad's chilliness that I think I sometimes do things like an automaton. And then I suppose I forget what I just did. Tiana, I never thought we'd have to live through a nightmare like we are experiencing right now."

"I know, OK baby. I know. I'm not sure what we have—no! what *I*—have to do to win your dad's approval. But I know there's a God in Heaven. And as sure as I am that we did not—neither of us—commit a crime when we fell in love, I know that your dad will come around sooner or later. I pray, *sooner* than later! This situation must find a way to work itself out. Here're my fingers crossed, for luck!" She raised her right hand to show Okocha her first and middle fingers crossed.

Okocha's smile was radiant. "You have a way, Tiana, of bringing bright light into the murky darkness of my life. But still and all, you have more faith in those delicate fingers of yours than I can summon from the dark depths of my troubled soul. But enough of my cries of woe! Let's go face my dad!"

He led the way to their Honda Accord.

*   *   *

Okocha did what he had not done in a long time: without sounding the door bell, he let himself and Tatiana into his parents' home with his key.

"Shouldn't you—" Tatiana began to ask, eyebrows raised in surprise.

"Shouldn't nothing, Tiana!" he cut her off, pushing the door open. "This is my parent's house."

"But this is America," Tatiana whispered fiercely. "Not Nigeria. And you've never done this in all the time I've known you. It's one thing not to call to say you're coming. I've gotten used to that. But it's quite another thing to unlock the door and enter without—"

"Doesn't matter, girl!" he said, taking her by the hand, and leading her into the house. Then, raising his voice, he asked: "Any one home?"

Still holding Tatiana by the hand, he strode into the living room, and led her to the two-seater, and made her sit down.

"Is nobody home?" Okocha asked again, more loudly. Picking up the TV remote control from a small basket on the oval center table, he switched on the TV.

"Okocha?" His dad's voice asked, from the direction of the master bedroom.

"Dad! Where are—?"

Chief Anigbo walked into the sitting room. He stopped when he saw Okocha and Tatiana, and turned and walked back to his bedroom. Tatiana, holding on to an arm-rest of the love-seat, fractionally rose from the chair, but was gently pushed down back into it by Okocha.

"It's okay, Tiana," he said softly. "He's only gone back to bring out my mom."

Chief Anigbo re-entered the sitting room, alone. "Your mom'll be out in a minute," he told his son. "Meantime, to what do we owe this visit?"

Okocha looked keenly into his dad's eyes, and saw no light in them. In the dozen or so years of what he considered his adulthood, Okocha was never sure he could read his dad's eye-language aright, especially—as now—when the old man deliberately wished to shut him out. Now, as his dad's eyes held his, Okocha saw no warmth, nor outright coldness, in them. It was almost as if they were relative strangers to each other; as if all the years of their intensely loving father-son interactions had been but a figment of his lurid imagination. Those were the years when his dad played ball with him. And not just soccer, one on one but, when they relocated to the United States, even the then strange American game of football. A game, his dad often remarked, in which the foot barely touched the ball. His dad loved to say that Americans never missed an opportunity to turn the English language on its head. "Why else," he would ask, "would they give a game, in which the ball is mostly thrown or carried by the hand, the exact same name as the game the British and other Europeans play with the foot? They should have called it American rugby!"

Those had been the years of his adolescence; years he could never ever recapture and, until he met and fell in love with Tatiana, the very best and happiest years of his life. He had learned, through the many years of loving his dad and mom, and being loved by them, that the affection that bound parent and child was the most pristine and incorrupt human emotion of all. As he reflected on this bindingly pure, elemental affection between parent and child, the thought flashed through his mind that the advantages of growing up to adulthood seemed almost grossly exaggerated. What would he not give, at this juncture of his life, to be able to roll time back to the years of his innocence? Except, of course, that the most adorable girl he had ever met was now in his life!

Tatiana coughed softly and startled Okocha out of his reverie. He immediately sat bolt upright, and then became aware that his mom was standing right in front of him, gazing at him. She had a gentle but diffident smile on her face as she held out one hand to him and the other to Tatiana. Like an automaton, he rose to his feet, gently pulling up Tatiana at the same time. His mom then clasped both of them in an embrace that endured for a long moment. In the meantime, Chief Anigbo, stiffly erect, stood to one side, eyes still focused on his son.

"Sorry, dad, you were asking me—"

"To what we owe your visit," Chief Anigbo said.

"Father's Day," said Okocha, stepping back a little from his mom's embrace. "Tiana and me, we thought we should come—er—just to say—er—a big thank you for being my dad. We—er—brought you a little something."

Okocha was angry with himself because he seemed paralyzed, by his dad's cold detachment, to the point of stuttering over his words. If he had ever sounded so unsure of himself, he could not recall when. He was searching for a way to recover his poise and aplomb, when Kanu and Somto walked into the living room from the entrance door.

"See, coz!" Somto slapped Kanu playfully on the shoulder, "I was right. Told you it was them. But you wouldn't believe me."

"And I know I'll never hear the end of this," Kanu retorted, smiling genially.

"The end of what?" Okocha asked Kanu, enfolding him in a bear hug.

"That he recognized you, when we saw you on the road, and I didn't," Kanu said. "But we're here, aren't we? That's all that matters. But I must say you were going at a fair clip, bro."

"Thank you, Kanu," Tatiana said, as they hugged. "I've told him he sometimes goes a little too fast—"

"Don't be too hard on him, Tatiana," Somto pleaded, in his turn embracing her. "He's a good driver. It's always good to see you."

"Same here," said Tatiana. "But where were you two going?"

"Nothing that can't wait," said Kanu. "Just to see cousin Nonye and our in-law, Nnanna. Some two or three days ago, Nonye invited us for today, and promised us some mouth-watering culinary delights, and that's something I don't ever want to miss—"

"You can say that again, little bro!" Okocha said. "We know you!"

"We'll still go, later," Kanu said, giving Okocha a dour glance. "But you're somewhat late, aren't you, big bro? Somto and I expected you more than an hour ago. When you did not show up, we thought you might—well—you know—"

"Not come?" Okocha asked deprecatingly. "Come on, little bro!"

"It's actually all right, coz," Somto said. "We know married life has its consequences."

"Such as?" Kanu wanted to know, looking from Okocha to Tatiana.

"Time!" Somto replied, smiling. "Can't always be master of your time, as before."

Okocha and Tatiana looked at each other, and laughed.

"Somto's got a point there," Tatiana said. "But don't blame it all on the wife."

Ekemma Anigbo clucked a few times. "So Okocha told you two they were coming, but not me or his dad."

"No surprise there!" Chief Anigbo said so softly it seemed he was only talking to himself.

"Dad," said Kanu, "he didn't need to announce he was coming. Today is Father's Day, and when did he ever fail to come see you on Father's Day?" He turned to Okocha. "You said you'd be going from here to see Tatiana's dad too, no?"

"Of course, little bro," Okocha said, with a nod, and an involuntary and nervous glance at his dad.

"Somto and I know you've come to see dad," Kanu continued. "So we must not be in the way. We've done our bit, in our own little way. Now's your turn. But we'll hang around just a little bit longer. Right, Somto?"

"Right, Kanu. My sis Nonye can wait a little, and I hope she'll still fulfill her promise. My only worry is that we didn't call her to be sure she's in a condition to receive us. But you said not to worry, that Nonye's word is her bond, and all that jazz!"

"That's for sure," said Kanu. "But these days, it isn't every day that I get a chance to be with Okocha and—" He caught his dad's eye, and the words dried up in his throat. He waved his arms vaguely, and then said to Okocha, pointing: "What's that you have there?"

"None of your beeswax, little bro!" Okocha said, smiling, clutching a sturdy plastic bag which he had just retrieved from behind the love-seat. He then took a smaller plastic bag out of it. Taking Tatiana by the hand, he pulled her up and closer to himself. Together they held the bag out to Chief Anigbo.

"Dad, this is from Tiana and me," he said, "with our love and eternal gratitude. This was what I was trying to say when Kanu and Somto came back."

Time stood still. It seemed, to Tatiana and Okocha, like an eternity. Their eyes were nervously riveted on his dad's face, as Chief Anigbo silently gazed at the parcel they held out to him. A smile all too briefly flickered at the corners of his mouth; his mouth worked, but no words came. Then with a shrug of his shoulders, Chief Anigbo reached for, and took the parcel from Okocha and Tatiana. He stared at it for a moment or two, and gently shook his head from side to side.

"Thank you both," he said softly. "Can I ask what it is?"

"Dad!" Okocha's eyes were askant as they regarded his dad.

"Sorry, son. I know I shouldn't have asked. Again, thank you both."

He turned and, carrying the gift parcel in both hands, was walking away, when he was brought up short by Tatiana.

"But dad!" she called out to him, smiling sweetly. "Don't you want to see what it is?"

Chief Anigbo laughed, but without his usual ringing, joyful sound. "I'm not in the habit of opening a gift in the presence of the giver."

"That's okay, Tiana," Okocha quickly interposed. "You know how it is with some of us. We often prefer to open gifts when the giver is not there."

"Right," said Chief Anigbo, with a firm nod of the head. But then he stopped suddenly and turned back. "But maybe I can make an exception this time. Perhaps there is no harm unwrapping the gift here and now." He gestured toward Tatiana. "For her!"

He did not add: *Because she's not one of us!* But he did not need to verbalize that thought because Okocha, though distinctly uneager to read too much into his dad's gestures, and the way his eyes shifted from Tatiana to himself, thought he understood perfectly. As Chief Anigbo placed the parcel on the center table in the living room and proceded slowly to unwrap it, he had his eyes steadily on Tatiana.

"Dad," Kanu said, "can I help you? You might find it—"

"Difficult, little bro?" Okocha asked. "Leave dad alone. He's doing okay, I'd say."

"Well! Well!" Chief Anigbo said slowly. "What do we have here?"

He took out a traditional chief's red cap, which he immediately put on his head, and a long Igbo jumper, embroidered with the patterned motif of an elephant's head, which he held up for all to see.

"Where—when—did you—?" he began to ask, turning to Okocha.

"From home," Okocha answered before his dad had completed the question. "And unless you have added some avoirdupois while I was not looking, you'll find it fits you to a tee. We ordered it from your usual tailor, through the good offices of a friend who went to Nigeria on a brief visit for Easter."

"Mike—?" his mom Ekemma asked.

"Egbuna, yes." Okocha laughed shortly. "Mike added the red cap though I didn't ask him to. And then he made me pay for it. But that's all right. Tiana and I hope dad likes the ensemble."

"What's not to like?" Chief Anigbo asked in a solemn voice. "But, you know, you shouldn't have gone to all the expense and trouble—"

"Because you have many such jumpers, dad? At least that's one item you can't have too many of. We're glad you like it."

"Thanks," Chief Anigbo said.

"Bless you, my children," mom Ekemma added. "I can see straightaway your dad'll look great in them, as always!"

"Just like Okocha himself, I'd say," said Tatiana, linking arms joyously with her husband and nestling closer to him.

Ekemma gestured toward the love-seat, in front of which Okocha and Tatiana stood. "You shouldn't be standing for so long, Tatiana," she said, and then asked, staring intently at Tatiana's belly: "How long more before the baby comes?"

"About two months, give or take," Tatiana replied. "I wish it'd come sooner!"

"Two months!" Chief Anigbo muttered, eyebrows raised in surprise.

Something in his dad's tone and inflection of voice caught Okocha's attention. He stared at his dad for a moment or two, and then shifted his gaze to his mom. But before he could say a word, his mom asked, waving an arm dismissively: "What do men know about such matters? Okocha, please don't mind your dad. Some men can't count; that's all."

The sudden ringing of the house telephone came as something of a relief to Okocha. Chief Anigbo immediately headed for his bedroom, closely followed by Ekemma. "I'll take this in the bedroom," he announced unnecessarily.

In the lull that followed, Okocha made Tatiana sit down with him on the love-seat. "You know," he said to her, as he cuddled her, "mom's right. You should take the weight off your feet as often as you have the chance."

"It's all right actually," Tatiana said, allowing herself to nestle really close to him. Then she added, chuckling: "Can't sit all the time! Or do you want the baby to grow up a lazy child!"

"Who told you that?" Kanu asked, laughing.

"Maybe that's what they believe, here in America," Somto suggested.

Kanu gestured angrily in the direction of his parents' bedroom. "Did you hear what dad said?" he asked Okocha and Tatiana. "Or, more to the point, how he said it? Can you believe the man? Anyway, nothing he says these days to you guys should come as a surprise to any of us."

He stopped, and beckoned to Somto. "Come, coz. Let's go! Nnanna and cousin Nonye are waiting for us."

Tatiana watched the two cousins as they walked out of the sitting room, and then pointed to the door through which they had exited: "What was that all about?" she asked Okocha. "What did your brother mean—?"

"Oh, that!" Okocha said with a dismissive wave of his hand. "Kanu obviously saw that dad seemed shocked you have only two months to go, which means, my dear wife, that—"

Tatiana raised an arm to stop Okocha. "I get it," she said. "I finally got it. Is it not this whole business about the conception preceding the church wedding?"

"It appears that any time he's reminded about your pregnancy coming before our wedding, we have to go through this drama. I suggest we'd better get used to the likelihood that this will repeat itself many times before the baby is born."

Tatiana shook her head gravely several times. "OK baby," she whispered in his ear, with a quick nervous glance in the direction of the master bedroom from which she feared Okocha's parents might re-emerge at any moment. "I think I'm missing out on something. You and me, we've talked about this matter over and over again in the early days. You made me understand—how shall I put it—that our marriage, as husband and wife, practically dated from when my family—I should really say, my dad—gave his consent to us after your group did the knocking on my parents' door, no?"

Her eyes searched his, earnestly. "Did I misunderstand something about your Igbo marriage tradition? My dad even went as far as actually accepting the token—er—bride-price, I believe you call it, from you—"

"Because, bless him," said Okocha, "he was determined to pay full respect to our Igbo customs in these matters, and especially because my own dad decided he would play no role in any of it. And, of course, my dad's role is just about the most important ingredient in the protocols of the thing."

"And, let's not forget," added Tatiana, "also because with a name like ours—*Karefa*—we might truly be descended from an *Okoroafor*."

"Your dad," said Okocha, cuddling her even more closely to himself, "is a dad in a million! That's for sure. How many American dads would do what he did?"

"So, OK baby, where does that leave us in the eyes of your dad? And perhaps also your mom? I suspect it's something to do with their Christian religion, no? If this scenario will repeat itself, as you suggest, I pray God gives me—us—the patience to endure it."

"What are you two whispering to yourselves about?" Ekemma Anigbo asked, as she re-entered the sitting room. She was alone.

"Nothing, mom," Okocha said hastily. "Only that it's time we left. We still have to go see Tiana's dad."

"Oh, of course, you must go. Well, I hope we'll see you two again soon. Tatiana, please tell your dad and mom we said hello to them."

"Sure thing, mom," Tatiana said, smiling radiantly. "We should say good-bye to dad before—"

"Of course, but he's still on the phone," Ekemma said. "It's something very important. Do you mind waiting just a little bit more? Maybe I should go tell him you want to leave now."

Chief Anigbo burst into the room. "That was Nnanna—"

"Oh, my God!" Okocha exclaimed. "Hope everything's all right with Nonye—"

"Nonye just had her baby!" Chief Anigbo announced. "And it's a boy!"

Ekemma ran to her husband, and hugged him so fiercely she knocked the breath out of him. "I didn't want to tell them before you came back. It's just so wonderful! God is good!"

"Easy, woman!" he gasped, struggling to ease her tight hold. "You might break a bone."

He relaxed her hold with some effort. "That's better. Mma," he called out to her, using his abbreviated and fond name for her, "I didn't know you were this strong. My! I've got to watch out, or you might inflict other surprises on me. Anyway, this is the best news of the year!"

"Dad," said Okocha, "I hope mother and baby are doing well. Me and Tiana, we've got to go to the hospital immediately, and see what we can do for them."

"Didn't Kanu say you were going from here to see Tatiana's dad?" Ekemma asked. "I think you should do that first. Today's father's day. Then you certainly should go and see your cousin and her wonderful new baby boy."

"Kanu and Somto!" Okocha cried out. "They're on their way to Nonye's house, in expectation of—"

"Doesn't matter," Ekemma said. "Those two kids can take care of themselves."

* * *

Tatiana and Okocha were very warmly received by Edna and Philip Karefa. Okocha hated to do so, but he could not help contrasting the effusiveness of their welcome at the Karefa home with the near-frigidity and chilling formality of, especially, his dad's welcome. His mother, poor woman, seemed, as often as not, to be caught in a bind, and unsure how much enthusiasm to show. Mostly she contented herself by keeping her eyes on her husband, as if she needed to tread carefully and to take her cue from his mood and disposition.

"I'm mighty glad you didn't forget me on father's day," Philip Karefa clasped Tatiana in a bear hug, even as he pumped Okocha's hand excitedly. "Come in and relax, and have a cold drink or something. It's a hot day, ain't it?"

"We could certainly use a cold drink," Tatiana said.

"Not for me!" said Okocha. "No, sir! It may be sweltering out there but, if anything, I need a cup of hot chocolate or ovaltine, to warm my spirits up."

Tatiana, surprised, turned her gaze on him. "What's up, OK baby?" she asked solicituously as they linked arms and followed Philip Karefa into the living room. "Are you sure—?"

"Let him be, Tiana!" her dad said. "If O'kcha wants a cup of ovaltine, or whatever, that's what he'll get. Edna!" he raised his voice to call out. "Tiana and her hubby are here!"

Edna was all smiles as she emerged from the bedroom and, the moment she saw Okocha and Tatiana, literally ran into the latter's arms.

"It's always so-o-o good to see you-all" she enthused. "And I can see you're looking great and glowing. Hope everything is hunky-dory with the pregnancy. Won't be long now!"

"If you say so, mom." Tatiana's voice was a little uncertain. "But two months seems a trifle long to me. I'm doing okay, anyway. And Okocha's been simply super."

"I do my best," said Okocha modestly. "I know it ain't easy."

Tatiana laughed. "How'd you know? But I thank God for you, OK baby. Every day!"

Okocha and mom Edna hugged each other and held on for a long moment.

"I hope you brought dad a good father's day gift," Edna said, smiling roguishly at her husband. "Something at least as good as what you gave me on Mother's Day. He's so jealous, and has never let me—"

"Woman! Watch your language!" Philip's harsh voice and tone were somewhat negated by the genial smile that curled up a corner of his mouth. "Why do you have to bring that up, now? Let them settle down, for Chrissakes, before you start questioning them about gifts or no gifts!"

"Dad'll love what we brought him," Tatiana gushed. "Here!"

She took a flattish oblong-shaped package out of her capacious shoulder bag and handed it to her dad.

"From us to you, dad, with love," she said softly.

"And gratitude for your unwavering support through thick and thin," Okocha added. "You have been a tower of strength for Tiana and me, and we appreciate you, and mom Edna, more than you know, or we can adequately express in words or gifts."

Philip held the paper package at arm's length for a moment or two, staring at it. He turned it over and over in his hands, and finally tore it open. Carefully, he reached inside and took out a broad, round, tasseled leather fan. The fan had a handle about four or so inches long. His eyes lit up, and his face broke in the widest smile anyone ever saw on his face. He held the fan up, waved it gently from side to side, as if fanning himself, and watched the tassels flap and dance in the air.

"This is a gift to beat all gifts," he said, clutching it to his chest for a moment or two, and looking at his wife with a triumphant expression.

"We knew you'd—" Okocha started to say.

"Just the question I was going to ask you!" Philip interrupted. "However did you know? What gave you the idea for this gift?"

"You, dad!" Tatiana said, and challenged him with her eyes.

"Me, girl? When or where did I ever so much as hint to you that I'd like something like this?"

"Tiana's right, dad," said Okocha with a smile. "At our wedding, you may remember—"

"Holy mackerel! That's it! You must have overheard me raving about just such a fan that—what's his name—the chairman—"

"Mr. Odogwu," Okocha said.

"Whatever! I remember he had such a fan. And I must say this one you just gave me is every bit as easy on the eye as that one." He paused, and held the fan at arm's length, and gazed on it for a brief moment. "What can I say? God bless you! You are the best children I could ever have asked for!"

"I'm glad you think so, dad" Tatiana said with the broadest of smiles. "So I don't expect you'll be mad at us if we cut our visit a little short today, because we have a most delightful obligation to fulfill in the next several minutes—"

"What's she talking about?" her dad asked, turning to Okocha.

"It's my cousin, actually," said Okocha. "I don't believe you'll remember her, although you've both met her. Nonye's her name. She's just been delivered of a baby boy, and we're so thrilled for her."

"I'm not sure I remember her, but I'm already excited for her," Edna said. "So what's keeping you here?"

"You don't have to worry about me," Philip said. "You just brought me a great father's day gift. So, off with you two! Go see your cousin."

CHAPTER 18

Tatiana and Okocha arrived at the maternity ward of the Memorial Hospital in downtown Elizabeth, NJ, to find the other members of the Anigbo clan, including Kanu and Somto, already assembled there.

"When I last saw you two," Okocha said, with a roguish smile, "you were heading for Nnanna and Nonye's home for—I believe you said—dinner. What happened?"

"This is much better than the best dinner," Somto quickly replied. He had eyes only for his sister Nonye, happily relaxed on her well-padded bed, and drifting in and out of sleep, and for his nephew—his first nephew—a cherubic, bouncing seven-pounder, bright-eyed, and in perpetual motion with his arms and any other body parts he could move freely.

"We got to Nonye's place," Kanu added, "only to find the doors shut and locked. Then a kindly neighbor—a woman—saw us and told us what happened. She said an ambulance had come and taken Nonye and Nnanna away. The woman said she knew it must be to a hospital because of Nonye's condition. That's how she put it: Nonye's condition. Of course we wasted no time but came straight here. It's a good thing Somto remembered exactly where the maternity was."

"If you're expecting your first nephew," Somto said, chest swelling with pride and happiness, "you've got to know about things. I'm an uncle now, and it feels mighty good, I can tell you. You're looking at the one and only uncle of the new baby!"

"Wrong, coz," said Kanu. "I'm also the baby's uncle."

"You?" Somto asked sneeringly. "You're only a cousin. Not the same thing, however much you wish it to be so."

Kanu was assertive, in voice and manner. "Just wait, and we'll see, as the boy grows, if he'll call me anything but uncle."

"Oh, that!" Somto said disparagingly, "I've no doubt he'll call you uncle, if only because of the age difference. But you'd better get used to the fact and reality that I'm the one, of us two, who's the *real* uncle. You're a *mere* cousin. Go look it up in any good dictionary, and then you may come back to me, and acknowledge that—"

"I'll acknowledge nothing, coz," Kanu said. "I'm an uncle to the baby, and that's all she wrote!"

Somto laughed, and said: "Why don't we ask Uncle Nat who's the boy's uncle and who's his cousin." He turned to Chief Anigbo. "Uncle Nat, please tell Kanu—and no offence meant—that he's not an uncle to the baby."

Chief Anigbo looked from his son to his nephew, and smiled and shook his head. "I have two infinitely more important questions to ask," he said, and turned to Nonye. "Nonye, my first question is: has anyone named this baby? Boy or girl, you must have chosen the baby's names in advance."

"The names," Nnanna said, "are Udechukwu and Nnanna. We hope you like them."

Chief Anigbo's smile split his face from ear to ear. "Udechukwu is my middle name, and I'm flattered. But please allow me to suggest that henceforth—and you all better pay attention to this—he should be called Nnanna Junior—"

"But Uncle—"

"Nnanna, you are his dad," Chief Anigbo said, in a voice that brooked little or no argument. "Your name must take precedence."

"If you say so, Uncle—"

"I do, Nnanna." He paused, looking from Nnanna Junior to his mother. "Now for my second question. Nonye, can I—am I allowed to pick up Nnanna Junior? Is it safe to do so—I mean, safe for the fragile newborn? I wouldn't want him to catch something from me. What do you say, Nonye? Can I carry him for a moment or two?"

The 'moment or two' turned out to be as close to a half-hour as made no difference. Chief Anigbo, from the moment Nonye nodded her approval, carried the baby and paced up and down the room, muttering happily to himself and—it seemed—to the baby also, his face aglow with delight and deep contentment. He would not let go of the baby, not even to his wife, Ekemma, when she asked if she could carry him for a little while.

"When I asked Nonye," he explained to her, with a smile, "it was for me only, not for you and me. You want to carry Nnanna Junior, ask his mom, not me!"

Ekemma Anigbo hissed, tightly shut her eyes at him and then, contemptuously, turned her head away from him, in the well-known Igbo woman's gesture that said: "I don't care!" She sat quietly by Nonye's bed, holding and gently tapping on the new mother's hand to a rhythm that was in her own head.

Nnanna, with studied nonchalance, looked on from the other side of the bed, opposite his auntie Ekemma, dispensing happy smiles all around, but especially to Nonye whenever she turned her head to look at him. One look at him, and Okocha could tell that his buddy and cousin-in-law, Nnanna, was straining nerve and sinew to play the role of a cool first-time dad.

"Who're you kidding, man?" he asked Nnanna softly, siddling up to him. "I can see you're as excited as hell."

"And so he should be," Nonye said gently. "He's come through with flying colors. He was very brave to insist on being present during the delivery. I must confess I didn't think he could—"

"Could what?" Nnanna interrupted her. As he spoke, he mopped her forehead and cheeks with a handkerchief. "I couldn't have been anywhere else in the world. There's absolutely nothing to it. Those husbands who're scared of the experience need a psychiatrist's help."

"Nnanna, my husband," Nonye called out to him, partially raising herself from her recumbent position. "You can't go on mopping my brow for ever. You haven't eaten a morsel of anything since we got here. They'll soon bring me something. Why don't you go to the cafeteria and find something to eat? You don't have to worry about me."

"Nor you, me," Nnanna said softly. "Right now, this is where I should be, where I want to be."

"Yes and no!" Chief Anigbo paused long enough, in his pacing of the room, to interject. "You're right you should be here at this moment. But you're not a permanent fixture here. You'd better listen to your wife. If she says you need to take a break, she must know what she's saying."

"Dad's right, man," Okocha said, his eyes wistful as he briefly peeked at his dad. "Let's go have a little something. You deserve a beer or something to recharge. Come on, man! Just you and me, maybe. And you can tell me how it all went during the delivery. Or would you like Tiana to come with us?"

"Not me," said Tatiana. "Oh, no! I don't feel like anything right now. Maybe Kanu and Somto might want to go with you. They just struck out on a dinner appointment with Nonye, to which they had been avidly looking forward. You all go right ahead. Let it be an all-men rendezvous in the cafeteria."

"Thank you, Tiana," said Kanu, all smiles, "for remembering something I'm sure Okocha completely forgot when he was inviting only Nnanna."

"Kanu!" Nnanna called out. "And Somto! I'm really sorry about disappointing you two when you thought you were coming for dinner—"

"Forget about it, Nnanna," Kanu said, with a dismissive wave of his hands. "Nonye giving birth to my nephew—"

"Cousin!"

"That's okay, coz," Kanu said graciously. "Whatever you call him! Point is, Nnanna, you and Nonye already apologized to us when we first reached here, and it was a situation you could not control. As I was about to say when Somto rudely interrupted me, the birth of—er—your son—er—Nnanna Jr., surpasses everything else. I'm sure even Somto would agree with that—eh coz?"

Before Somto could get a word out, Okocha gestured to Nnanna. "Are you coming, or what?" He turned to Kanu. "Sorry, little bro. To tell you the truth, I forgot about your dinner invitation to Nnanna's. But that's all past. Who's coming with me to the cafeteria?" He led the way out of the room.

"Come on, Somto," Kanu said, "what d'you say we troop along with them?"

"Do you need to ask?" Somto said, even as he began to inch towards the door.

Nnanna, casting a forlorn look at his wife, reluctantly got up and trudged after the threesome. "I'll be back in a jiffy," he muttered, over his shoulder, to Nonye who, eyes half-closed, waved him out of the room.

Chief Anigbo watched, in silence, as the young men trooped out of the room. Then suddenly he slapped his thigh, and turned to Nonye.

"There's something I forgot to tell you," he said. "Something you'd be thrilled to hear, because you've been worrying about it for some time now. I spoke with your mom yesterday, as I promised you I'd do. You'll be happy to know that she has successfully renewed her U.S. visa. The exact date of her travel has not been fixed, but it would surprise me if she's not here in another two or three weeks; a month, at the outside. I still remember what she said at your wedding—she pleaded with God to let her return to America within nine or so months to do her first *omugwo*. With the birth of Nnanna Junior, her first grandchild, you have now given her the opportunity to satisfy her passionate desire to be here to help you take care of him."

"Praise the Lord!" Nonye mouthed softly. "Nnanna will be especially happy about this."

"And you wouldn't, Nonye?" Ekemma asked, "Are you saying that you'd have been able to manage without your mom's help?"

"God forbid that such a thought will enter my head!" Nonye said, laughing. "If mom doesn't arrive soon, I'll want to know why!"

"Depends, doesn't it, on how soon is soon enough," Chief Anigbo said.

*　　*　　*

Okocha stared long and hard into his cup of steaming hot chocolate. Nnanna watched him anxiously for a moment or two, and then reached for and took Okocha's hand in his. They were seated at a table for four, in a cafeteria that was only about a third full.

"You know something, Okocha?" Nnanna's voice was solicitous. "You can't go on like this for ever. I know it's about your dad and mom, no?"

Okocha raised his eyes to his friend's, and shook his head sadly several times. "My mom?" he said softly. "Not really. She's caught between her love for her son, and her devotion and sense of loyalty to her husband. No, Nnanna, man. It's not my dad and mom. It's my dad!"

"You can say that again!" interjected Kanu. "I'm glad it's just the four of us here, and very few diners around. So, we can talk freely. And I say, it's not fair—not at all—what dad is doing to all of us—"

"*All* of us?" Nnanna asked. He took several little sips of his beer, and put his glass down. "You all know my case is very different from Okocha's. The difference, you might say, is like night and day."

"Couldn't have put it more graphically myself," said Okocha. "You could say that the day is yours, and the night, mine."

"That's what it looks like, right now." Nnanna's voice was gentle, and his tone pleading. "But your dad will come round some day, I promise you."

"I truly and earnestly hope so," Okocha said. "As I watched him carrying your son and pacing up and down, I said to myself that if it was my son right now, he'd probably not even go as far as picking him up. Never mind about pacing the room carrying him!"

Kanu suddenly got up, pushing his plate of potato chips and his glass of orange juice as far away from him as the table allowed him. He beckoned to Somto: "Come, coz. I want a word or two with you."

Nnanna and Okocha watched the two younger men withdraw out of earshot from them. They watched as the two engaged in what seemed from one moment to the next to be an impassioned disputation. Kanu finally nodded his head emphatically a few times, and then led their way back to Nnanna and Okocha.

"What was that all about, little bro?" Okocha enquired softly. "You were acting rather strange. What's going on, Somto? You can tell us, if Kanu doesn't want to."

"What can I say?" Somto spread his arms wide in a gesture of helplessness. "This is Kanu's—"

"Damn right it's my thing!" Kanu fairly exploded. "I've had it right up to here!" He raised his right hand up to the level of his mouth. "I don't care anymore. Okocha, you're my big bro, and I love you, and will do anything for you. But not even you can stop me now. Somto tried to stop me, but it is all too late."

Okocha put out a hand and placed it on Kanu's shoulder. "What seems to be the matter? I'm not sure I'm going to like this, whatever it is. But out with it, little bro!"

Kanu, eyes as wild as Okocha had ever seen them, brought his hands together and intertwined his fingers, resting his elbows on the table. He looked down briefly, then raised his eyes and looked first at Nnanna, then at Okocha. His mouth worked for a moment or two, but no words came.

"It's okay, Kanu," Nnanna said encouragingly. "Whatever it is, get it out of your system, and you'll feel better, I promise you."

In a slow deliberate voice, his eyes staring fixedly into his brother, Okocha's, Kanu dropped his bombshell. "My girlfriend is an *akata* girl! There! I've said it, and there's nothing anyone can do about it."

He looked at his three companions in turn. "Did anyone hear what I just said? Not you, cousin Somto. You've known about her for some time. I'm asking Okocha and Nnanna. My girlfriend is not Igbo. She's not Nigerian. She's not even African. She's as American as the apple-pie"

Okocha looked at Nnanna, and Nnanna looked at Okocha. Okocha was the first to recover from the shock of Kanu's announcement. "Do you plan to tell dad anytime soon about this? I ask because I believe you're really quite serious—"

"How serious can it be, really, when you think about it?" Nnanna asked. "Kanu's just eighteen, going on nineteen."

Somto shook his head slowly. "Eighteen or nineteen," he said, "what difference does it make? I know the girl; have known her for about one year. Take it from me, this is not a passing phase. Kanu has been going through hell over this matter, and the two of them agreed to keep their story—you know—not to tell anyone about it for as long as necessary, until the moment is right. That's what we were arguing about just now, the two of us. I do not believe this is the right moment for him to tell the family about her. Okocha, you understand Kanu absolutely had to tell her about you and Tatiana, and how uncle has steadfastly refused to accept the—er—situation."

"I understand," Okocha said, shaking his head sadly, a dejected look on his face. "I understand perfectly. But if he tells dad and mom about her, I don't know what dad'll do."

Kanu's bearing was defiant. "So what are you saying? That I don't tell dad—"

"Damn right, Kanu" Okocha said emphatically. "It'll kill him. So I'm asking you to hold off for the moment. Somto's right. Give our old man a little more time, and let's see how things develop."

"How much time do you have in mind, bro? One year? Two years? I hope you're not thinking that in the meantime me and Jonetta—"

"That's her name?" Okocha asked. "Jonetta?"

"Jonetta Smith, yes. You're not hoping me and her might break up, or something like that, are you, big bro? Because if you are—"

Okocha laughed out loud. "No, little bro. I'm not hoping for anything like that. But nothing's impossible. You're what, only eighteen—"

"Going on nineteen, as Nnanna just said" Kanu interrupted, a long-suffering smile curling up his lips. "You and Nnanna keep referring to my age, but what's that got to do with anything? I'll be in college, come September. That's just in two months or so."

"So?" Somto asked disparagingly.

"So, plenty, coz. I'm now an adult, and soon I'll be a college student. I have to start to think for myself and to act as a responsible grown-up."

"So wait until you're in college, and we'll see," Somto suggested, his tone pleading. "Give yourself a little time, coz. You must be stark raving mad to even think of breaking this kind of news to your dad right now. You've seen how it is for Okocha and Tatiana, and you know it's not going to be any different for you."

"It might be significantly worse for you," Nnanna interjected, pointing emphatically at Kanu. "Uncle might take it you're—you know—deliberately trying to provoke him."

"That's not my intention," Kanu stubbornly said, "and you all know that to be true. But what am I supposed to do? Fall out of love with Jonetta, so dad will let me be? I warned them about this. We simply cannot control whom we fall in love with. We cannot live in America, and continue to think that our African ways of doing things are the only right ways to do them. This is America, for Christ's sake! If dad didn't want to expose us to what goes on in other parts of the world, he shouldn't have brought us here. Sorry, folks! Now it's all too, too late."

Okocha rose from his chair, and went and sat next to Kanu. He put an arm around Kanu's shoulders, and drew him closer.

"Easy, little bro! Easy! So what are you saying?"

"I'm saying that I'll live my life the way my fate and destiny have preordained for me, and not for the cultural satisfaction of even my dad."

For a long moment, no one spoke. Okocha lowered his head, and stared at the top of the table. When next he looked up, his face wore an expression of acute agony.

"What's the matter, Okocha?" Nnanna asked solicitously.

"Do you need to ask, man?" Okocha said. "You'd say, wouldn't you, that dad's singularly unlucky, being who and what he is, to have two sons like Kanu and me, coming one after the other, and neither of us would tailor his life to fit in with the old man's world view. But what to do? What can Kanu do—mine is already too late—what can he do to make it easier for dad?"

Somto leaned towards Kanu, and engaged him with his eyes. "Kanu, have you thought this thing through—as thoroughly as you should?"

"I have, coz. Indeed I have thought of little else than about Jonetta and me, and where we're headed with our love, and how unfortunate—not for me, mark you, but for dad and maybe mom too—that we are in this—er—situation. You'd be surprised how far I've gone thinking and agonizing over this matter."

He paused for a moment, as he looked from Okocha, to Nnanna, to Somto. As their eyes met, Somto very gently—almost imperceptibly—shook his head.

"Kanu, please—"

"Too late, coz!" Kanu's voice was emphatic. "I started this conversation, and I aim to finish it."

He turned to Okocha, who now sat very quietly by his side. "Big bro, I might as well let you in on my plans. And you too, Nnanna. We're family."

He cleared his throat in a slow deliberate manner, as if conscious of the momentousness of what he was about to say. He even let his face crease in a faint smile.

"In about two months," he began, "I'll be a college student. I cannot help how I feel about Jonetta. And I'm not so naïve as to think for even one moment that dad will not react negatively when I tell him about her. But this is America—the United States of America! God's own country! I *will* go to college, even if dad disowns me—"

Okocha raised an arm to stop him. "Why do you think he'll do anything of the sort?"

"Because, big bro," Kanu replied smoothly, gently, "he couldn't do anything like that to you. It was already too late in your case. But in mine, I'll just have to be prepared for the worst. And this is where this country is the best of all possible worlds. If the worst comes to the worst, I'll take a job, and quite possibly a loan, and I'll see myself through college. I've made enquiries, and already have a job offer or two which I mean to follow up at the first sign of trouble with dad. I'll say this, however. If things turn out differently, then I'll certainly adjust accordingly. But I aim to be prepared for any eventuality. I mean to live my life the way—how do our Igbo people put it—the way my *chi*—yes, that's the word—the way my *chi* has preordained my life. I've heard dad and mom often say that everyone has this divine thing called *chi*, which is some kind of a guiding or guardian spirit that ordains the paths our lives must take."

Okocha rose from his chair, and took two or three steps back and away from the table.

"Kanu," he said, "would you mind getting up and coming towards me?"

"Why, big bro? Whatever for?"

"Just do as I'm asking you, little bro. Don't forget that's exactly what you are: my little brother. And little brothers are supposed to do what their big brothers ask them to do. Come on, Kanu!"

With wonderment in his eyes, Kanu slowly got up from his chair, and turned and took one step towards Okocha.

"That's enough, Kanu. I don't want you any nearer. I only wanted to take a good slow look at my little bro whom I can only just barely recognize."

Okocha placed both his hands on Kanu's shoulders, and slowly and deliberately looked him up and down. Then, with his brows furrowed, Okocha shook his head.

"What happened to you, little bro? I ask because the person standing in front of me appears to be the same Kanu I've always known and loved. But the Kanu who was talking moments ago sounds like someone else."

Nnanna burst out laughing. "Okocha, man! You don't have to be so dramatic about this. But you're right on one point. Kanu is talking kind of strangely. But it's not altogether surprising, is it? He's always had some—how to put it—some fire in the belly."

"I know what you mean, man," Okocha said, guiding Kanu back to his chair. "Please sit down. I don't need to tell you, little bro, how much I've appreciated you and the way you always stick up for me and Tiana. But I never thought things would get this far with you. It is one thing for you to feel as you do about dad and the way things are going between him and me. But it's quite another matter to suddenly find out that—in a manner of speaking—that same history is—sort of—just about to repeat itself."

He paused for a moment, with all eyes focused on him. "In some way, little bro," he continued, "I feel partly responsible for—"

"For my being in love with an *Akata* girl?" Kanu asked, with a quick burst of laughter. "How can you say that? How can you even think it? I'm a grown man—"

"I know, Kanu. You'll soon be a college student, as you say. And soon, who knows, I'll have to stop calling you little bro—"

"Not on your life, big bro! That's what I am to you—*little bro*. And it stays that way till—you know—the end of time, I suppose. The day you stop calling me little bro will be the darkest day of my life."

Okocha scanned his brother's face, a slow smile gradually lighting up his face. "You're quite serious about this, aren't you? Who'd have thunk it? But, as I was saying—"

"We all heard what you said, big bro. And you're dead wrong. Me and Jonetta had nothing to do with you and Tatiana. End of story!"

"I—kind of—agree with him," Somto said hesitantly, turning to Okocha. "Of course I wasn't here at the beginning of their story, but nothing I know about the two of them suggests to me that cousin Kanu was in any way, shape or form merely following your example. Still I wish he'd hold off from telling uncle about it for as long as it might take for uncle to come to terms with your marriage to Tatiana. Like Nnanna, I too am certain uncle will, one day, do a one-hundred-and-eighty degree turn around. You'll see."

"Good for you, Somto," Nnanna said. "You're quite an astute brother-in-law. So, go on. Tell these two brothers what you think. Maybe, just maybe, they'll listen to you. And Okocha will stop torturing himself. And perhaps Kanu will keep his story with Jonetta under wraps until this thing between uncle Nat and Okocha blows over."

Somto raised an arm to get the attention of his companions. "I'd like to suggest that we extract a promise—and I mean a *solemn* promise—from Kanu, that he will not breathe a word about Jonetta, especially to uncle and auntie, for—let me see—at least one year—"

"One year!" Kanu burst out, looking at Somto with wild eyes. "One year?"

"Easy, lad!" Nnanna said soothingly. "No one says you should not continue to see her. But discretion is called for, here. If, in the meantime, uncle Nat should find out about it, let it not be from any one of us, or because you recklessly flaunted it before him. We all sympathize with your situation because, like you've repeatedly said, you really cannot control whom you fall in love with. But at the same time, we should—if at all possible—think of our fathers and mothers, who may not find it easy to see the world as we younger ones do."

"So what do you say, little bro?" Okocha asked, looking at Kanu with a kindly light in his eyes. "Will you humor us in this matter? Please think about it for a moment or two before you answer."

Kanu slowly looked at his three companions in turn. He knew he was cornered, and that none of his interlocutors was going to offer him even the littlest avenue of escape. In the end, he shrugged his shoulders.

"I'll do my best," he muttered, "to shut my mouth, so help me God!"

Okocha threw his arms around Kanu, and pressed him close. "Thank you! Thank you! You're the best little bro anyone could have wished for."

CHAPTER 19

For her husband's fifty-sixth birthday, Ekemma invited a handful of their compatriots to dinner. She boasted to her closest friend, Ifunanya Odogwu, that she knew the favorite dish of everyone of her guests.

"I'm looking forward to tomorrow," she told Ifunanya, as they tucked into their chicken nuggets and fries at a MacDonald restaurant. "It always feels good to have friends like you around now and again—especially at a time like this, when my husband and I are going through a rough passage, on account of Okocha and his *Akata* wife."

"*Lolo*, I'm really sad about the whole thing," Ifunanya said, placing a hand on her friend's arm, and then patting it a few times. "I wish there was some way Chikezie and I can persuade—"

"Persuade us to accept the marriage?" Ekemma's eyes were reflective, as they stared at nothing in particular. "I have asked myself again and again why I cannot seem to be able to see this thing as so many others see it. And I don't know the answer, except that my husband is so dead set against it that I don't know what to think any more."

She paused, and regarded her friend for a long moment. "But enough of my tales of woe! Let's talk about happier things. Like, when you and Chikezie come tomorrow evening, come hungry! I'll not disappoint you, I promise."

"I know you won't," Ifunanya responded, smiling. "When did you ever disappoint? Don't worry about us. I'll make sure Chikezie does not eat a heavy lunch."

"You mean you'll—you know—?" Ekemma asked, laughing conspiratorially.

"Of course, Ekemma! He'll get what he doesn't care for, for lunch—peas and broccoli—those kinds of things—with boiled potato and stew."

"And if he doesn't—?"

"He will," Ifunanya assured her friend. "That's one of the reasons I love the man. He dutifully eats everything I put on our dining table; some of course with less enthusiasm and more sparingly than others—but almost always without complaining. Unless of course you serve him that kind of meal two or three times in a row. No! I wouldn't worry too much, Ekemma. Chikezie is one guest who'll come, really hungry, and ready for your—"

"Okro and bitter-leaf soup, one of his favorites?" Ekemma leaned nearer Ifunanya, and lowered her voice. "Do you know that those two brothers, Chuma and Chijioke Okwu, though their resemblance is plain for all to see, are nevertheless very different in their tastes. Chuma, our hardworking Vice-President, is one of those Igbo men who must have *swallow-swallow*, as we say, at least once a day, or they go around complaining that their wives are starving them. Like your husband, *Afulu-kwe*, Chuma doesn't like peas and carrots and such-like."

"And Chijioke?"

"As for that one," Ekemma said, laughing, "don't you know why they call him an *oyibo*-man? He's like the white man when it comes to food. The same peas and cabbage his brother hates, are like delicacies for him."

"Which just goes to show, Ekemma, that—as we say—the two of them may come from the same mother, but it is not the same *chi* that created them!"

*   *   *

A little over twenty-four hours later, Ifunanya Odogwu remembered every word of that conversation with Ekemma Anigbo, when her eyes lighted on the dishes that were arrayed on the dining-table. The dishes were covered, but Ekemma lifted the covers to give Ifunanya and her husband, Chikezie, a peek, seeing that they had arrived for the dinner much earlier than the other guests.

There was something to satisfy every palate. For the farina *foo-foo*, there were soup dishes of bitter-leaf, egusi, and okro in various combinations. There were dishes of mouth-watering jollof-rice, fried ripe plantains, roasted chicken drumsticks and mixed vegetables.

Chikezie Odogwu gleefully rubbed his palms together, as a smile of anticipation split his mouth in a wide grin.

"This is a feast for the gods," he said gushingly to Chief Anigbo. "Every time we are invited to dinner at your home, Ifunanya and me, we almost always consider it a duty to skip our lunch."

"But, of course, you didn't," Chief Anigbo asked, with a knowing smile.

"*Ugo-oranyelu!*" Chikezie Odogwu addressed his host by his praise-name. "Have you ever heard that I skipped a meal? But it is as if we—or rather, as if *I* did. Ifunanya plays this game with me, and she thinks she's being clever. For lunch, she served a mix of carrots, peas, cabbage and other vegies that have no name known to me, which I ate very sparingly. So, I'm ready for Ekemma's banquet."

"I knew you'd be!" Ifunanya interjected, smiling and sidling up to him where he stood, with Chief Anigbo, surveying the dishes.

"This is man-to-man talk, no woman invited!" Chikezie rebuked his wife.

"*Ugo-oranyelu,*" Ifunanya protested to Chief Anigbo, "you see what I have to put up with?"

Chief Anigbo laughed. "I know you two too well," he said, grinning, "to be taken in by your kind of talk. And the fellow's smiling as if you just paid him a compliment. But tell me something, Ifunanya—oh, by the way, I've been thinking of a suitable praise-name for you—something like—let me see—yes, *Ugodiya*—"

Ifunanya's face broke in a wide smile. "*Ugodiya?* What have I done to merit—"

"You're your husband's pride. That's what he tells everybody. So don't argue with me." Chief Anigbo turned to Chikezie Odogwu. "Right, *Afulu-kwe?* Or have I been hearing things in my day-dreams or what?"

Chikezie spread his arms wide, eyebrows raised. "You got me there, *Ugo-oranyelu!* What can I say? *Ugodiya!* I think I like the name. *Ugodiya*," he said again. "I like it. Suits her to a T!"

"That settles the matter," said Chief Anigbo, as he placed a friendly hand on her shoulder. "Now, back to my question. Seriously, *Ugodiya*, what's all this talk about *Afulu-kwe* not liking carrots and peas—you know, stuff like that? I've seen him eat those things a few times. So I don't understand."

Ifunanya laughed. "My dear husband only eats those things—he calls them whiteman's vegetables—he only eats them when he wants to shed some pounds, if you see what I mean. The man is an old-type Igboman, no doubt about it! The day God created my husband Chikezie, He must have broken the mold, because He didn't make many more like him thereafter."

"If you call me an old-type Igboman, just because of carrots and what-nots," Chikezie asked his wife, "what would you call our host, *Ugo-oranyelu?* A *modern* Igboman?"

Ifunanya threw up her arms. "That's not fair, Chikezie, and you know it. We're not talking about *Ugo-oranyelu.* He's—"

"It's all right actually," Chief Anigbo said, with a smile. "I'm honored to be called an Igboman, old-type or—how do they say it in English—a *dyed-in-the-wool* Igbo."

Chikezie Odogwu looked keenly at his friend. "I know you get quite a kick out of that kind of talk," he said. "You're so dyed-in-the-wool I almost expect to see you jump up every now and again, and raise your arm and shout

Enyimba! If the Igbo people were a nation, with a flag, I'd not be surprised to see you, on occasion, prancing up and down, furiously waving the flag, and raising the *Enyimba* war cry of the nation."

"Like at the Olympics?" asked Ekemma Anigbo. She wore an impish smile as she came through the kitchen door. She walked up to her husband, and whispered in his ear. Whereupon Chief Anigbo signaled to the Odogwus to follow him.

"Time to return to the living-room," he announced. 'I don't think it'd be a good idea for our other guests to arrive and catch us gawking at the dishes. There's a time for everything."

"*Lolo*, we were only doing what comes naturally," Ifunanya said, in an aside to Ekemma. "The eyes must first feast on the food before the mouth tastes it, as they say. And you gave Chikezie and me the opportunity to do so."

"That's because you two were the first to arrive," Ekemma explained. "And, you and us—you, Ifunanya, and me especially—we're like family."

"Family," Ifunanya nodded her head a few times, reflectively, muttering softly to herself. Then, suddenly, she put out a hand and stopped Ekemma in her tracks. "Let them go on back to the sitting-room. You and me, we have a little something to talk about."

*   *   *

Chuka Okpala leaned towards his wife, Akudola, sitting to his right, and whispered in her ear: "Watch it, girl! Too much of that stuff will do your figure little good."

"Too late, Chukky boy!" Akudola half-turned to him, as the last piece of the most scrumptious cheesecake she had tasted in a long, long while disappeared into her mouth.

"You know what that means, don't you?" Chuka said, and smiled. "Tomorrow, Sunday, you'll have to do at least a two-mile walk after church. As you always like to say, we have to pay, one way or another, for our sins of over-indulgence."

"No problem," Akudola said, nodding her head in agreement. "I'll do three miles, four if you like, so long as you are walking with me. You know that walking has never been a problem for me."

"May not be for you, Aky-girl. You're a bit of an athlete, and have a figure to match. But why do you always try to drag me along? I've never pretended or aspired to being an athlete. If you must punish your body every time you eat a morsel of food too much, please leave me out of your—what's it you call it—self-flagellation. I'll never understand why a girl with your trim, almost angelic figure—"

Akudola placed a hand on his arm. "How about we start, here and now, to help the body better digest all this food we've gorged on, with the kind of exercise you love to do—dancing? Ask our host if we can have some music—"

"And what if Chief Anigbo wasn't planning on any such activity, eh, Aky?"

"Can you possibly be talking of the Chief Anigbo I know?" Akudola asked. "*Ugo-oranyelu* loves music and dancing, however much he likes to carry himself stiffly. He's quite a dancer, and you know it."

"Did I just hear someone say 'dancing'?" Chuma Okwu jumped up from his chair. "What's a celebration without music and some dancing?" He went across the room to where Chief Anigbo sat in his *king's* chair. "What do you say, *Ugo-oranyelu*? How about some music, so we can dance in honor of your birthday? It's not every day that one celebrates something or the other."

Chief Anigbo laughed, and said: "Mr. Vice-President of AKPU, your wish is my command."

"That'll be the day any of us can command *you!*"

"You just did, Mr. V.P. And I have nothing if not good dance music cassettes."

He raised his voice, as he looked around him. "Where's that boy? Kanu! Where are you, boy?"

Okocha, who had sat quietly, with Tatiana, in a corner of the sitting-room farthest from his dad, came forward.

"When I'm here," he told his dad, "you don't have to call Kanu. I'll take care of the music. Kanu and Somto are having a great time with Nonye's son in one of the guest-rooms."

Okocha's gaze took in the entire assemblage, and finally came to rest on Chuma Okwu. "What would you like, Mr. V.P.? For starters, how about soukous—you know, the Congo beat? Or perhaps our good old West African highlife beat—?"

"Give me the old West African," Chuma Okwu said delightedly. "I know your dad has E.T. Mensah, Rex Lawson, and Victor Olaiya. Or, if those musicians are too ancient for some of us here, how about—?"

"Doesn't matter one bit," Akudola Okpala chimed in. "As long as it is good dance music—you know—*our* type of dance music, what does it matter, ancient or modern?"

For the next two hours and more, music filled the living and dining rooms. The West African highlife dance can sometimes seem uncoordinated and uneven to the Euro-American or the unpractised eye. But to watch a good highlife dancer is truly to observe, at its loftiest expression, the most natural and unchoreographed rhythm that the human body is capable of, as it flexes its parts, and gyrates and pirouettes in an access of pure enjoyment.

*   *   *

Nnanna and Nonye, with their baby, Nnanna Junior, were given one of the guest-rooms so that the baby could rest, or sleep, away from the noise and bustle of uproarious hilarity in the living and dining rooms. Kanu and Somto, perhaps finding the general company and conversation uncomfortably over their heads, spent lots of time with the baby. Even when Nonye and Nnanna—from moment to moment—left the room to join in the merriment of the occasion, the two cousins stayed put in the guest-room.

"I knew I couldn't bring Jonetta here," Kanu grumbled. "So what's the point pretending I'm part of what's going on?"

"But we were there at the beginning," Somto reminded him.

"Right," Kanu agreed. "We had to be there, especially for the kolanut ceremony—or invocation, as dad likes to call it. I had to be present to carry the bowl of kolanuts around, and show it to the guests, before dad did his thing—blessing and breaking them."

"And of course," Somto added, "one of us had to take the bowl around, with the broken pieces, so everyone could take a piece."

"And the damned thing'so bitter—"

"Watch your language, coz!" Somto admonished him.

Kanu waved an arm dismissively. "I couldn't even take a piece of the thing to eat, myself, because mom didn't have the peanut-butter paste—what do they call it—?

"*Okw'ose.*"

"Yes, *okw'ose,*" said Kanu. "At least it gives the kolanut an agreeable tang—you know what I mean—nicely spicy."

The guest-room door suddenly opened, and Nnanna poked his head through the opening.

"You two don't want to dance?" he asked, looking from Kanu to Somto.

"With whom?' Kanu asked, spreading his arms wide. "I couldn't bring Jonetta to the party—"

"Sh-sh!" Somto hit Kanu on the shoulder. "You don't have to shout!"

"Sorry! I forgot. But—"

"But nothing, coz," Somto said softly. "Anyway, Nnanna, Kanu's right. We have no girls to dance with. None of the older couples brought even their late-teenage daughters to the party because Uncle Nat's invitation card said '*no children*'! I don't even know how or why he let you bring Nnanna junior."

Nnanna laughed. "You're funny—very funny. But don't you understand that, for every rule, there's an exception? And, in this matter, Nnanna junior *is* the exception. He's almost like a grandson to uncle Nat, and there's no way Nonye could have missed her uncle's birthday celebration."

Somto partially covered his mouth in an obviously comic effort to muffle his words. "I'd better not voice the thought that just came into my head."

"Let me guess," Nnanna said, smiling. "Weren't you thinking that I could have stayed home and minded Nnanna junior, so Nonye could come?"

Somto stared blankly at his brother-in-law. His lips worked briefly, but no words came.

"That's all right, Somto. I know you would have said so only in jest."

"Thank you, Nnanna," Somto said, smiling. "But that was actually not the only thought that entered my head. I was thinking—like—where's my mom when we need her the most? If she had been here by now, as Nonye and I had expected, this problem would not have arisen—"

"Meaning, no doubt Somto," Nnanna said, "that we could have left Nnanna Junior in her tender loving care at home, so Nonye and me can be here without worrying about the little one? You may be right, but that might have been less than fair to your mom, don't you think? Don't they also go to parties at home in Nigeria, and dance away the night, as we do here?"

"You're probably right," Somto said, "about mom going to parties at home. And even if she was here, she would almost certainly not have wanted to miss her brother, uncle Nat's, birthday bash."

Nnanna spread his arms wide. "So you see," he said, "however you slice it, we would have all been here dancing. But seriously, Somto, about you not having any girls to dance with, you and Kanu could go and take turns with Nonye, and even Tatiana—"

"Too heavy with child!" Kanu said, before he could check himself.

"You'd say so, wouldn't you?" Nnanna said, and then beckoned to the two cousins. "I'd like you to step outside this room and see what's happening. Come on, Kanu, Somto, and see Tatiana dancing. She's not even dancing with Okocha right now, but with Mike—you know, Mike Egbuna. You don't have to worry about Nnanna junior. We didn't bring him here so you two will sit by him and miss all the fun."

Nnanna paused for a brief moment, and shook his head. "I see I might as well be talking to a brick wall. So, do as you please. And while you're doing so, thanks for keeping an eye on my son."

He stepped back into the corridor, and shut the door behind him.

*   *   *

Through all the noisy merriment, Tatiana and Okocha danced with quiet dignity, or sat quietly in their corner. Tatiana, by the best medical calculation available to them, somewhat less than three weeks to go before her baby was due, took it extremely easy. She had, indeed, not wanted to dance at all. But Okocha had been very persuasive.

"A little bit of dancing, you know, should be perfectly okay for you," he told her. "Might be even beneficial—"

"Says who?" she asked, with a chuckle.

Okocha played along. "*Dr.* Okocha Anigbo!" he said. "That's who!"

"Then I'm in good hands, *Dr.* OK-baby. But go easy on me, and on your baby."

"You have my word on that, Tiana. So let's go have fun!"

Okocha kept his word, as he guided Tatiana very gently around the floor. As they danced, several pairs of eyes, with varying degrees of anxiety, followed their movement. There was not a single individual among the guests who was not aware of their pain and agony. Okocha was there, everyone understood, principally because he was—as his friend Mike Egbuna fancifully put it—*a son of the soil.* But though many agonized with Okocha and Tatiana, none could offer a palliative for their mental suffering.

Mike Egbuna soon noticed, when he took a turn with her, that Tatiana looked a little weary.

"You okay?" he asked her solicitously. "You seem—"

"Thank you, Mike, for caring. Yes, I'm a little bit winded. Perhaps I should take a break."

Mike smiled appreciatively. "Thank you for agreeing to dance with me inspite of my clumsiness."

"Oh come on, Mike. You're quite a dancer and you know it. No need for modesty, especially not with me."

They stopped their gyrations, and she allowed him to lead her by the hand away from the dance area. Okocha was also taking a break, with Nonye and Nnanna. As Tatiana approached, Okocha rose from his chair and held out his hand to her. She grasped it, and gratefully leaned into him as his arms protectively encircled her waist.

"Thank you, Mike." She turned to him and smiled. "You've been the gentleman I always knew you to be."

"Thanks," Mike said. "Okocha, please take good care of her. She's tired, and needs some rest. So don't you even think of asking her—"

"I'm not as crazy as you think, man," Okocha cut him short, smiling. "*You* must have overworked her while you were dancing with her."

Tatiana jumped to his defence. "He most certainly did not, OK-baby! But I'm tired. Nonye, do you mind if I go to your baby's room? I believe Kanu and Somto are there with him."

"Great minds!" Nonye said. "I was just thinking of doing the same thing. So why don't you and me go there and see what Nnanna junior is up to?"

"And we can talk too, no?" Tatiana asked. "There's so much I want us to talk about."

"Like birthing and all that jazz?"

"No," Tatiana replied, with a faint and tired smile. "Not at all. It's about my perennial problem—your uncle—"

"You mean, *your* father-in-law," Nonye riposted. "Chief the honorable Nathaniel Udechukwu Anigbo!" Nonye spoke the name with an exaggerated gravity of tone, and then turned to Okocha. "I like the way Tatiana referred to *your* dad as *my* uncle. But, of course, I don't blame her. In light of what you two are going through now, and for the longest time, I fully understand. I think I'd have done the same thing. Uncle Nat can be a very difficult man to deal with."

"You can say that again!" Okocha said, and rose from his chair. "Come on, Nnanna man! Let's go with the ladies to see your son."

"Don't see why not," Nnanna said, also rising from his chair.

"Easy now, fellows!" Okocha spoke softly, gently gesturing with both his hands. "Let's just slink out of here without attracting too much attention."

"And how do we do that, OK-baby?"

"Simple, Tiana. We don't have to go, all four of us, at once. You and Nonye can lead the way. Then, after a moment or two, Nnanna can quietly follow. I'll take my time—after I've taken care of Mike, who seems to be watching us, even as we speak, and might notice that we've absconded from the celebration."

"Why do we have to adopt such a crazy tactic?" Nnanna wanted to know, shaking his head.

"I just don't think it'll look good," Okocha explained, lowering his voice to barely above a whisper, "for the four of us, the closest family members to the celebrant, to desert the celebration. Don't forget that Kanu and Somto have hardly shown their faces in this sitting-room. And now the rest of us just get up and vamoose."

Nnanna thought of something. "Are there enough chairs in there for all of us? With Kanu and Somto already installed—"

"We'll just need to pick up four or so folding chairs from the closet near the room," Okocha said. "Problem solved!"

The foursome carried out Okocha's strategy to the letter, and was soon ensconced in the guest room, with Nnanna junior, to the delight of Kanu, but not Somto.

"Sitting here like this, all six of us" he grumbled, "it looks like we've deserted Uncle Nat and his birthday celebration."

"Relax, man!" Nnanna said, patting him on the shoulder, as they sat next to each other. "We'll be here only for a brief while anyway."

"I'm here for keeps!" said Kanu, with some feeling. "If I cannot—or rather, since I dared not bring my girlfriend here, I might as well not have been present. Let me tell you guys something. If I'd been in Okocha's shoes, I think I'd have been strongly tempted to stay away altogether, I swear!"

Tatiana laughed softly. "That's easy for you to say, Kanu. But there's no way we—OK and me—would have missed the birthday dinner. I'll say one thing for your dad, Kanu. The old man has at least learnt to tolerate our presence, even though he has summarily rejected every olive branch we've extended to him."

"We know," Nonye said consolingly, as she picked up Nnanna junior from his cot. "I think he needs to be changed, or am I the only one who can smell something around Nnanna junior? But seriously, Tatiana, I wish I could just wave a magic wand, and your pain would go away. But, against the degree of inflexibility my dear uncle has shown towards you and Okocha, I'm afraid no magic wand, however potent, can bring him around as easily as we would all wish."

There was a faint knock on the door of the guest-room. The door opened and Ekemma Anigbo stepped into the room.

"Mom!" Kanu shouted, springing to his feet. "What's up?"

"You, Kanu!" Ekemma replied, pointing at him. "You're the only one that jumped up when I entered."

She pointed at Kanu and Somto. "I don't think I've seen much of either of you since the dancing began." She paused, looking from Somto to Kanu. "Don't both speak at once. Let me start with you Somto. You're the elder of you two. What's *your* problem?"

Somto gestured vaguely with both arms. "None, auntie," he said, with a nervous smile, and then pointed at Nnanna junior. "I thought someone should keep an eye on the baby so Nonye and Nnanna could join the rest—"

"A likely excuse indeed!" Ekemma retorted. "And what's your's, Kanu?"

She suddenly raised her right hand and stopped him before he could get a word out.

"Come with me, Kanu," she said. "And you too, Okocha. There's something I want to show you. It came a few days ago, and you two need to talk about how you'll deal with it."

"What's it?" Kanu asked excitedly.

"I have it in my bedroom." She turned to the others in the guest-room. "Sorry to take these two away. But it won't take long. Hope you don't mind."

"It's okay, auntie," Nnanna said. "Keep them as long as you want. We'll manage without them."

Okocha and Kanu followed their mom out of the room. The dancing in the sitting-room was in full swing as the three made a beeline through the room to the master bedroom. As soon as they entered the bedroom, Ekemma shut the door and turned to Kanu.

"I asked you why you've hardly shown your face in the sitting-room since after the dinner was over. And you didn't seem too eager to answer the question."

"Mom, you said you wanted to show us something," Okocha said, placing a gentle hand on her arm, as he looked keenly around the bedroom.

Kanu also looked around the room, searching for any unusual object of interest. Then he shook his head slowly at his mom. "That was just an excuse, mom," he said, with a faint smile. "There isn't really anything you wanted to show us. Big bro, I believe mom just wanted to talk to us privately."

"So, Kanu," Ekemma engaged him fully with her eyes, "what's your answer to my question?"

Kanu waved his arm vaguely. "Do I have to have a reason for everything? Somto and I just didn't think we fitted in—"

"Or," Ekemma said, "could it be that—and here I'm making a guess—could it possibly be because your girlfriend—what's that her name—Jonetta—is it because she isn't here?"

The effect was as dramatic as she knew it would be. Kanu and Okocha turned to each other, their eyes dilated in wonder and surprise. Ekemma took her time, as her gaze went from Kanu to Okocha, and back to Kanu.

"Your faces just gave me the confirmation I sought," she said, nodding repeatedly to herself. "So the story is true, about Jonetta. And neither of you had the courage to tell your dad and me about it? Not even you, Okocha?"

"I'm sorry, mom," Okocha quickly apologized. "I can see that there's no point trying to deny what I know—what we all knew, including Nnanna and Somto. But, mom, don't our people say that it is not everything the palm-wine tapper sees from the top of his palm tree that he recounts—"

"Even to your own mom?" Ekemma interrupted him. "And more so in a matter of this importance to the family?"

Kanu coughed loudly, reached out and held his mom by the hand, and then proceded to tell as barefaced a lie as Okocha had ever heard him tell.

"Mom," he said, his voice gentle and measured, "I swore him to silence. I swore them all to silence—him, Somto, Nnanna, Nonye and Tatiana."

Ekemma turned to Okocha. "You, too?"

"Especially Okocha," Kanu quickly cut in before Okocha could say a word. "Especially him, mom! And you know why, I'm sure." He stood directly in front of her and now held both her hands in his. "I don't know who told you about me and Jonetta. But, more importantly than that, I must ask you, have you told dad—?"

"And if I have?"

"Have you, mom?" Kanu was insistent.

"How—why is it of concern to you?"

"It *is* a matter of major concern to me," Kanu said. "And to Okocha too, if I may say so. I'm not sure how you are taking it yourself. But don't you see, mom, if you're taking it hard, the story of me and Jonetta will kill dad."

"What's that supposed to mean?"

Okocha could no longer restrain himself. "You know very well, mom," he burst out. "We—me and Kanu—we've talked endlessly about how you and dad have reacted to—" He paused and jerked his hand backwards, over his shoulder, pointing in the direction of the sitting-room and the guest-room beyond it, "how you two have reacted to my marriage to Tatiana. We can see that, if it's been hard for you, mom, it has been infinitely worse for dad. Tell me I'm wrong, I challenge you!"

Ekemma stared at her son, and though her mouth twitched as if she was struggling to say something, she remained silent.

"I didn't think you could," Okocha said very gently, as he came and put his arm around her shoulders, and drew her close to himself, even as Kanu continued to hold on to her hands.

"Mom," Okocha whispered in her ear, "me and Kanu, we love you dearly—"

"Yes, my sons. I can see I'm surrounded by love. And I thank God for both of you."

"Yes, mom," said Kanu. "But you've still not answered my question."

"About telling your dad? No, I haven't—yet. And you know why? It's because, like the poor frog, I don't know what, or how, I'll tell him, and water will enter my mouth, as we say."

Okocha gently spun his mother round to face him. Then, looking her straight in the eye, he pleaded with her. "You must not tell him, please, mom!" His voice was full of entreaty and earnestness. "I beg you, please don't tell him—not just yet, and perhaps not for a long time. Until, that is, we say it's all right. Let's see how things develop between him and Tatiana. We know it's been painful and difficult for you. But there's little doubt that dad just seems unable to get over his pain and suffering because I married an American girl."

"And mom," Kanu said, "you don't know how much I'm thankful that you seem to have softened your stand in this matter. You've been quite kindly in your attitude to Tatiana—"

"I've nothing really against her—"

"That's the point, mom," Okocha cut in. "I wish I could hear those same exact words from dad. But I despair, and only God knows how long it'll take him to come round to where you are now, mom. You have nothing against her, you said. That's at least, hopefully, a sign that you'll feel better and better about her, till the day you'll see my Tatiana for the great person she is, and a loving daughter-in-law to you and dad."

Ekemma freed her hand from Kanu's grasp, and raised it to stop Okocha. "Wait a minute," she said. "Is all this talk some way you've found to tell us something you seem to be hiding your mouth a little from saying clearly? Are you two hinting to me that Kanu will one day marry this girl—Jonetta? Is that what all this is about?"

"Who knows?" said Okocha. "And that's God's truth. They're two very young persons, mom, who happen to love each other. That's what they believe, and that's where they are at this moment. What's that great saying we Igbo have? Something about *today is enough for now, but tomorrow is pregnant with possibilities*. No one can predict how two persons will feel about each other in several years' time."

"And you're the best mom in the world," Kanu said, with a tender smile. "A mom who understands that her sons will do what comes naturally to all young persons, especially those of us who are growing up here. The United States is where our *chi* has placed us, for better or worse, and we cannot fight against our guardian spirit, can we, mom?"

"Enough, sons!" Ekemma cried out. "If this goes on any longer, you two will talk me into believing anything, even what my eyes haven't seen." She paused, and laughed shortly. "What I just said reminds me of Chikezie Odogwu. One might say that his praise-name, *Afulu-kwe*, as I believe you both know, supposedly means that he truly believes only what his eyes have seen—somewhat like Thomas Didymus, in the Bible story of Christ's resurrection. And by the way, Mr. Odogwu is one person who seems to have taken on your dad on your behalf, Okocha, at any and every chance he has. He keeps trying to convince both of us—as he likes to put it—to move on with the rest of mankind, and not to get too wrapped up in our narrow traditional ways. Okocha, you know you have him in your corner, a giant on whom you can lean."

"I know he is, mom. And I'm ever so grateful to him."

He went and stood side by side with Kanu, as both sons now faced their mom directly. Then, as if by telepathy, each reached for, and held, the other's hand. Okocha then spoke for both of them.

"Long and short of the matter, mom," he said, his voice as earnest as Ekemma had ever heard him speak, "is that you must not tell dad about Jonetta until we all agree it is okay that he be told. It's bad enough for me and Kanu that *you* know about Jonetta, though I'm wondering how you found out. But something tells me it would be futile to press you to reveal your source. And by the way, about what Kanu said—that he swore us to silence about Jonetta—that's simply not true. He was just trying to deflect your anger towards only himself. The truth is the exact opposite. We made him swear he would not tell you and dad until we say so."

"Nothing more needs to be said, for now," Ekemma said. She enfolded both her sons to her bosom, and squeezed them repeatedly as she spoke. "I don't like making promises I might not be able to keep—about not telling your dad. You two boys are a blessing to me—to us. But something—and I don't know what—has happened to you two, and you have become more American than is comfortable for me and, yes, especially for your dad."

"So, mom, you promise—?"

"I'll try, Okocha." She squeezed them one more time, and then let go. "But you two boys will be the death of us." She paused, as a shrill sigh exploded out of her mouth. "But as sure as I am that there is a God in Heaven, I'm sure, and I pray, that He will find a way to bring our pain to a resolution that will not tear us apart, as a family. That is my prayer."

Ekemma opened the door of the bedroom. "You should go back and join your companions. But, Kanu, I want to see you and Somto out there in the sitting-room, enjoying the party with our guests."

Kanu was at the door when he suddenly stopped, and turned back to his mom. "T'was Somto, wasn't it, told you about Jonetta?" he asked, but did not wait for her reply. "I'll kill him—!"

"You do so, son, and you'd have killed an innocent man. It wasn't Somto. If you must know, and I'm not saying more than that for now, I heard about—you know—your girlfriend—from the mother of one of the girl's friends. There!"

She gave her two sons a gentle shove, stepped out of the bedroom herself, and shut the door behind her.

CHAPTER 20

C hief Anigbo was in a deep brown study, slumped wearily in his king's chair in the living-room, when the phone rang, jarring him out of his reverie. His principal preoccupation had been how to bring some order—and quickly, too—into his family life. Only a day or two earlier, he had heard disturbing rumors of his second son's liaison with an American girl. *Another American girl!* He had taxed his wife on the matter, but could draw nothing concrete out of her. She had hummed and hawed, but—other than engaging him with her smiling eyes—had offered no information with which he could do anything. Nevertheless, he had had a distinct impression that Ekemma knew a whole lot that she was not willing to share with him.

"The damn thing doesn't have to ring so loudly!" he complained, sitting up straight. Wearily, he reached for the phone, which was placed on a side-table conveniently close to his chair. "Hello! Who's this?"

"You sound grumpy, *Ugo-oranyelu.* Is anything the matter?"

"Chikezie?"

"As in Odogwu, yes sir!"

"*Afulu-kwe,* you've come with your—"

"I haven't come—yet. As a matter of fact, I am calling you to ask if I can come to see you."

"Do you need to ask? When are you—?"

"Now!"

"That's okay. Only thing is Ekemma's not home—"

"Why do you think I want to come right now? I know she's not home. Neither is my wife. Those two women are as thick as thieves. But most importantly, I wanted our talk to be strictly between you and me—*mano a mano*—if you see what I mean."

"What's it all about, if I may ask."

"You may certainly ask, *Ugo-oranyelu*," Chikezie Odogwu said. "You'll know when I come. See you in a matter of minutes! Bye!"

So saying, he hung up on his friend. Chief Anigbo stared at the telephone in his hand, shrugged and, with a symbolic wave of his hand, dismissed Chikezie Odogwu from his thoughts.

Chikezie began to talk even as he stepped into the living-room. "*Ugo-oranyelu*, I greet you! I lower my cap in deference to you—"

"Which cap?" Chief Anigbo asked, laughing.

"Does it matter that I have no head-gear on?" Mr. Odogwu shot back. "Everything is symbolic. The gesture of removing the cap is what matters."

He looked around him, and then pointed to the *chaise-longue*. "When did you change the position of this chair? It used to be on the other side, behind the long settee. Doesn't matter anyway! "

He first removed his shoes, and stretched himself out comfortably on the *chaise-longue*, resting his head on the arm-rest. So installed, he was facing Chief Anigbo when the latter took his customary king's chair.

"Make yourself at home," Chief Anigbo said unnecessarily, smiling. He was familiar with the omens. When Chikezie Odogwu seemed at his most relaxed, expect trouble! "So, what's eating you up?"

"Why would anything be eating me up?"

"Because I can read you like a book. When you're acting the way you're doing now, I suspect—I *know*—all's not well. So, out with it, *Afulu-kwe!*" Chief Anigbo suddenly held up an arm. "But hold it! First things first! Let it not be said that I didn't ask after your family. How's everybody? *Ugo-diya*—"

"Ifunanya's okay," Chikezie said. "You know something? She glories in that praise-name. *Ugo-diya!* I must say I like it. The name has stuck, since you gave it to her—was it two or three weeks ago?"

"It was exactly two week ago—on my birthday."

"How time flies!" Chikezie said. "Yes, two weeks. Ifunanya herself helped spread the word about the name. Now she thinks she's my equal because we both now have titles. Women!"

"Is the name the reason you insisted on this meeting?" Chief Anigbo asked with a sardonic smile.

"Nope!" Chikezie's tone suddenly turned starchy. "It's about you!"

"Me? What have I done now?"

"*Ugo-oranyelu*, it's not what you've done. It's what you must do. It's about your sons."

"Sons?" Chief Anigbo's eyebrows rose fractionally. "Sons?" he repeated. "As in Okocha and Kanu? I thought it was only Okocha. Of course Kanu has been acting strange for some time now. But I'm well aware of his problem. He's decided to take on his brother Okocha's battle and, for quite a while, has been ranting and raving about how old-fashioned we are—me and their mother—"

"Mother, did you say?" Chikezie asked, frowning. "Please leave *Lolo* Ekemma out of this. I know her. She's mostly okay with Okocha and Tatiana. The way I see things, *you* are the clog in her wheels. It's just her loyalty to you that's prevented her from fully accepting what has happened and what's happening—"

"What's happening?" Chief Anigbo stared at his friend, and there was alarm in his stare. "What do you mean?"

"Kanu!" Chikezie said. "That's what's happening."

For a moment or two, there was silence. The two friends engaged each other fully with their eyes, as each struggled with his thoughts. At length, Chief Anigbo shrugged, and gestured with his hand.

"You've got to explain what you're talking about." The entreaty in his voice was unmistakable.

"If either of your sons knows that right now I'm here talking to you, they'd be mighty upset—"

Chief Anigbo shot up from his king's chair. "Kanu!" he called loudly. "Where's that boy? He was here in the house not quite an hour ago. But I shouldn't be too surprised. The boy moves like lightning—him, and his cousin Somto. They're inseparable, those two, and that's a good thing, I imagine."

"Let the boys be, *Ugo-oranyelu*. Let them be. We have more important things to talk about, you and me. Let me ask you something." Chikezie raised his body to a sitting position on the *chaise-longue*. "Can you stand there and tell me you have not heard anything about your son Kanu and an American girl? Tell me, *Ugo-oranyelu*, haven't you?"

Just as suddenly as he had stood up, Chief Anigbo now lowered his body into his chair. He seemed to be struggling to say something as his mouth worked, but no sound came. He looked from his friend's face to his own hands which he clasped together in his lap.

"It's funny, *Ugo-oranyelu*, but I don't remember when I last saw you this speechless. Come on, man! It would not be the first time—"

"That's the point, *Afulu-kwe*," Chief Anigbo finally found his voice. "I can't say I've never heard any such thing. It is quite common for our young boys and girls to have friendly relationships with their school-mates and what-nots. But the way you are raising this matter suggests that there might be more to it than the usual—"

"There is, I'm afraid." Chikezie's voice was gentle as he regarded his friend with compassionate, but challenging eyes. "Let me tell it as it is—I mean, as I understand the situation. Up until this moment, I know you have struggled to find some room in your heart to accommodate your son Okocha, and his American wife Tatiana—"

"What do you expect from me, *Afulu-kwe*? That I overlook everything and clasp them to my bosom."

"How shall I put it?" Chikezie asked. "Yes sir! Emphatically, yes! You must clasp them to your bosom. And what's more, my friend, you must find additional room in that bosom for—"

"I can't forgive Okocha—"

"But you must, *Ugo-oranyelu*. You've really no choice in the matter, unless you want to wreck your family. You must forgive."

"Forgive is an easy word to throw around," Chief Anigbo said. "But it ain't so easy—"

"I didn't say it would be easy," Chikezie said softly. "But it is doable. We all need to learn to forgive. I once heard a preacher say that forgiveness is a deliberate act. He said it is a deliberate choice we can make even when the offender has not asked for our forgiveness, and even when our hearts are not ready to forgive."

Chief Anigbo stared, open-mouthed, at his friend. "I never heard you speak like this before," he finally said. "Do you have any more where that came from?"

"I do," Chikezie said, and smiled. "The same preacher said that the trouble with many of us is that we see the world not as it really is, but only as our hearts incline us to do. I'm not sure I fully understood his message, but I think I understood him to be saying that we allow our hearts to rule our thinking more than we should. And the heart can only react to what our eyes see, and what our ears hear."

"So?"

"Oh, I don't know!" Chikezie said, throwing up his arms. "I've never claimed to be a theologian. The only thing I know is that—as I said—you've got to find room in your bosom, not only for Okocha and Tatiana, but for Kanu—"

"I have no problem," Chief Anigbo interrupted, "finding room in my heart for Kanu—"

"And Jonetta, his American girlfriend?"

Chief Anigbo froze. For a long moment he said not a word, but sat stiffly, staring rigidly at nothing in particular. He felt utterly alone in a world of his own, as he clasped and unclasped his hands in his lap. He seemed also to have lost control over his lips, which twitched nervously.

At length, his eyes came to rest on his friend and tormentor, Chikezie Odogwu, and there was desperate appeal in their gaze.

"No, *Afulu-kwe*!" he cried. "Please God, no! Not Kanu!"

"Yes, Kanu," Mr. Odogwu said, very gently. "You said you'd heard something—"

"Not anything concrete. Only the usual stories about boys being boys and that sort of thing—"

"Why do you think I insisted on coming to see you? You didn't really think it was to talk about the praise-name, *Ugodiya*, you gave my wife?"

"Kanu has an American girlfriend—I mean—a serious one?"

"Or I wouldn't be here! Yes, it is serious, as far as one can judge. *Ugodiya* told me, but asked me not to tell you about it."

"So, why are you telling me?"

"Because someone has to tell you about it, and help you get over your narrow prejudices—"

"How did *Ugodiya* hear about this?" Chief Anigbo wanted to know.

Chikezie Odogwu hesitated for a moment or two. Then he shrugged helplessly, and moved to the end of the *chaise-longue* close to Chief Anigbo's chair. He reached for, and briefly held his friend's hand and, looking him straight in the eye, began to talk.

"*Ugodiya* was told about the American girl by our second daughter, Janet. Janet is a friend of Jonetta's, and I've often wondered if their names—*Janet* and *Jonetta*—had anything to do with their being friends. But that's a side issue. The main thing is that it was Janet who told her mother, and then implored her not to tell me."

"But she told you," Chief Anigbo said, with a rueful smile.

"You know how it is. Nothing can be hidden for ever. I'm sorry I have to do this to you, *Ugo-oranyelu*. But it is a duty I owe to you and—like it or not—to your two worthy sons. No one else that I know, in our community here, would dream of coming to confront you on this issue. And I know several who wish and pray that, one day, you—Chief Nathaniel Anigbo, *Ugo-oranyelu*, our shining light—as some put it—that, one day, you will see that your attitude in this matter is terribly outmoded. More and more of our young men and—yes, even our young women—will find their life-partners from among Americans with whom we all live and interact daily."

"Am I the only Igbo parent—?"

"Of course you're not." Chikezie shook his head slowly. "But, don't you see, my friend, you are in a terribly, terribly outnumbered minority. And your opposition is futile because this is one fight you will win only when hell freezes over!"

"You think I'm concerned about numbers, and whether or not I'm in a minority?"

"Meaning—?

"Meaning, 'to each, his own'! Haven't you heard that saying?"

"So, what are you saying, *Ugo-oranyelu*? That you don't care if you are utterly alone with your prejudices and hang-ups? That you don't mind even if *Lolo* Ekemma—"

"What about Ekemma?" Chief Anigbo asked.

"Why do you think I chose to come to see you now?"

"You've asked me the exact same question two or three times already," Chief Anigbo said, with a tortured smile. "But that's all right, because I know you'll answer your own question again."

"Damn right, I will!" Chikezie exploded. "I knew she'd not be at home—"

"And you knew because—?"

"Don't tell me she didn't tell you she was going out with *Ugodiya*?"

"She told me," Chief Anigbo said, nodding gently. "She said she and Ifunanya had a rendezvous—"

"Where? Did she tell you?"

"No, *Afulu-kwe*. She did not. And I'm not in the habit of pressing her for every tiny, tiddly detail of her movements, especially when she's going out with someone like your wife. Women have their peculiar interests, like shopping, or meeting to gossip about this and that—"

"Yes, yes. Or meeting at a hospital to see someone important to them, no?"

"Is that where they went?" Chief Anigbo wanted to know, his eyes boring into Chikezie's. "Do you know who they went to see? If it's someone I know, I'm surprised Ekemma did not tell me, not to talk of asking me to tag along. But then, she might have had a thousand reasons for not telling me."

"She might indeed," Chikezie said, and stopped. There might have been the slightest hint of mockery in his voice, and in his roguish smile. But Chief Anigbo did not immediately catch on.

At length, Chikezie brought his hands together and intertwined his fingers as he looked steadily at his friend. When next he spoke, his voice was gentle, and his eyes pensive and tender.

"*Ugo-oranyelu*," he began, "I have to tell you that, at this very moment, your wife, *Lolo* Ekemma and my wife Ifunanya are at a Maplewood hospital visiting your daughter-in-law—"

"I have no daughter-in-law!" Chief Anigbo said forcefully.

"Stop it, *Ugo-oranyelu*! Or you blaspheme! Marriage is a sacred and holy state, and your son's wife is your daughter-in-law, like it or not!"

Chief Anigbo regarded his friend for a moment or two. "So? What's the girl doing there?" His voice was flat and neutral. "Is she not feeling well? I know she's almost due."

Chikezie shook his head sadly. "Sometimes I wonder how you can be so unemotional. Is it an act, or are you really unconcerned? But the answer to your question is that healthwise, Tatiana is doing well. So well indeed that, as we speak, she has already been delivered of her baby! A seven-pound beautiful girl, I'm told."

In a trice, Chief Anigbo was on his feet. He stared at Chikezie Odogwu for a long moment, and then abruptly turned, and headed for his bedroom.

"*Ugo-oranyelu!*" Chikezie called after him. "Are you all right?"

Chief Anigbo did not turn but, with a motion of his hand, waved aside Chikezie's concern. "I'm all right!" he said in a loud voice, and shut his bedroom door, none too gently.

He was gone for barely a minute and, when he came back to the living-room, he had not only changed into a fancifully woven Igbo jumper, he had a baseball cap on, and a bunch of keys in his hand.

"Let's go!" he said tersely.

"Where?" Chikezie asked, slowly rising from the *chaise-longue*. "The hospital?"

"Where else?" Chief Anigbo asked his friend. "Don't you see what's happening?"

Chief Anigbo abruptly came and stood directly in front of his friend, and put both his hands on Chikezie's shoulders. His smile was at once incandescent and beatific.

"We are talking about my granddaughter. My very first grandchild! Praise God!"

* * *

"Dad!" Okocha exclaimed, shooting up from his chair as Chief Anigbo walked into the hospital room, closely followed by Chikezie Odogwu.

A step or two into the room, Chief Anigbo suddenly stopped, and slowly looked around the room. Tatiana was stretched out on her bed with what seemed like a serenely happy and contented smile on her face. Chief Anigbo had to take a second look before he realized that she was asleep. He had expected to see his wife, Ekemma, and Mrs. Ifunanya Odogwu, but they were not there. Kanu and Somto were huddled with Okocha in a corner of the room, with the new-born baby in her crib, between them and the head of the bed.

Kanu and Somto, like Okocha, rose from their chairs, but more slowly and awkwardly, as if they were being pulled up by unseen and unsteady hands. Kanu's eyes, dilated in surprise, were riveted on his dad. Somto's smile was gentle and hesitant, as his eyes also focused on his uncle Nat.

Chief Anigbo turned and made a sign to Chikezie Odogwu. "Sh!" he whispered, and pointed to the sleeping new mother. "She must be tired," he added. He went and stood over the crib and gazed at the new baby. He stood like that for a long moment, in silence so unexpected it was deafening. No one in the room so much as moved a muscle! The only exception was Chikezie Odogwu who came and stood by his friend and then, very gently, put an arm around his shoulders.

"Your granddaughter," he said softly. His eyes moved around the room and finally came to rest on Okocha, with a glowing and triumphant smile. Then he squeezed Chief Anigbo's shoulders, leaned slightly forward, and turned his head so as to look directly into his eyes. "Your first—your very first grandchild, as you said when I told you about the delivery."

Chief Anigbo stooped over the crib, and slowly lowered his hands into it, with intent to pick the baby up. At the last moment, he hesitated and looked up at Okocha. "May I pick her up?" he asked.

"But of course, dad!" Okocha's voice, overcharged with emotion, was tremulous as he looked into his father's eyes. "Do you have to ask?"

Chief Anigbo slowly reached down and picked up the baby. Very gingerly—so gingerly he seemed to take ages to do so—he straightened his back, holding the baby almost at arm's length.

"Uncle Nat," Somto said, chuckling softly, "that's the same question, if I remember correctly, that you asked sis Nonye before you picked up her baby from his crib—that's like two or so months ago—"

"Exactly two months ago," Okocha said, "give or take a day or two. Nnanna Junior was born—let me see—in mid-June—"

"June 15, to be exact," Somto said glowingly. "I'm not likely ever to forget the date of my nephew's birth. It was June 15."

"Just two months," Kanu said, laughing. "But I can see the two of them, years down the road, arguing about who's the elder, in order to claim seniority and whatever advantages go with that."

"That'll probably be only in their years of adolescence," Okocha said. "In their more mature years, I doubt Chioma would even want to claim to be older than Nnanna Junior. She's a girl—"

"Chioma?" Chief Anigbo asked, and then repeated the name. "Chioma! That's her name?"

"Yes, dad." Okocha's voice was plaintive. "But why are you holding her like that?"

"Afraid I might drop her?" Chief Anigbo asked, with a smile, as he began to pace up and down the room. "I just don't want her to catch anything from too close a contact with my body and clothes. You know how they worry in maternity wards about new-born babies—that sort of thing. She's so fragile."

"I'm really sorry, dad, we didn't let you know the names we had chosen, in advance—"

"You knew it would be a girl?" Chikezie Odogwu asked.

"Yes—and no," Okocha replied. "At first, we—both of us—didn't want to know. But Tiana later changed her mind. So, eventually, she got to know the baby'd be a girl. But she respected my wishes on the matter, bless her! We decided on the names we'd give the child—boy or girl. The middle name we chose for her is Florence—"

"Florence! That's your mom's second name."

"I know, dad. That's why we chose it." He paused for a brief moment, eyes cast down. "Dad, I'm truly sorry—"

"What's that, Okocha?" Chikezie Odogwu cut in. "Did you say you're sorry? Sorry you didn't tell your dad? Who could blame you—seeing how things were between you and him? I'm sure even he would not think of blaming you for not telling—"

The words froze in his throat as he turned and stared at his friend. Chief Anigbo, still holding Chioma a little away from him, was no longer pacing the room but stood, rock-like, gazing at her rapturously. The glow on his face was almost transcendental.

"I thank whatever gods may be," he said, "for letting me live to see this day." His voice was soft and prayerful in its fervor. "I have lived to see and carry my grandchild in my arms!"

He looked around him, and continued: "There's nothing—nothing in this world—to compare with that. No feeling more powerful than how I feel right now. In a way, it is as if I have lived my life to its fullest. Anything else is like icing on the cake! I'm only in my mid-fifties, but if I were to die now, I know that in my heart of hearts, I'd die thanking God for putting this child in my arms."

Tatiana woke with a start and looked wonderingly around her. She then saw her father-in-law holding Chioma. Her eyes, seemingly unable to grasp the tremendous significance of what was unraveling right in front of her, turned to Okocha. Okocha, who understood immediately the cause of her wonderment, quickly went and stood by her side, and took and held both her hands in his. His smile was reassuring, and his eyes told her to relax. She focused once more on Okocha's dad, and took in the beatific expression on his face. She then let her body relax with a long drawn out sigh of deep contentment.

Just then, Ekemma and Ifunanya joined the crowd in the room. But they were not alone. A mere step behind them, were Tatiana's parents, Edna and Philip Karefa. They were talking animatedly as they trooped back into the room. And then, as if on cue, all four came to an abrupt halt, and stared at Chief Anigbo carrying the baby.

"You were gone for quite a while," Okocha said, looking from his mom to her companions. "Something happened here while you were away at the cafeteria. Something for which I had hoped and prayed for the longest time—"

"We have eyes to see," said Ifunanya Odogwu, looking at her husband, her eyes asking him questions. Chikezie Odogwu made a face at her, spreading wide his arms in a gesture that said he could not explain what they were all seeing.

"This is a sight," Philip Karefa said softly, half-turning to his wife Edna, "that I never thought I'd see." He strode up to Chief Anigbo, and placed a hand briefly on his shoulder. "Chief! It's good to see you," he said, and then let his arm drop to his side.

When she had sufficiently recovered from her surprise to trust herself to speak, Ekemma went and stood by her husband. Then she did what she always loved to do whenever her husband gave her the littlest opportunity, or cause. She put an arm around his waist, and held him close.

"May the eyes with which I'm looking at you at this very wonderful moment not go blind!" she said with a radiant smile.

Chikezie Odogwu laughed, shaking his head. "Nothing the eyes see will make them shed blood, as we say." He paused, and turned to his wife, and looked as sternly at her as he could contrive. "I was surprised you weren't here when we arrived. And now Okocha says you went to the cafeteria. Didn't you eat before you left the house, barely two hours ago?"

"Who told you I ate anything in the hospital cafeteria?" Her voice was mellow. "But the main thing is I didn't expect to see you here. You said you'd go to see *Ugo-oranyelu*, but you didn't say anything about you two coming to the hospital."

"Did I know?" Chikezie countered. "I thank *Ugo-oranyelu* for our being here. God works in His own mysterious ways!"

Ekemma stood on tiptoe, and cooed into her husband's ear: "Her second name is the same as mine—"

"I know, Mma," Chief Anigbo said. "I know."

He then disengaged her arm from around his waist, and resumed his pacing, with the baby now held closely to his chest, and dispensing smiles to his right and left, an ecstatic expression pasted on his face. Not a single person present had the slightest clue as to how his transformation had come about. Kanu especially—into whose ears, minutes earlier, Mr. Chikezie Odogwu had whispered that his Jonetta cat was out of the bag, and who therefore had the best reason of all to fear the worst—stared so hard at his dad that his eyes seemed likely, any moment, to pop out of their sockets.

Okocha suddenly knelt by Tatiana's bedside, and buried his face in the sheets. His body, powerfully athletic, shook with sobs. Tatiana watched him for a long moment, and then put her hand on his arm. Her eyes were misty, as she kept them helplessly fixed on her father-in-law as he paced up and down the room with Chioma in his arms. '*With Chioma in his arms!*' The thought reverberated in her head and in her heart. Then she shook her head at the incomprehensibility of what was transpiring before her eyes.

"What other proof do I need that there is a God in heaven?" she muttered to herself. The next she knew, Okocha's arm, as if in silent agreement with the barely audible words she had just spoken, suddenly lifted from off the bed and, though she lay prostrate on her bed, managed to encircle her waist.

Tears of joy rolled down her cheeks.

THE END

THE AUTHOR

Christian Chike Momah was born on October 20, 1930. He was educated at the St. Michael's (C.M.S.) School, Aba; the Government College, Umuahia; and the University College, Ibadan, where he earned a Bachelor's degree in History, English and Religious Studies in 1953. In 1959, he obtained the Associateship of the Library Association from the University College, London.

He was the first Nigerian graduate Land Officer (1954-1956) in the Public Service of the Eastern Nigerian government. Then he worked as a librarian in the University College, Ibadan (1956-1962); the University of Lagos (1962-1965); and the United Nations, first in Geneva, Switzerland (1966-1978), and then in New York (from 1978 till his retirement in 1990).

He has authored five other published novels: (1). FRIENDS AND DREAMS (1997); (2) TITI: Biafran Maid in Geneva (1999); (3). THE SHINING ONES: The Umuahia School days of Obinna Okoye (2003; reprinted 2010)); (4). THE STREAM NEVER DRIES UP (2008); (5) A SNAKE UNDER A THATCH (2008). He has written a few articles on Nigeria and on the USA.

Chike Momah has been married to Ethel, nee Obi, since 1959. The couple has two sons (Chukwudi and Azuka) and one daughter (Adaora), and has been blessed with seven grandchildren, and counting.

Among his contemporaries in high school and/or college are some of Africa's most noted writers: Chinua Achebe (Africa's foremost novelist, trail-blazer and essayist); Chukwuemeka Ike (acclaimed university administrator and prolific novelist); Wole Soyinka (1986 Nobel laureate in Literature); and the late Christopher Okigbo (considered to be Nigeria's "finest ever" poet, as per the 15th edition of the _Encyclopaedia Britannica_).

He is an involved member of the Nigerian community in the U.S.A., and has been honored with awards recognizing this involvement, including the first meritorious awards given by Songhai Charities, Inc., and by the Government College Umuahia Old Boys Association, Inc., both in 2003.

In 2003, he was honored with a chieftaincy _(Nnabuenyi-Nnewi)_ by HRH Kenneth Orizu, Igwe Nnewi, Anambra State, Nigeria.

In 2011, the Texas House of Representatives, and the Senate, by a Resolution in each chamber, recognized him for his contributions to the literature of his homeland.